Choosing Herself

I0587377

MAUREEN REID

EMPEROR BOOKS

Choosing Herself

Copyright © 2025 by Maureen Reid

All rights reserved.

Published by Emperor Books

Bellerose Village, New York

ISBN

Digital 978-1-63777-705-3

Print 978-1-63777-706-0 | 978-1-63777-707-7

No part of this book may be reproduced in any form or by any electronic or mechanical means, including information storage and retrieval systems, without written permission from the author, except for the use of brief quotations in a book review.

To Bridget, Caitlin, Maeve & Kelly
You are the sunshine of my life.

CONTENTS

CHAPTER 1

1906

Mama was light. When she entered a room, it was altered – candle flames burned more brightly, logs on the fire snapped a bit more merrily, women stared, and men stood straighter. She never noticed. Holding my hand, she would look for my father. We were the only world she wanted, just the three of us. *A trinity that becomes one,* she used to say. Three persons in one, the one was our family.

I was fourteen when the coughing started.

The blood stained her crisp white handkerchiefs. First, there were only drops. As the weeks went on, no amount of scrubbing could remove the red stains. These pieces of cloth became the symbols of her defeat, her flag of surrender. The illness had her in its grip, shrinking her, robbing me of both her and my father in the process.

I had not seen Papa in days. I was in school, a private school catering to the daughters of the finest Catholic families in Philadelphia, and had stayed late for the final rounds of a tennis tournament. I heard the whispering, the nuns shaking their heads. *Poor man, so tragic, what is he to do?* I kept my head down, refusing to make eye contact. I focused on conjugating French verbs and improving my overhand serve.

The day was autumn perfect, the Philadelphia air as crisp as the apples that now filled the crystal fruit bowl. The trees surrounding Rittenhouse Square were aflame with reds and golds. I turned onto Pine Street and threw open the door to our house, flushed with the excitement of victory. I had won the tennis competition, surprising both me and my opponents. Father was seated in the dining room, which should have been the first indication that something was amiss. He was never home this early in the day.

I was gushing out all the details about my triumph when he raised his hand to quiet me and asked me to take my seat. With a start, I noticed that Mama's sister, Aunt Helena, was seated next to him in my mother's chair. I did not know her well. She was older than Mama and I couldn't remember a time when they showed any sign of intimacy or affection toward each other. Up to that moment, she had only been a guest at the most formal of family celebrations. My eyes widened in surprise as Papa quickly said, *Your Aunt Helena is going to move in with us.*

I looked over at this woman I barely knew. *To help with Mama?*

Aunt Helena started to reply when Papa's sharp look silenced her. She lowered her eyes and closed her mouth.

No, my dear Nell, to serve as your chaperone and guide. If I am to keep your Mama, my precious Clare alive, we must move her to a better place. The Philadelphia climate is too harsh. She will not survive another winter. She must go where she has clean, dry air and sunshine. I have found such a spot; but it is in New York, a town called Saranac Lake where a famous doctor is looking for ways to cure the rattle in her lungs. There she will have the mountain air. It is Mama's best hope. It is my only hope. A shadow fell over his face.

Can I not go with her? my eyes welling up with tears.

Papa slowly shook his head. *No, this is not possible. We cannot expose you further to such an illness. Your mother is going to leave in the morning, I will go with her and get her settled. I will be back in two weeks. Until then, your Aunt Helena will be in charge of the household and life here. I know you will be a good girl and not give her any trouble.*

Aunt Helena gave a fleeting smile, a smile that was not reflected in her eyes.

Can I say goodbye? I couldn't stop shaking.

Absolutely, my dear child.

Aunt Helena spoke up, her voice as stern as the dark grey dress she was wearing. *Do not tire her. This is about my dear sister, not about you.*

Soon enough I was to learn that when it came to Aunt Helena, it was never going to be about me. Or about Mama. For the moment, I simply wanted my mother.

I knocked gently on her door and went in. Mama was sitting up. She looked beautiful, one of her Persian shawls draped around her shoulders, her auburn hair so like mine falling softly around her face. But pale, too pale. She had been spitting up blood, you could still smell its tang in the air.

Mama, I cried. She held out her arms and I ran to find the safety and comfort they always provided. *Papa just told me*, the words racked with sobs.

She started to speak, but the coughing broke in. Her breath rattled. After the fit ended, she was shivering.

I crawled under the covers to try to warm her. She kissed my cheeks. As she stroked my hair, she softly whispered, *This is the only way I know that may help. Consumption is a horrible disease; it is sapping my spirit. Yet it has also taught me how precious life is, how precious you are to me. I will go to this new place and get well. Then, when the long days return and the sun shines brightly, I will come back to you and Papa. We shall go to Cape May and play in the waves.*

She paused, gasping for air. Her hands, cold and so very thin, clasped mine as she put them to her lips. *You must love the sea as I do, my darling daughter. Think of me when you stand quietly on the sand. Welcome the waves as they come to you, for they rise and fall for only the briefest moment, disappearing while another one rushes to take its place.*

I nodded as I closed my eyes, the memories of our summer

days in Cape May washing over me as Mama continued. I could feel the sun on my back, the taste of saltwater in the air, the two of us running into the sea that welcomed our intrusion.

Mama stroked my hair. *The sun plays with the waves, changing their color, yet it is always blue. The sea is always moving, but it remains forever the same. Just like my love for you.*

On my dresser is my cross, bring it to me. I found it immediately, its gold finish shining brightly against the polished mahogany wood. I put it in Mama's hand as I sat down on the bed beside her. She slowly lifted my hair, every movement causing her body to flinch with pain. When the clasp was finally latched, the cross fell into the folds of my sashed dress. She took my face into her hands; her eyes seared into mine. *My mother gave this to me just before I married your papa. She told me it would bring me comfort even when life seemed difficult. These past weeks, it is the only jewelry besides my wedding ring that I have worn.*

You need the strength of the cross now. It will help you in the days ahead. When you wear it, remember that you are stronger than you think and loved more than you will know.

I was fingering the cross when Papa came in, breaking the spell. *Come, Nell, you are to have supper with Aunt Helena. Mama needs to rest to keep up her strength for tomorrow's journey. I will telegram you when we arrive and give you the address so you can write.*

And so he did; and so did I. Each week, I would write. Aunt Helena insisted that she read my letters, giving the excuse that she wanted to be sure my message didn't upset Mama. I believe she was more concerned with what I would say about her. Those 'Post Letters' addressed to Saranac Lake wrote that everything was fine. Each letter ended with a fervent prayer that Mama would be well enough to come home soon, the only sentence that was not fabricated.

What I couldn't say in those letters was that everything had changed. Our house was no longer a home. Papa would work for hours at the bank, his focus now on financing the latest railroad merger. Aunt Helena spent her days criticizing either me or the staff, usually both. She would demand rather than ask and look for flaws that were either nonexistent or irrelevant. The warmth that had filled the house when Mama was here had been replaced by the cold wrath that Aunt Helena delivered.

Despite her continuous 'suggestions' on how to run the house, Father would tolerate no changes to the world Mama had left. Stephens was still the butler in charge, Mrs. Williams remained our housekeeper, our maids, Bridget and her sister Eliza, who were not much older than me, were still with us. I continued to study at the Academy, the all-girls school for the upper-class Catholic, working even harder with the fervent hope that the accolades I received would have Papa congratulate me or at least acknowledge my presence. He did neither.

Although Papa was living here, he left his heart and his soul in Saranac Lake. I lost both of my parents to consumption.

I began to write 'Mama Letters.' Letters that no one else would see. Letters that would never be sent, letters for my eyes only that I kept locked in a wooden chest. I would put on my gold cross and picture Mama and me walking arm-in-arm through the Square, the wind gently blowing our hair out of its clips, or me lying in front of the fire while Mama sat in her chair reading me a poem from Emily Dickinson. With those pictures in mind, my world was right once again. I could talk about all my feelings, my worries. Mama would say the right thing or just hold me in her arms. All would be fine.

Dear Mama,

I miss you so much my heart aches. I pray every day for you to get better and come home.

Everything has been all wrong since you left. Aunt Helena says the most terrible things to Stephens and Mrs. Williams. She complains that her tea is too cold, her bed linens are not properly pressed, the food is either too rich or too bland. Nothing they do pleases her.

The same is true of me. She is perfectly polite to me when Papa is home; but as soon as he leaves for work, she changes. Her voice becomes cold and harsh. Most days I leave for school early so as to avoid her finger-pointing and criticisms. Papa seldom joins us for dinner, he is working more hours than ever before. It is just Aunt Helena and me at the table. She is either silent or scolding, I never know how she will act. Yesterday, Aunt Helena accused me of making Papa stay away. She said that I demand too much of him, my school is too expensive, I am not a dutiful daughter.

I am trying to be better, Mama; but I don't know what I should do or should not do.

I picture you and me in the library, reading our favorite books and talking. I close my eyes and have this conversation. I hear your voice. You tell me to be brave and do what I think is best. That is what I will do or at least try.

I love you, Mama.
Your Nell

CHAPTER 2

1907

A year later, Mama was still in Saranac Lake. I had visited her once during the summer. She was still weak, requiring constant nursing care. The cottage she lived in had a huge front porch; and we spent our days quietly sitting there, surrounded by the towering mountains. The pristine lake and rolling green hills made the entire area look like a painting. She asked about school, my friends, remembering the facts that I had written about. I continued the charade that my life was filled with friends and laughter. Mama was never going to get well if I unburdened my loneliness and disappointments upon her. She had to stay here where the best doctors and the best air gave her the best hope for recovery.

That trip to Saranac Lake was the first time in months I had had a chance to speak to Papa without Aunt Helena listening. I had practiced how I would tell him how life had changed with my aunt's arrival; but even though we were alone, I never found the courage to speak up. His thoughts were only about Mama. I didn't want to add to his sorrow. The nuns had taught us to offer up the slights we received for the poor souls in Purgatory. Given what I was going through, all the hurtful words and actions Aunt Helena slung my way, I calculated a fair number of those lost souls gained entry through those pearly gates because of my intercessions.

Papa never saw that side of her. The few times the three of us were at the same table, or in the carriage together, Aunt Helena was solicitous of him and him alone. The tone of her voice actually changed, kinder, lighter without the harsh, bitter cadence that was directed at me or to the staff.

CHAPTER 3

1908

The new year dawned and school was in recess. The winds outside were howling, the day called for a good book and a warm fire. I found comfort in both. I retreated to the library. The morning sun struggled to melt the frost whose prism of color clouded our leaded glass windows. I nestled in my favorite chair and was lost in the story of Jane Eyre's love for Mr. Rochester.

I didn't hear her enter and jumped when I heard her first words. Aunt Helena was standing over me, her eyes narrowed. Her voice was cold, its stinging bite vying with the winds of this early winter's day. *You sit here doing nothing while I have to make every decision for this household. This cook is robbing your father blind; and if I had my way, she would be out the door in 20 minutes' time.*

When I rose to the defense of Mrs. Williams who had been with us since before I could remember, her face turned the color of the red Oriental rug that covered the floor. *You and my sister never see the world for what it is. Your poor father works day and night to support you both. Neither of you cares about the toll it is taking on that dear man. He has much too much on his mind what with his comings and goings to that dreadful place in upstate New York. He can think only about Clare. You are a distraction.*

I was about to protest when she turned on her heels, *Get out of your morning dress and come to see me in the parlor. A decision has been made about your debut. I need to advise you of the details.*

I was stunned. My debut? I was just 15 and still wore my hair down. I was considered a child and at least two years away from becoming a *jejune fille à marier*, a woman ready for marriage. I was too young, too inexperienced. I could dance well enough but had no experience in dealing with boys, let alone potential husbands.

My hands shook as I changed my dress, making sure that my hair was hanging down my back. Wearing the gold cross, I descended the staircase slowly, step-by-step, like a prisoner about to face the executioner. Only mine was seated in the parlor.

Aunt Helena motioned me to sit at the chair farthest away from her but still so close I could hear every word coming from her snarled mouth. *I am going to get you out into Society. I have worked very hard to have you presented at the Philadelphia Dancing Assembly this May. It is taking place at the Bellevue-Stratford Hotel. Mme. Brodeur, one of the finest dressmakers in all of the city, will be here tomorrow to fit you with the dresses you need.*

But, but... I have not yet started to pin my hair up.

Nonsense. We will start to make the necessary introductions as soon as your dresses are on order.

A cold chill went through my body, this was a bad dream. I fingered the gold cross hanging from its chain and pulled the only string I could think of. *Papa, does he approve of this plan? Has Mama been advised?*

Enough, Nell. I spoke with your father about this last night and he agreed. I am going to get you into Society this year. No one will think it is too soon, given your mother's precarious health. I will simply explain we want to be sure my ailing sister has the comfort and pleasure of knowing you are about to start a life of your own before the Lord calls her to His heavenly home. A life that will take you away from this house and your father's protection. Aunt Helena smiled.

My eyes blurred with tears. I looked up and saw Mama's portrait, her wedding picture hanging on the wall. Her eyes downcast, her auburn hair, crowned by a wreath of lilies of the valley, fell softly to her shoulder; she looked like an angel. Next to it hung Papa's portrait, his kind eyes betraying the grave posture and stern smile the photographer had posed. Pictures of my childhood were scattered on the tables: riding a pony on my third birthday, dressed in white for my First Holy Communion, holding hands with Mama on the boardwalk. The room was a sanctuary of family memories. I prayed that somehow I could be protected from the fate that had been presented just minutes ago.

Do I have to do this? Can I talk to Papa? Can't this wait for one more year, maybe Mama will be home by then?

You heard me, Nell. You need to grow up. You have been coddled and spoiled since the day you entered this house. It is now time for you to pay this debt back. Your father and I have agreed.

And with that, Aunt Helena stood up, smoothed the folds of her dress whose golden hue was lost in the lackluster color of her mousey brown hair. She left the room. I was alone.

Now more than ever I wanted Mama to be with me. She would understand. She would not make me go out into the world for which I was totally unprepared. Papa would be of no support; he had turned over everything about the house and my care to Aunt Helena. Mama's illness had made him too weak to participate in the life that once was ours.

My plan was to write Mama pleading with her to let me be a schoolgirl, not a lioness on the prowl for a husband. I was composing the letter in my head when I entered the dining room the next morning for breakfast. Papa was finishing his morning coffee and was halfway out of his chair when Aunt Helena caught my eye.

John, Nell, and I were talking yesterday about the plans for her debut this spring. I know how much it would mean to our lovely Clare for her daughter to be settled in a home of her own. Nell getting married and accepted into the world would bring my sister great comfort and peace.

Papa looked up, his eyes widening as if the mention of Mama woke him from the stupor that dulled the pain of his daily life. *Whatever you think, Helena. I am sure you will do whatever is best for Nell.*

Aunt Helena's voice softened. *Thank you, John. You know I am only thinking of what is in the best interest of all of you. Nell and I will jointly write letters to tell Clare of all the preparations. It will be as if she were here every moment.*

That would be lovely, Helena, thank you.

Aunt Helena smiled triumphantly as she raised her cup to take another sip of coffee, her eyes only on Papa. *It is, and always will be, my pleasure, John.*

Papa got up and left the table, kissing me briefly on the cheek. Any thought I had of either enlisting his support or pleading with Mama to stop this charade had ended.

The debut was in May, there were but five months to get me ready. I was taken out of school, my education now focused on the hunt for a suitable husband.

The dressmaker, Mme. Brodeur, came two afternoons a week with her pins and silks, poking me in places where I had never been touched by someone other than Mama. She called my figure exquisite and my coloring a joy to dress. The price I paid for such compliments was to stand motionless for hours on end, like a doll being fitted for her place on a shelf. My afternoons were spent mastering the latest dance steps, practicing how and when to courtesy, and learning how to plan a formal dinner party. I thought it all quite foolish, but I was a pawn, and Aunt Helena the chess master.

While I was being pulled hither and yon, Aunt Helena was taking great pains to determine which of the eligible bachelors in this City of Brotherly Love should be my prime targets. Nothing would be left to chance. She had made a list of the best prospects; and to their parents' homes, she left her calling card with the invitation that we would be home on Mondays and Wednesdays from 3 to 5 p.m. to receive their company. I was expected to be seated at Aunt Helena's side, a picture of domestic bliss. I was instructed to chat about the most mundane of topics, with no discussion of literature or art. Subjects that Mama and I would discuss. The weather seemed the only topic that was safe to pursue; and Philadelphia acquiesced, offering an early spring of clear skies, warming temperatures, and early tree blossoms.

I smiled as Aunt Helena basked in the glory of having these women who, having ignored her most of her life, were now seeking her favor and advice. I wanted to shout, *This has nothing to do with you. They come to satisfy their curiosity: what china do we use? How many servants do we employ? What estate would be mine to inherit? Does this motherless child know how to behave in society?* I said nothing; it would make no difference.

My gold cross glittered in the candlelight as I wrote a Mama Letter.

Dear Mama,

> *This is no longer my life. I am not sure who I am or what I am to do.*
>
> *When Aunt Helena told me that I am to be presented to Society so I can find a husband, I thought I was having a bad dream. I wanted you to make her wait, wait until I finished school, wait until I grew up, and decided if I even wanted to find a husband. It was too late. Papa had agreed, or so Aunt Helena said.*
>
> *These past weeks have been torturous. I am no longer attending the Academy. Aunt Helena said it was a waste of time and money. I did not argue. I have learned that keeping silent and having her think I agree is my best course of action. Last week I went to see Papa in his study. I put on the gold cross for courage.*

It was a blustery night. The wind was causing the branches of the tree to make tapping noises that muted my cautious knock on the closed door. I called Papa as I opened the door. The only light in the room came from his desk, throwing a shadow, a man dark and hunched over his papers. It reminded me of Ebenezer Scrooge bent over his counting desk on Christmas Eve. Papa, I called again, my voice as shaky as the panes in the window vibrating from the winds that had now picked up speed.

Papa looked up, his eyes searching. I just stood there, waiting for him to recognize that I was there. He said my name more like a question, it was almost as if he was seeing me for the first time in months.

He motioned for me to sit down by his desk. My voice returned, just like I used to when I would bring my school work here to do. The memory made Papa smile, something he rarely does now. We talked about how nervous I was during my first days at the Academy's primary school, how you would hold my hand walking me to the building until the last two blocks. Then you would make me go on alone so I would look braver than I felt. Papa was lost in the memory of that simpler time.

I reminded him of how important my education was to both of you. Gathering all my courage, I asked if I could have a tutor come to the house in the mornings so that I could complete the requirements for my graduation. He agreed and promised to speak to the nuns to find an appropriate teacher.

The next Sunday morning as we were driving home from Mass, Papa mentioned that beginning on Tuesday a Mrs. Nisler, a widow who taught at the Academy before she was married, was coming to the house to assist me in completing my studies. She would come three mornings a week. Aunt Helena started to protest, but Papa looked at her sharply. She stopped in mid-sentence, her hands and mouth both clenched tight. He said that the decision was made and he knew it would make you happy. I almost clapped my hands in glee but kept my composure and said Thank you, Papa. I will write and let Mama know how happy I am and how hard I will work.

Aunt Helena said nothing, but her eyes narrowed, her face

taking on the color of someone who has spent too much time in the
sun without a proper hat.

When I am not with Mrs. Nisler, my days are spent under Aunt
Helena's control. I can now curtsy while keeping my eyes raised, pour
a cup of tea without spilling any drops in the saucer, choose what
wine to go with what food, and chat politely with people who care
nothing about what I have to say. I am acting the role of a proper
lady when, just weeks ago, I was a schoolgirl.

I don't want to be a grown-up. I want to be your daughter, to
have you brush my hair, to kiss me goodnight, to hold my hand.

I don't know why God had to take you away from me. It isn't
fair. I am angry at Him, and I know that is a sin. A sin I can't
confess, so that is a sin as well.

I am trying my best not to let my unhappiness show. I hope the
letters that get posted to you tell of a girl excited about the prospects
of new dresses, new friends, and a new life.

I don't want a new life. I want my old life back.

I love you, Mama.
Your Nell

After months of planning, the day finally arrived when I was to be presented to Society. If the moth emerges from the cocoon as a butterfly, I was primed to do the same, though I felt like every butterfly in the area had found its way into my stomach. After all the decisions about the color and style of my dress, Mme. Brodeur had outdone herself in its creation. I was wearing green chiffon over light green silk with a matching velvet ribbon draped from my left shoulder to the right side of my waist. Papa's gift of drop-down pearl earrings was my only piece of jewelry. Lilies of the Valley, Mama's favorite flower, and the only thing I insisted be included were pinned on the waistband and drawn on my dance card. When I finally had the courage to look in the mirror, I gasped. My dark auburn hair pinned up in large curls entwined with pearls was in sharp contrast to all this green. I looked to find the schoolgirl I had been just six months ago. She was nowhere to be seen. The image I saw looking back was not someone I knew. My heart seemed to stop. Then behind me in the mirror, I saw Papa.

Wearing a black tailcoat, he looked like his portrait in the library with only the slightest strands of gray now streaking through his hair. A small tear fell from one eye as I turned to face him. He put my hand in his and gently brought it to his lips. *You are lovely, my little Nell, as beautiful on the outside as you are on the inside. I will write Mama this evening and describe to her that you have followed in her footsteps. You will be the belle of the ball.*

Papa was still holding my hand when the sound of rustling silk broke the magic of the moment. Aunt Helena burst through the door wearing a bright blue evening gown so voluminous that she looked like she was engulfed in a small lake with her head and shoulders emerging to grab a last bit of air. Her breasts looked as if they, too, were looking to escape as they led your eyes to the jewelry adorning her neck. She was wearing Mama's sapphires – the necklace and earrings Papa had given her on their wedding day. I choked out, *You're wearing Mama's jewels.*

Yes, I think they go quite well with this dress. Your Mama is not going to need them tonight. She took Papa's arm, steering him away from me. *Come, Steven, our carriage is waiting.*

Turning her back to me, her arm now entwined with Papa's, she looked over her shoulder. *Stop dawdling, Nell. Your Papa has spent too much money on this occasion for you to ruin it by being difficult.*

I followed them out, the spring air reviving my sinking spirits. I would let no one see through my veneer. I would smile and dance. Flirt and flounce. I would be my mother's daughter, I would fulfill Papa's prediction, I would be the belle of the ball – witty, sophisticated, self-confident.

Bellevue-Stratford lived up to its reputation. The ballroom bore no resemblance to the plain, unadorned space where I had memorized this evening's planned formalities. Tall crystal vases held pink roses, and tree ferns banked the Italian marble fireplace and balcony. Small tables decked in white tablecloths were scattered like snowflakes on the gleaming hardwood floor. Candles flickered their approval of the scene.

Aunt Helena stood next to me when I was presented. I smiled, curtsied, and moved to my place in line with the other well-born young women, wearing gloves and the family jewels. Each of us being marketed as the complete package to any gentleman with the right name and sufficient fortune. The conductor received the nod and we took our places to perform the choreographed first waltz, all synchronized and well-rehearsed to flaunt a parade of smooth young bodies. To this day, I cannot remember the name of the young man who was my partner. He was followed by a string of good dancers and those who dipped me a bit too early, a blur of faces most of whom were not yet in need of a daily shave. Until the last dance, the final waltz.

This man was older than the rest. He walked with an air of confidence that comes from being accustomed to being looked at. He didn't shy away from the limelight, nor did he seek it. The light sought him.

All eyes, including mine, were on him as he strolled his way across the dance floor. I did not expect him to stop in front of me until I heard him say, *Miss Morgan, I believe this dance is mine.* I looked at my dance card and there, in clear, bold script:

Edward Walker

He led me onto the floor. He was tall with dark wavy hair, his frame athletic, his face chiseled, but his eyes are what captured me. They were striking – coal-black.

He put his arm around my waist as the music began. I started my practiced polite dialogue, *Are you enjoying the evening, Mr. Walker?*

I believe about as much as you are.

My lips twitched, I couldn't suppress a smile. *I take it you find such nights as this stifling and beneath you?*

Ah, you are both right and wrong, Miss Morgan. I do not consider evenings like this to be beneath me as they are the price you pay for having a doting mother and a financially successful father. I do, however, find them stifling, a well-mannered way of describing an event that costs too much money, allows for no real dialogue to be exchanged, and where a young woman is evaluated by the size of her fortune and the originality of her dressmaker. I would prefer a night at the opera or one spent in my library with a good book and a fine glass of wine.

I was so surprised by his comment that I missed a step. My companion quickly recovered and, moving his mouth to my ear, whispered, *Careful. My mother and her cronies are watching your every move. One false step and you will be left to being fawned over by boys who are years away from true manhood.*

I regained my footing and looked into the penetrating black holes that were his eyes. They empowered me to be bold in my response. *So, tell me, Mr. Walker, do you choose the wine to complement your book or your book to complement your wine? I am thinking if you are reading Tolstoy, you might need a powerful red to balance the prose. If you are in the mood for a lighter wine, perhaps a Sancerre, would you not be better off spending your time matching wits with Sherlock Holmes and his Mr. Watson?*

My dance partner threw his head back and laughed out loud. A dozen pairs of eyes looked our way, all from the corner where his mother was holding court.

I knew I would like you. I could tell from the moment you walked into the room, you are not like the rest of the flock they have gathered here tonight. What makes you different? He continued twirling me around the floor.

I followed his every move, easily and willingly, my eyes never leaving his face. *Perhaps it is because I share your preference that an evening with a good book and a warm fire is more to my liking than making polite conversation with people whose names I won't remember tomorrow.*

The music ended. Mr. Walker bowed, I curtsied and he escorted me back to my aunt who was smiling like the fox who had found his way into the hen house.

Aunt Helena was all abuzz on the ride home, and Mr. Walker was the only topic of conversation.

Nell, even you should remember meeting his mother when she came to call last month.

Indeed I did. It would be impossible to forget the infamous Mrs. Walker with her high cheekbones and aristocratic nose. That afternoon, her light brown hair was gathered in a bun at the base of her neck. Not a single hair was out of place. I don't think a strand of it would have dared. She maintained a cool disdain as she took us all in. She didn't have to say a word, her demeanor was of a woman whose will governed others as easily as the moon controlled the tides.

Mrs. Walker was barely into her carriage when Aunt Helena, flush with excitement, began to fan herself though the early afternoon sun had not caused the temperature to rise. *Rose Walker here! I can barely catch my breath. She is at the top of the hierarchy of Philadelphia society, the best of the German Catholic families that go back generations. They make the Kelly's look like Shanty Irish. You know, she has the most eligible son in the entire city? Edward must be in his late 20's by now and is clearly a catch. He lives right on the Square, #10 Rittenhouse Square, to be exact. That is the house he grew up in and is now his alone.* She nodded knowingly. *His mother moved out to the Main Line.*

Aunt Helena's arms were now flapping as the fan's intensity increased. *He is a lawyer and works only with the most elite bankers and railroad men. Rumor had it that J.P. Morgan wanted him to come work with him in New York City, but Edward refused as he did not want to leave his mother. He is an only child, and they are devoted to one another. The gossips say her husband kept other women in his life. I never put much stock into what those old rumormongers blabber about. Jealousy is what drives them. I abhor such low-life behavior.*

A smile escaped my lips as she continued. *I am sure Aunt*

Helena believed I shared her enthusiasm for having the Grande Dame Walker single us out. No, the glee I could barely contain was Aunt Helena's misconceived notion that she was above the worst of the gossips. She liked nothing better than to chortle about each person who came across her path once they were conveniently out of earshot: young or old, rich or not-so-rich. She would begin each tirade with the phrase: *It is not like me to find fault with others...*but, oh so untrue.

Father closed his eyes as Aunt Helena continued to prattle on about the Walkers. I was content to listen and think about Aunt Helena's perceived folly making it the perfect ending of the evening.

Within two weeks following that fateful waltz, Edward Walker started to call. He lived up to his reputation of being smart, charming, and devoted to his mother. On Saturday evenings, we would accompany her to the symphony or the opera. On Sundays, he and I would visit an art gallery or attend a lecture, followed by a light supper at his club. Edward thought the world was interesting, he was curious about things I had never thought about. He would ask my opinion, listen to what I had to say, ask me questions that clarified my thinking.

We had been seeing each other for over four months. It was a Sunday afternoon, a cool breeze was blowing a signal that days of too little sunlight would soon be on the horizon. We had stopped to sit on a bench in the Square, watching the leaves fall gently to the ground, their fiery reds and golds cluttering the paths that would lead us back to the addresses each of us called home.

Edward was quieter than usual, his eyes staring off into space. I called his name before he turned in my direction. *Your head is not with me at the moment, Edward. Might I ask what you are thinking?*

He looked up, startled, the thick lashes of those black eyes fluttering as if to awaken him from his thoughts. His hands opened up, framing the Square as shrugged. *This is the only home I've ever known. There was a quote in Harper's magazine that had all of us at the law firm in a bit of a tussle. It said that the "one thing unforgivable in Philadelphia is to be new, to be different from what has been." Do you agree? Is Philadelphia dull and content, not accepting change? Can that same thing be said of us who live here?*

I slowly shook my head. *I have never thought about it. Like you, Philadelphia is the only place I have ever lived, unless you count summers in Cape May.*

I scanned his face – the squared-off jaw, the strong chin, the nose sharp and defined, the eyes that pulled you in. *I do know that you are not dull. We go to the symphony and discuss the great virtuosos, we go to lectures at the Art Museum and debate the plans proposed for its expansion. You have enlightened me about local politics, the corruption that permeates this city's elected leaders. Perhaps another city would hold more excitement, but I don't think Philadelphia is dull. At least not at that moment and not with you.*

Edward took my hand, raising me from the bench. I thought he was going to kiss me. I wanted him to kiss me. He put my arm through his, the setting sun now the same color as the leaves of the maple trees that were basking in their final days of glory. *Thank you, my dearest Nell. You are wise beyond your years. Philadelphia has always been my home, though there are moments when I think of the adventure another world would offer. Another city where I could find my own way, a path that had not been pre-determined by others for me to follow.*

He said nothing else as he walked me to my door. He never mentioned it again.

It was after Thanksgiving, the air was turning colder and darker each day. Papa, Aunt Helena, and I had come home from Mass, finding our way to the dining room and its promise of a hearty breakfast. The smell of crisp bacon mingled with the aroma of freshly-baked bread, as Papa looked over to me as he sat down. *Edward Walker has made an appointment to see me this week.*

Aunt Helena jumped out of her seat, clapping her hands she shouted: *He is going to ask your permission to marry Nell. My prayers have been answered.* Papa looked startled. Aunt Helena sat back down but continued to shift in her seat, quenching her desire to want to say more.

Papa looked at me, *Are you happy, Nell?*

I nodded yes, *As happy as I can be without Mama here.*

That is true for all of us, my dear daughter.

Aunt Helena said nothing. Taking the dinner bell in her hand, she began to furiously ring for Mrs. Campbell. Papa looked at her. *Your coffee has gotten cold, John. It needs to be refreshed.*

Papa pushed his chair away from the table. *There is no need. I am finished.* He left for his study, and I quickly retreated to my room as Edward would be arriving soon. Aunt Helena was left at the table alone.

I understood what Papa meant when he said that Edward had asked to see him. The impending appointment was not something either Edward or I discussed that afternoon.

Later that night, alone in my room, I put on my gold cross and wrote a Mama Letter.

Dear Mama,

I wish you were here every day but even more these days. Edward and I are now a couple; that is how Aunt Helena refers to us.

I have told you all about Edward. He is a lawyer, very smart, and makes me laugh. He is interested in so many things and shares his curiosity with me. He asks what I think about the artists we see, women getting the vote, Sigmund Freud's U.S. lecture tour. Things the nuns never taught me in school. Mrs. Nisler is helpful with history and mathematics, but I need to know more about what is happening in the world.

I have started to read the newspaper each morning at breakfast. Papa was surprised when I asked if I could read his morning paper once he left for work. Aunt Helena objected, saying that it wasn't proper for a lady to fill her head with such things. Papa disagreed and he leaves the paper by my plate each morning. Some nights when he comes home early, we discuss a certain article or share our concern over that day's headline. It is good to have his attention, even for a moment.

Papa said that Edward has made an appointment to see him at the bank. Aunt Helena is convinced he is going to ask Papa's permission to marry me. I don't know if I want to marry Edward. I don't know if I don't want to marry him. It is all quite confusing to me, and I have no one to talk to about it. You wrote that I will know when I am in love. I only know what your love feels like and what Papa's love feels like.

How does it feel to be in love, Mama? Edward is kind, just like Papa. He never raises his voice or demands that only his opinion be heard. I feel safe when I am with him, as if no harm will come to me. He doesn't treat me like a child, he takes my arm, helps me in the carriage, and tenderly tucks the lap robe around me.

He is always the perfect gentleman. He has not tried to kiss me. He sometimes takes my hand and gives it a squeeze, usually when we are about to meet his mother. I think that is more to give me strength as his mother continues to be the most formidable creature. One that even Aunt Helena has let me write to you about in my posted letters.

I like being with Edward. I like who I am when I am with him. Perhaps that is love. Perhaps that is enough.

I love you, Mama.
Your Nell

I t was a week before Christmas. Edward and I were leaving his mother's house where the topic of conversation centered on her annual New Year's Eve Ball, one of the most sought-out invitations in Philadelphia. It had been her only topic of conversation since Thanksgiving. I learned to respond to her detailed description of the myriad specifics, not with words but in a language of nods. I agreed with who should sit at which table with a short nod and a knowing smile. Negotiating with the florist about prices and centerpieces? A medium-speed nod with my eyes growing larger to register my amazement was the required response. My slower 'how did you ever consider this' nod was used when she was expounding on her latest triumph while I was trying my best to stay alert.

You have learned how to deal with my mother, Edward smiled as we departed through the front door. The night was crisp, the stars sparkling like the frost on the manicured lawn. *I learned as a young boy that she is a force of nature. Everything she does, from planning the menu at this gala to raising me, is done with a clear eye to set a standard that will be the envy of her crowd.*

His voice changed, his eyes lit up. *Ah, there she is.* I turned thinking that Edward's mother must have unexpectedly joined us. Instead of Mrs. Walker, a large and shiny black chariot with white side-walled tires pulled up. It was a touring car, Edward's newest possession, a twentieth-century Clydesdale that puffed clouds of smoke. He had been keeping it at his mother's house until appropriate accommodations could be found near Rittenhouse Square.

You will love this, Nell, I know. From the passenger seat, Edward unfolded the largest piece of canvas I had ever seen. As he continued the unraveling, sleeves and buttons sprouted, making it look like a kite gone wrong. Edward held it open for me to put on. *A dusting coat, to guard you against grime for our drive back to town.* The coat engulfed me, I couldn't move, my head struggled to pop over the collar.

Edward shook his head, grinning. *I see my mistake. You just appear bigger than life, Nell. Tomorrow, I will find one half this size for you to call your own.* His eyes glistened with a tinge of mischief, *This one will get a proper brushing and bequeathed to my mother.*

Lifting me into the seat and tucking the coat around me, *She will never know. It will be our secret.*

Donning his own bright yellow driving coat with gloves to match, Edward took control of the wheel. Goggles now masking most of his face, his smile said it all. This is a man destined to take charge of the world he inhabited. I was now included in that orbit.

Two days later, Edward appeared at our front door. Stephens brought him into the parlor, now decorated with all the Christmas trimmings. Aunt Helena was out of breath by the time she found me in the library where I was absorbed in reading the letters of Abigail Adams to her husband John, Mrs. Nislers' latest history lesson.

Edward is here. Stephens brought him into the parlor. You should change your dress.

I slowly stood up. *Nonsense. Last time I saw him I was covered with dirt and grime, looking like a pin-up for an army tent. My attire this afternoon is a clear improvement.* I put the book down and walked into the parlor. Aunt Helena stayed behind, muttering that if I wasn't careful I would lose the prize.

I assumed she meant Edward.

He was seated on the striped love seat, cradling a large box on his lap. The light snowfall that recently laid a white carpet on the city streets and sidewalks left his hair glistening with melted flakes.

Edward, it is the middle of the week. Why are you not at the firm? Have all your clients decided to take an early holiday?

Standing up, box in his hand, he shrugged. *They will be there tomorrow. Even the titans of industry can wait a day to have their latest acquisitions secured.* Motioning me to take a chair, he handed me the box. *A trade. I think you will find this a better fit and more to your liking*

I sat down and untied the ribbon, wrapped in a mass of tissue was my new motor coat. A lightweight tweed with a sailor collar, it was tailored with precision, its black wooden buttons giving it both style and practicality. I stood up to admire it more closely and gasped. It was lined with the finest of furs.

Edward, this is exquisite. Lovely and so warm, you are too generous.

No, Nell. It is not too generous. Like you, it appears to be conventional when you first lay your eyes on it. Then you look deeper and find there is an underlying fabric that is soft to the touch but strong in its character.

Edward held out the coat as I slipped my arms into the sleeves. It was a perfect fit.

Edward stepped back and I did a small pirouette, letting the generous cut of fabric swirl around me. Edward clapped his hands.

I love the time we spend together, Nell. We are good for each other. I believe in all my heart that we can make each other happy. We can have a good life.

I stood still. My heart beating so loud, I had to strain to hear Edward's voice.

I have spoken to your father and he has agreed.

Edward took a small box from his breast coat pocket. *At my mother's New Year's Eve Ball, I would like to introduce you as my fiancé. Nell, will you marry me?*

A thousand thoughts went through my head as Edward slipped a pearl and diamond ring on my finger. I agreed with all that he was saying, I liked being with him, I believed he liked being with me.

My breath came in starts. I looked at my hand and the ring that now adorned it. It looked right, it belonged on my finger. Papa had already given his consent. I could think of no reason why I wouldn't agree. I looked up and met Edward's eyes, *Yes.*

E dward took my hand and put it to his lips. *Thank you, Nell. I shall make this work. You have my promise.*

I have one condition, Edward.

And?

Once we are properly wed, you will teach me to drive your motorcar.

Edward threw back his head as a great roar of laughter came bursting out. *Agreed, but not a word to either your father or my mother. I believe neither would think it proper and might banish me from seeing you again.*

I shook my head and smiled, knowing that Aunt Helena would never let that happen. The trophy was captured.

CHAPTER 4

1909

Once the announcement had been made, I became a spectator of the events leading up to the wedding day. There were parties where we were the main attraction. Edward was attentive, concerned for my well-being though our conversations most often began with the phrase, *Mother wishes* or *Mother suggests*. My opinion or wishes were not sought. Aunt Helena fawned over Mrs. Walker whenever the two met, agreeing with her every suggestion as if it was the best idea since God created Eve.

My bridesmaids selected by Mrs. Walker, whom I now call Mother Walker, were culled from the daughters of those she called her 'circle.' One or two I recognized from my schoolyard days, though they had never spoken to me prior to being tapped to lead me down the aisle. Three were fair-haired, the other three had raven locks, all were slim and chosen to complete the tableau of the perfect wedding. They were polite in my company but distant. I did not belong. They knew it and so did I. Only with Edward at my side did I feel steady.

It was my bridal luncheon, two weeks before my wedding day. Mother Walker's garden was the setting, so picture-perfect the editors of *Vogue* would have been envious of its layout. Small tables laid out in the finest china were scattered among the bonsai trees, their wooded boxes marking the manicured lawn. The flower beds were a riot of May color, nary a weed dared sneak its way in. In the center of all this splendor were the Walker prize-winning roses. White and red bushes were everywhere, their petals glowing under the unrelenting sun. I was mesmerized by their beauty and the intensity of their color. White and red. My eyes blurred, all I could see was Mama's handkerchief, white linen stained with red. I thought I was going to get sick.

I excused myself from the table, weathering Aunt Helena's scowl, and escaped to the parlor, needing cool air. A chair tucked in the corner provided the shadows for the respite I craved. Regaining my composure, I was about to rise from my perch when four of my 'maids' entered the room, their voices low and conspiratorial. My name was the first word I heard, coming from the one clearly in charge. *So this Nell wins. Not sure I would want Edward whose dark eyes look to burn your soul, but I envy her his fortune.*

I didn't dare move as the same voice pontificated. *I don't know what he sees in her. She is not much more than a child and clearly does not have the upbringing to further distinguish the family. My mother believes she must be Mrs. Walker's choice. That tyrant with all her prize-winning roses would never let her son choose a woman she couldn't control. She would have a hard time with any of us.*

The giggling continued as the quartet made its way out of the room, the voice fading in a conspiratorial tone. *The first thing I would do if this house were mine is to get rid of these awful drapes. Our esteemed hostess must have taken her decorating lessons from Queen Victoria, everything is old and musty. A bit like Mrs. Walker herself.*

I tried to catch my breath. This is what they think of me, a piece of clay to be molded and shaped. I returned to the garden and continued the charade of false smiles, graciously accepting all the empty wishes for my happiness.

I managed to make it through the next few weeks. Edward

was occupied at the law firm, he was 'clearing his slate' to free his time for our honeymoon. The doubts, the fears were mine alone, coming to me at night in a reoccurring nightmare. I was lost in a land I didn't recognize; flags, hundreds of white flags stained with red blocking my escape. I woke up to find my pillow damp with either tears or sweat. I couldn't tell which one.

I had one moment of sheer happiness. A brown and white striped box arrived from Henri Bendel, my wedding gift from Mama. My heart fluttered with joy.

I gently untied the ribbon and opened the box. Cradled in the reams of soft tissue paper nestled a peignoir, blue like the color of the morning sky and so delicate that it looked like it would break to the touch. It looked like Mama. I held the fabric to my face when a cold wind entered the room. It was Aunt Helena. She was standing in the doorway. *You are to wear it on your wedding night.* Aunt Helena's eyes shot daggers. She turned sharply, leaving me alone to gently repack this precious parcel, retrieving the scattered tissue paper to cover it from any unsuspecting wound.

That night, with the gold cross hanging down my nightdress, I wrote a Mama Letter. My tears blurred the ink on the page.

Dear Mama,

Your beautiful gift arrived this morning. Aunt Helena told me I was to wear it on my wedding night.

I am not sure I am ready to be a bride, let alone a wife. What am I to do that night? How am I to act?

I have never kissed anyone but you and Papa. Mrs. Nisler brought me a biology book last week to study. As a married woman, she explained what she called 'the act' to me. I was stunned. I cannot imagine what it would be like to have Edward on top of me, naked.

I understand that it will be my duty as his wife not to object, even if it hurts. I pray that I will find the strength to make it through my wedding night without collapsing either into fits of laughter or hysterical crying.

I am nervous. I do not want to be a foolish girl when my husband comes to my bed.

I so wish I could talk with you about all of this. And so much more.

I love you, Mama.
Your Nell

T he fateful day arrived. Like a play, I was given my role that did not include a speaking part.

My wedding dress hung on the wardrobe. Mme. Brodeur had once again been called into action. Beading, pearls, and silk fabric combined to make the dress a work of art. Mother Walker approved the design and Papa didn't blink at the cost.

Bridget held the dress as I stepped into it. I had forgotten how heavy the beading and embroidery made it. I sent a prayer to Mama begging that I would not wither under its weight. My headpiece was a halo of pearls, my hair tamed into a bun at the nape of my neck with matching pearls woven into it.

When she had finished, Bridget stood back and admired her work. She moved so I could face the mirror. *You look beautiful, Miss Nell.* The reflection showed not a girl but a woman. A woman I did not know.

Aunt Helena was at the bottom of the staircase when I came down. I looked anxiously for Papa. He came in from his study, his lips formed a smile but his eyes were trimmed in red. He took my arm in his. *You look lovely, my darling girl. If only Mama were here to celebrate this day with us.*

Before I could respond, Aunt Helena was next to us. She did not wish me well, her only comment was that the coachman was waiting.

The sun was blinding with no clouds taming its relentless

blaze as we walked up the stairs to the church doors. The organist began to play, and Papa and I started down the aisle as the assembled crowd stood up. The pews held hundreds of staring eyes, the very best of Philadelphia Society for the Catholic enclave. White ribbons and floral sprays were displayed everywhere, bringing a breath of summer into the dark and chilly ecclesiastical air.

Edward stood in front of the priest, awaiting my arrival. He was the epitome of what a husband should look like: tall, handsome, with a smile that evoked confidence, his black eyes twinkling with a slight bit of amusement at the approaching procession. He took my hand as Papa and I reached the altar. *You look lovely, Nell.*

I whispered back, *Don't let go of my hand.* He gave it a squeeze, and it stopped shaking.

The priest turned, took his place at the altar, and the Mass began. I stood, knelt, and bowed my head as I had done for years, my nerves settling down with the comfort of the familiar ritual. Edward took my hand as we stood to acknowledge our vows. His "I do" was loud and clear, a lawyer's declaration. My "I do" was softer, but I understood the words that I was agreeing to uphold. I was to be Edward's wife, no matter what life had in store for us *until death do us part.* I was not yet seventeen years old, our life together would be my life. Edward slipped a simple gold band on my finger, the priest blessed us, and we were wed. I walked back down the aisle, my arm entwined with Edward's. I was now his wife.

The reception was at Mother Walker's house. These were her guests; this was her celebration. Nothing had been left to chance, including the selection of the bride.

By late afternoon, Edward and I were aboard our private rail car, making our way to Cape May where we were to spend our first month together as husband and wife. Edward was charming, relaxed, satisfied at how well the day had gone. He leaned back in his seat, *I was a bit worried about our younger lawyers. Most are not too far removed from their university days where alcohol and willing partners were the norms of the day. Mother would have been scandalized had they repeated any of their previous escapades in front of her friends.* He spent the remainder of the journey sharing the tales of antics that had lionized the reputation of even the most senior partners for generations. I nodded and smiled, fiddling with my gold cross to hide my nervousness as I contemplated what new experiences the setting sun would bring me.

Edward signed the hotel's register as Mr. & Mrs. Walker, and we were shown to our suite of rooms. I touched nothing of the light supper delivered to our room, fearing any food I ate might reappear in the most vulgar manner. After finishing his brandy, Edward stood up and looked around the room, clearly satisfied with the accommodations. *Well, my dear, you might want to retire. It has been a long day for both of us.* I agreed, leaving for my bedroom and Edward departed into his.

My bedroom was lit by a roaring fire that illuminated a high four-poster bed, wall coverings in the most current French fashion, and white satin drapes heavy enough to keep the cold Atlantic breezes from seeping into the room. Despite the warmth, I couldn't help shivering. Bridget helped me undress and, slowly, the gauzy peignoir was draped over me. My hair, released from its pins, fell loosely over my shoulder, its auburn coloring a marked contrast to my alabaster skin. My hands began to shake.

She smiled, *I will add more logs to the fire.*

I could only nod my thanks, *Good night, Bridget.*

Have a lovely evening, Miss Nell, I mean Mrs. Walker. She giggled as she closed the door.

Mrs. Walker. I had no idea what that meant, to be someone's wife. To be Edward's wife. I looked around the room, not knowing what to do next. Was I supposed to be on top of the covers or under them? Should I be sitting or standing? My mind was awhirl, and I was standing there dumbfounded when the door finally opened and Edward appeared. The room went quiet, the only sound coming from the crackling logs.

He beckoned me to the bed and I climbed in. Nervousness ran through me like a cavalry charge. He came in on the other side and met me in the middle. Edward took my hand in his, brought it to his lips, and said: *Good night, my dearest, my lovely Nell. Cape May is such a delight. I so look forward to sharing it with you.* He did not let go of my hand and within minutes he was fast asleep.

I lay in the dark, bewildered. Was this how the wedding night was supposed to happen? I could think of no explanation or a thousand ones. Was I too young, too inexperienced? Was the wedding day with all it forced gaiety all too much? Did I look like a harlot? Did I appear too eager? Was I not eager enough? Is this to be done in daylight rather than in the shadows of the night?

I could not sleep while Edward slept like a man content with the ways of the world. I was afraid to move, afraid to let loose of his hand. After a while, when my shoulder had grown numb and my arm stiff, I released myself from his clasp and turned over onto my other side. At last, the exhaustion of the day demanded its fair compensation, I fell into a fitful sleep.

I woke as the dawn broke through the window with the first rays of sunlight. It took me a minute to remember what had happened or, more clearly, what had not happened. I had a brief thought that the morning would answer my questions. I turned over. Edward was gone. Tears of shame, of anger, of fear washed over me. I didn't know what I had done, what I was supposed to do. I lay in bed for what seemed like hours. My entire body ached.

I got out of bed slowly, like a cripple, and found my simplest dress to put on. I did a quick brush through my hair and looked in the mirror. There was no bridal blush returning my gaze. I looked older and wearier. There was a knock on my door. Edward appeared dressed for the day's outing. *Good Morning,*

Nell. Please excuse my presumption, but I have ordered breakfast for us though I think you will like my selection. And then let's talk about our plan for the day. It is a beautiful Cape May day.

When I joined Edward at the table, he poured me a cup of tea. *I know this may not be what you expected.*

I looked up stunned, ready for the explanation of what had not happened the night before when he lifted the silver cover off the tray. The most amazing titillating smell filled the air. My mouth began to water. Freshly baked rolls still warm from the oven, slathered in butter and topped with cinnamon icing, lay before me. Fifteen minutes earlier, I was certain I would never eat again, but now I was counting how many rolls were on the plate and dividing in half, calculating how many were mine to devour.

Edward saw the look, a smile overtook his face. *I know, my dear. I feel the same way about them. The cook here is famous for her baking skills, and I wanted to surprise you on our first day here.*

I smiled back and took my first bite. This was pure pleasure. I sighed. My wedding night may have caused me confusion, but this morning I was clear as to what I wanted. I wanted to clean this platter of delectable rolls.

Whether the satisfaction of that morning's repast or the ease of our conversation, the ache of the night surrendered to the blue skies and cool breezes of the Cape May landscape. We played in the ocean, Edward holding my hand as we jumped the waves. Childhood memories of Mama doing the same washed over me. Equally was the sense I was with someone safe. I could let down my guard, I could be me. I laughed as the waves knocked us down, the sand encrusting our toes.

Edward and I shared the love of the sea, the magic of the ocean that is dynamic, unpredictable. Calm and welcoming, it invites us to embrace it, to become one with it. Then, without warning, it can explode, attacking the shore that just moments ago welcomed its gentle waves. Such were my emotions those first few days – the days were warm and joyful while the nights alone in my bed brought shadowy condemnations for failings I thought were mine.

On the morning of our second week together, there was a box wrapped in a festive blue ribbon sitting on my chair as I made my way to the breakfast table.

Goodness, Edward, what is this?

Well, my dear, it is a glorious day and we are going bike riding.

My mouth flew open. Aunt Helena thought biking riding was unhealthy, and I was forbidden to even attempt such an adventure. I shared my aunt's rantings with Edward.

Poppycock! It seems to me when a woman wants to learn anything or try the unknown, there is always someone to solemnly warn her that such a desire is folly. Meanwhile, in the thriving metropolis of Philadelphia, a woman can work in a factory ten hours a day, stand behind a counter in a badly ventilated store from 8:00 a.m. to 6:00 p.m., and bend over the sewing machine for about five cents an hour without anyone caring enough to raise their voices in protest.

This is a new era, my dear. Fresh air and exercise are ours for the taking. Wait until you see the new places we can explore – country roads and seaside paths that will take your breath away. Cycling opens up all these new places for us to see and enjoy.

And then I heard his pause, and the word 'However,' started the next sentence. I held my breath, waiting to hear what restrictions were about to be placed on my potentially newfound freedom.

Edward pointed to the still unopened box. *Your current mode of attire, while lovely, will not do for our cycling adventures. I have taken the liberty of having a more practical, rational form of dress delivered for today's outing. We can always replace it if it is not to your liking, but it should serve today's purpose. A tandem bicycle is downstairs, a picnic lunch is packed, and we have the day to ourselves to ride along the ocean to our hearts' content.*

I literally jumped for joy as I tore open the box like a child on Christmas morning. There, carefully packed, was a divided checkered skirt, clinched at the ankles, with a tight-fitting jacket to match, and a pair of riding boots. I couldn't finish my tea for want of trying on these daring new pieces. I had lived in a world of corsets, large billowing skirts, and long-sleeved shirts with high collars. What lay before me relinquished all of that with the promise of unencumbered movement.

I grabbed the box, and with a quick "I'll be right back" practically skipped into my bedroom. After more than a few minutes of trying to figure what button went where I looked down and saw my legs peeking over the top of the black leather boots. My prim and proper look that marked the gentility of a woman hidden under yards of fabric was shredding. Now born was a new woman, sensibly dressed for an outing with her ankles exposed and not caring a fig for what others would say. I tied my hair back and returned to the breakfast table.

Edward looked up from his papers. *I knew you would. I knew you would look smashing.* He held up his coffee cup in a mock salute, his black eyes twinkling. *Here's to us not smashing this new cycle.*

I fell in love with the 'iron horse' from the first moment I sat on the seat and tried to find my balance. Edward had gotten us a Daisy Bell, a tandem bicycle where he sat in front and navigated while I sat in the back learning to pedal. By the third week of our holiday, he presented me with my own bicycle, black and shiny, and mine alone to ride and navigate. It was a Light Roadster, an English import with high handlebars and red-rimmed tires.

See how you do with it, Nell. He chuckled, patting the brown leather saddle sitting proudly on the glistening frame. *The saddle was made with the likes of you in mind. A bit more padding than the one you rode on last week. Take it slow, as we don't need to have you take a major fall. We need to return to Philadelphia with both you and the bicycle scratch-free.*

I was wobbly at first, and despite Edward's desire, a few mishaps left their mark on both me and the bicycle. It didn't matter. I was smitten. I had never known such freedom. I loved the feeling of motion, the speed, and the rise and the fall of the path beneath my feet. My pedaling became automatic as we explored new paths, new vistas. I was one with the machine, its wheels touching the earth, my eyes gazing forward. The early summer sun wrapping me in its shawl as I pedaled, the ocean breezes cooling me, pushing me ever onward. My eyes were able to see nature's beauty made even brighter by the closeness of the open sky embracing the sea that greets it.

Our days blended together, as did Edward and me.

Our days and nights started the rhythm of our life that was both comfortable and relaxed. We enjoyed each other's company and were equally content whether we dined alone or with others. At the end of the evening, Edward and I would sit in front of the fire, drink a final brandy, chat about what we had done, plan the next day's excursions, and then retire to our respective bedrooms. The fear and despondency that had gripped the first night were gone. Fresh air and exercise made me ready to escape into the folds of the silk sheets and warm comforter, mine alone to enjoy. Sleep came easily. I greeted each day with a sense of wonderment and delight as to what it might bring. I felt something that had long been missing from my life. I felt happy.

The month sped by. Edward was arranging for our bags to be taken for our return to Philadelphia. I adjusted my hat in the lobby mirror and scrutinized the likeness peering back. I blinked. This Nell looked stronger, more robust. My skin had a healthy glow, my eyes were bright and alert, their aqua coloring more pronounced. I nodded my approval, for this was the image of a 20th Century woman; one who owned a bicycle.

Hours later, walking up the sidewalk to Edward's home on Rittenhouse Square, a familiar wave of uncertainty rushed over me. This would always be Edward's house, his mother's home, and I the guest who never left. Six servants standing shoulder-to-shoulder, reminding me of soldiers dressed for battle in their black and white uniforms, were lined up on the steps awaiting my arrival. Upon being introduced, each either bowed or curtsied depending upon their gender. The butler and the house-keeper came from Edward's mother's home, there was no question as to whom would hold their loyalty. Then came the cook, a footman, and a housemaid who had served Edward since he had taken over its ownership. At the end of the line, with a broad smile, stood my own Bridget. Bridget had been with me since I was a child, and I demanded she stay with me. Mother Walker disdained the idea, but since I demanded nothing else, she acquiesced. I gave a quick prayer of thanksgiving, for the smile on her face was the only one I trusted.

The running of the house was now my responsibility. I felt awkward and too young. The lady of the house, indeed; an imposter, an interloper.

I repeated each of their names as I was introduced. Edward had already opened the door as I reached the top of the stairs. It was July, the air was thick and hot. My hands were moist from either the humidity or nerves, I couldn't tell.

I stopped just before the entryway and turned to face them with a smile. *I grew up just doors away from this house and always admired its beauty and quiet grandeur. I know your skill and dedication to the Walker family made it the star of our neighborhood. I believe that together we can make it a home.*

Thank you for welcoming me.

Taking my arm as we walked in, Edward whispered in my ear. *Well, that will create quite a buzz at their table.*

Whatever are you talking about? trying to remember what I had done wrong.

I am not sure any of those working here ever heard the lady of this house acknowledge their contributions in such a warm and inviting way. Well done, my dear. He gave my arm a squeeze.

I took a deep breath. So far, so good.

CHAPTER 5

1910

We were weeks away from our first anniversary. In less than the twelve months we had been together, my life with Edward had assumed a pattern. We would breakfast together, sharing the newspapers delivered to the table, ironed. Edward had grown up with such an indulgence; and I found it quite to my liking, no more ink-smudged fingertips. Edward, looking every inch the successful lawyer, walked out the door by 8:30 a.m.

My day was left to his mother to fill. There were specific charities and civic committees that required our presence and the Walker name. The same group of women was always there, discussing their roses, their housekeepers, and any of their so-called friends who were not in attendance. I rebelled inside but continued the pattern of endless meetings and luncheons where I was scrutinized for every word I uttered and the flatness of my stomach. The conversation of my 'maids' at my bridal luncheon forewarned me that Mother Walker was attempting to mold me, but I couldn't figure out how to stop it.

I looked forward to the evenings I shared with Edward where our conversations centered on art, literature, and politics. The more the discussion focused on Teddy Roosevelt's presidency, the better I liked it. And such debates – *did TR save the country from ruin with his involvement in the coal miners' strike or did he put the federal government at the table it had no right to sit at? Why did the relationship between Roosevelt and Taft end so disastrously? Would this Rough Rider commit political suicide and run again in 1912?* Edward asked for my views on topics I had never considered. My mind was challenged in ways no teacher had ever sought to attempt. The tedium of endless daylight meetings and social teas with seemingly no purpose was mitigated by the knowledge that my evening would be a delight. When the weather was fair, we found new paths and alleyways to explore on our bicycles. Aunt Helena disapproved and made it very clear my behavior was less than acceptable. Edward's mother either did not know of our escapades or chose not to comment. It mattered not.

I came home earlier than usual that afternoon. The Philadelphia heat was oppressive; you could see the air that cloaked the city in its smoky haze. The calendar said the first of May, too early for the hot weather to be controlling our lives and our temperaments. It would be weeks before we could escape to the Cape May breezes.

My ladies' meeting had run too long, and any air that was in the room had been taken up by discussions that were unable to distract me from the heat. I escaped as soon as I could, motivated by the desire to untie my corset and swallow any liquid that would cool me. The house was quiet; the staff had the afternoon off. I took off my hat and gloves, leaving them on the table in the entryway, when I heard a noise coming from the library. It wasn't a frightening sound, more like a whimper. I walked down the hallway to investigate, my heels announcing my movements with their click, click, click on the hardwood floor. I opened the door to the library, the curtains were drawn, the room dark.

My eyes were adjusting when I saw him. It was Edward sitting on the sofa with his head thrown back. His eyes closed, his jacket off, his right arm across the sofa's back. I thought he might be sleeping, except his lips were moving; and the sound coming from them was the groaning noise I had heard. I took another step, and the rest of him came into full view. His suit pants were down around his knees, a blonde curly head bending over him. The hair belonged to his newest associate, a young man whom I had met at the firm's Christmas party. I could not remember his name. He was bent over Edward's exposed penis, which emerged and disappeared in flawless rhythm through the perfectly shaped circle of the young man's mouth.

I watched, horrified. I could not move or utter a sound. Edward's moans coalesced into a few incoherent words; and his free hand moved with authority against the yellow curls of his supplicant, guiding his activity. Edward's hips bucked, but the young man held on tenaciously.

Edward's cry and mine were in harmony. I didn't know I had made a sound until the young man looked up with horrified eyes.

Edward froze, time stood still. I heard him call *Nell*.

I couldn't speak.

Edward looked at the young man, still kneeling on the floor. *Frederick, you should go back to the office now.* The young man, now labeled correctly as Frederick, jumped up, leaving his cap on the floor. Edward rose, placed the cap on the table, and readjusted his tousled clothes. He hadn't looked at me.

I started to shake. *My God, my God, my God.*

In less than five minutes since I entered the house, my world had collapsed.

I ran out the door and into the square, I needed air. I thought I would suffocate. The word *sodomite* shouting in my head. How could I not have known? Did others know? Was I the only one who would be surprised? Were there rumors that never came my way? Or, like a precious currency, were those rumors only given to a select few to spend as they saw fit? What was I to do? Where was I to go? Who could I tell? Who would believe me?

I stumbled onto a bench, everything around me blurring. The flowers in their full glory of spring freshness blended into a kaleidoscope of swirling colors. I lost track of time. A hand on my shoulder aroused me from my stupor. I jumped to my feet to find Edward, looking for the first time like a man not completely in charge.

He squared my shoulders and turned me so I was looking straight at him.

Nell, please look at me.

I looked up, unable to cry or speak.

Before you do or say anything, I ask you to think for a moment. Are you unhappy with me or our life? Do I not treat you as an equal? Do we not talk of literature, art, and politics as peers, each of us seeking the other's opinion? We have a marriage of mind and spirit. I know few married couples who could say the same. I am who I am and have been such since I could remember. This afternoon was a mistake in many, many ways. I give you my word it will never happen again in any home we share. I cannot and will not give you my word it will never happen again. I know my flaws and sins only too well to make such a vacant promise. I promise that if you return to me and our life together, I will never embarrass you or cause you harm.

Edward looked away, his dark eyes closed. *You do not have to make a decision at this moment as to what you want to do. I will come home for dinner; and if you want to talk about it then, we will. If not, I will wait until you are ready to have the conversation. My wish would be to have our life continue, that we have a marriage of companionship. I know many a man whose lusts are more conventional than mine who would wish for such an arrangement. What I will not do is make you unhappy.*

I love you, Nell, not as other men might love you, but love you I do. I love you for your wit, your intellect, your joy in the simple pleasures of life. We make a good pair, complementing each other so the combination of the two of us is greater than the whole of either one. If you can accept me for who I am, with my failings but also my word, I believe we can share a life together.

He kissed me gently on the cheek, a small tear falling from his right eye. Then he was gone. I had said nothing.

I sat back down. The sun had begun to form shadows through the trees when I stood up and walked back to the house. What might have taken others weeks or days to agonize over was clear to me. I was going to stay in the marriage, my reasoning pragmatic. I had no other place to go. Mother was still in her cottage in Saranac Lake, and a displaced daughter could hinder her recovery. Aunt Helena would never welcome me back. And try as I might, I could not fathom having a conversation with Papa as to what led to the break-up of my marriage. For the first time, I made a decision that was only mine to make. I would stay in the marriage on my terms.

That night at dinner, I told Edward of my decision. The week before, he had been offered a job with a prestigious New York City law firm, Sullivan & Cromwell. When I pressed for more details, he dismissed it. *Mother would never tolerate us moving farther than within a 10-mile radius.* I knew the argument was not mine to win. Today, however, the game had changed. I held a trump card.

I calmly told Edward that I wanted our life to continue on the one condition that we would leave Philadelphia. Only then would my life be my own.

He interrupted with one word, *Mother.*

I will handle your mother. Please pour me another glass of wine. He did.

That night I wrote to Mama, another letter I would never send. Though Aunt Helena was no longer reading my post letters, I continued to write the same messages addressed to Saranac Lake: life was good, I was happy, everything was fine. My Mama Letters continued to be for my eyes only. These words were my innermost thoughts, my fears, my dreams, my disappointments.

Dear Mama,

I have not been able to write about this even to you. I have been too ashamed, too confused, to put words on paper. Even now, my hand is shaking. I am afraid that someone will find this letter and our secret, mine and Edward's, will be known to the world.

Edward and I do not share the same bed. Even on our wedding night, I was alone. Edward showed no interest. At first, I was ashamed. I blamed myself, my inexperience. Then it felt normal, or normal for us, and I was content.

I thought someday I might broach the topic of having a child. It just never seems the right time to talk about it, and I am not even sure I want to have one. It is only the looks of women staring at my stomach to see if it is growing that reminds me.

This afternoon, it all changed. I came home to find Edward with a man. I ran out of the house, my eyes blinded with tears. Edward found me. He was contrite, honest, and asked me to stay in our marriage.

I thought about my future, my shock turned to anger and then resolution. I made the decision to remain in the marriage. Edward has agreed to my one demand, we are to leave Philadelphia.

Tomorrow I will meet with Edward's mother and confront her with the facts that I am sure she knows only too well. She is to give her blessing for Edward to start a new position at a law firm in New York City. I will let Papa know of our decision and will send you a 'post letter' explaining how excited Edward and I are to be taking this next step in our life together.

I plan to come to Philadelphia once a month to have dinner with Papa. I am not extending that invitation to Aunt Helena. I will continue to spend a week each summer with you in Saranac Lake. I will call Papa every Sunday after church after I have called you.

I grew up today, I took responsibility for my own life. A life that I have decided to share with Edward.

I feel strong, Mama, stronger than I have ever felt. I know what I am doing is right. I belong with Edward. We are good for one another, we complement and balance each other. I know that we will never have children but we can have a good life. A life that I have chosen to accept. A life that I will make my own.

I love you, Mama.
Your Nell

The next morning I arrived unplanned at Mother Walker's, a faux pas that at other times would never be forgiven. I shook my head no to the maid's offer to take my hat and gloves. *I will wait in the parlor.*

I went into the room, one that I had avoided since that fateful afternoon of my bridal shower. My 'maids' were correct; the draperies were outdated and stuffy.

Within 20 minutes, Mother Walker appeared, her hair fashioned, her make-up on, her deportment flawless.

Good Morning, Nell. What a surprise. I do hope you haven't inconvenienced yourself greatly by coming out so early in the day.

Not in the least, I replied. She summoned the maid to bring us coffee. I interrupted, *I will have tea.*

Of course, always slightly different and not surprising, my dear.

Minutes later as the maid was placing the tray on the table, I quietly said, *It is best we are alone for this conversation.* Without so much as an eyebrow raised, Mother Walker dismissed her with a curt nod, *That will be all, Kathleen. I will pour.*

Pulling Frederick's cap from my bag, I laid it on the table between us.

How long have you known?

She raised her cup to her lips, her eyes betrayed nothing. *Known what, my dear?*

I pointed to the cap. *Known that Edward prefers men to women, even women young, inexperienced, and naïve to the ways of the world.*

Whatever are you talking about? It must be the heat, our minds play games when the temperatures soar. I believe it is the hottest May on record for Philadelphia. You must be counting the days until you are running through the waves at Cape May. Have you reserved the same hotel? Her voice was calm, unflappable, only the slight shaking of the coffee cup as she replaced it in its saucer betrayed her.

My eyes never left her face. *I found him yesterday, in our home, with a man. Let me ask you again, how long have you known?*

Mother Walker clasped her hands together as if in prayer and turned her face toward the window. She said nothing.

Seconds passed. I asked again, *How long have you known?*

She turned to me, her voice soft. *Since he was a boy.*

Have you no shame, to allow a young girl to enter into a marriage with such a man? My voice rising.

Mother Walker's face darkened, she gave a brief laugh, casting me a look, a look that would have withered me days before. *You? You dare talk about shame? Your aunt had you on an auction block, hawking you to the highest bidder to take you away. Don't presume to talk to me about shame.*

She was right. The rush to present me to the 'right people' was a guise performed by the wiles of Aunt Helena to get me out of the house, a house that she continued to live in.

So your bid was accepted, and I am now your son's wife. Societal norms have been met. Any potential blemishes on the Walker name have been abated.

She paused, the muscles in her jaw tensed. She picked up the coffee pot and steadily reheated the liquid that had grown tepid in her cup. *What is it you want? Clearly, that is why you are here.*

I poured myself another cup of tea, feeling stronger. I was being treated as a worthy adversary.

I sat up straighter. *I intend for Edward and me to leave Philadelphia and start a life on our own. I know who I married and the sacrifice I will make in keeping my vows. There will be no grandchildren in either this house or my father's. I will not, however, stay in this City of Brotherly Love. Edward has been offered a position with a prominent New York City law firm. You are to give him your blessing to accept it and move on.*

Her mouth twisted. *And if I do not?*

I put my teacup back on the tray. *I will seek an annulment for my marriage. The tribunal will hear not only my story, but a doctor can testify to my virginity. I will be sure the young man with whom my husband was indelicately exposed yesterday afternoon speaks out, as well. Am I clear?*

Mother Walker raised an eyebrow, *Very clear, my dear. And my, haven't you grown up.*

She closed her eyes. The silence was deafening. At last her eyes opened, they looked dull, her complexion ashen. She nodded slowly. *I wish you and Edward the very best in this next venture. I will host a party to celebrate his new position and your move to New York City. I trust you will come to Philadelphia to visit.*

I nodded, victory had come easily; and while not sweet, there was a small amount of satisfaction. *I will surely visit my father, and Edward will come to see you. We shall both be here at your New Year's Gala, assuming that we make your coveted invitation list.*

Mother Walker bit her bottom lip, looking older than the woman who had greeted me minutes before. *A hard bargain, Nell. I will send Edward a note congratulating him on his new position and ensuring that he has my blessing in leaving the only home he has ever known.*

Thank you, Mother Walker, you are very wise. I took the cap off the table, placing it back in my bag.

No, Nell, pragmatic. Life is a game. There are rules and there are times when those rules must be broken. The hard part is to know what rules and when.

And with that, we both stood up, nodding in quiet agreement. I left without being shown out.

Dear Mama,

> *I met with Mother Walker today. I was unwavering that Edward and I must leave Philadelphia. I knew what I was doing is*

the right thing for me and the only option that Edward and I have to make this marriage work for us.

It is a bittersweet decision. Departing Philadelphia is leaving you and my childhood. This is the city of my memories, but it is not my future. I am not sure you would understand this. I am not sure even if I understand it. Moving from here feels right.

Edward was surprised when I told him that his mother was giving us her blessing to move to New York City. He didn't ask how she came to that decision, and I didn't share my conversation with him. He called Sullivan & Cromwell and accepted their offer the next day. This is a major career move for him. He will flourish.

Bridget is making the move with me, a link between my old and new worlds. So, in the midst of all this change, there will be continuity.

I am not sure what my new life will be like. The only thing I do know is that it will be my own. The decisions will be mine to make. The failures mine to acknowledge.

The Statue of Liberty in New York's Harbor lifts her lamp beside the golden door. I want to open that door. I want to see what is behind it.

I love you, Mama.
Your Nell

CHAPTER 6

1911

New York City doesn't allow you to be neutral – you either love it or hate it. I loved it from the first moment Edward and I changed our address. We spent the first three weeks in a hotel until we found our home, a home that welcomed me the first time I crossed its threshold.

Gramercy Park, like Rittenhouse Square, is an oasis in a world of brick-and-mortar. It has its own park, one that is protected from the outside world by black and steel rods that raise their spikes towards heaven. No spider would dare create a web between these spaces.

I knew the house was mine as soon as I walked through its door. This four-story brownstone, with steps coming down from the stoop, was unexceptional to the eye; but it said it belonged to this city and this area. More room than what we needed, it was the lovely library that made it feel like home, my refuge, my new beginning.

I sent Mama postcards from the best of the city's tourist sites, pictures of the Brooklyn Bridge, the Singer Building, the Hippodrome. Papa was more interested in New York statutes than its structures. Over our dinners, he wanted to hear about the recent changes in the legal marketplace. Edward had become an expert in securities reform. His reputation and stature within the legal community and at his firm were skyrocketing. Papa was impressed.

We were having dinner at the Belgravia, a hotel that graciously opened its doors to a woman traveling alone. *Moving to New York has been good for you, my dear Nell.* Papa was finishing his coffee but appeared in no hurry to leave the table. *Your Mama loves the picture postcards you send, preserving them in a special scrapbook so that unwarranted fingerprints won't do them harm. I believe she most covets the one of the Hippodrome. The theatre always called to your Mama. I think deep down inside she wanted a life on the stage,* giving me one of the rarest of his gifts, his smile.

Mama, an actress? I couldn't suppress a giggle.

Well, she never said it directly; but when we would go to the Chestnut Street Theatre, she always appeared somewhat wistful. Papa lit up his pipe. *She would have been adored by the masses, but I was the lucky one.* His eyes twinkled as the familiar smell of his tobacco filled the air. *I was chosen to be her adoring fan.*

He blinked, the memory of those days causing a slight stab in his heart. He moved the discussion to safer ground. *I hear from one of Edward's former partners that he is the rising star at his new firm. He is a great lawyer, with a keen mind and an affable manner. You have chosen well, Nell.*

I smiled, agreeing full-heartedly with his description of Edward. As to whether it was my choice would probably depend upon the date that decision was made.

———

The date was March 25th, a day that made me fall in love with the city all over again. The sun warmed the sidewalks, and the leafless trees raised their limbs as if praying for their buds to sprout and herald the coming of spring. I rushed through my morning's mail, responding to invitations to events that were of no of particular importance to me. Though we had lived in New York for months, I had not yet found my footing as to what I should be doing. I had fallen into the pattern I followed in Philadelphia and found there was little difference in the agendas and the conversations between the ladies' groups in Manhattan and their counterparts in Philadelphia. I was searching for something more. Something I had not yet found. Something that I knew I needed.

I retrieved my bicycle, knowing fresh air and exercise would help, making me a much more agreeable person by the time Edward returned home.

I was not alone in targeting Washington Square as my destination. Hundreds of New Yorkers were enjoying its simple symmetry, its curvy walks. I paused by a bench to observe the mixture of humanity parading in front of me. Giggling children calling to each other in languages few others understood mingled with the intellectual elite. Greenwich Village was a haven for radicals, rebels, and reformers. I was about to continue my journey home when smoke spiraling against the clear, blue sky caught my eye. I took my bicycle and walked closer to its source.

I found a building engulfed in smoke and flame. It looked like a fire-breathing dragon was inside, puffing away furiously. I looked up. There was a living picture in each window on the eighth floor – screaming heads of girls waving their arms, flames beating their faces. Shouts of 'fire' quieted the Square's natural cacophony of sound. A voice in the gathering crowd spoke up. *It's the Asch Building. The Triangle Shirtwaist Factory is on fire.*

Individuals who moments ago were strangers, acknowledging each other with only the slightest of nods, were now huddled together holding onto themselves and each other, mesmerized by the flames now burning a deep red and amber. A woman next to me shouted, *Oh My God! They are jumping.* She fell to her knees, sobbing. I saw him immediately, standing in front of an open window, flanked by girls on either side. It looked like a photo lit by the fire looming behind them. One by one, he took the hand of each girl, as if she was a lady being helped into a carriage, guiding her onto the window ledge. He would allow each girl the time to jump to her death before reaching for the next. As he brought the fourth girl to the window, she put her arms around him and gave him a final kiss. He picked her up and dropped her to her death.

I gazed in horror when he took his place on the same ledge. Tall and lanky with hair that the wind grabbed and then let fall softly around his face, he seemed to look directly at me; and giving a salute, he blew a kiss and jumped. His unbuttoned coat billowed around him like a balloon with no strings, the ground grabbing him as he hurled his way to meet it.

I was shaking, my hands gripping the handles of my bicycle for support. I added my voice to the crowd's plea to other girls stranded on the ledges not to jump. Two were intertwined, the taller girl hearing our cries placed both arms around the other and tried to pull her back towards the brick wall. But the shorter one broke loose from the protective embrace, twisted her head and shoulders loose, and jumped.

After her companion had fallen, the girl who was left stood back against the wall. Motionless. For a moment, she held her hands as if in prayer, her head tilted upward as if seeking divine intervention. A pillar of smoke rose out of the broken window, a few inches below her. Next to her, a tongue of flame licked up along the window sill and singed her hair. Just as the curling smoke was beginning to hide her from view, she stepped out like a spirit from the Netherworld. Feet first, she fell straight to the street.

I was hearing a new sound, so horrible it belongs in the worst of nightmares. The thud of a speeding, living body, hitting a stone walk. A noise so loud I was sure it could be heard all over the city.

Within minutes, the fire engines arrived, hindered by the bodies lying on the street. The smell of blood so pungent, the horses pulling their engines reared in panic. I stared in disbelief as the firemen raised a ladder that couldn't reach the burning floors. Others took out a life net, and two girls shot down. Their bodies broke the net. Their thuds were just as loud as if there had been no net, no attempt to save their lives.

After the first screams of terror, there was a massive hush, only the shouts of firemen broke the stillness. As the flames came under control, strangers hugged one another in disbelief at what we had just witnessed. Our tears flowed together in a stream of sorrow. Some stayed, unable to leave the hallowed ground, where bodies still laid. I joined the silent group of mourners, leaving one by one, needing to reconcile what they had just witnessed in a world where the sun continued to shine. It had all happened in less than twenty minutes.

I was numb with shock and disbelief. I found my way home, more by instinct than anything else. I didn't know who had died, their names nor their ages. The headlines the next day would tell me all I needed to know: 146 were killed, all but 21 of them women, most under 19 years old. I was the same age.

Edward came home early, the city grieving everywhere. He was stunned when I told him I had been there. My voice quivered, pacing in front of the fireplace. I pulled my sweater closer to my body trying not to shiver. *One by one, I saw, some not able to hold on any longer, they fell, their grip gave way. Others, their clothes aflame, would jump.* I fell into the chair, my eyes closed when I told the story of the young man and the last kiss.

Edward knelt by my side and took my hand.

It was living a nightmare. Even when the firemen arrived, their ladders didn't reach the top of the building and the nets couldn't hold the number of people jumping from that height. What were they thinking of in those last minutes of their lives? There was no escape. May this be their time in hell. My tears wouldn't stop, my body couldn't stop shaking. I cried.

When there were no more tears to be shed, Edward placed a glass of wine in my hand. *You have witnessed unimaginable horrors today. Drink this, Nell. You need a warm bath and a good night's sleep.*

We shall both rise early tomorrow and go to Mass. For the moment, I believe we can only offer our prayers.

I looked up at him, anger replacing the overpowering sense of grief and loss, my voice raised. *There must be something we can do. This can never be allowed to happen again. Whose fault is this? Buildings don't start on fire for no reason. Someone must have seen the danger. Someone must have known these lives could have been at risk. Why wasn't something done? Why didn't someone care?*

Edward stared at the fire, its blaze slowly dying. *You are right, Nell; but tomorrow is the time for that discussion. Today, you have seen hell on earth. There are people who share your anger and have been battling for safer conditions in our factories for years. Sadly, there have been more headlines than reforms, and progress has been slow. This tragedy may result in real change taking place, though it will not happen overnight. The interests that fight to keep the laws the same are powerful and politically connected.*

He sighed. *Perhaps in tomorrow's light, the world may find its way to doing what is right.*

While the next morning's newspapers headlined the horror that had taken place, I needed to see the harm that had been done. Despite Edward's objections, I found my way to Manhattan's Charities Pier, known as Misery Lane. This makeshift morgue was the final resting place of what remained of those who lost their lives the day before.

I shared my grief with Mama, another Mama Letter.

Dear Mama,

My heart is so heavy, I cannot describe its despair. I saw people die yesterday. Some because they had no choice, some because it was their only choice. It was the Triangle Shirtwaist Factory fire. You may read about it in the papers. I was there, Mama. The entire blaze from spark to ashes lasted less than half an hour but resulted in heartaches that will last forever.

I cannot shake the memory of what I witnessed.

Today I joined the mourners searching for their loved ones who never came home. The fierceness of the fire was hard to fathom even a day later. I walked alone, among the throngs of bewildered, grieving people who moved from box to box, hoping for a clue of recognition for a loved one lost. They spoke in dialects I did not understand, in words I did not know. Yet I understood their despair. Grief is a universal language.

I found myself standing next to one woman, tears streaming down her face. She stopped over one box and found a shoe charred and stained. She kept turning it over in her hands, hoping for a sign this could be the shoe of the one she had lost. I wanted to ease her sorrow, to provide some comfort. I took her hand, worn and crippled with too much sorrow to hold in too few years, and nodded yes. I am not sure why. The woman put the shoe to her heart and choked out the word Nicola. The morgue worker closed the box and handed the paperwork to transfer the remains to a mortuary to the woman still cradling the shoe. The woman tightened her thin shawl around her shoulders, looking to find strength in the shredding yarn, and found her way to the exit. I watched her leave, tears flowing freely, mourning for all that was lost and for the shroud of sorrow that enveloped the blue spring skies in this adopted city of mine.

I stood on the sidelines yesterday and watched horror play out before my eyes. I cannot sit on the sidelines any longer. This must change. There needs to be respect for all people's lives, no matter where they were born, no matter what language they speak, no matter how they pray.

I don't know what I am going to do, Mama. But I will do something.

I love you, Mama.
Your Nell

———

I was not alone in my anger and my resolve. Days later, Edward and I joined thousands of others at the Metropolitan Opera House. New Yorkers from all walks of life were uniting forces to ensure such a tragedy would never happen again. Sitting next to me, Edward pointed out Ann Morgan, daughter of JP Morgan, the industry tycoon, and Alva Belmont who had married her daughter off to an English lord prior to creating her own scandal when she divorced a Vanderbilt. Edward whispered they were part of the 'Mink Coat Brigade', socialites who spent their money and used their notoriety to support striking workers just a few years ago. I was straining to get a better look at the two when the crowd, restless up to this point, became quiet. Advancing to the podium was a young woman whose fiery red hair matched the passion of her speech. She did not thank us for our support. Rose Sneiderman, the daughter of Jewish immigrants, spoke of the harsh realities faced by her and the women who worked beside her. She challenged us to make a difference, she was clear in her rebuke. *This was not the first time young women have died or been maimed. The lives of these immigrants are viewed as cheap, replaceable. It is the owner's property that is protected as sacred.*

She spoke of the strife the workers have faced during their protests and then as if she was talking to me directly. *You hand out a couple of dollars for the sorrowing mothers, a charity gift. But every time the workers come out in the only way they know how, to protest against conditions that are unbearable, the strong arm of the law is allowed to press down heavily upon us.*

My head was flooded with memories of too many meetings when the agenda was to raise money for causes that we knew little about. Or at least I didn't. This woman, this Rose Sneiderman, was talking about real people, real problems. She was forceful. She was angry. She was right.

When she was finished, the crowd was silent. Then it began. Soon the building was shaking with the thunder of feet stamping and hands clapping. I was on my feet cheering, feeling part of something I had not felt before. Emotions were running high, amidst all the grief, a sense of euphoria captured the crowd. We were one, united in a cause.

The woman standing next to me shouted in my ear. *Isn't Rose magnificent? I'm working with women just like her, women who want to make a difference.*

Those were the words I wanted to hear. That is why I was there. I wanted to learn more, more about what others were thinking and doing. *I'm Nell Walker.*

Rachel Rosenthal, she shouted above the din.

Not trusting my voice would be heard above the uproar, I fumbled for my purse. Pulling out my calling card, I scribbled our address on the back and handed it to her. I mouthed, *Please come see me. I want to help.*

The next day, there was a knock at my door and Rachel entered my parlor and my life. She was dressed plainly, brown skirt and a simple white blouse, while I was wearing one of those shirtwaists that were the product of the exploitation of so many. I was the quintessential Gibson girl, fresh-faced, large-eyed, narrow at the waist, and slender at the hips. I was beginning to think of myself as a healthy, brave, independent woman. After all, I reasoned, I owned my own bicycle and lived in marriage with a husband who prefers other men to me. I had much to learn.

Rachel didn't wait for tea to be served before she began. *Well, last night set the stage, but it is up to us to get this act moving. What do you think we should do?*

Before I could reply, she rose from her chair and began to pace. I stood up, not knowing what I was to do, what I was to say. It mattered not. Rachel was speaking her mind, and I just happened to be the audience. *First, we have to show the world we care. We need to pay our respects to those who were killed, murdered by those shirtwaist kings, Isaac Harris and Max Blanck. They are the owners of the factory, they are the ones who locked the doors so no one could escape the flames. Murderers. They care nothing for human life, just for profits. Profits made by poor, young women whom they see only as anonymous cogs in their money machine.* Rachel looked like she was going to spit.

She sat back in her chair. As I poured the tea, she told me tales of horror. There had been many organized protests similar to those that Sneiderman spoke of where workers banded together to seek better worker conditions. Most of these were young girls led by an immigrant named Clara Lemlich. *Clara is a Jewish immigrant, as was my grandfather.*

My mouth dropped open.

What? You never met anyone Jewish before? Rachel smiled for the first time since she entered the house.

Not that I know of, I replied, feeling somewhat ashamed and incredibly naïve.

Well, now you have, and a New York Jew, as well. You may have hit the jackpot! She raised her teacup as if to toast.

I nodded, raising my cup in return while wishing I had a sheet of paper to record all she was saying. I was in the hands of someone who knew who she was and what she wanted to do. I needed to remember all the details of this conversation.

Clara was about 17 years old and was working sixty-six hours a week for the princely sum of $3.00. Not nearly enough to live on. Fed up with the working conditions and the poor wages, she formed a union. Later, she led a series of strikes that earned her the reputation of being a rabble-rouser. The owners knew they had to teach her a lesson so they hired two thugs to beat her up.

I put down my teacup. *They beat up a woman? Barely more than a girl.*

Rachel shook her head slowly. *She was beaten badly and left battered and bruised on the street, broken ribs and all.*

Did she die?

Those goons couldn't keep her down. Within days, she was back arguing for the workers to go on strike. And now she was mad, really mad.

I was trying to make sense of what I was hearing. *Couldn't she have gone to the police? My husband is a lawyer, couldn't she have pressed charges and had them go to jail?*

Rachel raised her eyebrows, shaking her head slowly and quietly. *Rose said it all last night. These workers don't have the support of the police or the courts. Tammany Hall only wants them for their votes. Striking workers have lost their lives because no one cares about people who look or sound different. For demanding better wages to support their families or wanting to be safe in their workplace, strikers are sent to Blackwell's Island, just across the East River from your lovely home. There they will dine not on your biscuits but on moldy bread. Our appointed judges agree with the factory owners, believing strikers are getting what they deserve.*

Rachel focused on the gold cross hanging from my neck. *I heard a story that one of your priests went to a factory where most of the workers were Italian immigrants and told them that striking was against God's will. So, if threats of violence and hard labor did not deter them from the picket line, there is always eternal damnation.* She smiled ruefully, shaking her head to my offer of another cup of tea.

What are we to do? I began to fidget, I couldn't sit still any longer.

Rachel stood up, a small smile lighting her face. *I knew from the first time I saw you jump up on your feet and cheer, you would want to do something. You have an energy about you. I could just sense it. So, first, we will walk in the procession to honor those who died. Then we will ensure they have not died in vain. I will meet you there.*

Her coat and hat retrieved, she was gone. The house was suddenly quiet, like the aftermath of a storm. A storm named Rachel.

Edward listened intently when I recalled the events of the day at dinner that night. He nodded, *The same issues were in Philadelphia, so it is not so very different. It is the political muscle of Tammany Hall that makes this city so unique.*

Can you explain this all to me in layman's language? I was trying to pull all the pieces together

Absolutely, Edward paused, his face taking on the contented look of a professor who had just been asked to expound on a favorite topic. *Tammany Hall has existed in this country for as long as it has been a country. Its history began in our home city of Philadelphia following the American Revolution as a social, fraternal, and benevolent organization. Named after Saint Tammany, a mythical Indian chief rooted in American Indian lore, the organization was designed as a means for exerting influence over the political process. At its very beginning, members elected their leader, known as the Great Sachem, and sought to influence legislation favorable to their own business interests.*

Nothing has changed much since that date. Their power grew with the arrival of the Irish following the Great Potato Famine. Those who came here worked their way into the Tammany structure like salmon swimming upstream to spawn. They became precinct captains, ward bosses, and aldermen, injecting energy and imagination into an elaborate ward system dispensing favors in exchange for a vote. The entire machine is well represented by the organization's official symbol, a ferocious Bengal tiger.

Edward was a master storyteller, I was getting my second tutorial of the day. *Gangs and thugs, like those who attacked that Lemlich woman, work at the behest of the political apparatus. They are the muscle, their unique skills most notably required on Election Day when all political parties unleash their bully boys to police the polling sites. Your new friend knows all this, of course. We will not get real change into those sweatshops or murderous workhouses unless you get the politicians on board. And that, in New York City, means Tammany Hall.*

There is not a lawyer I can think of that hasn't run into their power in and out of the courtroom.

Edward stood up, and for the first time, it looked like he was searching for the right words. He put another log on the fire that crackled when it hit the flame. He turned to face me.

One more thing, Nell, and this is difficult. Rachel is Jewish and with all her virtues and attributes, there are people we know, with whom we socialize, who will not accept her simply because she doesn't worship in the same way they do.

Trying to take in all I had just heard, I looked up, startled. *What do you mean? Rachel is educated with a college degree from Barnard, a major accomplishment for a woman in today's world. She is committed to making a difference.*

Edward refilled his wine glass. *You are a wise woman, Nell, but I fear there are few like you in today's world. There are places we go where Rachel will not be welcomed simply because she is Jewish.*

My voice went cold. *Well, my dear Edward, to quote you: Poppycock! We should not tolerate such people or places in our lives. It is unacceptable in this day and age. This is the 20th Century and Queen Victoria is dead. People should be accepted for who they are.* My eyes never left his face.

I, more than anyone, agree with you, my dear; but I wanted you to be forewarned. New York is now in mourning for the tragedy that it has faced. In too short a time, it will be forgotten and life will return to what it once was.

I got up from my chair, taking the last sip from my glass. *Not if I can do anything about it.*

It looked like all of New York City came out on April 5th to say farewell to those who came to work one day, only to be burned to death. The day was dreary, a bone-chilling depressing rain fell on the mourners, their sadness transparent. Rachel, Edward, and I joined the funeral march of more than a hundred thousand others. No one spoke, only the clicking of our heels and the clomping of the horses carrying the caskets broke the silence. The entire city was muted in black. Black bunting hung on the doors of closed businesses, while multitudes watching the procession created a man-made canopy of opened black umbrellas, their only protection from the rain draining the black storm clouds.

As we reached Washington Square and the Asch Building, emotions peaked. I began to weep, joining the piercing cries of joined voices now seeking relief from their grief. It was a continuous sound, like a roll of thunder in a raging storm accompanied by the marching of thousands of feet.

We will not forget, you will not be forgotten, was the mantra playing inside my head.

———

The following week, I was at odds with myself. Edward had returned to the firm, and Rachel was moving into newfound quarters in Greenwich Village. The weather was as dreary as my spirits.

Out of habit rather than desire, I had joined the New York City chapter of one of Mother Walker's charity groups. I was there because I didn't know what else I should be doing. I was there because I had no other place to go.

I was agitated entering the meeting room, its sense of complacency permeated the air. There was no energy, no height-ened sense of commitment that aroused the crowd when Rose Seiderman had spoken. The flowers on the tables, the tea service, the gentleman who took our coats, were all too perfect. As I sat at one of the empty tables, my foot began to tap, my eyes darting from one woman to the next to see if there might be one person with whom I could connect.

Then I saw her, across the room, a cup of tea in her hand, talking to no one. Everything about her said new – new money, new clothes, new to this circle. Her hat was having a hard time staying in place on top of a head of massive blond curls that could not be tamed, particularly given the damp weather. I caught her eye and waved her to join me at the empty chair next to mine.

She smiled as she sat down, trying to adjust her hat that had tipped precariously to one side. Before I could introduce myself, Miss Beekman, our no-one-would-ever-dare-run-against-her president, took the gavel in her hand and any idle chatter ceased. As the minutes dragged on, I was feeling caged in, like an animal ready to pounce at the first opportunity to escape. There were reports, following reports, following reports. I thought I would go mad.

Finally, I could stand it no longer and I stood up, looking directly at Miss Beekman whose face registered both shock and dismay by my boldness. *Forgive my interruption, but I am trying to better understand the mission of this group. Am I correct in assuming your purpose is to raise money and then give it away?*

Miss Beekman's smile changed from annoyance to self-satisfaction. *That is indeed what we do.*

My hands rose to my sides, my palms facing upwards. *Are you sure that your money is making a difference? That it is going to the right places to help the right people? I witnessed first-hand the deaths at the Triangle Shirtwaist Factory.*

Hats bobbed side-to-side, and murmurs of *Terrible, Tragedy* spread from table to table. No one other than the young lady seated next to me made eye contact.

Have you seen the factories where these girls are working? Most are no more than children. Do we know what working conditions they are being subjected to? How they are being treated? Where they live? What can be done to ensure their future? I couldn't stop, I heard Rachel's voice in my ear.

Miss Beekman's gravel hit the table with a force that awakened even the drowsiest in attendance. *We do not wish to expose ourselves to the perils within the tenement walls. It is up to others better adept and more experienced than the ladies at this meeting to go into such places. We send money to charities, ones that we have sponsored for years. They are run by the right people who are grateful for our help.*

I was not to be curtailed. *That is important, but perhaps we could be doing more. We should see for ourselves where the money should be spent. We are women of the 20*th *Century, we should raise our voices as well as money to bring about the change that is required. Young women, and men, are dead because others looked the other way. We should be different. We should be heard.*

The young woman sitting next to me spoke for the first time. *We should get the vote.*

Perhaps, responded Miss Beekman, her eyes narrowing, *it would be more reasonable for you, Mrs. Walker, to direct your involvement to another society as I do not believe we are the least bit interested in changing our direction. We wish you every success.*

Ladies, let us continue with our agenda.

I was dismissed. As I gathered my things, the young woman sitting next to me did the same. We rose and walked out of the room together. Neither one of us looked back.

We made our way to the sidewalk, the gray clouds had disappeared and the fresh air and blue sky refreshed my spirits. I turned to my new companion. *Thank you so much for your support, I have never done anything like this before. I can't stand this feeling of hopelessness. I do apologize if by sitting next to me, I made this difficult for you.*

Trying again to straighten her hat with its pins now sticking out, she gave a rueful smile. *No need to apologize. This whole lady's thing is my mother's plot to get us accepted into New York society. I told her Mrs. Astor would not be calling on us anytime soon, no matter how fine our clothes or how fancy our address. Three years ago we were dirt poor, living in not much more than a shack in the Colorado mountains. Then daddy's mine struck gold and we were rich, practically overnight. The first thing my mother did was to send me off to a finishing school so I could learn to talk and act like a proper lady. I am a mixed success. I can talk with the best of the lot now. My nouns and verbs all agree, but the last thing I want to do is act like one, particularly like those ladies at the meeting today. And you are so right, if we want to make a difference, we need to do something other than hosting teas.*

Having given up the fight to keep her hat in place, she took it off, a mass of blond curls that would have made the cherubs weep in envy was unleashed. *However, I could surely use a cup of one right now. I never did have one at the meeting. I was afraid that I would slurp and drips would end up on the saucer or, worse, on me!*

I threw my head backed and laughed out loud. A sound I hadn't made since I witnessed the fire. *Tea, we shall have. We are not too far from the Plaza, and they have the best scones in the city. I am Nell Walker.*

I love scones, her voice increased by two decibels. *I can never have them. Mother worries my fate in life is to take after my father's side of the family, women with too much flesh, which is her polite way of saying they are fat. I am only allowed a slice of toast with no butter for breakfast. If I beg for more, I get a half-grapefruit.* Her nose wrinkled. *I don't see what the fuss about being rich is if you can't enjoy it. And,* looking into my eyes, *trying to make a difference in other people's lives. My name is Victoria, Victoria Remy. Mother named me after the old queen herself. She always had the highest aspirations for me. I fear I am a bit of a disappointment.*

I took her arm in mine and headed for the hotel. The trees began to move gently as if to welcome their budding leaves and this new friend into my life. *Next week you will come to my house and meet Rachel Rosenthal. She has been active in trying to change the working conditions for both women and children. She is so dynamic and committed to the cause that, at times, she is quite exhausting. Wonderful, but exhausting. You will understand the first time you meet her.*

In less than a month, I had found something I never had before, friends. We were an odd trio. Three women: one nouveau riche who was a breath of mountain fresh air, one who had grown up on the streets of New York willing to engage in combat to make right the wrongs of the modern world, and me, a married woman who sleeps alone and wants to make a difference.

Edward was enthusiastic after meeting Rachel and Victoria. *Like you, Nell, they are as different as chalk and cheese, yet the three of you balance each other. Do be careful as you look to define your purpose, how you plan to make a difference. There are powerful men in this city and this state who don't want change, no matter how well-bred or articulate the person is making the argument.*

Spoken like a lawyer, Edward.

Spoken like someone who loves you, was his response.

———

Three days after the fire, Harris & Blanck put a notice in the trade papers. They were back in the shirtwaist-making business. Their new factory was the first one Victoria, Rachel, and I went to visit. It looked like all the others on the lower East Side, surrounded by brick buildings so close together no air could make its way between them. It was Sunday afternoon, and the building was empty. Rachel found an open door, and we walked in. We got up to the second floor when the guard, a plain, balding man with his necktie askew and his face red from exertion, came running up to us. He was thick-necked and narrow-eyed with temples gleaming with perspiration. *Trespassers, you have no right to be here. Get out! Get out! I'll call the cops.*

We were just leaving, Victoria retorted in her best finishing school accent and pointing her gloved finger over his shoulder. *I would suggest that you have Mr. Harris and Mr. Blanck remove the two rows of sewing machines to our right. They are blocking the fire exits. I believe that is against the law.*

As he turned in the direction, we hastily retreated down the stairs, never breaking our stride nor looking back. We didn't speak again until the factory and its guard were out of sight.

Nothing has changed, I sighed.

Rachel squared her shoulders. *Not yet.*

CHAPTER 7

THE TRIAL

Two weeks after the fire, a grand jury had indicted 'the shirtwaist kings' owners Isaac Harris and Max Blanck on six accounts of manslaughter stemming from two of the 146 deaths in their factory. Rachel was satisfied with the indictment and I concurred, thinking that justice would be served. The newspaper headlines echoed my sentiments.

We were at the breakfast table. Edward had finished his coffee, his newspapers, and had straightened his tie. This was his ritual. Next, he would look around the room as if he were taking in every detail, then he would stand up and announce that he was leaving for the office. He didn't deviate from his routine. This morning, as the sunlight cast a yellow glow on the silver tray with its freshly baked bread, was different.

Edward stayed seated and covered my hand with his, an action so rare that I must have registered my surprise. *This trial may not have the outcome you desire. You may be disappointed, Nell,* followed by his best lawyer's briefing on what to expect rather than relying on the newspaper's prediction. *Harris and Blanck are being defended by a giant among giants of the New York legal establishment, Max D. Steuer. I have never met him personally, but he is the best trial lawyer there is. He doesn't lose cases. Charles Whitman and his team in the District Attorney's Office may have public sentiment on their side, but Steuer never loses. Everyone, I mean everyone, in the legal community has the highest respect for him.*

I poured myself another cup of tea. *He is so good, he defends murderers?*

Nell, we take an oath as lawyers to defend the Constitution of the United States and the Sixth Amendment that established you are innocent until proven guilty. It is what we do.

I shook my head in disgust, *One more reason I am glad I am not a lawyer. What you do sounds boring; and if it is not boring, you end up defending crooks. You have chosen an odd profession, my dear Edward.*

He stood up, a small smile lifting the corners of his mouth. *Yes, indeed. One, I might add, for which I am well compensated.*

Touché. Well, Mr. Whitman and his crew may turn the tide of the successes this Mr. Steuer has won so far.

We shall see, were his parting words.

Along with most of New York, Charles Whitman was convinced that the door to the Washington Place stairway on the ninth floor of the Asch Building had been locked and had prevented the Shirtwaist Factory workers from escaping the fire. The survivors had the same version of the story: as the flames entered the crowded loft, the workers ran to the door. They pushed and pulled, twisted the knob this way and that. The door would not budge.

Heading up the prosecution team was Assistant District Attorney Charles Bostwick. It was up to him to make the case for the people. Rachel and I saw ourselves as part of the group for whom he was advocating, we were the people.

The trial began in early December when a sharp northwest gale drove five inches of snow onto the streets. The day was bitterly cold, a cold that found its way through the cracked windows and wooden flooring of the courtroom.

A crowd of about 200 people packed the hallway leading to the courtroom. English mixed with Yiddish as the crowd shouted: *Murders! Murderers! Merders! Merders! Give us back our chil-*

dren! Harris and Blanck blanched as they worked their way through the crowd. Steuer appeared unflinching, slamming the courtroom door shut through the shrieking that he did not seem to hear.

In the sea of humanity inside the courtroom, Rachel and I found seats. The smell of wet wool coming from the coats the spectators were still wrapped in choked out any fresh air, making the space both confining and suffocating. I leaned over to Rachel, *Edward told me that Steuer is the best lawyer money could buy. He has gone years without losing a case.*

Rachel looked grim. *Steuer is a Tammany boy. I predict he will get these crooks to walk out of here free and easy. He came up like the rest of them, went from hawking penny papers to working in a garment sweat-shop. He is smarter than the smartest, a blend of charm, good humor, and icy brilliance. Bostwick and the rest don't stand a chance against Max Steuer.*

I shuddered not from the cold but from despair.

The trial lasted days, days that had more darkness than light. Papa spent Christmas with Mama in Saranac Lake, taking my presents and wishes for the New Year with him. Though they knew I was attending the trial, I couldn't share my sadness, my fear that justice would not come from this courtroom. I wrote a Mama Letter.

Dear Mama,

I attend the trial despite the bitter cold. I find my way to the courthouse as the winds whip the snow, biting my face like shards of glass. I cannot stay away. I stare at the two owners of the Triangle Shirtwaist Factory, these men who had caused so much grief for so many. Blanck is a well-fed, moon-face man; he keeps his big beefy hands folded, clenching and unclenching his fists, his signature diamond stickpin sparkling in what little sun the courtroom yields. Harris is smaller, sharper, he looks like a beaver in his fur coat with piercing eyes that appear indifferent to what is happening around

*him. A young woman named Margaret Schwartz died in the fire.
Blanck and Harris are being tried for her murder. She represents all
the others who died that day.*

*I listen to the lawyers, the witnesses who swear to tell the truth.
The district attorney brings witness after witness, describing their
first-hand accounts of being locked into the burning building. All the
survivors told the same story. Dressed in their Sunday best, they said
the fire had cut off the escape through the Greene Street door. When
they ran to the Washington Place exit, the door wouldn't open.
Blanck and Harris had the door locked, supposedly to prevent
employees from stealing materials.*

*I became bored with the repetition, the same story being told
countless times, my mind wandered. Today, I looked around the
courtroom and noticed that everything seems worn out. White walls
aging yellow, covered by a lingering film of too much cigarette
smoke. The seat on my chair is cracked, forcing me to sit still or else
be pinched. Strong and unfamiliar smells from other people's
kitchens, packed in their lunch pails, permeate the air.*

*I was lost in my thoughts when she came to the stand and raised
her right hand. Her name was Kate Alterman, no more than a girl
herself. The courtroom fell to a hush, even Blanck's hands lay quiet
on the table.*

*Kate told of being with Margaret Schwartz as they tried to
open the door to escape the fire. Margaret was kneeling by the door.
Tears streaming from her face, Kate said she called Margaret's name
as she turned away from the smoke and heat. The last thing she saw
was the hem of Margaret's dress beginning to burn, the ends of her
hair being singed.*

Kate was sobbing, as was I and all around me.

The prosecution rested.

*I thought perhaps this would do it, the jury would be won over
by Kate's testimony. You could feel the sadness, the air heavy with
grief.*

*Steuer showed no emotion as he approached the witness box. He
was a short man who gave no appearance of the giant he was*

purported to be. He did not thank Kate for her testimony or offer any sign of sympathy of what she had witnessed. He simply asked her to repeat the account of Margaret Schwartz's death. Kate did. He then asked her to do it again. And then again. And then again. Each time, the words Kate used were very similar. Even I could guess he hoped the repetition of phrases would suggest to the jury she had been coached.

Edward had warned me. Steuer was living up to his reputation. Somehow he had succeeded in damaging Kate Alterman's credibility without ever directly attacking her. I was impressed and I was outraged. I wanted to applaud his skill; I wanted to slap his face.

I went home that night, unable to sleep, not wanting to stay awake.

Throughout the next couple of days, Steuer produced his case, witnesses designed to show that the ninth-floor deaths resulted from fire blocking the Washington Place stairwell, even though the door was actually open. Various salesmen, shipping clerks, watchmen, painters, and other building engineers told of their passage through the ninth-floor door – though, of course, none had attempted to exit through the door at the time of the fire. One witness said a key was "in the lock all the time," another that a key was attached to the door by tape. The district attorney couldn't prove they were lying. You just knew they weren't telling the truth.

Blanck and Harris smiled throughout these testimonies. They already knew what stories would be told.

By the end of the trial, Steuer's star power was not diminished. He approached the jury to give his final summation: "Gentlemen of the Jury, 1911 is drawing to a close. 1911 was a bitter year for these two men. Thirty years ago the defendants began in a shop not equipped with electric lights, with stairs made of wood and which they climbed together. I labored in one of those shops. The progress that has been made in those factories is wonderful. I do hope, I really hope I have brought to you the proof of their innocence."

The judge called a recess until after Christmas. We were to go home and celebrate. Yet, in too many homes someone would be missing.

I don't understand, Mama. I don't understand how people can behave so badly. Innocent people died that day. I saw them die. Someone needs to take responsibility. Someone needs to be held accountable. Someone needs to make sure this is not forgotten.

I am hard-pressed to join in the festivities of this season. It doesn't feel like Christmas to me. It feels like Good Friday, where darkness rather than light prevails.

I love you, Mama.
Your Nell

———

1911 was coming to an end, and New York greeted the holidays with open arms, like a child receiving a present on Christmas morning. Our tree was decorated, and tinsel seemed to be hanging everywhere. On the streets, strangers wished each other Merry Christmas while frantically completing their yuletide errands. I was hard-pressed to think of anything that could be merry.

I was dreading the annual Christmas party at Edward's firm, knowing that this over-produced extravaganza would do little to brighten my mood. My role was twofold: smile adoringly at Edward and not insult the managing partner's wife.

The firm had outdone itself in setting the Christmas tone. As we entered the foyer, we were greeted by a Christmas tree that took up most of the room's space. The top of the tree reached the ceiling, its multitude of branches lifting upwards as if searching for sunlight. Covered in ribbons and gold, trinkets and glitter, its natural beauty was masked. Decorations, lit candles, and the smell of pine combined to send the message that we were to be festive, to sparkle. I was in no mood for any of it.

We were seated at dinner with one of the firm's clients, a

newspaper publisher by the name of Monroe, and his wife. As our conversation with our dinner companions progressed, we began to talk about the trial. Mrs. Monroe's eyes widened when I said that I had sat through every session. She said nothing.

Mr. Monroe expressed a view that many believed the victims of the fire were at fault for their own deaths. I was outraged by the sentiment and couldn't contain myself. *Let me see if I understand your position, Mr. Monroe.* I dared not look over at Edward. *You believe because these girls, and we are talking girls, who had just arrived in our country with little or no education and could only find work in such places as the factories owned by the likes of Harris and Blanck were to blame for their own deaths?* I didn't pause. I wasn't looking for an answer.

Perhaps if they came from different backgrounds, had the privilege of good food, good health, and a fine education, they would not have had to jump out of windows that March morning as the flames leaped all around them?

Now, now, Mrs. Walker, Mr. Monroe began in a patronizing tone that only fueled my growing anger. *What I am saying is these kinds of women are prone to panic rather than thinking rationally about their options. If you and my wife were in similar circumstances, I am convinced you would have been able to escape this sorrowful but explainable tragedy.*

My voice started to rise. *So, now our sex is to blame rather than the owners who locked the doors, worked their employees seventy hours a week, and saw only profit and not people when they walked the factory floors, diamond stickpins in their lapels?*

Clearly becoming uncomfortable with how the conversation was going, Monroe turned to Edward for support in his position, *Nothing wrong with wanting a bit of profit, eh Walker?*

Edward didn't have the chance to respond. To this day, I don't know what possessed me but I was a woman on a mission. I broke in, *You publish newspapers, do you not, Mr. Monroe?* He was nodding his agreement, clearly not knowing how this conversation was headed. *I have an offer. What if I were to go into one of these factories and do the same work in the same way as one of these girls? If I reported on what I saw and how I was treated, would you be willing to publish my accounts?*

My mind was racing faster than I could speak. Edward tried to smile but his eyes gave me that 'careful Nell' look usually reserved for those rare moments when I was in his mother's company.

Mr. Monroe appeared stunned. He began mumbling to no one in particular that he had never heard of such an idea, a lady wanting to go into the slums. Then for the first time his wife, who had been silent for most of the evening, spoke up. *Splendid idea, our own Nelly Bly. My dear*, now looking at her husband who seemed dumbfounded by how quickly the conversation changed, *why don't you have your editor, Steven Bradley, meet with Mrs. Walker after the New Year? Together they can best determine the storyline to follow.*

My eyes must have registered my surprise. She quietly patted her husband's hand while looking directly at me. *The paper has been in my family for generations. My father was the publisher until the day he died and his father before him. I was an only child, so my dear Norbert has taken their place at the table. Ink, rather than blood, ran through my father's veins; and I seem to have inherited the same malady. As much as I love the newspaper, I leave the business to the men in my family, who have the head for such matters.*

She smiled demurely, a smile that belied the calculating mind that lay behind her deferential comments. *I am sure Mr. Bradley will be able to see you early in the New Year. Don't you agree, Norbert? And Mrs. Walker, if it is not inconvenient, would you consider joining me for tea tomorrow afternoon? Say about 3:00 p.m.? We are part of the pioneers who moved near the Dakota years ago. Although not quite the wilds that captured people's imaginations, the children do love exploring Central Park most afternoons.* She reached into her purse and handed me her calling card that, like its owner, was of fine quality and understated elegance.

Without taking a breath, she looked at her watch, *Goodness, my dear, look at the time. We must be on our way as the baby still refuses to sleep through the night.* She smiled ruefully, *we have four.* She gave her husband a look, and he stood up as if on command.

I was amazed, and though we had been in each other's company prior to this evening, I had never focused on them as a couple. She was a tower compared to her husband who was as short as she was tall. She was thin while his girth was bursting the buttons on his silk vest.

She took my hand to say goodbye. *I do hope tomorrow will work for us.*

Absolutely, I am looking forward to it.

I, as well, and after the normal exchange of pleasantries, they were gone.

Edward sat down and called the waiter over, *Two brandies, please.*

Well, Nell, do you have any idea...?

I know, I know, but I think this could help.

Help whom or what? His glass posed as if to raise a toast.

I raised my glass as well. *Rachel has begun working to get our politicians off their duffs and put laws into place that can protect these girls and children. Once women are given the right, we should be electing representatives who will agree that children less than eight years old should no longer be working in canneries.*

Whoa! Wait a minute, Nell. You know I agree with you that something needs to be done, but I am not sure putting you in danger is the best way to go about it.

Well, my dear Edward, now you know what it feels like.

Edward's eyes registered his surprise. *What does 'what' feel like?*

I smiled, clicking his glass with mine. *Wanting to have a vote.*

The next day I found my way through Central Park, an oasis wonderfully at odds with the buildings growing up around it, to call on Mrs. Monroe. That day, the land was barren, its rolling meadows blending into the dirt, its winding paths a marked contrast to the grid defining the neighborhood encroaching its borders. The address I was given led me to The Pasada on the

corner of West 65th Street. I had never been in an apartment
building before and was curious as to what the rooms would look
like. The outside of the building did not disappoint with its
frosted Beaux Art ornamentation and capped two-story mansard
roof. It proved a worthy introduction to the entry, all marble,
and stone with a large "Palm Room" complete with a fountain
and a stained-glass dome.

I was met at the Monroe apartment by the maid who led me
into the parlor with a mesmerizing view of the Park. Cast iron
bridges, flickering gas lights highlighted this oasis of quiet, all
transplanted into a city that defines the word energy.

In the midst of my deliberation, Mrs. Monroe appeared
looking more like a frazzled housekeeper than the woman with
whom I had dined just hours before. Her hair was falling out of
its bun, and she had one child on her hip and another clinging to
her dress. I must have registered a look of surprise as she lifted
her one free hand in a form of surrender. *Pardon all of this, but I
am afraid we are a bit of a madhouse. We are going to our home in the
Hamptons for the holidays, our nanny has come down with the most
awful flu, and I am trying not to let on that Santa may be too exhausted
to wrap any of the presents making their way down the chimney.*

She then gave the heartiest of chuckles and called for the
maid to take away the child that was glued to her skirt. She bent
down to kiss him as she put his hand into the outreached palm
of the maid. *Kathleen is going to take you into the kitchen where a
cookie or two will be yours to munch on to your heart's content. Your older
brothers will not know your whereabouts*, giving him a conspiratorial
grin. He broke loose with a gallop and never looked back. Mrs.
Monroe called after Kathleen. *Kathleen, I am sorry but could you
please ask Mary to bring us tea?*

With a quick, *Yes Ma'am*, Kathleen was out of sight being
pulled furiously by a determined towhead in search of the
promise treat.

*Again, Mrs. Walker, my sincere apologies. We are usually not quite in
such disarray, though with four children under age seven, life is never*

dull. She placed the baby between pillows on the sofa, *I need to keep Grace with me if you don't mind. She is still too young to be lured away by the promise of freshly baked cookies and a reprieve from being bullied by older brothers.*

She took a deep breath, the baby now sleeping soundly. *I did so want to talk with you. I think what you want to do is brave and so necessary. Before Grace was born, I was very active in the suffrage movement and plan to return as soon as my body is my own. Norbert, Mr. Monroe, has come around to believing that women should get the vote.* She gave a shrewd smile, *It took a fair amount of convincing and I do believe,* as she looked over at her daughter who looked like a sleeping angel, *Grace sealed the argument. He simply could not reason why she should not be given the same rights as her brothers.*

That is not true today. I could not inherit my father's business and his father's before him simply because I am a woman. Sheer foolishness. I was an only child, she continued, pausing only long enough to pour us the now-delivered tea, *as was my father before me. My job is to replenish the family tree, a role that is not without its pleasures,* her voice tinged with a smile. *Norbert is not without his skills.*

Now, tell me about you, how you found your way to New York, how you came upon the idea to write for a newspaper. I want to hear all now that the household appears to have settled down.

And so I did. Mrs. Monroe, whom I was to call Anne, listened intently, interrupting only to ask questions. Before I knew it, almost two hours had passed when the door opened and two identical scamps swirled in, yelling: *Mama, we are home and hungry.* The footman who had accompanied them looked in need of a warm fire and a hot toddy.

Boys, your manners, please, and the voice of the woman I met at dinner was evoked once again. *We have a visitor, and you are to be properly introduced before you make another move.* The boys stopped in their tracks, and in their very best private school decorum came to stand in front of me.

Good afternoon, they said in unison.

Nell, please let me introduce you to Benjamin and Franklin, my twin boys. Looking directly at the two boys with an "I will brook no nonsense" stare. *This is my new friend, Mrs. Walker. She is going to write for Father's paper.*

The boys bowed slightly, *I am the oldest,* offered Benjamin.

And I am smartest, was Franklin's retort. *I didn't know ladies could be reporters.*

Goodness. It is a pleasure to make your acquaintance though I don't know if I can properly tell you apart. And Franklin, this is a new century, wait until you see all the things that women can do.

Anne tousled his hair, *Starting with being able to vote.*

Looking over their heads, she went on, *You will soon be able to discern which one is which. Although they are mirror images of each other, they see the world differently, like Degas and Renoir painting ballerinas. Yet, as brothers, they are one and would agree they had painted a ballerina.*

Boys, there are cookies and milk in the kitchen. Timothy, thank you for taking them to the Park this afternoon. Please, help yourself to Cook's good baking, as well. The boys walked two steps before breaking into a run to see who would be first at the kitchen door.

Timothy tipped his cap and was gone.

I, too, realizing the afternoon had quickly passed, bid my farewell.

It has been a pleasure, Nell. I will be sure Norbert calls Mr. Bradley first thing tomorrow morning. We will set the appointment for 10:00 a.m. on the Monday after the New Year if that is convenient for you.

That will be fine. I can't thank you enough for opening this door for me, Anne.

She took my hands in hers, *Just tell the world their stories, Nell. The stories of those forgotten and those ignored. We may not be able to solve the problem today, but we can start to make a difference.*

As I closed the door behind me, I practically skipped down the street to my carriage. This was going to happen. I was going to write for a newspaper. I just needed to figure out how I was going to do that, what was I going to say.

First, however, I returned to the trial.

On December 27th, Judge Crain sent the jury out of the courtroom to deliberate their verdict. They were instructed that they must find beyond a reasonable doubt that the locked door caused the death of Margaret Schwartz and whether the defendants knew or should have known the door was locked.

When the jury had been dismissed, I leaned over to Rachel and recounted my conversation with Anne Monroe and my scheduled meeting with Mr. Bradley. The look on her face was priceless. *Tell me, what is it that you plan to do?*

I want to tell their stories. No, to be exact, I am going to tell their stories no matter what the outcome today. I will do everything I can to be sure that the world will not forget the pain Harris and Blanck caused. Because of their greed, people died. The lock was their gun, and they pulled the trigger. I want to tell the stories of these innocents. I feel as if their spirits are looking over my shoulder.

Rachel nodded, *Ahh, yes, I can think of a plan;* and before she finished her sentence, the judge appeared. My courtroom clock confirmed that the jury had begun its deliberation less than two hours ago.

The jury returned the verdict of not guilty. Harris and Blanck were free men.

Though not unexpected, Rachel and I were stunned. I felt numb. I understood Clare Lemlich's cry about the lack of justice in the system. What does 'reasonable doubt' mean? The question I could not answer. At home, I threw it at Edward the minute he came through the door.

I heard the verdict, he said quietly. *It is all over the streets. Steuer is being heralded as the lawyer of a century, a century we have barely turned the corner on.*

Tears welled my eyes, from anger or sadness, I couldn't tell.

Nell, I told you this was going to be difficult. The district attorney's job was to show that Harris and Blanck killed Margaret Schwartz.

But everyone said the door was locked.

That is of no consequence.

Stop using your lawyer tone with me, this is an outrage and you know it. I was shaking.

Okay, let us agree the door was locked. Did they prove Margaret Schwartz died because the door was, in fact, locked? You cannot simply state that she might have died because the door was locked. That is conjecture. Second, did Blanck and Harris lock the door?

I began to feel defeated. I slumped in my chair. *I want to fight back. I need to do something. I saw them die. They were on fire. They jumped to their deaths. It can't be allowed to happen again.*

Edward took my hand: *I couldn't agree with you more, and there are others equally passionate about these issues. Even if Harris and Blanck had been found guilty, it might not stop such a tragedy from happening again. If there is good to come of this, this horror story has to be turned into a political catalyst. The support of politicians is needed to make real change happen. I am sure Rachel knows this, as well. There is talk of a commission being formed come the new year, one that the legislature will listen to. You have to show the politicians the hazards so that they will believe they exist and do something about them.*

I stopped smoldering and sat up straight. *I was telling Rachel about my meeting with Mr. Bradley come the new year, and she has a plan as to what we might do. I never got to hear it because the jury was returning to the courtroom. Perhaps her idea will quiet my rage.*

Good thought, my darling. I will be thankful for this year to end in more ways than one.

On that, my good man, we agree.

CHAPTER 8

1912

On the first Monday of the new year, I found my way to the newspaper's office. *The Daily Sun* building reminded me of the owner's daughter, tall and erect with an imposing air that spoke of its reputation and respectability. I opened the too-heavy door and gasped. There, hanging in the foyer, were the portraits of the founding fathers. No mistaking Anne Monroe was from that same lineage. She may not have inherited the business, but she carried the same high cheekbones and aristocratic nose as her forefathers. Her husband's portrait, though the same size as his predecessors, shrank by comparison to the power oozing from their pictures. I shuddered to imagine how formidable these men would have been when they ran the newspaper.

A man approached me with a look that shouted: *No women need apply*. He eyed me from hat to boot, eyes almost violet in color and a voice as cold as the winds whistling down the street. Without so much as a *good morning*, he extended his hand: *If you have an ad to place, you can leave it with me.*

No, thank you. I have a meeting with Mr. Bradley.

Shock and surprise registered in those eyes now highlighted

by one cocked eyebrow. *He is on the fourth floor,* and he gestured toward the stairs.

I nodded and, with '*Have a pleasant day*,' I began the climb, trying hard not to catch the heel of my shoe on my coat.

As I made my way past the third floor, I heard cranking and thumping from somewhere behind the walls. Were those the presses? I had never given much thought to how the paper was printed; it just magically appeared at my breakfast table.

I found my way to the newsroom. The noise here was different from below. Here was a melody of the clickety clack of typewriters interspersed with male laughter. The room was engulfed in a cloud of smoke coming from cigars, cigarettes, and pipe tobacco. At each desk sat a man with a Remington typewriter, cluttered with blotters, inkwells, pencils, cigarettes, matches, tobacco, and baseballs. It smelled of cold coffee, yesterday's ashes, and bodily sweat.

Typing ceased the moment I stepped into their arena. Voices stopped in mid-sentence.

The man who met me at the entrance, Violet Eyes, cocked his head in my direction. *You're here to see Bradley, right? His office...*

How did you beat me up here?

Took the elevator, a slight trace of smile finding its way to the corners of his mouth.

You didn't tell me there was an elevator, my voice rising.

He shook his head, pointed to a closed office door at the end of the hall. *You didn't ask. If you want to be a reporter, you need to learn to ask questions. To be exact, to ask the right questions*, a response met with hoots and guffaws by its intended male audience.

Regaining what was left of my composure and feeling like an idiot on a fool's mission, I turned and found my way to the door with a small sign with its occupant's name, *Bradley.* I tapped on the door; there was no response. If I was going to survive in this world, I needed to show I was tough. I took off my glove and gave the door a hay knock.

Come in, snapped a voice that mixed exhaustion with impatience.

Taking a deep breath, I turned the handle and walked through the portal.

There behind a desk shrouded in a haze of smoke was Mr. Bradley with a full head of hair that was just starting to turn gray. He had the look of a man who never saw the sun, found fresh air overrated, and thought a suit coat only useful as a chair cover. He looked up without raising his head, *Who are you?*

Nell Walker. Mrs. Monroe, or rather Mr. Monroe, advised me you were expecting my visit.

Ah, yes, the call from the ivory tower, and you clearly fit the part of the fair maiden. His liquid brown eyes looked at me suspiciously. *You want to write for this paper?*

I stared back, *No, Mr. Bradley, I am going to write for this paper. A series of stories about the women who work in the factories, the canneries, the mills. I intend to reveal them as sisters, daughters, mothers. They will not be the faceless victims whose ashes needed to be sifted on Misery Lane. They will no longer remain anonymous. If we make them real to the politicians in this city, we can effect change. If we can make them real to your readers, we can sell newspapers.*

Bradley cocked his head. *I like a series,* putting out his cigarette in an all-too-full ashtray as he lit another. *Have you ever written for a newspaper before?*

No, but having read newspapers most of my life, there have been few, if any, articles whose prose and or content were of such a high standard that I fear I will not meet the criteria.

Bradley threw back his head and guffawed. My spirits soared for the first time in the handful of minutes that had passed since I entered this bastion. I thought this might actually happen.

Okay. Let's see how this is going to work. I don't have much choice about it anyway. He barked *O'Brien,* and Violet Eyes appeared.

Bradley made no introduction.

Mrs. Walker here wants to be a reporter, and our esteemed publisher has granted her wish. O'Brien's eyes rolled to the top of his head. *She tells me she intends to go to work in factories and canneries and tell the stories of the girls working there.*

O'Brien looked me up and down. I could feel my face getting warmer. *Have you ever actually worked, Mrs. Walker? I mean, gotten out on days that were too dark and too cold and found your way into a place where no one cared whether or not you were tired, or sick, or poor?*

No, Mr. O'Brien, I have not. Because I have not done it, does not mean I can't. I do not want to sit on the sidelines. That is too easy and won't make a difference. I saw young girls fall to their deaths, their hair on fire, their clothes in flames. It cannot happen again. Your paper can help make a difference, and I want to be part of that.

His look remained unconvinced. *You are looking to go into the bowels of the earth and write stories from the perspective of someone you are not. Men are stronger and more capable. They are cut out to be investigative reporters. We, Mrs. Walker, were never debutantes.*

I couldn't stop staring into his eyes. *So, that is the mark of Cain I wear because I am not, and never have been, poor? Or is it because I am a woman? I am confused as to what sin I am accused of?*

His mouth twitched as if suppressing a smile that was coming too quickly. *Neither and both.*

I don't have time for this, Bradley interrupted. *Before you go into these so-called bowels of the earth, write a piece on the Shirtwaist Triangle Factory Trial. Write it as a reporter, not a do-gooder. When you are ready, give it to O'Brien to edit. He is the best I've got, though he would rather tell a story with his camera than with his typewriter. Five hundred words, not one more, not one less.*

O'Brien shrugged, *Wave of the future, Bradley. The camera is going to chronicle history, it will provoke, shame, and enlighten the reader. Even those of this paper.*

Bradley grunted and went back to looking at the papers on his desk. We had been dismissed with no farewells to signal our departure.

O'Brien closed the door behind us. *Come back when you have the article written and ask for me.*

Well, this has been a delight, I said, my voice reeking with sarcasm. I turned and marched out of the newsroom only to find myself in a blind hallway.

I was looking for a way out when a hand took my elbow. I turned to offer thanks only to find O'Brien at my side. I jerked my elbow from his grip, *I can manage very well, thank you. We debutantes can find our way out of even the most forbidden passageways.*

He produced a damnable boyish grin, *Ah, but this is not a passageway, it is a hallway that leads to the printing presses downstairs and a dead-end. Go back to the newsroom and stay to your right. That will lead you to the elevator, I am sure your carriage awaits you.*

Mustering all the composure I could, I nodded briefly, turned my back, and was on my way out. *I will be back*, I muttered to no one in particular. *And the next time I come, I won't get lost.*

I went home and wrote, rewrote, and rewrote again. I focused on the story of the woman holding a singed shoe, crying for her Nicola.

I returned to *The Sun,* article in hand, found the elevator and made my way to the newsroom. The moment O'Brien saw me coming, he produced a blue pencil and beckoned me to follow him to what must be labeled an office. It had a small desk, two chairs, and no breathing room. I sat as quietly as I could while I watched him.

In twenty minutes, he looked up and put the pencil down. *Your writing is driven by emotion. You need to do real reporting, and that involves facts. Make these changes, and we will print it in Sunday's edition. Readers are most sympathetic after being railed at by their fire and brimstone preachers. I also have a picture that will work with the article.* He stood up, left, and was back in the room before I could gather up my things.

O'Brien remained standing, *You can write. You need a notebook to capture your thoughts – what you see, what you hear. Use this one. What you are planning to do is dangerous. The politicians and the owners don't want change and will do all they can to be sure everything stays as it is.*

Don't let them see you making notes. They won't like it, and they won't like you. Stay safe.

O'Brien left the room. I took the notebook, small and compact, vowing I would safeguard it as if my life depended upon it. I felt like a schoolgirl who had been awarded the school's prize for being the best at something. Praise for my writing, advice for being a reporter. 1912 was only a few days old and yet held the promise of being a great year.

I went home and made the edits O'Brien had suggested. The end result was a stronger piece. Bradley gave the article his nod and ordered it to be printed the following Sunday. The story appeared with a picture of a little girl sewing rose petals on a hat in a tenement apartment. She was looking directly off the page, her face told her fate – a child whose future was being sacrificed. The photo was haunting. The finished article was a perfect marriage of image and imagery.

The sun had barely broken through the horizon. I was peering out the window when I saw the newsboy coming down the sidewalk. He was carrying papers, papers that carried my article, my name. I ran out the door, my purse in hand but not bothering to put on my coat and gloves. He was in front of our stairs, and I took our regularly delivered paper from his hands.

Where can I buy more copies? It was so cold I could see my breath.

From me, lifting the stack he was carrying.

I took a dollar out of my glove and grabbed half the stack, not bothering to count how many copies I was taking. *Is this enough?*

Sure is, ma'am. You made my day. Though you best be getting back inside. It's mighty cold. He tipped his cap.

I realized I was standing in a snow pile.

I took my papers and ran to the library. There it was, my name in print. I kept re-reading the article. These were my words, words that were now being read all over the city.

Husbands and wives discussing what I had written over their morning coffee. Maybe even arguing over them.

I went in for breakfast to find Edward already seated and reading the paper; the only one I had left behind. I poured myself a cup of tea, trying to pretend that this was a morning just like any other. That this wasn't the morning that my first article was printed in a newspaper.

Edward looked up, took off his glasses, and raised his coffee cup in a toast. *To my wife, the reporter. Well done, my dearest. Well done, indeed.*

I smiled, giddy with the praise.

And who is the photographer? This picture is provocative.

A man called O'Brien. I don't know his first name, but I can tell you he would make the Public Library's Patience leave her new home on Fifth Avenue to seek respite in the jungle.

Edward chuckled as he reached for something underneath his chair. *I have something for you.* From beneath his chair, Edward pulled out a wrapped package. *I believe that you will need an album to preserve your articles.*

Inside the box was the most beautiful leather book with clear pages to store my articles. Navy blue, Italian leather, and engraved on the front cover were the words: *Nell Walker, Reporter.*

I screamed with glee. *This is perfect. You are perfect. This is a perfect day. I have already bought enough copies of today's paper to fill most of the book. When we get home from church, I plan to send a copy of the article to Papa and one to Mama.* I tucked my new present under my arm, *Best, I believe, not to include your mother in the distribution.*

Very wise, Nell, very wise indeed. I, however, am very proud.

Thank you, Edward. You are so very good to me. I stopped and looked at him sitting there. He was my connection to life – a tie to my past, the light in my present, the road to my future. He was my best friend. He made a difference in my life. *I love this gift. I love you.*

And I you. He poured himself another cup of coffee, his third. A rare indulgence, even on a Sunday.

———

T he next day I met Victoria for tea and told her of my plan. She shook her head so hard, her blond curls escaped their pins. *You'll never get away with it. You look and sound too refined; and your hands, your hands will give you away.*

I looked down at my hands, *What is wrong with them?*

Absolutely nothing. They are the telltale marks of a lady of leisure. Have you ever looked at the hands of the domestics in your house? You know, not Bridget, but those that work for your housekeeper? The ones who prepare your meals, scrub your floors, do your laundry?

Chagrined, I shook my head *no*, unwilling to make eye contact. Here I was seeing myself as a warrior for the oppressed, and I had never even noticed those who worked for me as individuals with their own needs and wants.

Oh, stop being so mortified, it happens all the time to those who are to the manor born. It is my opinion, however, there are those of us who remember the days that weren't all that fine are the worst when it comes to respecting those who now work for us. But, my dear Nell, that is a conversation for yet another day. Are you convinced you are going to do this?

Yes.

And Edward has agreed? her eyes asking more than the one question.

Edward understands that I am my own woman. It is the pact we agreed to not many years ago, I said to myself.

Victoria nodded, a bit more convincingly. *Okay then, starting tomorrow, I will give you a crash course on how to look poor. There is nothing I can do, however, to prepare you for the pain and fatigue of hard work. There is no tutorial on that. I believe my father referred to it as the 'school of hard knocks.' Do not bathe tonight or wash in the morning. Such rituals are for only those who can afford a tub, hot water, and clean towels.*

Victoria arrived the next day with my new wardrobe. My

cloth dress was replaced with coarse wool and a frayed hat accompanied by a mismatched flannel coat that itched when I put it on and was too big for my slight frame.

When I looked in the mirror, I could barely recognize the image reflected. This was a Nell I had never seen. I looked ragged. There was no sheen to my hair. My face, devoid of cream and rouge, was pale and dry.

Though I had known fear and uncertainty, my sense of desperation had stemmed from the sense of being alone, of having no place to go, of trying to seek my place in the world. I never feared for a roof over my head or food on my plate. This person staring back looked in need of both. I was going to be playing a role, being someone that I wasn't. Could I be her? Could I find myself at home with others who looked like her? Could I make this happen?

For the first time, I began to doubt my ability. Was I being reckless? Was I being self-righteous? More questions than answers. But I had gone too far down the road to turn back now. My smile was weak when I looked back at Victoria,

Let's go find Rachel. I wonder if she will recognize the transformed Nell.

Victoria was shaking her head, *That will never do.*

What, not finding Rachel?

No, she snickered. *Nell will never do. It smacks of the upper class.*

Then what would you name me?

Agnes might do.

Agnes, I replied my nose wrinkling at its sound.

It is my mother's name.

Perfect. Agnes, it is.

We found Rachel at the National Women's Trade Union League. Women were shouting to each other across desks, from hallway doors, as they ran from one person to the next. This was not just flurry and flutter, for, despite the chaos, these women were united in a cause to bring about protective labor legislation.

Rachel didn't look up when I approached her desk with papers piled so high you could only see the top of her head. I called her name. She didn't look up but responded with an impatient, *I'll be right with you.*

I called her name again.

She looked up. *I just need to....*She fell back on her chair. *Nell? Is it really you?*

Victoria appeared from off to the side, *Pardon me, ma'am, but you are in the company of Agnes Miller, recently of the lower East Side of New York City, looking for a new start in life.*

Rachel was hooting, she couldn't catch her breath, *What's with the name?*

I am named after Victoria's mother, my lips curving into a smile. *As long as no one engages me in what life in that part of the city is like, I should be fine.*

And don't smile much, Victoria warned.

I shouldn't be friendly? I asked, my eyes darting between Rachel and Victoria.

That is not it at all, Victoria was clapping her hands. *Your teeth are too perfect, as is your complexion, even without powder. I am not sure how your ivory and roses will look after a couple of days in those sweatshops, but we can't do anything about your pearly whites. Pull your scarf tight around your mouth whenever you can. Maybe nobody will notice.* And she pulled the woolen, slightly moth-ridden scarf hanging off my coat around my face. I sneezed and sneezed again.

The three of us fell into gales of laughter

Rachel's firm voice brought us back to the real world. *This is going to be hard, Nell. Are you up to it?*

I don't honestly know, the mirth giving away to the enormity of the task I was committing myself to. *I have asked myself the same questions. But I have been given an opportunity few others have. I want to make a difference, just like you are doing here. I need to try. If I fail, it is my failure and the fight will continue. We need to have people understand what is happening in those factories and to women and children who work there. I want to tell their stories.*

Rachel nodded her okay. *Then we have work to do.* Rachel pulled two rather shaky chairs around her desk and motioned for Victoria and me to sit down. *Let us confirm where and how Miss Agnes Miller is going to try to make her living. I think the sooner the better.*

We agreed that three weeks, a week each in a factory, a mill, and a cannery would be enough. I was to arrive by train, find my own accommodations, and then set out to find work. I had a list of contact names at each location who were attempting to organize women into unions, should I need help. Rachel was clear, I was not to contact them directly unless I was in danger. These women were putting both their lives and their livelihood at risk and needed to be protected. I understood, but a sense of relief passed through me knowing I would not be alone if I ran into trouble.

I was to leave on Sunday, I had only three days to prepare.

Edward was at the club when I got home. I knew what that meant, he had kept his word that he would not give in to the 'passions of the flesh' in our home. The evenings at the 'club' were the code name for the way he maintained his promise. We never talked about it. We didn't need to, we both understood what it meant.

The following morning at breakfast, I outlined the plan to Edward. He was not convinced.

I'm not sure about this, Nell. It all sounds very dangerous. You have never been without protection, and now you are going off to parts of this state and pretend to be something you are not. I am not sure you will be safe. I am not sure of any of this. I am not sure I can allow you to put yourself in harm's way.

Edward, you must understand why I need to do this. Part of me wants to right the wrong I felt when the young man blew me a kiss as he fell to his death. Part of me wants to expose the Blancks and Harrises of this world who see their workers as objects to be used and then tossed away. Part of me needs to do this because I need to. And, my dear

*husband, as much as I respect and care for you, I do not, and will not, seek
your permission to live my life.*

Edward looked into my eyes as if he was seeing me for the
first time. *I wed a girl not so many months ago, but today I see I am
married to a woman. I want you to be safe, Nell.*

*I will send a card to you at the office each week so you will know I
am well. I also have money sewn into the hem of my coat. I am not as
brave as I am pretending to be, Edward.*

I think you are very brave indeed. I will miss you. He straightened
his tie. He was leaving for the office, not breaking his routine.
He kissed me tenderly on the cheek.

Sunday morning dawned. We had gone to early Mass, and I
came back home to change into my "Agnes" apparel. Edward
went with me to the train station. We were an odd match, he at
the height of men's fashion with his single-breasted jacket with
narrow lapels and straight trousers, and I transformed into my
new look. He asked one last time if I was sure I wanted to do
this. One last time I said, yes, though the butterflies in my
stomach felt that they were about to take flight.

I had taken the train to Philadelphia to dine with Papa regularly, leaving from the majestic Penn Station. There, under its
150-foot ceilings and iron and glass roof, the ticket masters
would politely inquire about my health, conductors would tip
their caps, and porters would take my bag and escort me to my
seat.

Today, I was changing my direction and traveling north. Until
the shrine that Commander Vanderbilt's wealth and power was
completed, I had to navigate my way from one of the decaying
terminals in Grand Central Depot. I found what I thought was
the right location and went to take a seat.

I heard the loud voice of the ticket master boom, *Hey, girly!
You don't belong here. First-class passengers only.* He was right. I was
traveling third-class and had not seen the restrictive sign.

It was not my imagination, I was being treated differently.

Holding my bag close to my body, I tried to smile, *I was just looking for a place to rest.*

Well, it ain't here. Keep moving. If you can't read the sign, you'll see the rest of the likes of you huddling together. If you can't see 'em, you'll be able to smell 'em. He turned his back.

I found the right platform and saw the crowd of bewildered men, women, and children waiting for the train door to open. I had met my first challenge. I was being viewed as one of them, a person of no consequence in need of help that no one offered to give.

As soon as the door train opened, the stampede began. People pushed, elbowed, and ran to get a seat. Porters, infuriated by the flurry, shouted their way through the throng. One child who had lost her parents stood still, screamed steadily to the point of shrillness. I was about to turn to go to her when a woman picked her up, cuffed her with her free hand, and drove back through the crowd.

Through the jostling and shouting, I found my way to the third-class car and what appeared to be an open seat. There was scarcely elbow room for two on the bench, but three of us jammed our way onto it. Noting that I was the only single woman in the compartment, I kept my head down and my eyes closed, putting my bag on my lap both for its safekeeping and mine.

In mid-afternoon, my fellow passengers produced food from their bags. Bread dark and crusty, pungent cheeses, thick cuts of sausages, smells that made my mouth water and my stomach growl. It hadn't occurred to me to pack a lunch.

I found my way into the dining car wanting a bowl of soup and a cup of tea. The waiter said I needed to pay my bill before my order could be placed. I complied. Shortly thereafter, a group of knickered-clad college boys, their sweaters sporting their athletic prowess, came in. The din in the car increased dramatically. While I waited for my soup and tea, these eight were served, fed, their drinks refreshed, and departed. I was still sitting, becoming angrier and hungrier. The soup and the tea finally arrived, both were cold.

I found my way back to the third-class coach car, now less crowded. Many of my fellow passengers had departed, lured by the promise of work in the factory towns and cities along the train's path. Three hours later we were in Buffalo. This Queen City was engulfed by a black cloud, as the smokestacks lining Lake Erie's shores spewed their smoke, like serpents reaching for the skies.

Rachel had given me the address where I could rent a room. Night had fallen by the time I found the house, its clapboard weathered and cracked, the wire fence bordering the property sagging in the spots where the wind had knocked it down. The sign in the cracked front window told me all I needed to know: lodgers were welcome.

I was not the only boarder in the house, and the room was not mine alone. Nor, much to my amazement, was the bed. I climbed a ladder to reach the loft of the attic and saw another woman lying on the bed I had just paid to occupy. She grunted as I came near the sheet of wood covered by a tattered sheet. She clutched the thin blanket that could barely cover one of us, let alone two. I kept on my slip, folded my dress, and wrapped myself in my coat, both for warmth and safety.

I fell into an uneasy sleep and woke before the sun rose. Pulling my dress over my shivering body, I found my way into the hallway. The sun offered a glimmer of light on an old oak table where a basin stained with age was filled with water so cold that bits of ice had formed around its edges. Not allowing myself to dwell on how many hands had used it before me, I closed my eyes, threw the water on my face, ran my fingers through my hair, clipped it in a bun, and went downstairs. The price of the room included breakfast. I was handed two pieces of bread that looked to be older than the girl who shared my room. You could barely see any remnants of the promised butter, but my stomach growled at the sight. For the first time in my life, I understood hunger.

I waited with the others for the cannery doors to open. Barely acknowledging me, the factory boss sent me to the top of a long flight of stairs to press cork liners inside tin pickle jar tops. In the first three hours, I had fitted fifty caps. I looked around for some recognition this was a job well done, but no one spoke or even made eye contact. I was simply one more factory girl in the machine who corked, labeled, and carried the full jars away.

My fingers stiffened and slowed, and the clock had not yet struck noon.

I was rubbing my hands together when one of the young girls caught my eye.

You better not stand there doin' nothing. If he catches you, he will give it to you.

I knew 'he' was the foreman; and while I didn't know what he would give me, I knew it wouldn't be good.

How old are you?

Ten.

Are you sure?

Don't care much.

Do you go to school?

She looked at me incredulously, *I work.*

Are you tired?

She shrugged, bowed her head, and continued to work.

By the end of my first day, my hands were beginning to blister and I was tired. It hurt to stand up straight. I realized no one had called me by my name.

I was given my pay for the day, seventy cents. With twenty-five cents going for my room, I still had to buy dinner, and I longed for a cup of tea. I had to put aside money to have laundry done and was told a Saturday bath would cost me extra. I needed to be careful, so no tea this evening.

The next day, I asked the little girl how she came to work here. She nodded to a woman about three feet away from me.

With my Ma, she's an inspector, one of the few women who got that job. Pays pretty good, her voice touched with pride. *My Gran is here and two of my sisters.*

I knew the universal rule that talking in the factory during work time could get you fired, so I waited until we were on our lunch break and sat with the little girl and her family. On the second day of joining them, they seemed to accept my presence. They all looked alike, the same shape mouth, the same color eyes. You only had to look at the oldest seated, the one with gray hair, to know how the rest would fare in the years to come.

I asked the mother, who was dividing the food she had brought among them, how she got to be one of the inspectors.

The bosses like our quick fingers and that we pay attention to the little things. Us women inspectors make sure no bad stuff gets packed in the jars. We do it better than the menfolk, and we are a whole lot easier to work with. My son started out here, but he couldn't take it. The boy could never sit still, and he got to looking around. Said it's not right that we didn't have enough light to see our work clearly. He started to stir up trouble. He talked back to the foreman one day and got sacked. Left home that night and haven't seen him since. He was my only boy.

My daughters give no lip to anyone. Worse they do is cry a little.

I nodded. *I understand, I cry a little, too.*

The older woman smiled, *You understand. Stop by our house tonight, some of our neighbors are making quilts to be sold at the state fair to raise money for the church. You'd be welcome to join us.*

And so I did. Despite their best efforts and patience, I never learned how to quilt. Yet, in the evenings I shared with those women, I heard them. I listened as they spoke of fear, fear of being fired, fear of not being able to feed their family, fear of being hurt. I listened as they spoke of love, love for their children, for each other, and for their God.

I was afraid to take notes, I didn't want to be seen with a pen in my hand. Later when I left the house and throughout the next days while the routine of the work dulled my senses, I kept telling their stories in my head, recalling and memorizing the details. There would be time for me to write this all down, but not then.

Saturday arrived and I was looking forward to my promised bath. I was putting on my coat when the factory boss gave me a shove. *Where do you think you are off to, it's the end of the week. You have a floor to scrub.*

He handed me a pail of hot water, a dirty rag, and a brush. I watched the other girls who were on the floor scrubbing and knelt down next to them. My hands went into the slimy water and came out brown. I slopped the suds around until one of the girls drew near.

Have you never scrubbed before? she asked, her voice carrying the lilt from a faraway land. What could I say? No, we paid people to do this where I live, and I don't know their names. But I replied: *Yes, but not a wood floor.*

Her eyes rolled to the top of her head: *Just watch what I do and don't let him see you wasting the water.*

That was the day I learned to scrub floors.

I mailed Edward the postcard on my way back to the boarding house, going blocks out of my way so no one would see me at the post. The world I had left behind seemed like a dream.

By the time I got back to the boarding house, I had missed the opportunity for a bath. There was no warm water left.

The next day I took the train to Utica. I pulled out the notebook O'Brien had given to me and started to write. I wrote about the drudgery, the monotony, the physical pain. I wanted to get this right, to have the reader breathe the stifling air, to feel invisible. I wanted to be able to have them feel the bond and strength these women gave to each other. They laughed together, worked together, cheered each other on. Life was hard, but it was a life they shared.

Utica was a smaller version of Buffalo. I found my way to a

boarding house that was a duplicate of the one where I had previously stayed, only cheaper.

Monday morning, I joined the line at the mill gates – men, women, and children all sharing the same sickly, sallow paleness – all looking for work. I was given the job of a doffer, replacing spools of thread on the looms.

I found my way to the designated spot. The spinning wheels gave off lint that looked like a thousand dandelions gone to seed, waiting for children to blow their wishes into the wind. Their fluff lingered in the air, making it difficult to breathe.

I was soon part of the rhythm spinning threads into cotton.

I couldn't help but notice her, she had long black hair that curled softly around her face. She stood straight, her back not yet bent by the loom she operated. I thought her to be in her early teens, but I couldn't guess the age. There seemed to be only two categories: the young and the worn-out.

Her name was Grace. I learned that on my last day.

We had not yet taken our lunch break when he silently came up behind her. I recognized him as the one who had given me my assignment. He smelled of tobacco and old sweat, his shirt spotted with the remnants of his last meal. He had the look of someone who liked to be mean. I kept my head down as I saw him gripping her waist with one arm, pushing her into him. She continued to operate her machine, never taking her hands off the loom as he pressed into her. His free hand began rubbing her breasts as the bulge beneath his trousers grew larger. For a moment, his eyes closed and I started to make my way toward her to stop this, this degradation. She shook her head ever so slightly as he pulled her back hard. He gave out a moaning breath that only the two of us could hear.

She kept on working. Minutes later, when he was finished, he smiled and walked away. He hadn't said a word. Neither had she.

She and I kept at our tasks as if the humiliation hadn't occurred.

The next day the same thing happened. And the next.

That afternoon, I fell into step with her as we left the factory.

Why? I didn't have to explain the question I was asking.

I need the work. My Mama has four more like me at home and Pa died almost a year ago. The only money we got coming in is what I bring home. He knows I need the job, he worked with my Pa in this same place. They never got along much. Pa once told him that he was a sorry specimen of a man. I think this is the way he gets his revenge.

She continued walking, never looking in my direction. *I'm not the only one. He has his routine. He picks three or four girls, and he rotates among us. I think he has been around me more this week because he has his eye on you.*

She looked around to be sure no one was watching. The wind began to howl, and I put the collar of my coat up to ward off both the cold and hide my face.

He'll wait till he catches you doing something that he says is wrong. Says he's going to fire you unless you are nice to him. Then it begins. The older girls say that sooner or later he gets tired of you. Likes his picks younger and fresher. That hasn't been true for me. It's been over six months, but I think it is more about Pa than it is about me.

A tear found its way down her cheek, and she quickly brushed it away.

Cold is making my eyes water. She walked away before I could reply.

The next day it happened, just as she predicted. I could smell him as he approached me.

You're too slow. Not worth the good money we are paying ya. Gonna have to get me a new girl to do this job, you're no good.

I stammered, *I need the money.*

He leered back, *Well, perhaps if you're more friendly to me, I'd give you a second chance.*

He started to walk behind me, putting his hand around my waist. I froze. I shouted *Mama* in my head. And then I heard a voice. *Cough. Cough like Mama coughed.*

I did. A hacking, can't-catch-my breath cough. I pulled my

handkerchief out of my pocket, making sure that the bloodstain from my finger that I had earlier pricked on the loom was in plain sight. I coughed into the linen but made sure he could see the red blot.

He gasped as he pushed himself away. *You're diseased. You got the consumption. Gotta get you out of here. Y'all kill us all.*

No, please no. I need the money.

He couldn't get away fast enough.

That night when I was leaving, I was given my pay and told not to come back.

She was waiting for me as I turned the corner. The air was cold, the sun's rays not strong enough to warm the earth.

He sacked you, huh?

I nodded.

I never heard you cough until this morning.

I shrugged.

Who are you?

I lost all pretense, she deserved me to be honest. *My name is Nell. What is yours?*

Grace.

Grace, I will be leaving here first thing in the morning. Could I talk with you?

I need to get home, and it does me no good being seen with you. They'll say I have caught the cough.

Please, Grace. We have to start making a difference in this world. I am writing articles for a New York City newspaper about what goes on in these factories. I would like to hear your story.

She pulled her coat tight around her body. *There is a bench outside the church on the other side of town. I can meet you there around 7:00. Don't let anybody see you.*

The night had grown colder and darker as I found the bench. Its slats were broken, the surrounding trees barren. It looked like it had given up, that life had worn it down.

Grace arrived minutes later, out of breath. She was jittery. I couldn't tell if she was rubbing her hands together to keep them warm or to give her strength. She sat on the edge of the bench, her back straight, her legs locked into a position that could have her up and running in a split second. I knew I wouldn't be able to keep her long.

I shouldn't be here. I lied to my Mama, said I just needed to get some fresh air. She looked straight at me, *I never lie.*

Tell me what happened to your father.

He was the best of men. Didn't drink and spend all his money at Smithy's like most of the others. He was smart, though he couldn't do much more than write his name. He wanted all of us kids to go to school. You can make something of yourself, he used to tell us. I loved being in school, thought I could be a teacher.

Her voice got stronger, a defiant tone proclaiming, *I can read and write. Read to Ma from the bible every night. It is those passages I think about when...,* she stopped.

I wanted to hear the rest of her story, *you were talking about your father.*

She looked up, startled as if I had awakened her from a deep sleep.

He was killed in an accident, or at least that is what they told us. Pa didn't think the workers were being treated right, and he started talking about forming a union. The other men began to listen, and soon they were having meetings in the back room at Smithy's talking about how to orga- nize. They had begun putting together a list of things they wanted, and it wasn't just more money. Pa didn't want the little ones in the factory. We got kids as young as seven working, and he didn't think it right. He wanted safer looms, one of our neighbors lost his arm and couldn't work. Pa thought it was wrong and said so.

One day, he came home very excited. Said we were going to have a visitor, someone was coming from New York City to help the men get organized. That night, he went to a meeting at Smithy's.

Her voice broke. *He didn't come home. Ma was up all night about out-of-her-mind with worry. At first light, she went off to find him. She found him on the side of the road, his clothes all bloody and muddy, his arms and legs broken, his head bashed in. They said he got drunk and fell* on the side of the road. But he never had a drink. Ma got one of the neigh-bors to put him in their wagon and bring him home. He never woke up, died two days later.

The rumor went around that if you stir up trouble like my Pa, you end up in trouble, just like him. Ma's heart and spirit were broken. I started at the mill as soon as I could. I keep my mouth shut and do what I need to do. That's my story. I'm not going to say anything else.

Who do you think hurt your father?

She didn't look at me. Who do you think? I'm going now. My Ma needs me.

She left under the shadows of the night; the moon remaining hidden by the thick black clouds threatening the onslaught of a winter storm.

I walked slowly back to the boarding house, the wind howling its restlessness. The coldness numbing my hands and feet was no match for the chill I felt take hold of my heart. I couldn't stop shivering. Grace's story had unnerved me. I was hungry, grimy, and tired. I wanted to go home, to sit in front of the fire, to be taken care of, to talk about books and the arts.

I mailed Edward the postcard and wanted it to be me.

Life here was too hard to do anything but survive. This was Grace's story. Whoever killed her father also destroyed his family. A young girl's dream of a better life was broken along with him.

The next day, the town was buried under a blizzard, three feet of snow had fallen through the night. It was two days before the trains would run again. I couldn't stay where I was, the walls were closing in. I wanted to be away from it all while still in its midst. I needed to start to write, to get my thoughts and words down on paper.

I counted the money I had earned, it looked like it would be enough for two nights' lodging if I didn't go to too grand a place. I wasn't going to dip into my 'coat-hem cash', that would admit to being beaten. I was not conceding defeat.

I picked up my bag and trudged through the snow and ice

until I came to a hotel near the train station. The lobby smelled of oil and grime, its usual occupants being the workers who kept the rails working. The carpet was a faded pattern of large flowers interrupted by worn and threadbare patches. The hotel clerk barely looked up as he took my money and handed me a key. The room held a bed, a small table, a lamp, and a small coal-burning stove. I felt a sense of relief, this was mine alone, an oasis of solitude. I knew I was one of the lucky ones. I could escape.

For two days I barely slept, going downstairs only to eat whatever stew was passing for the special of the day. I was writing not just to remember but to tell myself the story. I was talking to myself, the words on the page were recording the dialogue. By the time the tracks were clear for travel, I had pages written. I was ready to move on to Troy, the last stop on my journey.

I followed the same routine, finding a room to stay in, joining the line of others looking for work on Monday morning. This time it was in a shoe factory. I was told to go to the 6th floor. There was no elevator. I joined others on the climb, the air smelling more and more toxic with every step. There was dust everywhere you looked, inches of it, the footprints of those who walked before us leaving their mark. The windows were shut tight, their cracks allowing only a sniff of fresh air to offset the fumes. As I clambered up, I looked for fire escapes and found none, there would be no rescue from a flame. I felt a kinship with the Triangle Shirtwaist Factory workers and said a small prayer for history not to repeat itself.

By the time I reached the top, there were few of us left. The space was tight and dark, and the air thick with the smells of leather tanning. I was one of the last to reach this summit and the only one not wearing a scarf around my nose and mouth. I found a handkerchief and did the best I could to give myself the same protection.

My job was simple. I was to clean the caked glue from leather boots to prepare them for sale. There were no chairs, but I could sit on a crate. Somehow, I thought I had gotten lucky. Pulled up next to me was a crate full of boots and a glass of hot, soapy water. I dipped my fingers into the glass and rubbed the soapy mixture over the leather to loosen the glue. At some point, I looked at the girl sitting next to me. She couldn't have been much more than eleven. I stared at her hands, they were as leathery as the boots and stained nearly as dark. The nails of her fingers looked chewed. A dirty bandage wrapped one thumb.

What happened? I whispered.

My nail rotted off. It's the water, it's poisoned from the shoe dye.

I gasped.

Don't tell 'em, I told ya'. But you'll lose your forefinger nail, all right. And she gave a little cackle. I looked at my hands, they were already turning brown. Days later her prophecy proved correct.

I knew from my conversation with Rachel that there was talk of the workers here going on strike. I listened to the women talk at lunch and on their way home in the evening. I quietly asked what they wanted, wanted to change. Their answers were always the same: money wasn't the only issue. They wanted cleaner air, safer machines, shorter workdays, and hope. These were not women to be pitied. They were strong, they were wives, mothers, daughters. They fell in love, gave birth, mourned their dead. They shared one dream, the dream of a brighter future.

I would soon be home, but a different Nell would be returning. I had seen too much. I thought of Miss Beekman and her committees and shook my head. Raising funds wasn't enough, we needed laws to protect these workers and their children.

As I was leaving my shift, I saw the foreman talking with a group of men, their heads bowed. I thought I saw him point to me but wasn't sure.

Night had fallen quickly, the wind had stopped howling. The evening was pristine, the newly-fallen snow even made this factory town glisten. I left the boarding house in need of fresh air and walked aimlessly in the direction of the town, my notebook safely secured in my coat pocket. Lost in thought, I didn't hear the footsteps behind me until I heard a voice, deep and dark. One that I had not heard before and never want to hear again.

Well, well. What do we have here, a damsel about to be in distress?

He came from behind and grabbed my arm pulling me toward him, his face only inches from mine. His breath smelled of bad cigars and too much whiskey. Another, smaller version of himself, was at his side.

You've been asking too many questions, my pretty one. My friend and I are here to give you all the answers you need.

He took my arm and twisted it behind my back. The rusty handle of a knife was clenched in his other hand, its blade jagged and curved.

I was too terrified to scream. I didn't know where I could run, where I would be safe.

It will be a shame to scar this face. No reason to hurry and maybe if you are nice to me, I won't hurt you too much. He started to lick my neck as he ripped open my coat and began tearing at my dress. Panic turned into stone-cold fury. This was not going to happen to me. Not today. Not here.

I spit in his face and screamed as loud as I could. He raised his hand, knife poised: *You bitch. Now you are going to get what's coming, first with the blade and then,* rubbing himself hard against me, *with this.*

His friend snorted, *You first, Taylor, and then me. Make sure there is enough left – ain't much to her to begin with.*

Then I heard a voice as cool as a cucumber, *Gentlemen, if I may. I am going to take your picture.*

Taylor stopped, spinning around, his hand still gripping the blade. He threw me to the ground. I looked up to see O'Brien. He was poised with his camera and was beginning to prepare for the shot.

Get out of here picture-taker, this ain't none of your business.

I disagree, sir. A picture of you assaulting a lady on the street will sell newspapers. And that is my business. The camera was now in place.

Taylor seemed unsure of what to do next.

He looked around for his buddy who had run like a rat into an alley as soon as O'Brien had appeared. He lurched towards O'Brien, his knife still clenched in his hand. *Let me start with you, Mr. Picture Taker, and then I can get on with her.*

Probably not.

O'Brien produced a pocket pistol out of his coat pocket and aimed it directly at Taylor. *You have two choices. One, I can shoot you and I will not miss. Or you can turn around and run back to the cage you were let out of. You have until the count of three to make your decision.*

One.

Taylor looked confused, his eyes darting from side to side like a cornered animal.

Two.

If it isn't me, someone else will get this trick. She asks too many questions, and I was the... and before he could finish, O'Brien cocked the gun.

Taylor ran away mumbling, *Bloody hell. She ain't worth getting shot over.*

O'Brien kept the gun pointed at Taylor's back until he was no longer in sight.

I got to my feet and started to button my dress, my hands shaking so badly I couldn't put the button through its proper hole.

O'Brien turned around.

Good evening, Walker. Aren't you going to ask me why I am here? Or thank me for saving your life, among other things?

Yes, of course. How and thank you, oh thank you. I can't imagine what would have happened. I started to cry. I couldn't stop the tears from falling. They were tears of anger, of gratitude, of relief.

So much for my role as an investigative reporter, I blurted out between the sobs still trying to button my coat.

They were after you because you were doing your job, O'Brien handed me his handkerchief.

A pistol and a clean hankie, you are truly my savior tonight. I was beginning to regain my composure now that my clothes, torn and wrinkled, were somewhat intact. *How and why are you here?*

I think we should discuss that over a cup of tea, or something stronger if you would prefer. A whiskey may be just the thing you need after being practically murdered in the street.

A whiskey sounds perfect. Though I am not sure a respectable place will welcome the likes of me tonight.

Not to worry, none of the places I go to are the least bit respectable.

Within minutes and in less than a mile, we were in what would be described as a saloon. Just one more of my 'firsts' for that night.

While we waited for our drinks to arrive, O'Brien talked about the role that photojournalism was beginning to play in the newspaper business with an excitement that was in sharp contrast to the coolness of the man who had just saved my dignity, if not my life.

I took a sip of the whiskey, which was a slap to my senses. I now needed information. *How did you know I was here?*

He shrugged, *Bradley suggested that I follow you, taking pictures.*

You've been following me?

Well, not really. I convinced Bradley your stories would need pictures. He called someone, figured out where you were going, and sent me and the camera out on the same route. The storm curtailed my traveling so I waited and just figured I would start in Troy and move on from there. If I hadn't heard your scream, I wouldn't have thought to look for you. My assignment was to take pictures, nothing more.

Thank God. I could be dead or wish I was. And the gun?

My equipment is expensive and my work controversial. I find it to be a deterrent to a potential thief or heckler. I want to hear about your story when we are back at The Sun. I suggest you not go back to where you have been boarding. There may be other Taylors. I can lend you money for a hotel, there is one about four blocks away that looks respectable.

Well, I smiled, pulling the fake hem out of my coat and producing the wrapped-up cash. *I came prepared in case things went bad and I had to quickly get out of town. I think tonight meets that criteria. By the way, is there any chance I can get a hot bath at this hotel? It has been three weeks and, of all the things I've missed, this ranks number one.*

O'Brien's laughter smoothed my still jagged nerves. *I am sure it can be arranged, though there is not much you can do with your current attire.*

Well, at least I can be clean.

I got my bath. I came to realize that feeling dirty or, to be more exact, not to feel clean takes a toll on the mind and the spirit.

O'Brien met me for breakfast the next morning. *It's time you get back to your world and begin to write your stories.*

They are swirling around me, their ideas here, showing him the notebook he had given me. *It is all here, in bits and pieces. What I saw, what I heard, what I felt. I am just not sure where to begin.*

You will find your voice. You just need to listen to your heart and then to your head. I will have my edit pencil sharpened and wait for your first installment.

The weather had turned fiercely cold, my eyes were watering as O'Brien and I walked the few blocks to the train. He boarded his train to Utica as I was buying my ticket back to New York City. My train was late, and I decided to wait inside the station house rather than on the platform. As the minutes ticked by, I became more and more agitated.

The entire incident of the previous evening was etched inside my brain, and I kept replaying it. I could feel Taylor's hands ripping away at my buttons, his hot, tobacco-whiskey-smelling breath on my neck. What if he was still looking for me? What if others had been sent to finish the task?

I tried to look relaxed, to stop my eyes from darting between the clock on the wall and the doorway. Every noise set my nerves on edge. I was so close to going home, but what if I was stopped? What could I do? Where would I be safe?

Finally, I heard the whistle of the train breaking the silence of the frigid air.

I trudged back onto the platform, the prized notebook clutched between my hands as the train pulled into the station. There was not another soul boarding. I made eye contact with the conductor who stared out his ice-encrusted window.

I found a seat, turning my head to the window to watch the landscape slide away. I was lost in thought as the buildings faded and white fields appeared when I heard the heavy tread of feet outside the compartment door. I thought Taylor had found me.

I was about to scream as the handle moved and the door opened. On its threshold was the conductor wearing a soiled cap and a jacket that did not stretch over his round belly.

May I have your ticket?

I laughed out loud, startling him. *It is my pleasure.*

I was on my way home, to write these stories that were burning inside of me.

I had to remember how it felt, how gray the days were, how lonely the nights. I also had to remember the connection to women who banded together to make a quilt or organize a strike. Women who put aside their own individual needs, who came together for a common cause, and who worked for the common good.

As I thought of what I had seen, what I had felt, I knew I wanted the pleasures of my life back. I felt guilty that even having seen so much poverty, so many struggling for so little, I still longed to take a hot bath, to have men tip their hats as I pass, to read a newspaper. I questioned whether I was any better than those committee ladies who opened up their pocketbooks but not their neighborhoods to the less fortunate. The conductor interrupted my thoughts.

Last stop, New York City.

I walked onto the street among the throngs of people absorbed in the business of living their lives, forging their own path. No one looked at me, and I didn't make eye contact with them. I was home. I said a brief prayer, thanking God for bringing me back to the city I loved and the life I longed for.

The cab driver wanted to see my money before he let me open the door to his carriage. I was no longer either surprised or outraged.

You sure you got the right address? Pretty posh, and if you don't mind my saying, most of the servants are better dressed than you.

I have the right address, thank you.

I rang the bell and turned around just in time to see the driver's look of astonishment as Phillips opened the door and called for Edward. Before the cabbie could depart, Edward stepped over the threshold and held out his arms to me. I quickly ran to them, calling his name.

I am glad you are home and safe, my dear, but you do look awful. You are so thin, I am going to tell Mrs. Campbell that the dinner desserts need to be extra tempting the next few weeks. Where is your bag? What happened to you?

I leaned against him for one more second, comforted by the simple smell of him: Pears soap and starch. I was safe. I was home.

Oh, Edward, I am so happy to be here. I have learned so much and there is so much to tell. First, however, I want to take a hot bath and change into clothes that should fit better. There are things in my life may I never take for granted again, beginning with having a bath and a bed to call my own. Give me an hour to get myself back together and then stoke the fire in the library, open a bottle of wine, and wait for me. Prepare to listen as I am not sure where I can even begin. I gave him a quick kiss on the cheek and practically ran up the stairs to my room.

I offered God my thanks as I lay in the bath. I had warm water, fresh towels, and privacy. Pleasures which just days before I had been denied. I vowed not to forget the lessons I learned in the three weeks I had been away. I would remember the people I met. I would remain grateful for what I had been given. I would try to make a difference.

The logs were crackling, warding off the late afternoon chill, their flames casting shadows over the rug that mirrored its red and blue hues when I opened the library door. Edward was in his chair, his black hair lying against the oxblood leather so that at first glance it looked like a stain upon the fine leather. His eyes were closed, his glasses had slipped down his nose, a book lay on his lap unopened. A mid-afternoon nap, one of the privileges of class.

I squeezed his shoulder gently, his eyes opened. *Welcome home, my dear.*

I took my place across from him in my wingback chair with its tapestry covering. Like us, our chairs complemented each other, different in style and texture but pleasing to the eye and a comfortable blend.

I missed this, my hands raised as if in supplication. *I missed the gentleness of our life. There were moments these past weeks when I didn't have the energy to think. It took everything I had just to stand up and keep going. I thought I couldn't manage, I wanted to give up.*

Edward said nothing as he poured me a glass of wine.

Yet, I couldn't. The women and children I worked with, the men too, didn't have that option. No matter how tired, how hungry, how weak, they rose each day just to survive. And they were nameless.

Only a few ever called me by my name. I smiled for the first time. *Victoria and I had made such a game of my needing a new name and it didn't matter. Nobody cared. I was just a body, a stranger to the workers so most kept their distance. A nameless figure to the owners who only saw me as part of whatever production line I was placed on.*

I paused, moving from memory to the present day. *Do we know all their names, Edward?*

Who are you talking about, Nell?

The people who help us in this house. Bridget, along with Mrs. Campbell and Phillips, but the others? Those who help in the kitchen, who clean our clothes, dust these shelves?

Well, yes, I think so. It would take me a minute or two, but Phillips keeps me informed of any new people on staff. We do pay them well, you know. I think we are good to the people who work for us. The tone of his voice changed, he sounded like the expensive business lawyer he was.

I asked if you know their names.

You are making me feel defensive, Nell. This is not how I expected this conversation to go.

I know, Edward, and I am not trying to sound accusatory; but I felt invisible the past three weeks. I want to make some changes in the world that I can control. We are good people, but we live in a sphere few others inhabit.

I understand. What do you have in mind exactly? he asked, his voice softened.

I gave this some thought on the train coming home. I am going to ask Mrs. Campbell and Phillips to give me a list of the names of the staff we employ and the names of their children. At Christmas time, we will continue the traditional staff party but also have a special celebration for their children, complete with presents and games. Once a year, on my Mama's birthday in May, we will have a birthday celebration for the children. Ice cream, cake, presents, and pony rides. That is how I remember my birthdays as a child. I would like others to have that same memory.

That would be lovely, Nell. Thinking the conversation over, Edward stood up to pour us another glass of wine.

Oh, I'm not done yet. For the staff, after a year's service, they each will get one week of paid vacation. We will have reduced staff on Sundays; I will leave it to Phillips and Mrs. Campbell to organize, but we can make do on our own that day. I want each person to have two full days off each week. We will need to think about how to work the Christmas and Easter holidays so the staff can spend time with their families rather than just serving us. My guess is Mrs. Campbell knows how other households manage during that time, and she could propose what arrangements could work for us.

Edward looked up from the now-filled glasses he had just poured. *That all seems sane, Nell. I think you should proceed as you just said, but first, you must promise me two things.*

I reached for my glass of wine, *They are?*

First, you need to tell me all that happened to you these past weeks and second, you are never to enlighten my mother about your plans for the staff. Edward grinned mischievously.

I clinked my glass with his. *You have my word.*

The remainder of the night and for the days following, I told my story to Edward, complete with my encounter with O'Brien. Edward's emotions ranged from shock to empathy to anger. I was vivid in my descriptions, thorough in my accounting of the events, and tried very hard to keep emotions out of the telling. I was preparing to write my stories.

My first series was about the children, the headline ran: *Childhood Canceled.* I wanted parents reading the articles to see the difference in lives: the lives of their children and the lives of children working in the canneries and factories. Children who could not dream about the future. I then wrote about the mothers, the women who sacrificed not only for their families but for the right to have a say in their own lives. My last article was Grace's story, *Saving Grace.*

By the end of the year, my blue album was full of articles. O'Brien's pictures captured the emotion of the story. Neither sensational nor sentimental, the picture and the prose carried the same message: this is what no future looks like.

I was at *The Sun.* O'Brien was back in the office. He was now officially the paper's photographer and spent his time telling stories with his camera. I had my final article in my hand.

This is the last one, ten all total. I have heard from Mrs. Monroe that the paper is pleased with the public's response. I think we may have made a difference between my stories and your pictures. The legislature may be more open to labor reform, particularly for the children.

O'Brien shook his head slowly. *Don't be naïve, Walker, it doesn't become you. The only thing that changes New York City pols is the vote. If they think making the workplace safe will keep them in power, they will support it. Women still can't vote in either this state or this country, no matter what this paper reports or what pictures I take.*

What these Tammany men care about is getting the vote, not doing the right thing.

As for The Sun, if the newsies can hawk its headlines on the street and sell more papers, then the powers-that-be are content. At least for the moment.

O'Brien reached for the article in my hand. *Is that the Grace story?*

I nodded.

I remember you telling me about her. I've got the picture already selected. What are you going to do next?

I don't know, but I am sure I will think of something.

O'Brien arched an eyebrow. *I am sure you will.*

CHAPTER 9
RACHEL

To describe Rachel is hard. She is one of those women whose intellect is heralded by the look in her eyes, the gestures she uses to make a point, her ability to end a sentence that makes you want to hear the next one. Broad-shouldered and barely reaching five feet, her dark brown eyes are the passageway to her soul.

From the beginning, Rachel was a leading figure among a network of radical women: reformers with open minds and unwavering convictions to make the world a better place. Outspoken and determined to exercise the freedom she and the others were clamoring to win, Rachel opened my mind and my consciousness. She was more than a mentor, she was my friend.

Rachel introduced me to Brooklyn, another world and more than just a few miles away from my epicenter, Manhattan. Her family had lived in the same apartment building for two generations – surrounded by family. On my first visit, Rachel played tour guide, pointing out the landmarks of her childhood: the deli that served the best pastrami sandwiches in all of New York, Ebbets Field where the best baseball team, the Dodgers, broke their fans' hearts every season, and the corner soda fountain that made the best egg creams one could imagine. When I pointed out she used the word 'best' to describe everything about Brooklyn, she merely shrugged, *it is what it is.*

The first time I met her parents, I was treated like family. I learned Rachel seldom brought friends to visit, so they deemed me special. I had never heard the word *goyim,* but I fit the definition, I wasn't Jewish.

I was invited to her family's Seder, the annual ritual when family and friends gathered. Rachel's father, who was as short as his daughter and equally passionate about what was important, sat at the head of the dining room table that was built for six. We were a squeezed-in-nine. The gouges on the back wall gave testimony that this was not the first time it would be difficult to get in and out of a chair.

Rachel's father extended his arms as if embracing all around the table, but his dark brown eyes locked into mine. *Ah, Nell, let me begin by explaining why this day is important. As Jews, we must teach the next generation in the same way we were taught. We hand down the story of our deliverance out of Egypt. We come together to remind ourselves that once we were slaves.* He pointed to the plate in the center of the table. *On the Seder plate, we have bitter herbs to remind us of the bitterness of bondage. And the paste, the charoset, is a reminder of the mortar our ancestors used in captivity. The parsley you will dip in salt water reminds us of our tears. During the meal, we shall drink four cups of wine – grape juice for the little ones – to remind us of the four promises God made to us.*

Let me begin with a blessing. And with that, the Seder commenced.

All over the world, this ritual was taking place in Jewish homes, the youngest child being instructed to ask, '*Why is this night different from all other nights?*' I recognized some of the lessons being shared, I heard them from the readings in our Old Testament. Yet this evening they came alive not as passages but as messages being sent from God himself thousands of years before. Messages of life and freedom. Messages that were the pillars of Rachel's life.

It was the summer of 1914 and Manhattan was in the midst of a heatwave. The day was hot and sultry, the sky cloudless. Rachel had been gone for weeks. We agreed that I would meet her in Brooklyn, and the ferry ride was a welcome respite. The breeze from the deck was gentle as I watched the Gothic towers of the Brooklyn Bridge ebb away.

It was weather like this that greeted me in North Carolina, was Rachel's response to my droning about the heat and humidity that made my hair take on a life of its own. We were walking in Brooklyn Heights, miles from Rachel's home but an integral part of my continuing education about Brooklyn.

I was the neophyte joining much more experienced union organizers. The local union advocates who were supporting the movement among mill workers had never quite seen the likes of me. A woman, a New Yorker, and a Jew – I was the trifecta of all that was foreign. It took me a while to gain the trust of the organizers, but I did it. The wrath the mill owners and the local authorities let loose in my direction helped. I was labeled an agitator. Rachel jumped up on a large stone that nestled a nearby elm tree. Standing on her tippy toes and her arms stretched to the heavens, she pointed to the lowest limb that she could not reach. *The only thing stopping a noose from being put around my neck was my gender and my height. They weren't quite sure they had a platform high enough to hang the likes of me!*

Throwing her hands up in the air, she landed back on the ground and continued her tale without taking a breath. *A week after we arrived in town, the workers stopped their looms, shut off the power, and came out into the streets. They were waiting for a sign, and we were it. The strike was on.*

Rachel was lost in the memory. She was back in a mill town with dirt roads and ramshackle shacks. I alone was on the brick walkway with its brownstones and private parks. *The first of the workers leading the strike were rounded up by the sheriff. They were framed by the mill owners who had their paid stool pigeons accuse these women of stealing bits of cloth. Women who were no more thieves than we are.* Rachel chuckled. *Or at least me. Your husband is a lawyer, so I can't speak for the caliber of the company you keep.*

We passed a mother wheeling her baby in a steel and chrome pram that would have been the envy of Queen Victoria's brood. Rachel shook her head slowly, turning in the direction of the mother and child now a block or so away. *The women I met, young girls really, would not understand this. They did not have free afternoons for a casual stroll. They only wanted the one thing that had been denied them and those who had toiled before them. They wanted hope. Hope for better working conditions, hope for a better life not only for themselves but for their children and their children's children. Children who never had the opportunity to enjoy a summer day clean, well-fed, and healthy.*

Rachel started walking faster, her breath coming quicker, her words pouring out without pause. I could see beads of perspiration forming tiny rivers staining the back of her dress. Rachel seemed oblivious. *The odds against us were amazing. The mill owners had the local police and judges in their pockets, not to mention the town and state politicians at all levels. All the demonstrations had been peaceful until about two days into the shutdown when the governor called in the National Guard. These guards used their bayonets, slashing more than a dozen of the strikers, men and women, who were defenseless against these attacks.*

Along with a handful of other women, I was rounded up and made to stand on the back of an old wagon. The police paraded us through the town with the idea we would be put to shame and ridiculed. Well, that backfired. Our message became stronger and the workers more resolved. More women joined the picket lines. We were seen as martyrs for the cause, and our ranks began to swell.

I put up my hand in surrender to the heat. *I understand martyrs, and I want you to continue your story, but I need something cool to drink.* We found a vendor hawking ice-cold lemonade and took a seat on a shaded park bench that offered a brief respite from the unrelenting sun.

Taking a sip of the tart, sweet concoction, Rachel continued.

I was staying in the house of one of the organizers, who was putting her and her family at great risk. She had a six-year-old granddaughter, just as sweet as you could imagine. Her name was Maribelle. She kept staring at me, her eyes unblinking and questioning. I finally got her to come over to sit next to me.

Do you have a question? I asked.

Yes, ma'am, she replied, her eyes downcast.

And what is it?

Are you a woman or a sheep?

I am a woman, but why would you think I was a sheep?

She shook her head, still in doubt. *I asked my mama what a ewe was, and she said it was a sheep.*

Your mama was right, but why do you think that I am a ewe?

My cousin said that mama and I are going to hell because we had a ewe staying in our house.

I took her in my arms, she was thin, too thin for a child at that age. *No, my little one,* I responded, *they were talking about my belief in God. I am Jewish, and like Jews all over the world, we are waiting for the Messiah.*

You don't believe in Jesus? Her eyes widened at the thought.

Oh, I do, but I think he was a great prophet and a man we should admire and respect.

That response seemed to satisfy her, she squirmed her way free from my grasp. *Okay. I am glad you are not an animal. You seem like a nice lady, though you're not much taller than me.*

Rachel's eyes got a faraway look. *I thought, this is why I am here. Maribelle needs a better world, the chance to be all she is capable of becoming.*

Refreshed, we walked towards the river, finding a meadow with a grove of trees that captured any cool air the river was offering. We found a large maple and sat down, our legs jutting out straight in front of us, our backs resting against its centuries-old trunk.

Rachel began quietly tearing at a leaf that had fallen to the ground. *The next day, things got darker. The divide in the town was developing into another Civil War with the owners on one side and the workers on the other. Three of the male strikers were arrested, having been framed for causing an explosion in the factory that caused no real damage. The company had done its job and framed the three accused with the so-called evidence they had placed within the factory.*

The night after the explosion, a couple of goons had gotten one of the three men drunk on local moonshine. They forced him to sign a blank sheet of paper, lying that they needed to verify his signature so he could get paid. The next day, a paper stating the three men accused were guilty was submitted to the judge and signed by that same man. The blank piece of paper he had originally signed now had 'confession' over his name.

The trial, if that was what you could call it, was the next day. Once again, justice was turned away; and the three were found guilty and sentenced to ten years of hard labor. Their families, destitute already, had no means of financial support from that day on. The spirit of the strikers was broken and they returned to work, downcast. The owners had won, but I knew they had only won a battle. We were still at war.

That is when I came back to New York. I am angry and tired. It is good to be home.

I looked at my wristwatch. *Yikes, speaking of home, I need to get back but I need to hear more. Come for lunch on Tuesday.*

Brushing the twigs from her skirt, Rachel stood up. *Perfect. Shall you ferry or the subway back to town?*

In this heat? The IRT and hell would compete with the least favorite places I would willingly choose to be at the moment. I need to hurry, I will see you on Tuesday.

We gave each other a quick kiss on the cheek. The heat had not abated, and I was walking at a fast pace. My dress was damp, the sweat trickling down my back attaching it closer to my skin. I arrived at the ferry just in time. As I stood at the ship's rail, the waves gently rocking the ship, I thought about Whitman's poem. "Crossing Brooklyn Ferry." He assumes that the crowd of strangers he sees every day sees the same things he does, reacts in the same way he does, and this binds them together. I look around at my fellow passengers – a lone girl, her head bent in an opened book, men in suits impatiently pulling out their pocket watches to check the time or absorbed in the evening newspaper with headlines on the potential rise of Woodrow Wilson as the Democratic candidate for president. The injustices that Rachel witnessed were miles away. I wondered as the ferry pulled into the pier, can we ever see another world? A world that we are not a part of. A world that we may not know exists but can be seen if we open our eyes to it.

The day was no cooler when Rachel came for lunch. We opted to eat in the library, its dark walls guarding the heat against taking over, oscillating fans on tables moving whatever air there was.

Rachel took her seat in Edward's chair. I marveled at how someone so small in stature could command the same perch as the 6 foot plus Edward. She sipped her Coca-Cola. *Ah, as the ad says, 'satisfying and delicious.'*

I clinked my glass with hers. *Edward thinks it is the trend of the future. He says when the time comes we should invest, the public will become addicted.*

Rachel swirled the caramel-colored liquid in her glass, *Conversations I seldom have.* She rolled her eyes and pitched her voice two octaves higher. *Such decisions, where should I invest my money? Or should I simply buy a new hat, perhaps one with an ostrich feather around the brim?*

My cheeks burned, *I didn't mean to imply...*

I'm teasing, Nell, but let's continue my tale on how the other half lives. It all started for me when I heard Clara Lemlich speak. I was still at Columbia. She was the young woman I spoke to you about following the Shirtwaist Factory fire horror.

I nodded my head in recognition of the name.

That speech aroused such emotions that more than twenty thousand young shirtwaist makers went on strike. The press dubbed it "The Uprising of the Twenty Thousand," as these workers, most of them merely teenage girls, silenced their sewing machines. Their demands were simple – put an end to child labor, limit the workday to 8-hours, and offer a minimum wage.

Rachel's eyes grew merry for the first time. *Did you ever hear about the ladies of the night and their role in this strike? Will you be scandalized if I proceed with this part of my tale?*

I got up, my dress sticking to my back. *I am a woman of the 20th Century, I assume you are talking about prostitutes. Let's continue the conversation outside in the park, I swear there is not a breath of fresh air moving in this house.*

I gave Rachel one of my newest parasols to ward off the heat of the sun's rays. Looking at us on the park bench, you would have conjectured our conversation to be focused on fashion rather than the ladies of the streets.

Rachel twirled her parasol. *Your favorite fellas, Blanck and Harris, the esteemed owners of the Triangle Shirtwaist Factory, dreamed it up. They hired prostitutes to infiltrate the picket lines in an attempt to sully the strikers' reputations by association. When the girls working in the oldest profession suggested to the strikers that there were more lucrative ways to make a living, fights broke out, cops were brought in, and arrests were made. I'm sure the Boys in Blue had more than one story about the jailhouse antics to share that night.*

We both started laughing.

Rachel put down her parasol, throwing her hands in the air.

It got worse. There continued to be an escalation of police violence against these young women, and we were beginning to feel powerless. There had been over 700 arrests, most made with harsh physical assaults. Two weeks into the strike, we led ten thousand of the strikers on a march to City Hall to demand the mayor rein in the police. He promised an investigation, but it was all talk. The judges were no better. In sentencing one of the strikers for 'incitement', he pronounced from his bench: "You are striking against God and Nature whose law is man shall earn his bread by the sweat of his brow. You are on strike against God."

Rachel's eyes moved once again to the gold cross hanging from my neck. *This pronouncement being pointed at women who toiled in the worst conditions imaginable for hours on end. It is he who should be answering to his God.*

Rachel averted her eyes, brushing a strand of hair behind her ear.

Your friend Anne will recognize this next part. Ladies from your part of the world joined our cause. The press loved them, and the police feared them. There was no more clubbing of women, the police would not risk hitting a member of the Social Register, someone perceived to be powerful, so no one was touched. Our striking women understood immediately what was happening. The distance between the 'mink brigade' and them was made abundantly clear, only the poor were subject to violence.

I had a flashback of Grace standing at her loom. Violence came to the poor in many forms.

The strike lasted until February 1910 and ended in a "Protocol of Peace" which allowed the strikers to go back to work with better pay, shorter hours, and equal treatment of workers whether they were in the union or not. But it was not enough, young women were still dying.

I stood up, not able to sit still any longer. *I know. I saw them die.*

Rachel was passionate about what she believed in. She was nourished by the excitement of picket lines, street corner rallies, and strategic debates. In the aftermath of the Triangle Shirtwaist Factory Fire, few things seemed more important to her than enacting laws to stop people from dying needlessly.

Edward loved talking with her. They would verbally joust over what issue the press had found to rally around. It would make for discussions both bracing and exhausting. Rachel was at the house for dinner, the newspapers were predicting the overthrow of the Russian Tsar. Edward was not a fan of any of Queen Victoria's offspring, be it the Tzar, the King of England, or the Kaiser, nor was he a proponent of revolution, on anyone's behalf. He and Rachel passionately debated the pros and cons.

Edward argued his point on the Russian Revolution: *It is impossible to predict where all this is going to end, but I am fearful. The*

French Revolution may have been splendid, but it still produced a reign of terror.

Rachel smiled. *I foresee bloodshed, but it is hard to blame the Russians for wanting a change in government.*

Even by socialists?

Rachel raised her wine glass. *I dare to say that if I were Russian, I would think so.*

Edward roared.

CHAPTER 10

ON THE ROAD TO REFORM

Tammany Hall was at the height of its power and seemed to be thawing in its support of reform. Light was breaking through at the end of the tunnel. Rachel was in the center of it all. It was 1915.

It was early morning, Edward had just left for the office and the household was coming to life. Our newest acquisition, the Hoover, was making more noise than I thought earthly possible; and Mrs. Campbell was raising her voice to be heard over its roar. I was retreating to the relative calm of the library when the front door opened and Rachel blew in looking as if a tornado had dressed her – her hat was askew, her blouse hung out of her skirt, her gloves mismatched.

Without so much as a proper hello, she started: *I know I look a mess, but I have your next assignment. You must meet and write about him and her and the work they are doing.*

Him and her? I shook my head, not comprehending what she was saying. It was too much, too early for a guessing game.

Goodness, Nell. Al Smith and Frances Perkins. They are embracing the spirit of progress, the spirit of the age. I have never been so excited. Reform is going to happen. The legislature is going to change workplace laws beginning in New York, and that will set the stage for the rest of the country.

Rachel skipped into the library as I led the way, the Hoover's roar over the hallway rug blotting out any hope of conversation.

I closed the door of the library behind us, welcoming a moment of quiet, but Rachel hadn't paused. *Smith is a Catholic, just like you, and a true product of this city. He was born and raised on the Lower East Side and left school when he was 12 years old. He is a true man of the people, with the ability to get along with everyone. Tammany Hall loves him; he is a magnet for voters who have just crossed our shores.*

Frances comes from an entirely different world. She was raised by a strict, conservative Republican family which read to her in Greek. She went to school at Mount Holyoke, and the experience changed her life. She talks about visiting the mills along the Connecticut River and being horrified at the conditions that women and children had to endure. She was there at the Shirtwaist Factory Fire and knew first-hand about the inadequate exits, the fire department's useless ladders, and life nets that didn't hold. Frances believes in labor unions and the vote for women and is a card-carrying Democrat. And she always wears a hat.

They are going to make a difference. We are going to make a difference. Rachel clapped her hands as she pirouetted around the library. I didn't know whether to laugh or take her temperature.

I knew the names. Smith, along with Robert Wagner, were two of the most influential New York City legislators. They were the proteges of the infamous Charles Murphy, a reticent politician, a first-rate political chess master, and the head of the Tammany organization. I tried to keep my voice calm as I replied, *I would love to do a story on them and their work.*

Rachel flopped down in Edward's chair, her feet dangling in the air. *I could use a cup of coffee with extra cream and sugar and then I will tell you what is happening. I think you could help.*

Rachel gave me an overview of what was happening and left with the promise that she would know more shortly. I would need to wait until then to figure out the details of my role. Two days later, the calm and collected Rachel returned. She was to accompany Perkins, Smith, and Wagner, along with other appointed politicians, on a fact-finding tour of the upstate factories and canneries. She had gotten them to agree to have me join them for a part of the trip. I was to write articles on their findings for publication.

Edward was as excited as I when I told him what Rachel proposed. *The perfect next step for you, my dear. I will go out tomorrow to order another album for your articles. These three pols are powerhouses, and I believe that they will soon be making national headlines.* And with a smile in his voice, *You should find your accommodations vastly improved since your last journey to these upstate towns.*

The next day, I walked into Bradley's office after only a brief rap at the door. He looked up, not pleased that I had interrupted whatever he was doing. *Walker, what? Your stories are done.*

I moved the papers off the lone chair, sat down, and slowly took off my gloves. *I believe I have more you may want to publish.*

Before he could respond and without taking a breath, I continued. *I have been invited to join Al Smith and Frances Perkins on their fact-finding mission for the Committee on Safety.* I paused, *I believe Bob Wagner will be joining us, as well. I have their permission to write an article or two — perhaps more — on what they find and what they plan to do.*

For the moment, Bradley looked like he was gasping for air. *You are going to see what they see? Hear what they say? And then write that story?*

I nodded in the affirmative, *For this paper, unless you think otherwise.* Knowing I held the trump card, *I expect the paper to reimburse me for my expenses.*

Bradley grunted his approval. I stood up, gloves in hand, and opened the door. Then he smiled. I had never seen him smile, an emotion I believe few had witnessed. *These are headline stories. They should sell papers. Well done, Walker,* he said, as he returned to the papers on his desk.

I closed the door and walked smack into O'Brien, who was

looking quizzical. *What was that all about?* pointing to Bradley's office. *That is the highest praise I ever heard Bradley give anyone.*

Trying to keep my composure rather than jumping up and down in delight, I pulled out the notebook he had entrusted to me not so very long ago. *Oh, I was just giving him the particulars for my next assignment.* Then, in front of the gawking rookie and seasoned reporters lurking in the hallway to see what the fuss was all about, I shared the story particulars. Stunned silence filled the room.

When I finished, O'Brien threw back his head, his laughter bounced off the walls. *Well, Nell Walker, an insider to the workings of Tammany Hall. Beyond my wildest expectations, Walker.*

I could feel the flush coming to my face as I basked in the glory of what I knew to be high praise.

O'Brien picked up his camera. *Let me know if you need any pictures. Stay out of harm's way.*

I was filled with nervous energy. Once home, I changed my clothes and got out my bicycle. The day was fine, sunshine finding its way through clouds that looked like castles in the air. I needed both fresh air and exercise to gather my thoughts. Without any destination in mind and in need of a good stretch of the legs, I found myself in front of Anne's apartments across from Central Park. Just as I was turning the bicycle around to head home, she emerged from a cab, Benjamin and Franklin on either side.

Oh, Nell, what a lovely surprise. Boys, you remember Mrs. Walker, the reporter for Father's newspaper.

The boys nodded. *Did you get your story printed, Mrs. Walker?* Franklin blurted out. Now looking even more intrigued at me as I gracefully slipped off the bicycle.

Yes, Franklin, a series of articles, and I just came from The Daily Sun's offices to tell them about the next one I am set to do.

Anne hustled up the twins, moving them towards the building's entrance. *This is wonderful, Nell. What will you be writing about?*

I wasn't long into my description when Anne shared her view that Tammany Hall was one of the blockades to women getting the right to vote. *Politics is all cigars and backroom deals. The men are either corrupt or dull as dishwater. Sounds like Smith may be different. Let me know, or more importantly, let our readers know. It would be good to have him on our side as we take to the streets demanding the vote.* The twins were losing their patience, shifting from one foot to the next. Anne sighed, *Women may not be any better at getting the right people elected, but we sure can't be any worse.*

I straddled the bicycle. *I will call you when I return.*

Being pulled towards the door by two identical engines who shouted their good-byes in unison, Anne wrestled free one hand and gave me a salute. *Good luck, Nell. This is splendid.*

Franklin, however, was to have the last word. Over his shoulder he shouted, *I like that you ride a bicycle.*

Me, too. I raced back to the house, one with the wind and this city.

Edward's take on New York City politics was even more pragmatic. *Irish Catholics are running New York City from borough to borough. Some might say ruining it.*

I looked at him quizzically, *Are we talking religion or politics?*

Edward shrugged, *In this city, they are one and the same. You will learn soon enough. At least on this trip, you will be safe from thugs, or at least the hired thugs. I worry about you, Nell.*

I smiled, *The worst thing that can happen to me on this trip is I join up with the Tammany Hall crew. I understand Al Smith is quite charming.*

Edward nodded his agreement. *He is. He likes to credit his charm to his alma mater. Unlike the Harvard men and the Yalies who clang about in Albany, Smith declared himself an F.F.M. man. Fulton Fish Market. He grew up in the same place and at the same time as the Brooklyn Bridge.*

I smiled. *Sounds like both are New York City landmarks. I like him already.*

I was part of the entourage, a group of 15 who visited the

plants and mills all over New York State. In Auburn, we were up at dawn, as the night shift gave way to the day workers. Husbands and wives worked alternating 12-hour shifts at the local rope factory, kissed quickly as they passed through the gate. We saw a Buffalo candy factory, steamy, suffocating work that was all done standing up. Chocolate boiled over into an open gas flame. Hour after hour, workers hovered over simmering cauldrons, scars on their hands and arms, badges left by the scalding of the confectionary brews.

On the third day, Rachel and I finally got a chance to catch up. Her eyes registered a determined look. *Perkins is really pleased about how this is going,* she began. *Smith is already calling the trip the best education he has ever had. And did you hear what Perkins had Wagner do?*

No, I haven't spent much time with the inner circle, but before I could begin my grievance about not having time with Smith and Perkins, Rachel continued.

It happened at the candy factory. There was a small hole in the wall that gave egress to a steep iron ladder that was labeled the fire escape. Perkins beckoned Wagner to the hole, 'Come on, Robert,' she taunted, 'this is the same type of fire escape the girls at the Shirtwaist Factory had. Let's see how quickly you can escape.' Well, Wagner started the descent and then realized there was a 12-foot drop to the ground from the last rung on the ladder. He scurried back up like a rabbit. Perkins couldn't stop smirking. She gave him a hand-up and said loud enough for all to hear, 'and don't forget the doors of that factory were locked.' Point made. The moment was priceless.

I joined them for one last stop before I was to return to the City. It was a cannery not far from the Buffalo boarding house I had first stayed in. As we were leaving, Smith stopped one of the women, a child no more than seven was working at her side, and asked. *Is this your daughter?* The young woman nodded yes. Smith asked one more question: *How long is her day?*

He was visibly shaken by her response. *Until she passes out from exhaustion.*

I watched Smith pause as we were leaving the site, taking in all that was around him. There was a single stairway with no handrail and only two toilets. On the day we visited, one of them was broken. *These were the same owners along with their candy-owner collaborators who blocked the 54-Hour Bill, legislation that would have limited the number of hours women could work to 54 hours per week and prohibited children from working until the age of 14.*

That night at dinner I found myself sitting next to Perkins, wearing the tri-corner hat that was her signature. My opening line was simple: We *share the same memory of the Shirtwaist Factory Fire.*

Perkins stared at me. *You were there, as well?*

I nodded my answer. *It changed my life. It is why I am here.*

Perkins's eyes glazed over as if recalling the memory of that day. *Mine, as well. I believe it will change this country.*

Smith, who was seated next to her, leaned over, looking to be included in the conversation. *Sure as shooting! Wagner and I will get the 54-Hour Bill passed despite the owners of these canneries and candy hell-holes. They argue that if we regulate the number of hours a woman can work and prohibit her children from joining her, it would ruin their business.*

My husband, I broke in, *would say Poppycock! to that argument. And he is a lawyer.*

Smith nudged Perkins, *Absolute poppycock!* He then looked directly at me with a voice that both commanded and cajoled. *Now, Madame Reporter, get out your pen and get the public to support us. This is the best education Wagner's ever had. Not sure any of us will ever recover. Bob and I know where to find the votes. Frances will figure out how to make it all happen.*

Despite the growing sentiment that reform needed to happen, there was strong belief coming from those both in and out of government who believed that children were destined for factory work. Rachel couldn't believe that such sentiments could exist in the 20th Century.

We were back in our library, Rachel returning to her spot in Edward's chair. She had been meeting with Perkins to finalize the voting on the 54-Hour Bill. Wagner and Smith were throwing their full political weight at getting it passed.

She shook her head no to my offer of a cup of tea as well as to the political arena surrounding the vote. *It is beyond reason. One of the upstate politicians whom the cannery owners clearly have in their pockets announced that many children were destined for factory work, that it gave them the chance to develop good habits. In the same breath, denouncing the 54-Hour Bill, he said its passage would have dire outcomes, factories and canneries would close.*

Rachel, unable to stand still, stood up and started to pace around the room. *He told them a tale of that little brave boy who was looking forward to getting money to give to his mother for food. Pass the 54-Hour Bill and he would be left empty-handed, the family would be hungry. People believed him, Nell. People clapped when he finished his speech. When we get the vote, politicians like him will be gone.*

From your lips to God's ears, was my reply. *No matter what god you pray to.*

Despite the intense opposition, the 54-Hour Bill passed. Rachel invited me to join in the celebration at one of Tammany Hall's choice spots. It was a night where there were too many toasts and not enough bread to absorb the alcohol that was freely flowing.

I woke up the next morning with only the slightest recall of how long I had been in bed. My body hurt to get dressed. I was standing on the stoop, in need of fresh air, my eyes squinting, unable to tolerate the brightness of the day.

Edward was leaving for the office and chuckled when he saw me a bit worse for wear. *How was your dinner with New York City's favorite pols?*

A bit too much for me. My head feels like a marching band is parading through it and my tongue has grown about three inches in thickness.

Edward chuckled. *Did you meet the powerful Silent Charlie Murphy, the head of the entire Tammany operation?*

Indeed, sir, I did. Not only did I meet him, but I am also to continue our conversation tomorrow afternoon at Delmonico's. Happily, it is not today, as my head would not be up to the challenge.

Edward was practically stuttering. *Murphy has invited you to the Scarlet Room, his inner sanctuary. How did you manage that?*

I shaded my eyes from the all-too-bright sun. *We were introduced and when he realized that I was the reporter who wrote the articles on the Commissions' upstate tour, he asked me one question. 'What needs to be done next?' Without hesitation, I replied, 'the widow's pension'. He asked 'Why?' I told him of my experience in the factories, of women who had no time to grieve, who were left destitute when their husbands died. The party was in full steam while we were talking, I could barely hear him over all the hoopla. He told me he would like to hear more of my thoughts but that he needed to leave as the party appeared slated to continue well into the early morning's light.*

I should have taken his lead. Remind me the next time someone says 'just one more,' to turn and run the other way. I need a glass of water.

Edward shook his head, adjusting his tie that needed no tweaking. *This all too much, Nell. First, you write articles that expose the hardships women and their children encounter in their daily lives of labor. Then your published words fuel the public acceptance of one of the most controversial labor laws this state has ever seen, and now Charles Murphy has asked you to call on him. There are men in politics and business that would give their eye-teeth to have such an invitation extended. By the way, he likes to be addressed as Commissioner.*

I gave him the best smile I could muster. *I shall remember, but do remind me tonight. My head is throbbing so I am not going to count on it to remember anything at the moment. I plan to have a cup of tea and dry toast and retreat to my bed.*

Edward chuckled again, gave me a quick kiss on the cheek, and we both left the stoop.

The following day both my head and my stomach had settled down. Spring was on the horizon, the sunshine warmed me, as I found my way to 45th Street and entered Delmonico's on Fifth Avenue. Edward had prepared me with tales of the infamous Scarlet Room on the second floor, where Murphy held court.

The doorman registered a look of surprise when I handed him my card. The card and I then began our procession from him to the elevator boy, to one of the liveried attendants standing guard at the anteroom, and finally to Murphy's gate-keeper, 'Smiling Phil Donohue.' Twenty minutes later, I was still sitting alone and started to doubt if I had imagined the conversation with Murphy. It had been a long evening, and my recollection of parts of it remained fuzzy. I was thinking of quietly slipping away when the massive panel door swung open. Donahue reappeared, his infamous grin never leaving his face, and beckoned me in.

Murphy's private sanctuary lived up to its reputation. The walls were hung with red fabric and the floors thick with carpeting in the same bright color. The chairs were red plush and the buffets highly polished mahogany. My first thought was I was glad I had chosen to wear navy blue so as not to clash with the furnishings.

Seated alone at a table with legs carved into tiger paws in honor of the Tammany mascot was Murphy.

He rose to greet me. *Mrs. Walker.*

Commissioner.

He motioned me to take a chair. *Are you one of those people who managed to get the 54-Hour Bill passed?*

Yes, sir, and proud of it.

He looked straight at me, *I opposed that bill.*

So, I was told.

He did not immediately respond, the quiet was deafening. This was the Silent Charles Murphy the press wrote about and then finally, *It is my observation that the bill brought us many votes. I will tell the boys to look into this widow's pension bill. Thank you for coming.*

I stood up, *Thank you for taking the time to speak with me.*

He nodded, *One more question. Are you one of those suffragettes?*

Yes, was my quick and only reply.

Murphy's shrewd eyes never left my face. *Well, I don't believe that women should get the vote.*

I stopped, my hand now on the door, *Well, Commissioner, beware. Our ranks are swelling from farmers' wives to millionaires with minks. Women are marching to the ballot box, and we are going to get the right to vote sooner or later. You will want their vote, and you will want mine. Good day, sir.*

I didn't wait for a reply.

Murphy was true to his word. Six months later, the pension bill was passed without fanfare. By the end of the year, Charles Murphy was on the record endorsing women's voting rights.

The calendar turned 1916. Cars were clogging the streets, European countries were entangled in a series of political and conflicting alliances, newspapers were focusing their stories on the turmoil caused by the assassination of an archduke no one had ever heard about until his assassination. O'Brien left New York to photograph the unraveling. I was working with Anne to garner support for the passage of the right for women to vote in New York state. Wilson was president and Henry entered our lives.

CHAPTER 11

HENRY

W e were dining at the Plaza the first time I met him. He was the kind of man who took your breath away at first glance. Closing in on six feet, dressed in black tie with a coat draped over his arm, he looked like he would be welcomed anywhere. His blonde hair was gelled in keeping with the current style, and his royal blue eyes belied a merriment that was well hidden in the composed man-about-town studied look he wore. From the vantage point of the doorway, he let his eyes adjust to the half-light and then surveyed the crowd. He nodded when he found us, smiled, and meandered his way through the labyrinth of tables until he sat down at ours. Edward introduced him as Henry Wordsworth.

No relation to the old chap, he said as he took my hand, *but it is a great conversation starter when I am trying to impress a beautiful woman*. His gaze dropped to my face, and I felt my cheeks begin to burn. Throughout the rest of the evening, Edward couldn't stop staring. Neither could I.

The pattern of our life was altered from that moment on. Henry would join us for dinner at least once a week, always with a budding starlet on his arm, each was more stunning than the one before. They all smelled of lavender soap, cigarettes, and gin.

Henry defined the word charm. He was always attentive, listening when I spoke, not merely nodding while politely waiting for his turn to change the subject. When I asked him about this one evening, he replied that his mother raised him to treat ladies with respect and not to bore them with men's talk. *But you, my dear Nell, are different. I believe you prefer to talk about the rights of others rather than DW Griffith's filmmaking. I really do prefer the company of smart women, most of the time.* And he winked at me.

Henry was in show business. Given most of the men in Edward's circle, he was a breath of fresh air. We were back at the Plaza, Henry loved the Men's Bar. When I protested that women weren't allowed in, he shrugged his shoulders. *My dear Nell, first you get the vote, followed by a seat at the table, then and only then will you be able to get a stool at the bar. Till that moment comes, I will drink in peace with no distractions brought upon by women with eyes as lovely as yours.*

Henry had ordered us martinis, instructing the waiter that *they should be shaken as if the bartender were conducting a Viennese waltz.* When his drink arrived, Henry lifted it with reverence as the priest raising the chalice at the consecration. *To the martini. As H. L. Mencken, once said, it is the only American invention as perfect as the sonnet.*

Ah, he said, putting down the glass, *Where were we? You, my lovely Nell, were scolding me over my choice of watering holes and you, my dear,* looking over to his current lady of the evening, *want to hear more about the movie business.*

That was my first and last martini. I thought it tasted like nail polish remover, or at least what I thought nail polish remover would taste like. The effect was immediate, my body was warm all over, my senses blurred, my voice louder. I put the glass down, convinced by the courage seeded by the juniper berry that whatever the next conversation would be, it would be one of the most brilliant discussions I could engage in.

I pronounced *The Birth of a Nation* an absolute horror, loudly enough that heads at the next table turned our way.

Henry ordered another round of drinks. I had the good sense to decline the offer. *DW would have never understood why,* Henry replied, his voice for our ears only. *Griffith may be viewed as a trailblazer by those outside the motion picture industry, but he is stubbornly backward in his views, preferring the mores of the 19th Century to our new world order. It is well known his actresses will be dismissed if they develop blemishes on their skin, as DW believes such imperfections are the mark of a debauched character.*

Henry looked over to his latest date, *And you, my darling, have the skin of the angel; but that is the only characteristic of those heavenly beings you have inherited.* She cooed her response. I rolled my eyes.

The martini's effect ebbed, and my head began to clear as I listened to Henry talk about the entertainment business. *This new breed of movie man, of which I am one, grasps that the picture business is a business. If the audience doesn't like a picture, they have a reason. The public is never wrong. They want to be entertained. I prefer the grit and glitter of theater to the polish and light-heartedness of today's films. Yet the public disagrees. So, give them Charlie Chaplin and Clara Bow if that is who it takes to bring them to sit in our seats.*

Then one night, I noticed a subtle change, a change only I would have seen. Edward smiled a special smile when Henry spoke, as if there was a private joke only the two of them shared. The following evening, Henry's hand lingered just a second too long on Edward's shoulder as he passed. Nothing was said. Nothing had to be.

The next day was Saturday morning. Like most starts to our weekends, we were casually reading the morning newspapers over a late breakfast. I poured milk into my tea, stirring it carefully. I looked up at Edward. *Are you and Henry lovers?*

Edward choked on his coffee. *You know?*

Not until last night and confirmed by you just now.

Edward looked into my eyes. *I love him, I dearly do.*

I returned his gaze. *I understand completely. I love him, too. I just wished he would have chosen me over you.*

Edward's eyes danced with amusement. *Oh, I do love you, Nell. You are like no other woman the Lord created.*

Well, I am not sure about that. What I am sure of, however, is that there are few wives who discuss their husband's male lovers over breakfast.

Our world changed with Henry as the catalyst.

———

H enry took us to the Cotton Club up on 142nd Street, a part of the city most New Yorkers thought of as the frontier. Harlem was a cocktail of races, the ingredients all mixed together, resulting in something new, exciting, inebriating. It gave me quite a rush.

The Cotton Club with its brightly lit entrance looked like a movie theatre to the untrained eye. Inside, this garishness was forgotten as it shouted expensive and elegant. Its patrons appeared both bored and engaged, a look only the fashionable New York crowd owned. They sat at small round tables, each with a single candle in the center of a spotless white linen tablecloth. There was room for dancing, but the stage was the focal point. The proscenium was large, floodlights on each side predicted that something wonderful was going to happen. And most nights it did.

On our first trip, Henry shared the gossip that no one cared the place was owned by Owney Madden, a Brit who was a born-and-bred Yorkshire man who bore no resemblance to the stereotyped English gentleman. He bought the Club when he was still in prison at Sing-Sing doing time for murder.

Henry whispered in my ear: *Rumor has it that Madden has no problem killing people who cross him; but he runs the best jazz club in the City, so no one seems to mind, including New York's finest. The police safeguard all who enter here. And there, to confirm my pronouncement, look two tables over. You will set your eyes on none other than the man who will be the mayor of this city one day.* I looked over and there was Jimmy Walker who would have his own rule book when it came to wine, women, and politics.

I loved going there. Henry knew everybody from the cigarette girl to the star of the show. Edward and I were warmed by the spotlight shone on him.

Henry took us to his private club, a haven for those whose family names had been on the Social Register, the 400 families that could fit in Mrs. Astor's ballroom. This was a world foreign to Edward and me. These were the families who traced their ancestry to Dutch landowners and English merchants; they had known and married each other for generations and cared equally for wealth and social standing. You didn't ask to join this circle; you gained admission slowly and only after proving yourself worthy. It could take lifetimes.

After navigating our way through a myriad of idling limousines, a valet in top hat and with the briefest nod to Henry opened the door to the club's dining room. It was a tableau, men in tailored suits adorned with perfectly tucked-in and unused breast pocket handkerchiefs stood next to women wearing black, sleek and shiny, with more pearls than could be found in the oyster beds resting in Long Island Sound. I whispered to Edward as he took my arm, *At least we look like we belong, though my lone strand of pearls seems too understated.*

The maître d' approached Henry with the ease of a man who meets and greets the famous with the same style and affectation. *We've been expecting you. Please. Follow me.* Never have I heard the words sound both like a command and an invitation. Henry ordered martinis. I deferred, preferring a simple glass of white wine. Our glasses clinked. Life was lovely. Life was elegant. Life was easy. Here I was seated between two men who were lovers, one of whom was my husband; but it felt right, it felt complete. We all three loved each other, though differently.

Dear Mama,

    Edward has a lover, his name is Henry. Oddly, I love Henry, too. It is hard to describe, even to you.
    I am comfortable when I am alone with either Edward or Henry. I am comfortable when the three of us are together. Edward has been true to his promise. I am not aware of when Henry spends the night. If he stays, he is gone by morning and there is no mention of it.
    This works for me, Mama. I don't know why. It feels like we are a family. An odd family, but a family nonetheless. I am not sure you would understand. I am not sure I understand. I know I am happy. I think that is enough.

                        I love you, Mama.
                        Your Nell

———

1917 dawned with Henry and I finding our own spot, the Trophy Room, though no one ever knew why it had been given such a name. There was not a trophy to be seen unless one of the young willowy blondes holding the arm of a man old enough to be her father fit that definition.

We went there for the first time on my birthday. Edward was away on business and felt less guilty knowing that I was not going to be left alone. Henry was quiet about the plans, telling me that I was about to have a night that I wouldn't quickly forget. We got into his car and headed south on Sixth Avenue.

I remember my first reaction when I saw the place. There was no doorman to greet us, the flashing neon sign heralding its name was missing an 'O.' Henry said nothing, he just led me down a flight of dingy steps as the smells of the city engulfed us. Yesterday's garbage that had baked on the street, topped with today's debris, created an aroma that made my stomach turn and my eyes water. Henry opened the door and all of this was soon forgotten by the sounds that came from somewhere within the inner sanctum. This was the best jazz south of 96th Street; this was downtown. Nobody called anybody by their last name.

My eyes took a moment to adjust, the air a smokey haze. There was a long wooden bar and everything, including the liquor bottles, was layered in an inch of dust. Henry found us a small table. We were surrounded by starving artists, starving artist models, poets, musicians, lost souls, and a few that looked like we shared the same telephone exchange. Henry stood out while fitting in. The bass player was his friend who joined us between sets. The bartender put his drink down before he could order it. Everyone smoked. Everyone drank. Everyone listened. No one spoke.

The music danced out of the instruments, some notes deep as the soul, others sweet as maple syrup. My foot began to tap, my head nodded and swayed. No sadness allowed here, no worrying over the state of the world, only a feeling of being one with the music.

It would be 'our place' – the one that belonged to just Henry and me. Edward never minded. He gave both of us this space, a space that was filled with sounds both joyful and mournful.

———

The sun had given up the day but left the heat behind when I first heard the word 'summer' used as a verb. We were seated on the porch of Henry's house in Brigham. I had just finished reading the paper with headlines of young men dying on barbed wire fences on French fields for a cause I couldn't describe. I looked at the view, the water and the sky were so blue you couldn't tell where one ended and the other began. I thought of all the young men who would never leave the mud and blood of Flanders Fields. The contrast was jolting.

I heard Henry's voice, I wasn't sure he was addressing me or speaking his own thoughts. *We have summered here for as long as I can remember. The family cottage is in the next town over. I bought my own place as soon as I could. I love this part of the world, but staying under the same roof with my family ruined the peace and tranquility of a day such as this.*

Henry was wearing his finest doeskin trousers, a light bright blue cashmere sweater, and spotless custom-made shoes. It all seemed too perfect, like one of the pictures in a travel brochure that makes you yearn for parts of the world unknown.

I shook off my gloom and looked over at him, my hands sweeping as if to embrace the picture posed before me. *You are magical,* I said, raising my glass in a toast.

He smiled a rueful smile. *Magic is ever a trick, and yet the viewer believes. Wave a wand, cast a spell.*

He clicked my glass.

CHAPTER 12

A WORLD AT WAR

I t was early March 1916. France, Germany, and Great Britain continued to kill off their youth while Wilson still claimed neutrality. It was Monday morning, the prisms of morning sunlight had found their way into the dining room. Edward shook his head, *We are going to war*, he took off his glasses and rubbed his eyes.

I looked up. *Unless there are headlines in this paper I haven't read yet, I believe our Professor-President is refusing to involve us in the madness of foreigners.*

I'm reading between the lines, Nell. Today's paper tells of a 'captured' document that supposedly the German Foreign Minister sent to the Mexican government urging them to attack the United States. Their prize for doing so would be to retrieve their so-called lost lands of New Mexico, Arizona, and Texas. This is all Wilson needs. We will be in the thick of it all within weeks. Shaking his head, Edward put his glasses back on, stood up, and straightened his tie.

I nodded. *Papa agrees with you. He told me last week that he believes that the banks have loaned too much money to the Allies and are afraid they will never be repaid unless we enter the conflict.*

Papa and Edward were proven right. A month later, our peace-sprouting president turned the ship of state in the direction of Europe and the nation cheered. The United States was at war.

It was April of the following year, Edward and I were walking back from the Wake Up America Day! celebration. Our mayor had arranged for bells of Trinity Church to be rung as floats depicting scenes from American history made their way along Fifth Avenue. The day was bright, the daffodils that had been patiently waiting under the cold earth were pushing their cheerful colors through the earth. The sun on my face welcomed me back to the outdoors. It was the time of year that I normally feel renewed. But not this day, not this year.

I took Edward's arm. *I don't understand this. I don't see that the test of loyalty to this country is to show your enthusiasm for sending young boys to places they had never heard of for a cause that I still can't articulate.*

Edward paused, a group of school-age children blocked our progress carrying large signs equating loyalty to this country with buying war bonds. *Wilson sees a new America, one taking center stage in this war and in the international arena. It is as if he has experienced a religious conversion and, like Saint Paul, saw a blinding light and heard the voice of the Lord calling him to do battle. The former peace-sprouting professor has now been transformed to be the intermediary between the Almighty and the nation, assuring us that this crusade was God's will and God's work.*

Well, to quote you, my dear husband, Poppycock! I believe this new world we are entering will bring more, rather than less, conflict to our shores. Edward simply nodded. We walked the rest of the way home each in our own thoughts.

It was two weeks later, we were with Henry, a quiet evening with just the three of us at home. Edward had said little over dinner, picking at his food, his eyes had a faraway look. I looked over at Henry, whose nod affirmed he was equally concerned. I tipped my wine glass with my knife as if to start a toast. Edward looked up, startled.

Are you well, Edward? You are not yourself tonight.

I am fine, physically, my dear, he responded shaking his head ever so slightly. *While our boys* are *fighting in France, there is a war being fought in this country, as well. Not with bullets or barbed wire, but with anti-German hysteria that I find heart-wrenching. One of our partners today refused to hire a young lawyer because his last name was Schmidt. My colleague, a so-called esteemed member of the bar, was adamant that our clients would be 'uncomfortable' – that was the word he used – to be in the company of someone who could be a spy for the enemy. He referred to the young man as a Hun. It was a ridiculous accusation, but no one called him on it, myself included. He is a powerful man at the firm.*

Edward looked into his wine glass as if it were a crystal ball, showing images of days past. *My great-grandfather came over from Germany many years ago. He made his fortune in the Midwest brewing beer and then found his way to Pennsylvania and real estate. I never gave it much thought. We never spoke German at home, and I don't even like beer.* He pushed his plate away, the food barely touched. *I didn't do the right thing today, and I am not sure I will do the right thing tomorrow.* His black eyes became even darker.

Henry looked to save the evening. *Well, I for one am certainly not going to stop listening to Beethoven or reading Goethe and Schiller because of the politics being forced on us. I do have a greater concern*, he continued, fingering his wine glass slowly, staring into the final drops of the fine white Sancerre that we poured that evening. It was said with such a mix of sadness and force that both Edward and I turned our complete attention to him. We said nothing but waited for him to continue. *If the dreaded Prohibition gets passed, I will blame it on this war.*

Whatever are you talking about, Henry? Edward is concerned about the backlash the war is having on our fellow Americans, and you are worried about alcohol being outlawed. I don't see the connection. My voice sounded scolding.

Oh, my dear, Henry sighed, *the only effective lobbying group that is keeping the wolves at bay in this dilemma comes from the brewers. Like your ancestor, my dear Edward, they have German names and are becoming increasingly unpopular. Our taps and our barrels will be taken from us, I fear. I am going to do the courageous thing and begin stockpiling cases upon cases of good wine and better whiskey. Once these dark days are a memory, we will need the nectar of the gods to lighten our mood*, he said as he poured himself the last few drops from the bottle.

He held his glass up to the light. *Trust me, my dear friends, there will be a time in the not-too-distant future that this 'noble experiment' will become the law of the land; and enjoying the fruits of the vine will be problematic. Our country is changing. There will be more name-calling like you heard today, Edward, as our government looks to legislate our morality. I was hoping for better from Wilson.*

I added my view. *So did I. Women still need the vote.* I stood up and fetched another bottle of wine.

———

Two weeks later, we saw bigotry first-hand. We were meeting Henry at one of the new restaurants that had just opened on 52nd Street, and Edward had persuaded Rachel to join us.

Rachel and I stopped in the Ladies Room, leaving Edward to wait for Henry. As we opened the door, we ran directly into Miss Beekman, looking as priggish as when she crossed me off the welcome roster for her meetings. She and I exchanged the necessary greetings as befitted our station, but no more. When I introduced her to Rachel, her lips curled and her eyes narrowed, focusing on the Star of David, the symbol of Judaism, hanging from a chain on Rachel's neck. Now, seemingly in a hurry, Miss Beekman bid us a brief farewell with barely a nod.

I thought nothing more of it. Minutes later, Rachel and I went into the dining room to find Henry and Edward in an agitated conversation with the maître d'. Miss Beekman was watching the exchange from a table visible to all who entered but far enough away to avoid the front door's draft.

Henry's voice was rising in protest, his eyes never leaving those of the increasingly red-faced maître d'. *That, sir, is complete rubbish. I made the reservation myself; and even if it isn't in your book, there are plenty of empty tables where you could seat us.*

The maître d' mumbled something about being completely full for the evening. Edward exclaimed, *Poppycock!*

Rachel understood immediately what was happening; and in a loud but amiable voice responded, *My friends, I know a spot nearby where both the management and the ambiance are more agreeable. I ate there last evening with Frances Perkins and Al Smith, and both found it to be quite to their liking.*

The maître d' looked dumbstruck. This woman dined with two of the most influential politicians in the city, and he was refusing to admit her and her party into his restaurant. Stumbling for the right words, he began to say something else when Henry gave us his best rakish smile, threw his coat over his shoulder, took Rachel's arm, and in the loudest of possible voices for all in the room to hear: *That is the highest of recommendations. And we will be sure to tell Al and all our friends at Tammany they needn't bother coming here. Its reputation as a fine dining establishment is clearly overrated.*

I looked over at the table where Miss Beekman was seated. Her look of smugness changed to surprise as the focus of *maître d's* displeasure was now directed at her.

Edward, having now put the puzzle together, whispered in my ear, *May Miss Beekman enjoy this evening's meal as I suspect it will be the last time this establishment opens its doors to her.*

CHAPTER 13

1918

I t was mid-October, one of those days that dawn not sure if it should remind us of summer or foretell the coming of winter. It was early, most of the household was just beginning to stir. I heard the phone ring but gave it no thought. Minutes later, Bridget knocked on my door.

Your Aunt Helena is on the phone. I can't make much sense, but she is asking for you.

I put on my robe and went into the parlor. I hadn't spoken to Aunt Helena since Mother Walker's funeral six months ago. She had arrived with Papa. We were cool but polite to each other.

Aunt Helena? It's Nell.

She was choking out words between sobs. *He's gone. He's gone. My heart is broken. What am I to do?*

My throat started to swell. I tried to speak the words screaming in my head. I stuttered, *Papa? Is something wrong with Papa?*

Aunt Helena kept up her mantra, *What am I to do?*

Aunt Helena, put Stephens on the phone. Do you hear me, put Stephens on the phone! Now, Aunt Helena. Now!

Stephens, who had been our butler for as long as I could remember, was soon on the line. His voice strained.

I am so sorry, Miss Nell. Despite my marital status, in my parent's home, I remained Miss Nell. *Your father came home early yesterday afternoon, saying that he felt poorly. He declined supper and went right up to his room. I asked if he wanted me to call Dr. Ruehl, and he said no, he just needed a good night's sleep. When he wasn't down for breakfast this morning, I went to his room. He didn't answer when I knocked. I found him in his bed, he wasn't breathing.* Stephens paused. *I called the doctor and had Eliza wake up your aunt. Dr. Ruehl is still here. Do you want to speak with him?*

I didn't want to speak to anybody. I wanted this conversation to be a bad dream. I looked up to find Edward at my side. He was tying his morning coat around his waist, his hair uncombed. He took the telephone from my hand and asked Stephens to stay on the line. He took me in his arms, the stubble on his cheek feeling like sandpaper against mine. It occurred to me that I had never seen Edward shave. Edward called for Bridget. I followed her into the library. I shook my head at her offer to bring me a cup of tea. Staring out the window, I realized the day was gray, dreary. As it should be.

Within the hour, Edward joined me. *I spoke with Dr. Ruehl. Your father died suddenly last night of the 'Spanish flu.' The doctor confirmed what the headlines are reporting, hundreds are dying all over Philadelphia.*

I shook my head as my voice trailed off. *I spoke to him on Sunday. He talked about going to the Liberty Loan Parade and how proud he was to see so many show up and buy war bonds. For Papa, the floating biplanes that were built in Philadelphia's own Navy Yard were the highlight of the event. He told me it was worth fighting the crowds just to see those floats. Today is Thursday. How could this have happened? We talked about this war ending. He was fine. How could he be dead? What about Mama? Who is going to tell Mama?* I shuddered. *It can't be Aunt Helena. It mustn't be Aunt Helena.* I started to shake.

Edward covered my hand with his. *It is taken care of Nell. I have asked Dr. Ruehl to call your mother's doctor. Best if she has her doctor tell her. I said you would call her this evening and would be coming to see her within the next few weeks. I am going to change and go to the firm. I will speak with Stephens about making arrangements for your father's funeral. This 'Spanish flu' is killing thousands, so I don't know what we will be able to do. It will be easier if I make the calls from my office. I called Victoria and she is coming to spend the day with you; and I expect Henry will be at your side, as well.*

I took a deep breath. This is what it is like to be taken care of, to have someone care enough about you that they think for you and about you. *Aunt Helena? Can you let her know the arrangements once they are made? I don't have the energy.* Aunt Helena had continued to live in the house after I left. She explained she was sacrificing her life to ease the mind of her poor ailing sister. When I came to Philadelphia to have dinner with Papa, she was not included in the invitation, nor was she a topic of conversation. The same was true when I went to visit Mama.

For the next few hours, I was a caged animal, pacing throughout the house. The day had turned cold and rainy, there was no escaping into the fresh air. Victoria came quickly and, looking to distract me, offered to help me pack the bag I would need to take to Philadelphia. It gave me a purpose. We were pulling out the dresses that I had worn to Mother Walker's wake when Edward came home.

Henry was steps behind him and came rushing towards me. The air was growing heavy with sorrow as if the damp from the outside had followed Henry in. A wave of emotion overpowered me and exploded into a giant sob. Henry put his arms around me. *I got here as soon as I could, Nell. I am so sorry, my dear friend. There are no words, only heartache.*

Edward took control. *Let's all go to the parlor. Henry, Victoria, please stay and have dinner with us. The news is difficult.*

The four of us marched in place, the start of the first of the funeral processions. A fire had been lit, providing the only light and warmth this day had seen.

Henry poured us each a glass of port. Edward motioned me to sit next to him on the couch as he handed me a glass. *You need to drink this, Nell. It will calm your nerves.* I sniffed the dark red liquid, it smelt of plum and berries. I took a sip, the sweet taste ended in a bite, jarring my senses.

No one spoke as Edward continued. *I spoke to one of my former colleagues as soon as I got to the office. Philadelphia is suffering. This flu is killing hundreds, and it looks as if the city is about to shut down. It is as if Philadelphia is in the plague-infested Middle Ages. Horse-drawn wagons are patrolling the streets collecting corpses draped in sackcloths and blood-stained sheets, priests follow giving the Last Rites. Hundreds upon hundreds of bodies are being collected, and there is no place to take them. The city is expected to ban wakes and funerals this week.*

I gasped. *But Papa, I need to bury Papa.*

We will, my dear, we will. I spoke to the priest at my mother's church. We can have the Funeral Mass at his parish. There have been fewer cases of the flu there. There will no wake, there can be no public gatherings. I've talked to Stephens.

Henry interrupted, *This entire mess is inexcusable, no one was warned. The papers wanted the news to talk of cheerful things instead of disease. They didn't want to scare everybody to death. Now they have brought people to the death. They should be tried for murder.*

I took another sip of the port, my throat now more accustomed to the burning sensation it evoked. *I've seen how well our courts deal with those responsible for the deaths of the innocent. It never occurred to me that my own father would be counted in that circle.*

Edward spent the rest of the evening describing the arrangements that had been made. We were to leave for Philadelphia the following morning. There would be no wake, no viewing of the body. We would meet anyone who wishes to pay their respects in a private suite in the hotel. We were staying at the Belgravia. Stephens was arranging it all, including having the staff checked by Dr. Ruehl to be sure they had no symptoms. Edward had spoken with Papa's lawyers, and we would meet with them following the burial. Everything was arranged, everything was as it should be. Except Papa was dead.

I stepped out of the parlor. I needed to call Mama. The dark skies had made the evening come much faster than the clock on the wall chimed. I went up to my room to put on the gold cross. I placed the call, wishing with every fiber of my being that we could have this conversation in person. I wanted to be held.

Mama, I am so sad. I can't believe Papa is gone.

Her voice was strained, but it was all I could hold onto for the moment. *I always thought I would be the first. When you are sick as I am, my darling Nell, you live every day as though it could be your last. People die around me all the time. I am comfortable with the thought of death. My own and your Papa's.* I heard a smile in her voice, and the memory of me sitting on her bed as she braided my hair came rushing back. It was the voice of love. *I believed I would pave the way into heaven for him. It looks as though he will now do that for me. He loved you, Nell. I know he wasn't always good about telling you that. Or telling you how proud he was of you, how you wrote articles that made people take notice.*

I loved him, too, Mama. Though I never told him so, it was simpler to say nothing. Oh, how I wish I told him. Now it is too late, too late to tell him how much I loved him.

It is never too late to tell someone you love them, my darling daughter. Tell him in your heart. He will listen and whisper back that he loves you, too.

I love you, Mama.

I love you, Nell. I will see you soon. Stay strong.

Aunt Helena cried uncontrollably from the moment we greeted the first person who was brave enough to come and pay their respects to the moment the last mourner left. She was dressed in widow's black, looking like a mirror image of Queen Victoria, though taller by five inches.

On the day of Papa's funeral, the sun shone brightly, the changing color of the leaves sparkling in its brilliance. It all seemed too bright and cheerful. I wanted the day to be dark and damp, the air heavy. I was burying Papa. I stood in silent grief as we waited for the casket to arrive at the church. We would go through the ritual of the Mass, drive to the cemetery, and watch

Papa's casket be lowered into the ground. I thought how he would have hated this, how he would have rebelled at being the center of all this attention, as simple as it was.

As we lined up to enter the church, Aunt Helena positioned herself directly behind the casket. Edward quietly went over and walked her to the second pew. She started to sputter and looked at me to revoke the perceived slight. I did nothing. This was about saying my last farewell to Papa. I was not sharing my grief with Aunt Helena.

Then it was over, or at least that part. The following few days melted into each other. Edward stayed with me, taking care of the myriad of details that needed to be resolved. My thinking was fuzzy. I would wake up in the middle of the night wondering where I was. I knew I wasn't home. In a moment or two, the fog would dissipate and I would remember that I was at the Belgravia. I was in Philadelphia. Papa was dead. A worldwide virus was killing innocent people

In the hotel, the smell of disinfectant was overpowering, assuring us we were safe and secure from the virus. The streets around the hotel, usually bustling with the citizens of the city hustling to and fro, were eerily quiet. The shock of so many deaths in such a short period of time kept people behind closed doors.

When I read the headlines of the Philadelphia newspapers, I wanted to scream. It was not just 815 dead, it was my Papa. My Papa was dead because these papers had told him it was alright to go out into a crowd. My Papa was dead because of what had been published. And so were other fathers, mothers, sisters, sons. These were real people, not just numbers to be reported on, not just numbers that helped sell newspapers.

A week after I had received the phone call from Aunt Helena, Edward came to breakfast, dressed as if he was going to the office. *You are wearing your lawyer's uniform, Edward.*

Indeed, my dear. Remember, we are meeting with your father's

lawyers this morning. I have arranged for them to meet us in a conference room here at the hotel.

Us? Do I have to go, can't you go as my husband and my lawyer?

It is best that you attend. It will follow a standard protocol and shouldn't be too onerous. These lawyers do this all the time, so they have it down to a science. Edward poured himself a cup of coffee and puffed himself up a bit as he did his best imitation of a stuffy lawyer, a role he had seen played often enough.

'Ahem, my dear Mrs. Walker, on behalf of my fellow partners and myself, I wish to extend my sincere sympathy to you and your husband on the passing of your father. He was a fine man and a respected client of the firm. We hope we can continue the tradition of being a service to you and your family.' He will look sad, consoling, and the minute he finishes his sympathies, his voice will change as it starts to go over the particulars of your father's will.

I felt myself smile for the first time in days.

Ah, there you are, Nell. I knew I could get your eyes to twinkle again, if only for a moment. Trust me, my dear. It shouldn't take more than an hour. Then, if there are no outstanding issues, I would like to take an early afternoon train back to New York. Stephens has had the house scrubbed and sanitized, so whenever you are ready, you can visit. If you want me to stay to go with you, I will.

I put up my hand. *No, I can handle this. I think I need to say goodbye to the house and all its memories on my own. Let me finish my tea, and then get ready for the meeting.*

Despite my heavy heart, when Mr. Clark's baritone voice expressed his deepest desire to retain his relationship with the family, I almost chuckled out loud. He had acted as if on cue and proceeded immediately to begin the reason we were assembled, the reading of the will.

As Mr. Clark droned on about the particulars of the disbursements of my father's assets, I was shocked by the dollars. I knew we were comfortable and wanted for no material things, but these numbers were staggering. I was a wealthy woman. Not Vanderbilt wealthy, but these monies gave me something I never had thought about before, financial independence. After agreeing Edward would call Mr. Clark later in the week to discuss the release of the funds, Edward whispered in my ear that he had no idea he was married to an heiress.

I leaned into him and responded. *I always thought you married me because I looked like a Gibson Girl.*

Exactly. Beauty, brains, and now a bonus. My wildest dream come true, he squeezed my hand. *Are you okay?*

I squeezed his hand back. *A bit overwhelmed but okay. Thank you for being there for me and for making me be here, as well.*

Edward and I went back to the Belgravia. He needed to pack and return to New York. As we finished lunch, Edward explained in layman's terms that Papa had thought of every contingency, laying out his wishes clearly and succinctly. Stephens, Mrs. Williams, Eliza, and Antonio, the gardener, were each awarded a handsome sum based on their position and service to the family. The remainder of the estate was split. Half of the proceeds were to go into a trust fund to care for Mama. Mr. Clark and Edward would serve as the trustees. I would inherit the remaining funds at the time of her death. Aunt Helena was to receive a one-time distribution of $50,000, and I was to receive an annual allowance of $25,000. The house and all the furnishings were mine.

The lawyers would advise the others of their gifts the next day. Edward suggested that I write to Mama and explain it as best I could.

Edward and I said our goodbyes, and he left for New York. I took out a pen and began to make a list of what I needed to do tomorrow and the days ahead. The house would be sold, I had no desire to return to Philadelphia.

That night I slept fitfully. I pulled open the thick red velvet curtains that hung around the mullioned windows and the blackness that had enclosed the room disappeared. For some reason, seeing the early dawn's light break its way into the space made me feel more at peace. I called for tea and sat down to write Mama, a letter that would be posted, about all that happened since I had spoken to her after the funeral. I wanted to be clear about the details of my meeting with Mr. Clark, my astonishment at the size of the estate, my thinking on how I might proceed. By noon, I was satisfied with what I had written.

I needed fresh air, the sun on my face, movement. I left Mama's letter with the hotel manager to be sent and began to walk. I was walking home, back to Rittenhouse Square and the house I had been raised in as a child. The house where Papa had died. Stephens came to the door as he heard me open it.

Miss Nell, how are you holding up?

It is one day at a time, Stephens. Thank you for all you did to help with his funeral. I am not sure we could have made it through without your assistance.

I stepped into the foyer, it all seemed so familiar and yet so strange. *It doesn't seem possible we will no longer have the smell of his pipe tobacco wafting through the house.*

Stephens nodded: *He was a good man, your father* and before he could finish his thought, I heard a crash from the second floor. Startled, I looked at Stephens who said: *Your Aunt Helena arrived from the lawyers' offices a few minutes before you.*

I quickly ran up the stairs, expecting to see her hurt or in pain. I found her in my mother's room, pulling the draperies from the window. The crash was the shattering of the dresser mirror broken by mother's antique jewelry box which now lay amidst the broken shards of glass.

Aunt Helena, I shouted. She turned to me, her black eyes narrowing, spitting out her words. *Irish whore...thief...who are you to be thinking this house should belong to you. It should be mine. He should have been mine. I was with him before he set his eyes on her. All smiles and sweetness. She stole him from me and then went to the gutter and found you.*

What are you talking about? Who is she?

She who can barely take a breath on her own — my poor invalid sister, that's who, her words dripping with sarcasm and hate. *I saw him first. I wanted him. But when he came to call, he saw her, little Miss*

Perfect. He courted her. He wed her. And when she couldn't produce a babe, they went and found you. There is not an ounce of my family's blood in your veins. Just because you resemble her doesn't make you her daughter. And whose daughter are you? Found in some orphanage in godforsaken Buffalo, New York. You come into this house and call it your own. You have no right, she shouted and lunged at me. I stepped aside just in time as she lost her footing and fell to the floor.

Whatever are you talking about? Nothing she said was making any sense to me.

Stumbling as she got up, *He was to love me, this house was to be mine. Then she stole him from me. You don't belong to them. Who knows who you belong to? You with your fine airs and silk dresses. You are nothing but a guttersnipe. This should be mine.*

Picking up a piece of glass from the floor, she lunged at me with all her might and fury. I raised my hands to protect my face from her wild slashings. Blood was running from the cuts on my arm. I stepped back and out of her reach. *Get out! You have hatred running throughout your entire being. You could never understand what it means to love or be loved.*

What? She stepped back, almost losing her balance, dropping the jagged piece of glass now stained with my blood. Her face was contorted, her eyes trying to focus as if she was seeing me for the first time.

I stood frozen, ice water now flowing through my veins. This was my house; and though I didn't know what she was talking about, I wanted no more of her ravings. I wanted no part of her.

My eyes never left hers. *Pack what you need for tonight, I will arrange a place for you to stay. But this is the last time you will be in this house. You are correct, this is now my house. And you, Madam, are no longer welcome. You are to leave immediately and will never be invited back. From this day on, you and I will never meet.*

And with that, I turned and left the room, my hands shaking as I walked down the stairs. Stephens was on the bottom step looking to make his way to the top when he saw me. *Are you alright, Miss Nell? You are bleeding. Should I summon the doctor?*

No, Stephens, it is but a scratch and has already stopped bleeding. Please call the Bellevue-Stratford and arrange a suite of rooms for my aunt, she will be staying there for an indefinite period. Tell them Mr. Walker and I will be responsible for the bill. Send Eliza up to Miss Helena's room and pack just enough for tonight and tomorrow. Tomorrow we will arrange for her things to be delivered to her lodgings there.

Yes, Miss Nell, at once.

Oh, and Stephens, my father remembered you, Mrs. Williams, Eliza, and Antonio in his will. His attorney will be contacting you tomorrow with the details.

He already has, Miss Nell, we were advised today. Your father was most generous, and we are grateful.

You are a member of this family, Stephens, and we will discuss what the future holds but not at this moment. I am going to my father's study. Please advise me when my aunt has left. Have the cab take her directly to Bellevue-Stratford. One last thing, could you kindly open a bottle of my father's finest cabernet and bring it into his study?

At once, Miss Nell. Just let me make the arrangements for your aunt.

Of course, you are very kind.

I found my way into the library, the dark wood flooring, the loose chintz-covered sofas, the Persian carpet, worn in just the right places. It was the room that I loved more than any other. I tenderly touched the sofa, remembering how Mama would pat the cushion beckoning me to sit next to her. In the comfort of the room and her touch, she taught me my letters, taught me to read. She was the perfect teacher, imaginative, demanding in a way that made me want to learn more, understand more, question more. My nerves began to quiet down. This was the room that brought me peace.

I moved slowly down the hall, opening the door to Papa's study. The streetlights flooded the room with their amber glow. I closed the curtains and sat in the chair behind his desk. I took a deep breath, the room still had Papa's scent: old leather, pipe smoke, and whiskey. I am not sure he loved me, but I knew he loved Mama. Aunt Helena has said that I was not their daughter.

I shook my head, this couldn't be true. Was I not their child? I started to shiver, remembering nightmares as a child when I thought I was on a boat and people were dying. Mama dismissed them, and eventually, they went away. There were no pictures of me as a baby. A fact I had never given any thought to until today. Was Aunt Helena right? Was this not my heritage? Do I belong to someone else? Somewhere else?

A cold, tingling kind of numbness spread across my body. My knees began to shake, my skin was cold and sweaty. I started to tremble all over.

I didn't hear Stephens knock and let out a small gasp when I saw him next to me. He held a tray with wine poured in our best decanter along with one of our finest crystal glasses and a bit of cheese and crackers. *You're cold, Miss Nell. Let me start a fire.*

I hadn't yet said a word. I wasn't sure what words I could say. I blinked and nodded yes.

She is gone, Miss Nell.

Gone?

Your aunt, Miss Nell. The cab took her to the Bellevue-Stratford about 15 minutes ago. She was hysterical, but Eliza was able to get her packed and out the door.

I can't thank you and Eliza enough. I reached for the now-poured glass of wine. *One last thing, would you please call the locksmith and have the locks on all the doors and downstairs windows changed first thing in the morning.*

Of course. Will you be spending the night here, Miss? I can get Eliza to put fresh linens out for you.

That won't be necessary, Stephens. I am going to ask Mr. Walker to return from New York, and I want to be at the Belgravia when he returns. And thank you for everything. Not just today, which was one of the worst this house has seen, but for all your days with us.

It has been a joy watching you grow into the woman you are today, Miss Nell. Particularly, today. I'll arrange for a cab to pick you up later this evening.

Thank you, Stephens.

Good evening, Miss Nell.

Good evening, Stephens. We will talk again tomorrow. The door closed and I was alone in the room. The sunlight was fading, throwing shadows across the glistening hardwood floors. Father's presence surrounded me like a blanket, not quite suffocating but making it difficult to breathe.

I knew if there was an ounce of truth in what Aunt Helena was saying, there would be a record of it somewhere in this desk. I opened drawers looking for something that I didn't know even existed. There were receipts from workmen on changes made to the house, files with the pay records for the staff, a complete drawer containing Mama's health reports, and the arrangements for her stay at Saranac Lake. The next drawer was mine, it simply read Nell. My hands were shaking when I spread the contents on the desk. There were my school reports, my confirmation certificate, a booklet with all the articles I had sent him from *The Sun* preserved between the plastic sheets. Then, like a beacon whose light draws you to its center, there was a plain white envelope sealed with Papa's stamp. It was addressed to Eleanor Mary, my baptismal name. Up to this day, this moment, I never thought about who I was. Now there were questions. I knew by looking at it that it contained the answers to the questions swirling in my head. *Did I not belong to this life? To this place?*

I held the envelope in my hand. *Do you have the answers? Are you going to tell me who I am?* I couldn't open it here. Alone in this house. I needed Edward to be with me. I called Edward and told him all that transpired, Aunt Helena's accusations, the finding of the envelope, and my decision not to open it.

I need you with me, Edward.

I will be there before you awake in the morning. Go back to the hotel, take a bath, try to sleep.

Two out of three I can do. I am not sure sleep will be mine tonight.

The warm bath water and aromatic soaps provided by the Belgravia did their best to soothe my frayed nerves. If it were not for the cut on my arm, I might have thought the encounter with Aunt Helena was a bad dream.

When sleep was finally mine, I dreamt I was on a ship, crying. I could find no other passengers. I saw a woman at the foot of my bed. She had long black hair and was wearing a white flowing dress that I could see through. Her voice was soft, it was almost as if she was singing. She told me that I was never alone, she was always watching over me. She blew me a kiss and then she faded away.

I woke up, my pillow wet with tears, to find Edward, still dressed in his business suit, standing over me with a steaming cup of tea. *Thought you might need this, my dear,* he said putting it down on the stand next to my bed and kissing my forehead.

Oh, Edward, I sighed, *what would I do without you?*

Probably more things than you could imagine, he replied, his eyes twinkling. I burst out laughing, a sound I hadn't heard in so many days.

Are you okay, Nell? You had me worried last night.

I think so. I had a strange dream that somehow comforted me. Whatever we learn from what is in the envelope, I am going to be okay.

Edward the lawyer took over, *I could use a bath. I will have them bring us up breakfast, and you can tell me in greater detail all that happened yesterday afternoon.*

I took a deep breath. *Always good to have a plan, counselor. This is the envelope, and that is Father's seal. I suspect he knew someday I would be in search of answers to questions that had never been asked. I didn't open it, I wanted you to be with me.*

And so I shall. As soon as I get the grit and grime of the railroad removed from me.

I got up and dressed, putting Mama's gold cross around my neck.

I came into the sitting area to find Edward taking off his glasses and rubbing his forehead. I knew this simple gesture was a sign he was thinking, both of what to say and what to do. The air was thick with the scent of freshly-brewed coffee, and I drank in its aroma but not its taste. I found a teapot and poured another cup, adding my usual bit of milk to its blend.

I took my first sip, my voice measured. *Well, what have you found about me?*

He took a sip from his coffee cup and in a gentle voice started: *Helena is right. You are not their child. Your father's will is much clearer now.*

My hands started to shake. *Can I have a cigarette?*

You don't smoke, Nell. Neither do I.

I know. I just thought it would quiet me down.

Well, it won't. Not now, not never.

Edward took my hands in his. *Let me explain what I have found. There are only a few documents in the envelope.* Edward's voice took on his lawyer tone, a timbre of assurance and measured concern that would invoke a sense of trust even in the most distressed client. *The most telling is a letter written in 1896 by a nun who refers to herself as your father's cousin and appears to have run an orphanage for German girls in Buffalo, New York, the German Roman Catholic Orphan Home. There is also a receipt for a generous donation your father gave to the orphanage a month following that letter. If we can trust Helena, I believe your parents went to Buffalo, met you, and gave the donation as a 'gift' for taking you home with them. It all makes sense.*

What makes sense? That I am not who I thought I was? And never was? I felt cold, my legs began to twitch.

Sorry, my dear. This is my legal mind taking over. In reviewing your father's will, he refers to you always by your full name: Eleanor Mary Denton Walker. There is no reference to you as his daughter. For your mother's trust and your aunt's allocation, he states the relationship: my wife, my sister-in-law, and such. I found it odd he did not do so in your case. Now, I understand. He wanted to be sure no one could contest his wishes by claiming you are not his daughter. He must have anticipated that his death could open up the possibility of making the past a stumbling block to your future. This was a brilliant move on his part, and I must commend his lawyers for their drafting skills.

The chill in my body could be heard in my voice. *Really,*

Edward, you are commenting on the merits of a legal document while I am not sure who I am.

Forgive me, Nell. This is jarring for you. There is a letter from the nun that begins to make the picture clearer. Whenever you are ready, let me read it to you.

I took a deep breath. *You can read it now, but please don't let go of my hand.* Edward rustled through the few papers on his lap and found the one he was looking for – the handwriting was clear and strong, speaking to the strength of its author. Edward squeezed my hand and softly began to read.

My Dear Cousin Steven,

I hope this letter finds you and your wife Clare in God's good graces.

I write to let you know that last week a father came to the orphanage to leave his two motherless daughters. Mr. Clancy is from Cork, Ireland, and the children's mother died on the voyage over. The eldest named Margaret is about six years old with a strong temperament. It is her younger sister, Eleanor Mary, who is called Nell, that I write to you about.

Nell is just three years old and closely resembles your beloved Clare. She has the same auburn hair, fair complexion, and sweet temperament. Nell has been raised in the Catholic faith and can recite her morning prayers. Although she is Irish, her accent is not as pronounced as her older sister's and has lessened during the short time she has been with us.

We are always looking for good homes for our girls, and we would be happy to have Nell live with you in Philadelphia. Should you have any interest in meeting her, please let me know.

In Christ's love and with the blessing of St. Francis.

Your Cousin,
Mother Maria Celine

I took the letter, the paper rattling in my shaking hands, and re-read the words, wanting them to tell me more than what they did.

So, my life has been a lie?

No, my dear, that is not the case at all. You were raised as the daughter of two people who loved you deeply. You know how much your mother loves you. It is only her illness that keeps you separated. Your father took care of you as a father should, providing for you both while he was alive and ensuring your well-being when he died.

I could no longer sit. My heart was beating a dull steady hum, I stood up and walked to the fire, drawn to its flame and promise of warmth. The roof of my mouth was dry. I couldn't swallow. I clutched at the gold cross hanging from its chain. *And I have a sister? And I am Irish by birth? What does this all mean? What am I to do?*

Edward got up and put his arm around me. *I believe we should do a number of things. First, you need to see your mother. She is the only person who can answer your questions. I will contact the orphanage in Buffalo to see if they have any records of your sister and her whereabouts. Do not get your hopes high in this regard, there is very little record keeping in adopting children. And since we are talking about over 20 years ago, I would expect there are few nuns left who would remember you and your sister.*

I released myself from his grip. *Her name is Margaret.*

Who?

My sister. Margaret. Margaret Clancy, to be exact.

Two days later, I was on the train to Saranac Lake to see Mama. I left it up to Edward to finalize all the legal papers. The house would be put up for sale, the proceeds earmarked to subsidize Dr. Trudeau, the physician who established the lab there, to continue his work searching for the cure for consumption. The lawyers were instructed that should Aunt Helena become difficult, they were to deal with her directly. Stephens and the rest of the staff were given the highest letters of recommendation. Whatever else needed to be done, Edward would take care of it.

At that moment, I needed to take care of myself. I was in the hotel room in Saranac Lake and ordered supper to be delivered to my room. A meal that I knew I should but could not eat. I found the hotel's stationery and began to write.

Dear Mama,

I will see you in hours, but first I must get my thoughts in order. I am angry, sad, and questioning.

Papa's death was the first shock. He seemed fine when I saw him just two weeks before he died. We had dinner at his club, he ordered the same things off the menu: a sirloin steak, baked potato, and a small green salad. Nothing out of the ordinary, nothing that hinted he wasn't feeling well. We talked about you, Edward, the war in Europe, and women getting the vote. The same topics we covered most every time we met.

I think that is what I will miss most about Papa. I always knew what to expect. I always knew I could count on him. There was never indication from him that I was not his daughter or, perhaps to be exact, he always made it feel that I was your daughter.

I will not share with you how Aunt Helena told me that I was not your child. It was too cruel. She is your sister and repeating her harsh words will not take away their sting.

Not your child? If not your daughter, who am I? Why was I never told? I would not have loved you less. Why did you pick me?

I have a sister. Did you meet her? Does she look like me? Do you know where she is? Did you ever try to look for her?

I was born in Ireland. I never thought to ask where I was born, only now does it seem to matter. I think about the young girls who died in the Triangle Shirtwaist Factory fire, many of them were Irish. Is that the fate that you saved me from? What would my life be like if you had not found me? So many questions rushing through my mind at the same time, my brain aches.

Where do I belong and to whom?
This is hard.

I love you, Mama.
Your Nell

I read the words and started to cry. There was no sobbing, just tears. Water dripping onto the paper, leaving its mark. I climbed into bed and pulled the blanket to my chin. Shivering with cold, I curled into a ball. I would see Mama tomorrow.

The snow fell soundlessly throughout the night. I woke up early, the time of day between night and day when you could still see the moon through a thin veil of clouds. The ground was covered in a smooth layer of fluffy white snow, I thought it looked like clouds had found their way to stay on earth. You could see the cold air. It was too early for winter, but this was magical.

This was January weather, I had packed for early November. One of the maids at the hotel, in looking at my shoes, lent me her boots to walk the few short blocks to Mama's cottage. I could see my breath when I stepped out to walk. The cold air was bracing, it awakened every part of me. I understood why this spot beckoned people to come and be cured. It was healing me, as well.

Mama was feeling stronger and held my hands as she confirmed all Aunt Helena had so cruelly divulged. For three days, we talked. She told me how nervous she was when she and Papa went to meet me at the orphanage. How she knew the minute she saw me that I was to be her daughter. She never met Margaret but she told me that I insisted that I had to tell Maggie I was going to Philadelphia. She meant to tell me that I was adopted but then she got sick.

Mama was still in bed the morning I came to say goodbye. She made room for me to lie down next to her and held me.

These were the same arms that had cradled and loved me my entire life, and I found comfort in her embrace. Her words did the same as she whispered in my ear, *My darling Nell, we cannot erase the sorrow that happens in our life. It is up to each of us whether we let it dictate who we are. Try to hold on to what has been good and do the best you can with the burdens that are yours to carry. Let the good be what colors your life, what gives you a sense of purpose. I love you, my daughter.*

I left her bed feeling stronger. The storm clouds had drifted away; and though they might reappear, they will not be as dark and as threatening. I would try to find my sister, the family I never knew. Not because I didn't know who I was but because I wanted to know who they were.

Six months later, Mama died in her sleep. I believe Papa couldn't wait for her any longer. Though she had not been part of my everyday life, she left a void that would never be filled. Edward agreed that we would have her Funeral Mass in Saranac Lake. It had been her home for years. I sent Aunt Helena a telegram telling her of the arrangements. It was the first time I had been in touch since Papa died. I never got a response.

It was Mama's Funeral Mass, I lifted my eyes and pulled my jacket a bit tighter around my shoulders. Edward looked over, his eyes questioning if I was alright. I nodded yes. I felt chilled, though the day was warm. It struck me that I often feel this way in the old churches, all those stones must not be able to absorb and retain the sun's warmth. I decided that priests must approve, the chill makes us stay awake and alert even during the most boring of sermons.

My mind wandered as the priest continued his Latin recitations.

———

Dear Mama,

I buried you today. We left Saranac Lake after the Mass and took the train to Philadelphia. You are buried next to Papa. He called you to him as soon as he could.

My heart is heavy.

You will always be with me. I will hear your voice when ocean breezes swirl the sand on the shore. Your hand will be holding mine as I clutch a bouquet of Lilies of the Valley to my heart. Rainbows in the sky will be a sign that you are thinking of me.

Nothing separates us. Not illness, not distance, not even death.

> *I love you, Mama.*
> *Your Nell*

I was back in New York, but I couldn't settle back into the routine of my life. Too much had happened. Edward and I were in the den, he had lit a fire and settled into his armchair with the evening newspaper. It was six months after we had buried Mama, and I was still restless. One moment I was sitting, the next standing up gazing into the flames, the next minute sitting again.

I stood up to pick up a glass of wine, my hand shaking. The glass dropped to the floor, shattering into a thousand different pieces. Tears began to spill onto my cheeks. Edward looked up startled. *I broke the glass*, I sobbed.

It is only a glass, Nell. We have plenty more, his face softened with concern.

I feel lost, Edward, lost. I took a deep breath, my hand shot to my mouth. *Who am I, Edward? I am just not sure.* My chin began to quiver uncontrollably. *This is so hard, so very, very hard. I've buried the only parents I have ever known and found that I had parents who I can't remember. I have a sister who we can't find. I have a past for which there is no record. I was born in a country that I know nothing about.*

Edward wrapped his arms around me, I stopped shaking. *It's all right, Nell. Cry out your pain, unleash the heartache.* He helped me back into my chair as I wiped my eyes with shaky fingers.

I took a ragged breath. *What am I to do?*

For the moment, you are to sit here and enjoy the warmth of the fire. I am going to get the glass swept up and then pour you another wine. Though we can't trace your Irish family, you can surely learn about Ireland. It is said that the Irish built New York City. You will have no problem satisfying your thirst for knowing more. He smiled tenderly.

Do we know anyone who is Irish? Other than Al Smith who I am sure doesn't have time to be my tutor? looking at Edward for an answer.

Well, clearly Bridget and Mrs. Campbell, though I suspect they may be uncomfortable sharing their family history with you. He paused, the rumble of the evening traffic the only noise that could be heard in the room. *What about that photographer you worked with for those articles in The Sun?*

O'Brien.

Yes, O'Brien. My guess is he could help you in your mission.

He was in Europe during the War, Some of his photographs were published in the paper. I'll check with Ann, she might know if he is back in New York. I closed my eyes for a second, I could feel my cheeks begin to flush. Perhaps I was too near the fire? Perhaps it was the relief of releasing my grief? Perhaps it was thinking about O'Brien?

CHAPTER 14

O'BRIEN

The next morning, I saw the article in *The Daily Sun*. The paper was sponsoring an exhibit of O'Brien's wartime photographs and the opening reception was the following week. I called Anne to reserve two tickets to the event. She was surprised by my request. *I didn't know you knew our famous photographer or soon-to-be-famous is more like it.*

His photos accompanied my articles on the factory women, I reminded her. *He was quite the character. And why do you think he is soon to be famous?*

His pictures are creating quite the controversy; and now that the war is over, the paper is thrilled to be showing them.

I'm still not sure what you mean. I hadn't read the reports she was referencing about O'Brien's work.

The paper will print the whole story tomorrow, or at least we hope to do so. During the war, our government was censoring all photographs coming from the war zones. Officials placed a ban on combat pictures, citing they would lower morale at home. That was true for the English and French, as well as the Americans. The newspaper protested, and we ended up only being able to print pictures taken after the battle had been fought, without showing the dead or dying. Rumor has it the photographs taken by official government photographers were staged – happy soldiers, local residents welcoming our troops into their war-torn villages that looked none the worse for wear.

Anne's voice registered her disgust, *Nothing but propaganda, a censored memory of war. Pure rubbish. Whatever happened to freedom of the press in this country?*

Before Anne began touting her First Amendment Rights, I interrupted. *This doesn't sound like the O'Brien I knew.*

No, no, that is the point exactly, Anne replied, now breathless in her explanation. *He didn't enlist as a photographer but as a member of The Fighting 69th. From what I could gather, he knew their Chaplain, Father Francis Duffy, who let him use his camera whenever he wanted. The pictures O'Brien took are extraordinary. They tell the untold story of the war, images either editors didn't want to publish or our government objected to. They show the horrors of battle, bearing witness to the tragedies of what happened on the fields in France. Perhaps when we see what this war cost in lives and not in dollars, it will be the 'War to End All Wars.' But Nell, I have been warned these photos are not for the faint of heart. That is why the exhibit is by invitation only. Are you sure you want to attend?*

Now, more than ever. O'Brien, a famous photographer? I wondered if he would even remember me.

The evening of the event, Edward was at his monthly partners' meeting, so Henry and I were going to the Trophy to hear a new jazz group. I insisted that our first stop be the O'Brien exhibit. *You must come with me, Henry. You will be the perfect companion to see O'Brien's work. You understand the power of film, whether moving pictures or still frames. You produced many war films for the government.*

That night, the lobby of *The Sun* had been transformed into part art gallery, part reception hall. The portraits of Anne's predecessors were replaced by black and white photos, simply framed in varying sizes. I expected more of a sedate, scholarly affair; but this had a festive atmosphere. Small groups of men and women were huddled together, their eyes on each other rather than the photographs. This was the 'smart crowd' and I gave myself an unseen pat on the back for having chosen my outfit wisely. I was in a forest green taffeta lined with silver ribbon that formed a deep double flounce. My ankles were exposed, highlighting my most favorite acquisition, my silver t-strap shoes. I waited while Henry left my side fighting the crowds to get two glasses of champagne. Returning with his prizes in hand and a look of triumph, he whispered, *I believe there are more people here to drink than to think. I was practically assaulted by a drunken young woman whose bobbed hair accentuated, rather than flattered, her still baby-face. I am not sure who the current gods of fashion are, but I believe they should be selling mirrors so that their lemmings can see how they really look.*

Taking his arm and my glass of champagne, I smiled. *You are incorrigible. Come, let's look at the photographs.*

We walked along the wall at an unhurried pace. I thought I had prepared myself for the exhibit; I had not. The pictures were raw, images of machine guns, barbed wire, mortars, bayonets, hand-to-hand battles, and more. I couldn't tear myself away. One was more troubling than the next. The images yelled at me. *Understand this is war. Understand that we died.*

Our progress became slower, the photographs absorbed us. Henry was the first to speak. *I wanted to join, to wear a uniform, to have crowds cheer me as I climbed aboard the train with the band playing 'Over There, Over There.'*

You never talked about that. Why didn't you go?

Flat feet and family connections. Everyone thought I could best serve the country by making newsreels. This isn't the war I edited. My war showed young men with fair hair, rosy cheeks, and duffel bags on their shoulders. Farm boys looking for adventure, waving to their sweethearts or mothers. That was the war I had wanted to fight. It did not look like this. These images yell: We are cold. We are scared. We are dying. This is war.

Henry stepped back. *I need more champagne.* He took our glasses to be refilled. I kept moving, walking past the pictures until I saw it, stark and real. A priest was giving the last rites to a young soldier. Tears were staining the priest's face as he blessed the young man who would be left in Flanders Fields. My eyes filled up. I sensed someone at my side, he didn't have Henry's smell of aftershave and good wine. I knew immediately, O'Brien.

Good to see you, Walker.

O'Brien. Moving my hands to embrace the room. *They are powerful. I knew you were good, but these defy description. These pictures should bring our government to their senses of the horrors that happen when young boys are sent to war.*

I hadn't realized tears were filling my eyes until O'Brien reached into his pocket and handed me his handkerchief. I nodded, *Once again, thank you.*

O'Brien nodded. *You understand better than most. The camera is my weapon and my mouthpiece. I want to show the best and worst faces of men. Future generations must see the mistakes we made so history doesn't repeat itself. There is nothing worse than war, both sides lose no matter who is declared the victor.*

My eyes moved to the picture I had been staring at. *Tell me about this picture, the priest and the dying soldier, I need to know more.*

Father Duffy is the finest man who ever walked this earth. He was always there for the Fighting 69th and me. We had brought this soldier back to camp, and we all knew he wasn't going to make it. Duffy was starting to give the lad the last rites when he recognized him. The soldier was a member of his parish. Duffy had baptized him and heard his first confession.

The Fighting 69th? Dare I ask what or who that is?

A bit of Irish history, Walker. My grandfather told the story of a time around 1860 when the Old Sod's recent immigrants formed an Irish Brigade to defend their interests here along with a fervent wish to return home and fight for Ireland's independence. When the Civil War arrived, the boys in the Irish Brigade were called on for the toughest of missions. They were called the "Fighting 69th" and the name stuck. Until the day he died, my grandfather would cross himself every time he heard the name.

This is exactly what I wanted to talk with you about, I interrupted.

You want to sign up to join the Fighting 69th? Not even you can make that happen, Walker.

No, no, I want to learn about what it means to be Irish. I just found out I am Irish, or at least I was born in Ireland. Can you help me?

O'Brien shook his head. *You can't learn what it is like to be Irish. You have to feel it, it is part of who you are, part of your heritage, it is in your blood.*

Please, O'Brien. It is my blood. I have 100% Irish blood.

O'Brien cocked his head. *Something we have in common. I've got to hang out here for the rest of the evening and most of the week. How about I meet you at Grand Central Station on Monday at 11:00 a.m.*

That would work, I replied.

Good. It's a walking tour, wear the right shoes. He looked down at my shiny, sparkly T-Straps and grinned. With a quick salute, he disappeared into the crowd.

Henry appeared at my side, *So you are on a last-name basis with the man of the hour. His work is extraordinary.*

In more ways than you can imagine, I replied, tucking my arm into his.

———

The calendar said it was late winter, but the day was tempting us with a hint of spring. The sun was bright and warm, the sky a translucent, flawless blue. I met O'Brien under the clock at Grand Central at the appointed time. I had taken more time than usual to select what I was wearing for the day. I settled on my newest acquisition, a sport suit – a plaid skirt with a short black jacket. Thinking about the warning I was prepared to walk, I went with my broken-in black shoes with a Cuban heel.

I got the approval I needed by the look in O'Brien's eyes. *Good Morning, Walker. Let's get started.* And we did.

We started our climb up 41st Street. O'Brien began the tale of his family's history. *My grandfather came over when he was 12 years old. He was the second oldest in his family and the only one, according to him, who had both the wit and the drive to make it in the new world. The year was 1847 and Ireland was starving. You can read about the failure of the potato crop in any history book, Walker, but Grandad had no use for the English. This was no famine, my lad, he would say, it was starvation. He called it the Great Hunger. Disease was everywhere, dead bodies were buried on the side of the road. Men who had pride, who worked the same land as generations before them, were put into work-houses. When they died, they were buried in mass graves.*

Grandad was put on one of the famine ships with a bag of food for the three-week journey, a change of clothes, a five-dollar bill, and the name of a man he was to meet, James Corcoran, who was called Paddy. O'Brien chuckled, a sound I had never heard from him. *Actually, he was supposed to meet a man named James Cullen, who was his mother's second cousin, but the handwriting was so bad that Grandad couldn't make out the name. He used to say, 'best mistake I ever made.'*

O'Brien led me east into a part of the city I had never seen. The area was dark and dreary; tenements and breweries bordered the streets, and the dreadful smell of slaughterhouses coming from the banks of the East River made it hard to breathe.

Where are we?

O'Brien's voice became merry. *Well, it depends on who you ask. This is called Dutch Hill. In Grandad's day, it was known as Corcoran's Roost.* He paused. *I'm not quite sure how he found his way here from that frightful ship; but knowing him, he charmed or connived someone to take him. He had a way about him that captivated all who met him.*

I muttered under my breath, *Must run in the family.*

Grandad found his way to Corcoran's home. He said when he first saw the spot, he thought he was in the army, an army of Irishmen who could shoot better than any militia. Hooligans roamed freely, and my grandfather knew he found the right place.

If you recall our conversation about the Fighting 69th, he said, taking my arm to navigate the muddy ruts in the road, *many of those lads joined that brigade and their sons after them, and their sons* *after them.* His touch sent blood rushing to my face. I lost my footing, and he caught me in his arms. I couldn't catch my breath.

Are you okay, Walker? A look of concern flashed across his face.

I'm fine, thanks. Removing my arm and trying to regain my composure. *Remind me to tell Mayor Hyman there is a need for sidewalks around here.*

O'Brien piloted me to the turn, as we began walking along the river. *One of the many things that I believe our good mayor should add to his agenda.*

And he continued his tale. *So, Grandad finds his way to Corcoran's home, which was not much more than a shack, knocks on the door, and Kitty Corcoran appears. Now comes the real Irish part, Walker, so pay attention.*

I am hanging on your every word, sir.

Now Kitty and James Corcoran, whom everyone called Paddy, were married for years. She gave him ten children but was rumored to be sickly and stay in bed for weeks at a time.

My words came out quickly, *With ten children, she was probably looking to get some rest.*

Whatever, O'Brien rolled those lovely violet eyes.

On the day before my grandfather arrived at her doorstep, as the sun was rising, Kitty heard someone calling her name. She opened the door to find a woman in a red cape. Believing she was in the presence of one of the fairies, Kitty offered her a cup of tea and a slice of bread. In payment for her kindness, the old lady told her the reason for her illness was that her children threw out what she called the 'dirty water' at the same place and at the same time every day. 'Find another place and another time, and the sickness will leave you' were her last words.

Before Kitty could thank the woman, she was gone, never to be seen again.

Was she really a fairy?

O'Brien smiled, *The first indication that you are feeling what it is like to be Irish – believing in the little people is key.* He took my arm as we began the rocky descent down the road on our way back. The ease of his touch sent shock waves through my body. I had to concentrate on what he was saying, my pounding heart dimming the sound of his voice. *Well, no one knows for sure; but the next morning, at the same time as Kitty had answered the knock of the sprite, my grandfather knocks on her door wearing a bright red sweater, a bit tattered and torn, but still holding its color.*

Well, Kitty Corcoran takes one look at him and thinks that the fairy has returned to her in the human form of a little lad. That was it. Kitty returned to good health, and my grandfather became part of the Corcoran clan from that day forward. Oh, and just so you don't believe all tales end happily-ever-after, his job was to throw out their 'dirty water' twice a day, finding a new spot each time to dispose of his task.

O'Brien stopped talking and looked around as if to get his bearings. *What if we stop for a cup of tea. There's a shop a bit of a walk from here and I can continue my tale from there. While we walk, tell me your story. How did you discover you are Irish?*

And so I did, beginning with hearing the startling news from Aunt Helena to Edward's findings that no records of my adoption or my sister could be found. We walked for over an hour. His reporter's instinct to ask questions to clarify was the only interruption. I just talked. When I finished, I sighed. *This is why I need to understand about Ireland. What it means to be Irish.*

I am sorry, Walker. To know you have a family that can't be found is a loss I can't imagine. Your story is not uncommon. Families broken up by death, poverty, or injustices too brutal to discuss were the heartbreak of too many of our countrymen who came to these shores searching for a better life. The Irish understand sadness. My Ma would say that the only way you can know joy is to experience sorrow.

We had stopped in front of a small shop, and O'Brien opened the door. *Is that what it feels like to be Irish? To be sad and happy at the same time.*

A small smile found its way across O'Brien's face. *I think my tutorial is working. You're a good student, Walker.*

We found an empty table, its checkered cloth stained with

memories of those who had sat in the chairs before us. A pot of steaming tea and two mugs were brought to the table. As the tea finished brewing, O'Brien and I both reached for the pitcher of milk.

Ladies, first.

Thank you, kind sir. Now that you have heard mine, please continue your tale.

O'Brien took a sip of his tea and sat back in his chair, *Would you mind if I had a pipe? A cup of tea and a pipe are perfect accompaniments to an Irishman's story.*

Oh, please. My father smoked a pipe. He performed quite a ritual in preparing it to be lit. I think he enjoyed getting the pipe ready as much as he did the smoking.

I understand. I've never gotten into the cigarette habit, though I was tempted during the war. There was neither time nor tobacco to fill the bowl. He took the pouch out of his pocket, filled the pipe, and slowly lit the tobacco. Wisps of smoke, rich and pungent, touched with both sweetness and spice, filled the air. He smiled, the smile of a man content in his world. I was content just looking at him.

He took another draw of his pipe. *So, back to my grandad and Paddy Corcoran. The years progressed, and Paddy Corcoran started a construction company. Things haven't changed much since then, his Tammany Hall connections were great business referrals. My grandfather, a strapping 17-year old who could read and write, was supervising the construction of new homes that were moving out of the city and into the countryside in an area called The Bronx.*

I've heard of it, pouring myself another cup of tea. O'Brien shook his head no as I lifted the pot in his direction. *I walked across the High Bridge with my friend Victoria.*

Adventuring into unknown territories again. You never cease to amaze me, Walker. He took another draw on his pipe.

You were telling me about your family. I tried to sound harsh but could feel my lips twitching into a smile.

Ah, yes. By that time, Mrs. C, the name Grandad called her all his life, had found him a wife. Peggy Malone, the third daughter of one of her friends, came without a penny to her name; but my grandfather didn't care. She had long dark hair and violet eyes, and he was smitten from the first moment he saw her. On Sundays, they would take the train to Van Cortlandt Park where he convinced her to make the dramatic move to the countryside. It is the house where my family still lives. My father was born there, just squeaking into the over nine-month permissible time frame. He was followed by five more.

Today, if you walk within four blocks of that house in any direction, the name O'Brien will be on every other mailbox. Those who have a different name are the married daughters of one O'Brien or another.

He put the pipe down. *Ready to continue our journey?*

Give me a few minutes to freshen up and I will be ready. There is more to your story?

I should be ending the tale in the time it takes us to reach the pub and continue your education.

I returned to the table ready to continue, and we were out the door. The broken-in shoes were a good call; the dirt streets we were walking along were ruddy and beyond repair. O'Brien walked with the stride of a man who knew where he was headed. Thanks to the time spent on my bicycle, I was able to keep up.

So, closing the family history, O'Brien replied. *My Da followed Grandad in the construction business. He spotted my mother on a day he had to deliver lumber to one of the houses being built. He was carrying a load on his shoulders when he saw her coming out of the local bakery with a fresh loaf of bread. He couldn't put down the lumber and speak to her as the bundle was too big and he was covered in sawdust. He just followed her to where she was going, more than a mile out of his way. Every day for the next two weeks, he went by the house with the hope of seeing her, but it never happened.*

Frustrated, he went into the neighborhood pub and asked where the local Catholic church was. He was told St. Barnabas and confirmed it was the Irish parish. He found the church and wrote down the times for Sunday Mass.

The next Sunday, he went to every Mass hoping to catch a glimpse of the 'bakery girl' as he was now calling her. He said God must have answered his prayers, because at the 11:00 a.m. Mass she appeared, looking as lovely as he remembered. He caught her eye as he was leaving the church and tipped his hat, but she made no sign that she had seen the gesture.

He was there the following Sunday and the Sunday after; and each time, he would take off his hat when he saw her. Finally, on the fourth Sunday, she stopped, 'you are not from here so why are you praying at our church?'

'Because I wanted to meet you', was my Da's reply, introducing himself as James O'Brien.

O'Brien's eyes twinkled.

My ma was as much of a spitfire as one could imagine. She said her name was Nora Garrity and since he done what he planned to do, he could be gone. So my da responds, 'I plan to marry you.' Ma would have none of it. Told him that she wasn't going to marry anyone. She planned to be a lady's maid in one of the fine houses on Madison Avenue.

Well, that was the first and only time she ever underestimated James Patrick O'Brien. They were married one year from the date she told him her name was Nora. My brother Matthew was born less than a year later, followed in quick succession by Mark, Luke, and John. All four carry the middle name Patrick, so as never to forget the saint who we are to pray to. Ma, however, was not one to give up until she had a daughter. Four years after John was born came my twin sisters Mary Katherine and Mary Ellen, born on the same day but as different as the sun and the moon, although pulled together by a source of gravity that is frightening to behold and get in the way of.

He laughed, laughter so contagious I joined it. *And where do you come in, now the family should be complete?*

I was not planned and quite a surprise. Ma called me a 'miracle' and Da said I was the reason he would have to work until he was 60. Ma was pretty well done with parenting by the time I was weaned. She started to devote most of her time to the church and left my daily upkeep to my grandad, whose house we lived in, and the twins. My sisters were thrilled to have someone to boss around. By the time they were 10, they had both decided to become teachers and I was their first pupil. Mary Katherine had me reading and writing before I was 5 and Mary Ellen, who is a fairly well-known artist in her own right, taught me to paint, to see color and shapes in different ways. They both take credit for my being a reporter and seeing the camera as my third eye.

I nodded, seeing the value in each of their arguments. *I think they are right.*

Me, too. My ma died when I was 10, she felt sick one day and was gone within three months. My father was never the same. On one of her last days, she made Da promise to send me to Fordham. He worked himself to death to pay for it, but you are looking at the first of the O'Brien's to have a college degree. My father died shortly after my graduation, a proud man. He had kept his promise to his Nora.

And your grandfather?

O'Brien smiled. *Lived to be over 80, said it wasn't right to have to bury a son. Think it broke his heart when my dad died. All my brothers and sisters are married. Mary Katherine and her brood live in the same house we grew up in. Me, too. It will always be my home. Everyone lives within shouting distance from each other, although Matthew is making noises about moving to Westchester. All told last Christmas, we numbered 60. Quite a legacy for the boy who came over with nothing but a $5.00 bill to call his own.*

We were standing in front of a pub in a section of the city called Hell's Kitchen, as rough and tumble a neighborhood as one could find. O'Brien grew quiet. *I've never thought about what it would be like not to have a family. They are my touchstone.* And he swung the door open.

I didn't respond. I was lost in my own thoughts. I was not unhappy with my life with Edward. He had been right, we were good together. Yet what O'Brien was describing sounded quite wonderful, and I felt a longing I never had before. A yearning to belong to a family. O'Brien's voice jarred me from my thoughts. *You need one more lesson today. Have you ever tasted Guinness?*

I shook my head, no. *Never heard of it.*

Well, you are about to savor what being Irish tastes like. A pint of

Guinness and a bit of Irish stew will fortify you as you learn about Irish politics. If you want to know what it feels like to be Irish, you also must know why we hate the Crown. Those who frequent this establishment have strong views on the right to Irish independence. Most are employed as part of New York's finest, the others are members of its fire department. The Irish have found their niche in this great city of ours.

The pub was misty with body heat and smoke from an open fireplace, and it was noisy. The clamor of voices hushed a little, the locals were craning their necks to see who O'Brien had brought in. By the looks that passed our way, O'Brien was a regular and I was a source of curiosity.

We sat down at a high-top table and O'Brien went to the bar, returning with two glasses of a dark, creamy brew followed by a server who placed a hearty, steamy stew before me. My stomach growled its acceptance and my longing. O'Brien's eyes gave away his amusement, *You are indeed Irish, nothing quite like a good stew except this,* pointing to the two glasses he had just brought over. *So, my lovely Irish lass, taking your first sip of a pint of Guinness should be a mindful experience. Like a fine wine, Guinness must be appreciated.* O'Brien began the first-class imitation of a French sommelier, *Madame, if I may,* and he raised his glass. *Observe how the colors change as the pint settles, the bubbles mysteriously rising instead of sinking. Feel the coolness and the heft of the glass in your hand,* and I raised my glass, meeting his, *the condensation collecting on the outside. Prepare to feel the creamy top touch your lips.*

Sláinte, and he clicked my glass.

The cream head looked appealing as I brought the glass to my lips. The liquid that went down was strong and bitter, burning my throat.

I choked, *This is strong.*

O'Brien smiled, *Tis grand. Like the family's kitten, you have left a trace of cream on your lips.* He took out his handkerchief and gently wiped the top of my lip. He handed me the now-used handkerchief, *I'll have to start buying these by the dozen if I spend more time with you.* Our eyes met, my heart skipped, we both looked away.

O'Brien started talking about the struggle for Irish independence beginning with the Easter Uprising in 1916. *There is trouble in the land and the politics are heating up. The Sinn Fein won a landslide victory in the last election and declared Irish independence. There is a guerrilla war being fought all over the land, and it won't end until we have our country back. The boys you see here are big supporters of the fight for a free Ireland, so it's best that we not engage in any political talk within their hearing distance.*

The bar was filling up, big, burly men jostling for an open spot. Two came over to the table, carrying two glasses of Guinness they put in front of us. O'Brien introduced them as Brian and Sean. Brian took my hand, *A lovely lass, indeed. Your eyes are the same color as the lakes of home. One would not be missing her green hills and misty mornings if you were by his side.*

O'Brien was about to respond when the other man put his hand on O'Brien's shoulder. *Haven't seen you since I heard the news. Sorry about Jimmy.*

Thanks, Sean. It's been hard on Mary Ellen and all of us. There's a memorial Mass for him this Sunday. The ten o'clock High Mass.

Sean poked Brian who was still holding my hand. *We'll be there with the family.* The two doffed their caps to me and left. I looked at O'Brien, my eyes questioning.

My nephew never came home from France.

Is he the boy in the picture, the one with Father Duffy?

No, but it might as well have been. The boy in the picture was Jimmy's buddy. They went to grammar school and high school together. Jimmy was caught in an ambush and never made it back to camp. He is buried over there somewhere, we don't know where. Mary Ellen is having a tough time. Before he could say much else, three musicians appeared from nowhere and started to play, one the fiddle, one a guitar, and the third an instrument I had never seen before and asked its origin.

It's bodhrán, better known as the 'poor man's tambourine,' O'Brien explained, trying hard to be heard over the voices who were now putting words to the music the trio was playing. Minutes later the name 'O'Brien' was being shouted. It started with the boys at the bar; but soon the rest of the crowd followed, shouting his name while banging their fists on the table.

What's going on? I asked, the clamor continuing to rise.

They want me to sing.

You sing?

A man of many talents and the soloist in Our Lady of the Angels' choir. I might as well give them what they want or it will just get louder.

Okay, everybody, and thank you, lads, grinning to the bar crowd, he stood up and took his place with the musicians. *We've had a touch of sadness darken our doors, as you know. So here's to our Jimmy and all the lads who never came home.*

O'Brien closed his eyes and started to sing:

Oh, Danny boy, the pipes, the pipes are calling
From glen to glen, and down the mountainside...

The crowd was quiet. I was sobbing by the time he had sung the last line, *Oh Danny boy, I love you so.* His handkerchief was again being put to good use. The bar erupted with clapping and shouts of never again.

O'Brien worked his way back to the table, grabbing hands that were extended, taking pats on the back, and affectionate clips to the head. *Time to go, Walker. I can say you now know what it feels like to be Irish. It is about being able to laugh and cry, happiness and sorrow. All at the same time.*

We walked out the door, I stopped in front of him. *Thank you, I couldn't have asked for a better day.*

O'Brien took my hand and caressed the skin with his thumbs. I could feel the blood rushing to my temples, my heart pounding, a warm feeling creeping softly throughout my body. He was looking into my eyes, smiling, he softly placed his hand on my cheek. He leaned over, I could feel his breath on my face. I wanted him to take me in his arms, to surrender myself to him.

I was beginning to lose reason when a cab pulled up. I longed to pull O'Brien into the car with me. Given the special arrangement of my marriage, I justified I wouldn't be betraying Edward. In the split second I was weighing my decision, one word rang in my ears: *Poppycock!* I pulled myself back. No matter the arrangement, I had made a vow to stay with Edward as his wife. I couldn't cross the line, afraid if I did the house of cards would fall around me.

O'Brien was still stroking my cheek, pulling me closer to him. *You are...*

Before he could finish, I took his hand away and said *Married.*

O'Brien looked like I had thrown a pail of ice water on him. He paused for a split second and quietly repeated, *Married.* I rushed into the cab, not looking back.

———

Dear Mama

I hear some who speak with the slightest lilt of an Irish brogue, and I look hoping to find him near me. I see pictures in the paper and search to see if he is named the photographer. When his hand touched mine, my stomach turned to jelly. I close my eyes and I see his face. His name is O'Brien. He saved my life one night.

I couldn't sleep last night, wondering what it would be like to be with him. To be with him as a man and a woman. What would have happened if I hadn't pulled his hand away?

Despite the longings, I couldn't do it, Mama. I couldn't betray Edward. I know that sounds odd since Edward and Henry are lovers; but in my heart, that seems different. I can't explain it. I just believe it is different. I took a vow to be Edward's wife, one I intend to keep.

I spoke to Anne today. She told me that O'Brien was taking his camera and leaving for Ireland. He talked about the troubles in the land and his concern that there would be more turmoil than peace in the days ahead. I felt a sharp pang of loss. It is best that he is miles away. My resolve is much easier to maintain when temptation is not in sight.

My feelings are as jumbled as this letter.

I love you, Mama.
Your Nell

I took the wooden chest from its place on my closet shelf, unlocked it, and placed this letter on top of all the others I had written to Mama. Letters that were mine alone to read.

CHAPTER 15

1919

Victoria, Anne, and I were celebrating the upcoming passage of the 19th Amendment. Women, at last, were going to be given the right to vote in every state. Anne had been active in the Suffragette movement, first in New York and then on a national level. I wrote articles garnering the increasing support for the movement, but it was Anne who was the driver. She was clear that next on the agenda was the passage of the Equal Rights Amendment. Rachel shared Anne's commitment to the ERA. Rachel was expected to join us for lunch, though we were never quite certain if she would show. Her involvement with the International Workers of the World competed for our time and most of her attention.

It had been a long and cold winter. That particular day, the sun broke through the clouds, the earth welcoming its warmth, the breeze moving the air gently from cold to warm. You could sense the promise of daffodils and forsythia. Anne proposed that I open the gate to Gramercy Park so that we could inspect the recently-dedicated statue of Edwin Booth that stood in its center.

Victoria agreed but only if we minimized the amount of walking as she was wearing her new spat two-tone boots, back with ivory, and side buttons that topped at her calf. *This new look is quite fashionable, but my feet are killing me. Why can't they design women's shoes that both look good and feel good?*

Victoria was continuing to bemoan the sadistic practices of cobblers when Rachel appeared. She was soaked from head to foot, her hair looking as if she had just gotten out of the bath.

Anne was the first to comment, *Goodness Rachel, what have you done? Slipped into the reservoir on your way to meet us?*

Oh, I have so much to tell. Rachel was out of breath, beads of water falling from her red hat producing puddles that now lay on her coat's collar. She looked up at the statute, head shaking, gently showering us with any leftover drops of water. *I can't believe that they erected a statue to the brother of the man who killed Lincoln. I don't care if he knew every line that Shakespeare ever wrote.*

I shook my head. *You know that it is in recognition of his founding of the Player's Club. Henry says it houses the largest private collection of American and British theatre history in the world, and it is all quite remarkable. Edwin did write a letter to the public apologizing for the actions of his brother and wouldn't let his name be uttered in his home.*

Before she could respond, I put Rachel's arm through mine. *Let us not debate. Come into the house to dry off and tell us why you are so wet.*

We went into the house through the kitchen so Rachel could hang her coat and hat to dry. She hugged Mrs. Campbell as she entered. *I hope my clothes retain these aromas. Your kitchen always smells of sugar and cinnamon.*

Back in the library, taking a freshly laundered towel to tousle her hair, Rachel continued her story. *Well, Palmer is at it again. This country's illustrious attorney general has a new henchman, another Justice Department lackey named J. Edgar Hoover who is leading witch-hunts against those who stand up against the wrongs this country imposes on the uneducated and unrepresented. This city is corrupted at every corner, yet the police are coming after those of us who carry banners, not weapons. It makes me so mad.*

Today, over 100,000 of us marched to City Hall to air our grievances about police harassment.

I looked over at her. *You should have let me know, I would have joined you.*

Rachel put the towel aside. *I meant to call you, but it was organized so quickly that we were on our feet before I could pick up the phone.*

I gave her a quick smile. *Forgiven, but tell us why you are so wet!*

Where was I? Oh, yes, yes. Our esteemed mayor must have been scared as there was a sea of blue in front of us as we left Union Hall. Police rode their horses among us, threatening, intimidating. Rachel threw her head back, like a mare preening for the race. *We were not to be thwarted. We began to cheer, a rustling of voices raised in a united cause. Then we took out our weapons.*

Victoria gasped, *You were carrying a gun?*

No, silly. We had long hat pins in our hats. We pulled them out and put them to good use, sticking the men in blue, who were shocked and turned away. We were jubilant.

The four of us clapped our hands. Anne raised the question that needed to be answered. *But how did you get so wet?*

Rachel continued her story. *Ah, it seems that our local officials sought the help of the fire department to quell our so-called uprising. As we were continuing the march, the firemen opened up their hydrants and their hoses. We were attacked by water, literally fired upon by water.*

I put the wet towel next to the fire. *Well, I am glad you came here to dry out. The champagne is opened to congratulate Anne and her fellow Suffragettes for getting women to the ballot box. I have something I want to talk about and get your advice on. Shall we have lunch?*

I am starved, Victoria added. *I can't wait to see what delights Mrs. Campbell has prepared.*

Rachel left after we toasted Anne for her efforts and before we had finished our lunch. She stood up to say goodbye. *Too much is going on, and I don't want to miss a minute of it.*

But your clothes are still damp, Anne admonished, using her best mother-of-four voice.

My badge of courage. I want to be sure I am recognized for having been there. *Thank Mrs. Campbell, my coat smells heavenly. Anne, there are no words that can express the gratitude that the women of this country owe you. I am proud to call you my friend.* And she was off.

The conversation turned to me. *So what is on your mind, my friend? You have been preoccupied for weeks,* Victoria asked, though her focus was on the dessert plate Mrs. Campbell had just brought in.

I have been reading in the paper about the troubles in Ireland. It sounds like our Civil War, brothers against brothers. I understand the issues that I've read, but I don't understand the emotion. That is what I am missing. Even after I heard the shocking news that I was born in Ireland, it didn't really occur to me that I was Irish. O'Brien said you can't learn to be Irish, you must feel it. And I did feel it the day I spent with him – the poverty and anguish of the immigrants not wanted and scorned, the love for a land that was left behind, and the joy of tradition. I do want to know more, to learn more. I feel like an empty bottle that needs to be refilled.

Victoria's voice got serious. *I understand. Despite my mother's best efforts, I still feel a pull to the life we had before all that gold came our way. It defined who I am. It is where I came from.* And then she paused, *I have an idea. I have a friend, well not really a friend, more like an acquaintance from school. Her name is Maude, and we were at the Sacred Heart Academy together. She stopped taking classes a year or so ago and we fell out of touch.*

Why is her name popping up, Anne asked as Victoria stopped speaking and reached for her second cake.

I can't resist this strawberry tart. So, Maude is Irish, Victoria continued, the crumbs from the tart fringing her now-satisfied lips. *She knows all about Ireland. Its history, its legends. Seems her grandparents came over about 60 years ago, before the famine and all of that.*

The Irish call it the Great Hunger, I interrupted, though Victoria never paused.

Maude told me her grandfather was a teacher, and on the boat coming over from Ireland, he wrote down all the stories and legends his fellow passengers shared. Maude has the book and treasures it. I could ask her to join us for lunch and share the stories with us.

Anne was the first to agree. *That would be great, and I would love to hear what she has to say. I have often thought of going to Ireland and would love to hear its history. It would be like having our own study group without the pressure of exams.*

I agreed. *That would be perfect, particularly if the two of you would join me. Victoria, do you know where she is now? Can you find her?*

Victoria nodded. *I am pretty sure the school will have a record, even though now it is called Manhattanville College. I heard she has fallen on some pretty hard times. Her mother died on the Titanic which is why her father had her boarding at Sacred Heart. Then about two years ago, her father suddenly died, not sure what happened. I heard she was living with one of his brothers. Maude was the smartest of all of us, and it is a shame she didn't continue with school.*

And then Victoria's eyes squinted. *Nell, you look like her. I think it is your eyes. You both have the same eyes and the same coloring. Must be an Irish thing. I will get right on this; and at our next gathering, I will introduce you to Maude Herlihy.*

Three weeks later, Victoria introduced Maude, who was now working as a dressmaker for a family not far from my house. Seeing her for the first time, I was stunned. As Victoria forewarned, we looked alike. Maude had my eyes, though her hair was as red as the morning dawn while mine was dark ginger. She had an ease about herself, a sense of knowing who she was. Yet her eyes reflected a story of sadness and heartache, a life that had taken a difficult turn.

We were in the parlor, a room that was designed to encourage conversation. Tall windows looked out over the park and were framed by blue and yellow curtains that broke onto the rug, complementing the patterned blue silk wallpaper, that was the height of fashion.

We sat down around the fireplace, Maude on one of the

sofas, me on the other, Victoria and Anne found the two armchairs.

Maude, I am so happy you agreed to come. I want to know more about the land of my birth. Somehow, I feel it is the missing piece of my puzzle. I nodded towards Anne. *Anne is one of my dearest friends and the mother of four absolutely splendid children. She was very much involved in organizing the newspaper's support for the right of women to vote. I couldn't be prouder of her.*

Anne smiled. *Independence is often a hard-fought fight. I am interested in hearing your perspective on what is happening in Ireland. O'Brien, one of The Sun's photographers whose family is Irish has just landed on your shores to start to record the country's road to self-rule.*

My heart stopped at the mention of O'Brien's name. No one seemed to notice.

Maude shook her head sadly. *I can tell you, the seeds of discontent have long been nourished and flourish throughout the land. While I am not embroiled in politics even though it has spread to these shores, the animosity towards the British runs deep and strong.*

Victoria needed no introduction. *Oh, Maude, it is just so good to see you again. You were sorely missed when you left Sacred Heart.*

Maude's voice got quiet. *Those were magical days. I think about them a lot.* Then her voice got stronger, *I was very excited when Victoria asked if I could join you. I love talking about Ireland and sharing the stories and legends my grandfather wrote down. It is as if I can hear their voices.*

She pulled a tattered notebook from her bag. *This has been in our family for three generations. My grandparents left Ireland before the Great Hunger and landed in Quebec where my mother was born. When the famine ships started to arrive on the St. Lawrence, my grandmother railed at the Canadian government for their failure to help those ravaged souls. With little money and no connections, she packed up the family and came to New York. Before they left, they adopted my Uncle Mike. I never got a chance to meet him as he was killed in the Draft Wars in 1863. A time this city and this country should be ashamed of but is seldom spoken about in all of our history books.* She shook her head in disgust.

Maude looked at me. *I know you want to understand what it is like to be Irish, Nell.* A smile lit up her face, *the first thing to remember is that we Irish have a long tradition of never forgetting or forgiving.*

I smiled back. *I now know where I get that from, it is in my blood.*

Maude continued. *Once my grandparents landed in New York, the first years were hard. My mother remembered living in a makeshift tent that had been pitched on the ground and playing with barefoot children whose accents were as thick as the fog that rolled in from the river. The tide of immigrants was flooding these shores. My grandfather was trying to find work, but an Irish teacher was not in high demand. He started to help his fellow countrymen fill out the necessary papers to find work. His efforts paid off in unexpected ways. He came to the attention of one Mr. Boss Tweed who hired him to continue the work on behalf of Tammany Hall. My grandmother pronounced that Tammany Hall was a moral swamp, but it paid the bills and got them a place of their own. My gran was a woman ahead of her time. She and I share the same red hair. It is a warning label you are not to mess with an Irish woman.*

Another lesson, Nell. Though your hair is not quite as fiery, I would guess that the embers beneath burn bright.

Anne and Victoria clapped their approval.

Maude's eyes gave a far-off gaze, *I still have family in Ireland, though I only know them through their letters. My mother was coming back from one of her visits when she boarded the Titanic,* her voice broke as she continued. *My grandmother was good with the needle and had a successful dressmaking business in Quebec.* She gave a quick smile. *My mother and I inherited the same skills. Give me a bolt of cloth and some thread, and I produce magic. I am employed by one of your neighbors, Mrs. Morgan, to be the dressmaker for her and her daughters.*

Maude sighed. *But you are probably bored with my telling about my family and not about the land I still think of as home.*

I stood up, motioning the others to do the same. *No, not at all. This helps me understand. I was recently told you can't learn about being Irish, you must feel it. But first, let's go into the dining room for lunch.*

Sound advice, Maude's face lit up. *I am going to have a bite of a sandwich and then start with the first of the readings, a tragic tale of Conall, nephew of the High King of Tara, and his fierce love for the beautiful Deirdre.*

For the next three months, Maude would join us for lunch as often as she could, her grandfather's notebook clutched in her hands. Stories of Viking invasions, Norse gods, and the Norman conquest fueled our conversations and imagination. Maude interspersed the lectures with articles from the local Irish press reporting on the politics that was ripping the country apart.

During those conversations, we developed a connection hard to describe. More than the darkness of the confessional where we ask God to forgive our transgressions and a mysterious voice fetters out our penance, we talked about our hopes and dreams, our fears, and our failures. We developed a trust, a bond of sisterhood born not of blood but of sharing and confiding.

Still, I could not share all that was hidden in my heart. The secrets of my marriage were mine and Edward's alone; a covenant I would not break. I could cleanse my soul of the loss of my mother to a disease that took her from me before I was old enough to have that tether broken. I talked about the uncertainty of not knowing where I came from. I shared my fear of being abandoned by those who love me.

Even Edward commented one day over breakfast. *You have a new spirit about you, Nell. There is a lightness about you I haven't seen before.*

I paused for a moment and put down my teacup. *It is nothing new but rather capturing the old that is doing this. I am more content, more at peace. Knowing more about the land where I was born has grounded me. It has given me roots. Our luncheons with Maude and all her tales of the hardships and the hopes of a land that has a history of magic, mysticism, and mirth are the missing link to who I am.* I smiled. *I may never know the particulars of my birth or my family; they have been lost to me. What I do know is my parents, like so many before them, came to find a new life. A life that would never have been afforded them had they stayed in Ireland. I wonder now what my life would have been like had my mother lived and my father not given Margaret and me up for adoption. I could have been working at the Triangle Shirtwaist Factory that fateful afternoon or living amidst the lint of the mills in upstate New York with no hope for my future. I have enjoyed the finer things in life because of what others had to give up: their life, their children, their dreams, and ambitions. I need to be grateful rather than angry.*

Edward put down his coffee cup. *You are a wise woman, Nell. Always have been and even more so now.*

Well, I am not sure about that. But I do so like being Irish. It gives me an excuse to tap my feet when I hear a fiddle play and have a good cry when a ballad is sung.

Well, I am happy for you. Edward laid his hand over mine. *As one who can go trace where he came from for generations, I have never thought about what it would be like to not know.* He looked thoughtful as he added, *to not know who I am.*

The day was dark, the skies heavy with clouds, the air cold and damp. Maude came for lunch. Her mood in direct contrast to the weather, she had a spring in her step and a smile that wouldn't leave her lips. Victoria was the first to remark, *You look like the cat that just finished dining on the canary.* For the first time ever, Maude's face turned only a slight shade lighter than the color of her hair. *I think I am in love. He is wonderful and it can never be.*

Oh, I envy you being in love were the first words out of Victoria's mouth. *All I ever meet are men – boys really – whose fortunes have evaporated and want my father's gold to replenish their bank accounts more than they want me. I am determined that I will never marry…*

Before she could go on, Anne put her finger to her lips. *Hush, Victoria, we need to hear what Maude is hiding.*

Maude was in her own world. *A week ago Sunday, I went down to the market and then I saw him. He was walking among the vendors, and you couldn't help but notice him. He has hair as dark as midnight and stands taller than most men. I was looking for Mr. Seiderman, my favorite pickle vendor, when I stumbled and fell right into him. Saints preserve me, I swear I didn't do it intentionally. I think maybe my guardian angel gave me a bit of a shove.* Maude's eyes twinkled.

After he said three words, I knew he was from Ireland. Without so much as a polite introduction, I blurted out, "where in home are you from?"

He smiled a smile that would melt the coldest of hearts and said, "From Ulster, just a bit north of Belfast. And I knew you had to be Irish, though your dress and ways shout America. I am Billy Conlon, and you must be one of the fairies of the old land come to make my eyes long for the blue-green lakes of home. Please tell me you are real and not a dream I wish never to wake up from."

He took my arm and it felt like we belonged together. We walked around the open carts the rest of the afternoon. I can't remember much of what we said, we just talked. I might have been a star in a picture show, falling in love with a handsome stranger. It has been years since I felt that happy.

The three of us were hanging on her every word.

We agreed to meet the following Sunday, and there he was standing at the bottom of the church steps. She looked over at me, focusing on the cross hanging around my neck. *He's not Catholic,* Maude looked back up as she continued. *His hair was all slicked back, and I thought I never had seen such a handsome man. I couldn't believe he was waiting for me. He held a picnic basket in his hand, and off we went down by the river. The day was cool, but the sun was bright, and we walked as one. Billy laid a blanket down on the bank and held my hand. He is easy to talk to, the easiest man I have ever been with. He talked about how much he missed home, his love for Ireland, the troubles the country was facing. I love him, I do. I love that he loves Ireland, and that makes me love him even more.*

I am seeing him again this Sunday and that is only four days away, and she got a dreamy look.

We were all rooting for her and this romance.

Over the next few months, we heard pieces of how the courtship was progressing. Then, as the weeks wore on, Maude seemed to withdraw and become less sure of herself. Victoria, who initially was green with envy with Maude now having found love, was the first to notice. We had just started lunch when she looked straight at Maude and asked the question that was on all our minds, *Are you alright? You just haven't seemed like yourself lately.*

Tears fell from Maude's eyes. *Billy and I are as doomed as Romeo and Juliet. Our families are enemies. Billy is a Unionist and sees the Independent Republic Army as the enemy. He says I am the only Catholic he has ever cared about. He says he loves me and wants me to come back to Ireland with him. He is leaving to go back soon and wants me to follow him over once he has found a place for us.*

Maude sobbed, *I don't know what to do. My family will never accept him. Never. And I think the same will be true about his family welcoming me. There is too much bitterness on both sides. The English stole our land, our language, our dignity. The Unionists support the Crown; they see themselves as defenders of their land and their birthright.*

I love him, but can I live with him? What am I to do? She couldn't catch her breath.

Victoria put her arm around Maude's shaking shoulders, I went to fetch a bottle of sherry, and Anne waited until all was quiet and then spoke. *You must listen to your heart, Maude. Too often the past and the future conspire against us finding happiness. You must find your happiness in the present.*

I poured each of us a glass of the golden nectar, adding a bit more to the one I set in front of Maude.

I looked over at Maude. *Shakespeare's play is the story of children. You and Billy are adults who can make up your own minds and find your own way. Let us raise our glasses and propose for peace to come to Ireland and may all lovers, past and present, be united forever. May Maude and her Billy live happily ever after.*

Two weeks later the Maude of old returned to our luncheon table. Before we could get started, she blurted out: *Billy leaves for Ireland next week. I have agreed to join him before the end of the summer. That will give him the next few months to finish whatever work he has left to do and find us a place of our own. We agreed we would stay in Ulster but far away from Belfast and the politics he has been involved with.* She gave a brief smile, *and we are married.*

The three of us shouted, *Why were we not invited?* Victoria pouted, *I should have been your maid of honor.*

Maude giggled. *There was not much planning. I took a day off from work last Thursday giving the excuse that I was to see a cousin who was visiting from Ireland. That was the day we went and got the license. On Monday, we met with the town clerk first thing, signed all the right papers, said all the right things. I know I am not married in the eyes of the Catholic Church; but as far as New York State is concerned, I am Mrs. William Conlon.* She slipped a simple gold band on her finger, her face the happiest I had ever seen.

We descended upon her, hugging her and hugging each other. Bottles of champagne were brought out and poured. Well into our third bottle of bubbly, Victoria looked around the room, *I see your Victrola, but where are the phonographs? We need music, and I am taking off these boots. I can no longer feel my feet.* I pointed to the cabinet, and Victoria pulled out the Scott Joplin recordings that Henry had given me for my birthday. *These will do quite nicely. It is time that all you married ladies learn the latest steps. It is time to shimmy, follow me.*

Edward came home to find music blaring from the parlor and four slightly intoxicated women wiggling their shoulders back and forth to get their breasts moving side to side. He entered the room, his lips and eyes all smiling, *May I ask if you all have gone mad?*

Victoria shouted over the music, *Bet you can't shimmy and shake with us, old man.*

Old man! Poppycock! Make room ladies. Edward threw his jacket over the divan, unloosened his tie, and began a lascivious shake of the torso and chest as we four clapped, cheered, and stomped our feet in approval. Laughter and music filled the air. I don't believe any of us remembered what time the sun set that night.

Three months had passed since our shimmy lesson. Spring was in the air, and I was in the park surveying the daffodils that had finally found the sun they craved. Bridget came to find me saying that Maude had come by. *She doesn't look well, Ma'am. Not well at all.*

I found Maude in the foyer, her eyes red-rimmed and looking lost. I called her name twice before she looked my way.

Billy's gone. He's gone, she said in a voice so low I could barely hear her.

I know, Maude. You told us he was back in Ireland.

Her body started to shake *No, no, he's gone. He's dead. I read it in yesterday's Irish paper. He was killed. He was murdered following the Bloody Sunday killings in Croke Park in Dublin. What I was able to figure out is it happened on the 26th. Ireland was supposed to be at peace, and they weren't after him. Their prey was his uncle, his mother's brother. The IRA thought the uncle was a spy. Billy told me all about him, how much of a patriot the uncle was; how folks thought they looked so much alike. My Billy wasn't the one who was supposed to be killed. His uncle was the one they were after.*

I don't know what I am to do now. I am a widow before I was barely a bride, her eyes glittered with tears. I wrapped her in my arms and squeezed her tightly. Maude gave in to her despair and sobbed, her grief coming in gasps, hiccups, and sighs.

She looked up at me, her aqua eyes glistening with the tears that now were spent. *What am I to do?*

My voice softened, *For the moment, you are to do nothing. You are to stay here. I will have someone go to the Morgans and tell the house-keeper you are ill and are staying with a friend. Then we will figure out what to do, but not today. There is a room on the second floor where you can lie down. You need to rest.*

Maude couldn't hear me. *This is a bad dream. God is punishing me for marrying outside his holy church. This is my penance. Billy was killed because of me, because I am a sinner.*

Nonsense, I shouted, shaking her as hard as I thought fit. *That is utter nonsense. Billy was killed because of man's inhumanity to man. It is not the first time this has happened; and despite our prayers and our power to vote, I am sure it won't be the last. You are not to blame today nor will you ever be the one at fault.*

Billy, my darling Billy. What am I to do now? Her eyes, so like mine, glazed over like an animal in pain.

I walked her upstairs, removing her coat and hat along the way. *You are to lie down and try to close your eyes. We will figure out something. Just not at this moment and perhaps not this day.*

Once she was settled, I called Victoria and Anne and gave them a brief report. We agreed to meet after lunch the next day. I could think of no next steps. Maude was in no shape to resume her duties in the Morgan household, her heart was too broken. Going back to live with her uncle and his family was out of the question. We had heard enough about her life with them to know she would not be welcomed. I went upstairs to check on her. She was sitting looking out the window, her grief engulfing her like a fog. I had her change into a nightgown and brushed her hair. She shook her head no to the offer of any food. I put her into bed, tucking the bed covers tightly around her shivering body. Her eyes closed, her body was worn out by the heartache that it had in its grip.

I explained it all to Edward that evening. He knew nothing of the killings. *It doesn't make the regular press here in the States. I feel for Maude. To lose someone you love is hard enough, but to find out by reading it in the newspaper defies description. You are right to have her stay with us.* He paused for only a second, *when she is ready, I am sure I can find a role for her at the firm. I am not sure why I hadn't thought about it before. You always talked about how bright she is. There will be no need for her to return to the Morgan house.*

You are wonderful, Edward. I am sure we can work out a plan for her now.

The next day, Victoria and Anne came to the house. Maude joined us in the dining room, her face tear-stained, her listless gait the mark of a person who has lost all hope. I poured her a cup of tea. She was pale, with dark circles shading her eyes; and she picked at any food offered saying she didn't think she could keep it down. Twice while she was sitting with us, she had to leave abruptly saying her stomach wouldn't settle down. When she returned to the table, Anne reached over and took her hand. *When was the last time you had your monthly?*

Maude's eyes widened. *I don't know. Let me think, it's been a couple of months. I've never been too regular, so at least a couple of months for sure. It was before Billy left. So I am late for sure, later than usual.*

Anne's grip tightened around Maude's fingers. *You may be pregnant, Maude. I know the symptoms well enough. I need to take you to my doctor to be sure.*

Maude started to shake. *For the love of Jesus, no. If Billy were alive, we would be celebrating; but no one other than you three knows we were married. I can't return to my uncle's home with a baby about to be born. I will be thrown out on the street and labeled a whore.*

Anne stood up and pulled Maude to her. *First, we make sure what your condition is, and then we will decide what to do next.*

Victoria and I waited at the house. Three hours later, Anne and Maude appeared. Anne just gave the briefest of nods affirming the news. Maude was indeed with child, the baby was due in five months.

We went into the library. Maude collapsed to her knees, raising her arms in supplication. *What have I done? What am I to do? I can't raise a child on my own. It wouldn't be fair. But the thought of Billy's and my baby being raised by strangers breaks my heart in too many ways.*

I blurted out: *I will take the baby, Maude. Edward and I will raise your child as our own.*

Victoria looked stunned. *Are you sure, Nell?*

Anne spoke quietly, *That would be best. The baby will have a good home, Nell and Edward will make great parents; and Maude's heart, though broken, will rest easy.*

I looked at Maude, my heart pounding. *My dear Maude, you alone can make this decision about the baby; and it is not one you need to make now. I will talk with Edward tonight though I believe, truly believe, he will welcome your child as his own. He is the best of men.*

Maude took my hands and looked me in the eye. *This could ease my pain. You talk with Edward, and I will think about what I want to do with my life. If Victoria will oblige, I will stay with her for the next few days. You need to talk with Edward, and we all need to think.*

Edward was shocked when I told him what I had offered. He repeated Victoria's concern, *Was I sure this is what I wanted to do.* Then the other questions: *Did I know what I was getting myself into? Did I really want to be a mother? Did I realize how this would change our life?*

We were in the library. I couldn't sit still, my offer to raise Maude's child surprised even me. I couldn't give a reasonable explanation for why I made the offer. It had come from my heart, not from my head. *I know, Edward, and I don't know. It feels right*, was the best I could muster. *We are good together; and I believe we could raise a child, be a family. It is not like I am taking a stranger's child into our home. Maude, as good a person as I know, is the baby's mother and she loved Billy. This is much less a risk than when Mama brought me into her house and raised me as her own. I believe this is a gift I have been given. It feels right and I can't explain why.* A small tear fell down my cheek.

Then we shall do it, was his only reply. *My father, no matter what you may have heard, was my hero. He and my mother were often at odds but never about me. I would hear my father talk to his cronies about how proud he was of 'his boy.'* Edward stopped speaking and looked into the fire as the dying embers were fighting for their last bit of flame. *I have never thought of myself as a father and the idea may take a bit of getting used to, but, my dearest Nell, we could be quite the combination. If it is what you want and Maude is willing, I am ready.* He took my hand and raised it to his lips. *We will need to tell Henry he's about to be an uncle.*

Indeed.

I went to bed wondering what I had done. My life with

Edward had developed a rhythm of its own, one that we both understood and accepted. Bringing a child into our life would change that balance. I prayed that Maude would decide to keep the baby. I prayed that she would give her baby to Edward and me to raise as our own. I wasn't sure what prayer I wanted the Lord to answer.

The next morning Maude called and said she would come over later in the afternoon. Edward had not gone into the office and neither one of us wanted to discuss how our world could or could not change. It would be Maude's decision. We would respect whatever she wanted to do. We waited for her in the library, Edward reading his legal briefs. I hadn't turned the page on the book in my hands, my mind wandering with images of walks in the park with a pram and the sound of a child's laughter filling the house. I kept fingering Mama's gold cross clasped around my neck when Bridget knocked on the door and Maude entered.

She looked lovely. The harried, unsure woman of just days before had been replaced with the calmness and confidence of the Maude I knew. She wasted no time in coming to the point. *I have made up my mind. I will give you our baby – Billy's and mine – to raise as your own child.*

I gasped out loud. The decision was made, my heart started to beat uncontrollably. I got up and walked over to Edward's chair, putting my hand on his shoulder. Edward reached up and covered my hand with his.

There is one condition, Maude continued, *I want the baby born in Ireland. The child must be Irish. It would be Billy's wish. I will remain in Ireland after the birth, to start my life there.* Her voice broke, *New York holds too many painful memories.*

I looked at Edward. *I will go with you and stay there until the time comes. I have talked about how wonderful you have been in teaching me about the history and lore of Ireland. My story will be that I am returning to the land of my birth and have asked you to serve as my guide.*

Edward nodded his agreement. *Nell, we can then say that you found out you were pregnant while you were there and made the decision to stay until after the baby was born. I will make all the necessary arrangements, including getting you all passports.*

A passport? Maude shook her head. *I've never heard of such a thing, and my mother traveled to Ireland more than once.*

Edward poured each of us a glass of wine. *One of the many outcomes of this last war,* Edward responded. *You are to worry about nothing except your health and that of the baby. My office will handle all the details. Until such time as you board the ship, you shall stay with us.* I nodded, giving his shoulder a squeeze.

A sob escaped from the depth of Maude's throat. *I am so grateful to have you in my life. I would be lost if it weren't for all of you. My uncle would have called me reckless with no moral standards.*

Poppycock, was Edward's reply.

Maude's cries ebbed, a smile slowly crept over her tear-stained face. *I have heard you say that before. What does that mean?*

I shrugged my shoulders, *Who knows? It is his favorite word and seems to be the right response on so many different occasions.* I paused, *If it is alright with you, Maude, I would like to have Victoria join us in our travels. It would be good to have another woman to help with the baby, particularly on the trip back to New York.*

Maude's eyes widened, registering the realization of what was about to happen: she was to have a child; I would leave with that child and come back to New York; she would stay in Dublin.

Her eyes closed for just a second, and I feared that she would withdraw her offer. *That would be lovely. I have known Victoria for a very long time.*

Maude was not with me when I asked Victoria to join us. *We are not touring the countryside, Victoria, no matter what I tell others. We are there to safely deliver Maude to Ireland, to stay there until the baby is old enough to travel back, and then sail back to New York.*

Victoria's enthusiasm was hampered by her newest boot — fawn antelope with a gold brocade satin leg whose two-plus inch heels curtailed her ability to dance around the room. *I under-*

stand, Nell. I am just happy that you have asked me. I do so want to help Maude. Her mood was tempered. *She had been so happy when she met Billy, then to have him killed, and now she must give up her baby. It is all just too sad.*

I know, Victoria. I pray that God will give us the strength to help Maude. It is hard not to have your dreams come true.

It took Edward a month to get it all arranged. England was still recovering from the war, and Ireland was pushing for its independence. The ensuing politics required the patience of Job and connections that only an international law firm could draw on.

During her stay with us, Maude would join Henry, Edward, and me for dinner when we dined at home. If she suspected Henry's relationship with Edward, she never let on and I provided no insight. We all have secrets we take to the grave.

CHAPTER 16

BIRTH AND REBIRTH

Victoria, Maude, and I arrived in Dublin two weeks after we had sailed from the New York harbor. As I stepped foot in Ireland, I had expected to feel some sense of belonging, some awakening of a seed that had been planted and then uprooted all those many years ago. It didn't happen.

There was too much to be done, too much to be settled. Edward had given us a list of contacts. We had to confirm Maude's doctor, the hospital, the wet nurse, where we were to go once the baby was born. We were staying at the Shelburne Hotel in the heart of Dublin. It was a grand hotel with high ceilings, marble floors, and tall windows looking out onto St. Stephen's Green. Victoria claimed that the scones served with our tea were unmatched by anything she had tasted in New York.

The local headlines talked of a country awash with politics. This was not the land of song and mirth; tension was in the air.

We had been in Ireland for six weeks. I had not been able to sleep and got up to get some fresh air. I crossed into St. Stephen's Green as the dawn was breaking, firing the sky with reds and grays that made the lake dance with color. I thought I was alone until I saw Maude sitting on a bench. Her eyes registered no surprise as she moved, making room for me to sit down next to her.

She looked swollen, her hands cradling her stomach, her face peaceful. *This baby will come into this world before nightfall.*

I took her hand, the skin now stretched like a sausage. *Maude, I know you said it would be too hard for you to hold the baby, knowing that you will never see it again. You can change your mind at any time, my dear friend.*

She shook her head slowly. *I know I am doing the right thing for both me and the baby. I don't even want to know whether it is a boy or a girl. It will be too painful. Best for all of us if you take the babe immediately and leave. Please don't even stop to say goodbye. You have been kind, Nell; and I know the baby will be loved and taken care of.* Her voice was gentle, almost fragile.

My heart and my eyes filled up. *Do you want me to write or send pictures at any time?*

Maude shook her head, the haphazard set of pins holding her hair in place giving up its struggle as her curls fell softly around her face. *No, best not. I need to forge ahead. The memory of Billy and what might have been will sustain me. At least for the moment. You and Edward have been generous. Once I am ready, I will set up a dress shop here in Dublin. I believe coming from New York will have the society ladies beating down the door to buy my dresses and hats.* A smile flickered across her face. *The O'Shea women have a history of being good with a needle and mending the silver lining in the darkest of clouds. I will have time to recover; and when I am ready, I will begin a new life.*

I softly brushed her hair away from her face, my lower lip trembling. *You are giving me a new life, as well. Perhaps it is not only the same eyes we share but a heart, and that withstands the hardships life casts upon us. God bless you, Maude, and keep you in his care. I will miss you.*

The same to you, Nell. She took my hand and brought it to her lips. *In so many ways, you and Edward have become more like family than I could have imagined. I have always felt a bond with you that can't be explained. Now we should go to the hospital, the pain is coming quicker. I need to do this on my own, Nell. No hand-holding or wiping my brow from either you or Victoria; best if that comes from strangers.*

I kissed her on the cheek, the taste of salt left by her quiet tears stinging my lips. I helped her up, her legs staggering by the weight she was carrying. We walked arm-in-arm back to the hotel as Dublin woke up to a new day.

Maude and I had said our last good-bye but my heart would not let her go that easily. It grieved me to lose her. She was my friend.

Three hours later, we were in the hospital. Victoria and I were in the next room as Maude gave birth before the sun had set. I telegraphed Edward that we had a son.

———

Dear Mama,

Last night I cradled my son in my arms for the first time. He had just entered this world. I cannot describe the emotion. When the nurse put him in my arms, I was scared to hold him. He is so tiny. Then I looked at his face, and I couldn't catch my breath at the miracle of it all. Here is a new human being who holds the promise of everything good, of sparkling hope, of fresh beginnings. I feel like I have grown another heart, one that is all love for this magical child who will be christened Edward but we will call Teddy.

When Edward agreed for us to raise the baby as our own, I knew we were doing the right thing. Is that how you felt when you brought me home? That you knew from the beginning it was the right thing to do? I always felt that I belonged to you. I feel that Teddy belongs to me. I believe that God has given me a precious gift, one that I will be eternally grateful for having received.

I keep staring at the baby who excites feelings in me I never knew I had. Life has taken on another meaning. When I held him in my arms, I never knew such happiness nor such terror. I know I would die for him; I know I would live for him.

I wish you were here. I know you would understand.

I love you, Mama.
Your Nell

Living in Ireland for the first three months following
Teddy's birth introduced me to the land of my birth.
Victoria, the wet nurse, and I had left Dublin with Teddy the day
after he was born and went to the Irish countryside. Dunmore is
a small village that gently slopes to the sea. Our cottage blended
with the rest, built of clay with a high thatched roof and cut
dormer windows whose frames had been painted red to match
the door. It was perfect. When I first saw it, I had a fleeting
thought, O'Brien would love it here.

Victoria and I got into the routine of taking a walk while
both Teddy and the nurse napped. Victoria was looking out to
the Irish sea, now wearing oxfords. She no longer complained
about her feet hurting. She turned to look at me. *I don't miss the
noise of New York; you can feel the quiet here. It is like a soft embrace.
You lose yourself in the moment, feeling both comforted and safe. It pulls
you in. I am so glad I am here with you.*

I took her arm in mine, *I couldn't imagine being here with anyone
else.*

We had been in Dunmore about a month when a small, withered woman approached us with a grin as broad as her face.

*You're the American girls with the newborn, are you not? I have a
cousin in Chicago, never met him, left fore I was born. Do you know the
O'Leary's?*

Victoria shook her head. *Sorry, Ma'am. We're from New York,
and Chicago is a long way from there.*

Quite all right, the woman sniffed. *The O'Leary's were never
much good anyway. My ma would say that they would only come for
Sunday roast and never raise a finger to give a hand. The eldest daughter
went away with a tinker, never to be heard from again.*

She looked closely between me and Victoria. One gnarled finger peeking out from her crotched glove pointed directly at me. *How long have you been gone for?*

Gone for? I wasn't sure what she was asking.

Aye, how long since you left here?

I smiled. *Since I was young. My Ma died on the voyage over, and my father put me and my sister in an orphanage. I was adopted by a family in...*

Before I could start my tale, she shrugged, *I knew you were one of us. I could feel your spirit. With that color hair, you have Viking blood flowing through your veins. God's land this is. See that lighthouse, that is Hook on the other side is Crook. The devil incarnate who called himself Oliver Cromwell said he would invade Ireland 'by Hook or by Crook.' Those he didn't kill were not allowed east of the River of Shannon on pain of death. We showed 'em, we showed 'em all. He could massacre us, but he couldn't keep us down.*

She tilted her head back as I watched a ball of saliva float in the air making its way to the dirt in front of her well-worn boots.

I spit on his grave. She looked up. *We'll break the shackles of the Crown before your lad speaks his first word. Slán.*

With a wave of her hand, she was gone. Maude was right, the Irish never forget or forgive.

It was the day before we were leaving for our journey back to New York. I stood on the hill overlooking the sea. The wind blew inland off the water in chilly gusts, and I wrapped my coat tighter to ward off the cold. The waves rose and fell in ever-changing swells as their peaks extended upward as hands in prayer. They crashed against the rocks, leaving white foam bubbles. The water rolled in and out in a rhythm that only God could orchestrate. I thought of O'Brien. I wanted to tell him that I understood what it feels like to be Irish. To love Ireland. Wild, mysterious, and indescribably beautiful.

Three weeks later, Edward and Henry were waiting for us when the ship docked. Teddy looked up at the man who was to be his father and smiled his first smile, his face crinkled with happiness as he grasped Edward's finger in his tiny hand. Edward was hooked.

On May 6, 1921, Edward John William Walker was formally christened at St. Patrick's Cathedral in front of a crowd of 150. He was named after his father, my father, and the father he never knew. No one questioned the name, and I felt somehow Maude would approve. We agreed Henry and Victoria would be the godparents. There was some fast footwork to get them approved by the church hierarchy; but somehow, Edward made it happen. Rachel took on the title of 'honorary godmother,' she took the baby from me and gave him to Henry to hold during the ceremony. Rachel smiled, *I'll teach Teddy I was his kvaterin, the woman who took him from his mother's arms to give him to his godfather. He will be the only Catholic boy to understand Jewish traditions before others fill his head with false stories.*

I was warned most babies cry at their baptism, too many people and cold holy water being the main culprits for their collapse. Not Teddy, he smiled and cooed throughout the entire day.

It was Teddy's first birthday, a celebration that was lost on him and left Edward and me exhausted. When the house was finally quiet, Edward and I retreated to the library. As we stood up to end the day, he took my hands and raised them to his lips. *I love being a family, Nell. I wasn't sure of the decision the day I agreed to bring a baby into our home, but I cannot now imagine another life. There are moments when I look at Teddy and he babbles 'Papa', I think my heart will burst with happiness. Today was one of the best days I could have imagined.*

I looked at him, his eyes glistening with tears, and put my arms around him. *I know, my dearest Edward, and I am so thankful. Teddy is lucky to have you as his father. We have been blessed in so many ways.*

And you, my darling Nell, are a wonderful mother.

———

Teddy was easy to raise. The most charming baby grew to be the most charming child, surrounded by the love and devotion of so many. Throughout the years, it was Rachel who challenged this thinking, giving him books to read on an almost weekly basis and then demanding a report on the same when they would meet. She took him with her to political meetings and opened him to a world that was not as bright and beautiful as the one he inhabited.

As he got older, Henry introduced him to the finer things of this world – how to introduce himself to strangers, what knife and fork he should use for what course, and gave him an appreciation for theatre with all its wonders and exploits. Victoria played with him. Amusement parks, jump ropes, and merry-go-rides, all were in the purview of Tory, his childhood name for her that stuck. Anne's family gave him older cousins to look up to and admire. Bridget became a mother's helper, a role she excelled in.

I simply loved him. He was my full-time job.

CHAPTER 17

1925

T he night was wild and stormy, the wind so violent it shook the trees bare of any remaining leaves, a sure sign winter would be our next visitor. We were scheduled to join Henry at the theatre, but Edward had opted for a quiet evening at home. He had given Teddy his bath and read him his first story of the night. The two of them came down to the library, hand-in-hand, for the 'final story.' It was our nightly ritual; and we scheduled our evenings out to occur after all the stories had been read, Teddy's prayers had been heard, and we had tucked him into bed.

Edward and I were coming down the stairs from Teddy's room. *I believe this weather has chilled my bones, my dear. Let's have a quiet supper in front of the fire.*

Mrs. Campbell must have read your mind. She left a pot of her soup on the stove before leaving for the day. Even my limited culinary skills can produce a salad and cut the bread.

Excellent. You chop and toss, I will pour the wine.

I headed towards the kitchen and Edward to the library, our tasks at hand.

I had pulled out the lettuce and tomatoes and had just picked up the knife to start the salad when I jumped at the sound of crashing glass. I shouted Edward's name and ran into the library, still gripping the knife while small droplets of blood made their way down the thumb that I had nicked when I heard the noise.

I found Edward lying on the floor surrounded by crystal shards. He was still. It looked like a scene from one of those dreadful plays, the howling of the wind the only sound accompanying my screams. There was no response. His eyes never opened. There were no final words.

Bridget, hearing the screams, appeared at the door.

Oh My God, Ma'am. Mr. Walker? Crossing herself, *Is he dead?*

Tears streamed down my face. *Call Dr. Jenkins, Bridget. His name is in the book by the telephone. And Henry. He is at the Lyceum. I don't know the number.*

I was on the floor cradling Edward's head in my lap, whispering his name, when I saw his white shirt, so crisp and starched just an hour ago, was now splotched with dots of red, spilled red wine and my blood which had dripped from the small cut on my finger. My mind blurred with white images stained with red. Stains that rob me of the people I love.

Bridget arrived with Dr. Jenkins, his stethoscope already hanging from his neck.

I stood up as he knelt by the body. I thought Edward would hate this, the indignity of lying prostrate on the floor, his mouth opened, his body growing cold. In a few short minutes, I heard the words I already knew to be true: *He is gone, Mrs. Walker, I am sorry. God has called him home.*

I fell on the floor, my legs no longer having the strength to hold me up. A noise escaped my soul, a sound between a sob and a shout. Through my haze, I heard my name being called. I looked up to find Henry at my side. He pulled me up, and I fell into his arms.

Henry, no, no. This is a mistake. I am in a nightmare and will wake up.

Henry said nothing, his face pale, his hands shaking. He just held onto me.

I need him, Henry. Teddy needs him. Couldn't God have waited?

Bridget came back into the room with a young man who introduced himself as George Macken. He was the undertaker that Dr. Jenkins had called. All the burial arrangements would be handled by him. He had the kind yet deferential demeanor of those in his line of work. Looking at the body on the floor, *Edward Walker?*

Dr. Jenkins nodded.

Macken was pulling out a linen bag that lay near the stretcher he had brought in. Henry took my hand.

We need to leave the room, Nell.

I felt like I was on shifting sand. *I need to say goodbye. We both do.*

I knelt by the body. This was not the Edward I loved, a man strong and sure of himself and his place in the world. I tried to pray, but no words would come. I took his cold hand, pressed it to my lips, and laid it back down. The first of my tears rolled down my cheeks. *This is poppycock, Edward. Poppycock!*

Henry helped me to my feet, tears streaming down his cheeks. *Poppycock,* he repeated. He turned to the doctor and Macken who were busy doing whatever needed to be done to move Edward away from his home and our life. *We will be in the parlor if you need us.*

Jenkins reached into his bag, producing a vial of pills that he placed in my hands.

Take two of these. You will need to sleep tonight.

I mumbled my thanks.

We were in the parlor when Rachel and Victoria arrived and rushed to my side. Dr. Jenkins had left, leaving Mr. Macken to finish the last phase of his task. He excused himself as he entered the room shrouded in sadness. *Does the deceased have a favorite suit to be arranged in?*

I stood up, raising my hand in a fist. *He is not the deceased. He is my husband, and two hours ago he was alive.* I looked around, a blur of grief-stricken faces surrounded me. *Please, no.*

The wine and the pills took their effect; I have no recollection of what happened next. I woke up to the sound of rain pelting against my bedroom window. I lay a moment in the semi-darkness, listening to the wind. For a split second, I didn't remember that Edward had died. Then the memory came crashing in, Edward was dead. Though still warm under the covers, I shivered. My heart stopped, I had to tell Teddy.

I found my dressing coat and went to his room with no thought of what I was to say. He was so little, so young. What would he understand?

Bridget had already dressed and fed him, her eyes welled with tears when she saw me. She left me alone with him, closing the door quietly behind her. Teddy was on the floor playing with his train. *Mama,* his outstretched arms reached for me.

Ah, my little love, picking him up, I kissed the top of his head. Tears started to trickle down my cheek. How could he understand what has happened? How our life would change? He was a child, just five years old, not much older when I had been placed in the orphanage. A memory I could not recall. There would be a time to keep the memory of Edward alive for Teddy. I would be sure of that.

Mama, are you crying?

Yes, my darling boy. These are my tears for your Papa, who loved us very much. Papa died last night. I am very sad. We will miss him very much.

Teddy stood up, shaking his head, he put his hands on his hips. *No, he needs to be here today. He promised we were going to play in the park if the rain stopped.*

I knelt beside him. *I know, my love; but he won't be able to keep that promise. When someone dies, they leave this world and go to heaven to live with the Lord. That is where Papa is now. We will always remember him, and Papa will always be here in our hearts.* I put my hands on his heart and on my own.

Teddy's eyes squinted. A look of disbelief came over his face, the same questioning expression he gave me the time I told him that thunder was just the noise the angels made when they were bowling. *Papa is pretty big to be in such a small place. He will not fit.*

Through my tears, I smiled. *You are so right, my son. It is our love for Papa that we keep in our hearts.*

Bridget came back into the room, her eyes bloodshot. *Should I take Master Teddy to the park, ma'am? The weather has cleared up quite nicely.*

Teddy's eyes lit up.

Absolutely. Just dress warmly.

I took him in my arms once again, and he started to squirm. *Victoria and Rachel will come to have lunch with you.*

You, too?

I shook my head. *Mama is going to have to prepare for Papa's funeral. In a few days, you and I will go to St. Patrick's together where there will be hymns and prayers for your Papa. We will hold each other's hand and will remember all the good times we had together. You can bring your favorite stuffed animal with you.*

I shall bring Bear, he is my favorite.

A perfect choice. And for the first time in hours, I thought my heart might not break.

Teddy went quiet as he looked up at me, *Mama, will I ever see Papa again?*

I hugged him closer to me. *Not until we are all in heaven together.*

Okay, I am glad to know that I will see him then.

Bridget came and took his hand.

Thank you, Bridget. We will get through this somehow. Can you let Phillips and Mrs. Campbell know that I will meet with them once the arrangements have been finalized?

Yes, ma'am, You and the wee lad are in our prayers. May the Blessed Virgin look over you during these dark days.

The following days were a blur. I had to make decisions I never thought were mine to make: where was the body to be buried, whether I should reserve my spot next to his for when my time came. I thought I was going mad. If Henry hadn't been there, I believe I would have lost my mind.

The wake lasted three days. The parlor was filled with floral displays. The house smelled of death, the overpowering sensation of too many bodies and too many dyed roses, tinseled leaves, and inane expressions of grief. I stood to greet the mourners, uttering the stock phrases of *thank you for coming: yes, he will be missed.* My gaze kept returning to the satin ribbon of one floral arrangement, the message on its ribbon curling like a hand pointing to Edward laying in the casket. He should not be *At Rest*, he should be standing among us.

Teddy, clutching Bear, and I followed the casket into St. Patrick's followed by a procession of his law firm partners all looking very solemn while calculating who was to move into his office, take his clients, assume his role as a leader of the firm.

Following the Mass, the procession of cars found its way across the 59th Street Bridge to Calvary Cemetery. I didn't have Teddy come to the cemetery. I was afraid that seeing the coffin disappear into the hole of dirt would be too much for his young mind. It was all I could do to stand strong and not wail with a feeling of sorrow I couldn't articulate.

Later we returned to the house for the funeral luncheon. Anne, Victoria, and Rachel rotated between being either at my side or in the nursery with Teddy. He was too young to hear words that rang empty. Henry watched me from a distance. Our heartache was shared. I had lost my husband, he had lost his lover, and we both had lost our dearest friend.

I was numb with grief, a grief so deep I could not find its source. Like an egg that had its contents blown out, I was a shell, going through the daily acts of living but with no sense of purpose.

When somewhat of our daily routine had been resurrected and the house clear of the lingering scent of mourning, St. Patrick's became my sanctuary. I would take the trolly up Fifth Avenue, oblivious to the construction that continued to change the landscape of the city, climb the stairs to the heavy doors, and push them open.

Dipping my fingers into the holy water, I would find a back pew. Once on my knees, my eyes would close. In that quiet solitude, I asked God to show me the way, the way to do what was right for Teddy, for me, for those whom I had come to love. And amid these silent cries for help, I would open my eyes and marvel at the stained glass windows, the carved arches, the marble statues, the candle flames flickering their petitions to the saints whose complexion caught their light. I began to feel a reverence for the creators of this place itself, for creating a space to worship. It was here I felt safe from the void that too often overcame me. It was here that I could cry. Silently, quietly. Not the sobbing of the distraught or the weeping of the too-young widow, but soft tears. Tears that were mine alone to wipe.

Henry had quietly removed his things from Edward's room. He came by most days to see Teddy with a ball in his hand or plans for an afternoon outing. Most often he would stay for dinner. Teddy once asked him if the Lord would let Papa come back and play with them. I am not sure how Henry responded, but it seemed to satisfy Teddy.

Edward had been gone for about three months. Henry had taken Teddy to the Museum of Natural History to see the dinosaurs. He had stayed for dinner when I asked, *Is the sadness manageable?*

Henry stared into his wine glass as if seeking his answer there. *Some days, I wake up and don't realize he is gone. I feel normal for the moment, and then I realize that life as I knew it has ended. There are moments of pain so severe my body feels like it will collapse. Then a numbness takes over that is a blessing, a welcome respite from the gnawing, burning ache.*

Henry shrugged deeper into his body. *I wasn't with him when he died. I shouldn't have gone to the theatre that night, I should have stayed in with you both. I should have been here for him. I should have been here for you.*

Henry started to sob. Sobs that made him gasp for air. I went and took him in my arms. Together we cried, for how long I don't remember. When there were no more tears to shed, we looked at each other, smiled, and sat back at the table.

Henry raised his glass. *To my dearest friend.*

Clicking my glass with his, *And mine. I do love you, you know.*

And I, you.

We finished our meal in the comfortable silence that comes when there is nothing more to say and nothing more that needs to be said.

I stood on the steps after I walked Henry to the door. The air was cool, but the chill was invigorating. Through the darkness, I saw light – street lamps throwing their shadows on the park's gates, the beam of car headlights guiding their passengers on the crowded streets, the flickering gas lights on doorways reminiscent of days long past – each glow providing a collective spotlight on my world.

I closed the door. I would miss Edward. I would survive.

CHAPTER 18

A VOICE FROM THE PAST

The next day the letter arrived. The address and the handwriting clearly marked the author, there was no mistaking the handwriting. Aunt Helena. I had not seen her in years. The last time I had written to her was to tell her that Mama had died. A note that was never acknowledged.

I was not sure what to expect. The letter was on cream paper, trimmed in black, a condolence note. I had received dozens upon dozens of such notes following Edward's death, all requiring a personal response.

I poured myself a fresh cup of tea and went into the library and sat in Edward's chair, a practice I adopted following his funeral. Sitting in his chair made me feel that he was still with me, at least in spirit.

Dear Nell,

How distraught I was to read in the papers of Edward's death. Such a young man and so sudden. The Inquirer spoke of how respected he was in the legal communities in both Philadelphia and New York City. A man of intellect, integrity, and position, who was a good son to his mother.

I was surprised to learn that he has a young son. There had been no announcement in the local papers about the boy's birth, a breach of protocol given the standing his grandparents had in the community that I am sure was your decision. You never understood how to properly behave in society.

Now that you have inherited the Walker fortune, you are in no need of the monies set aside for you by my sister's husband. Following the death of Clare, I received no additional income from her estate. As her only sister and living relative, I should have been entitled to her money. I intend to pursue every recourse of action until they are returned to me.

I do not wish to make this unpleasant for either of us. I just want what is my rightful due.

I anticipate a speedy reply to this letter.

Sincerely,
Helena

I shook my head slowly. The years hadn't changed Helena. There was no expression of sympathy. Rather, she hurled insults accompanied by threats. I knew my course of action. Helena would be dealt with by lawyers, there would be no response from me. She had shown me no comfort when Mama had left for Saranac Lake nor when Mama had died. All she wanted from me was money. Papa may not have shown me the affection I sought as a child, but he had ensured I would be provided for. That was how he showed his love, the one way he could tell me how much he cared about me. I was not going to tarnish that gift by sharing any of it with Helena.

I called the lawyer who had been handling Edward's affairs and set up a meeting for the next morning.

The day shone bright, and I awoke with a renewed sense of purpose. Helena's letter curtailed the ebb and flow of my grief. I had to protect Teddy; I had to protect us. I knew little about finance, that had been Edward's domain; but I had a mind and will of my own. I would rely on both.

I arrived at the S&C office with its wood paneling, high ceilings, ornate moldings, and Oriental rugs that showed just the right amount of wear to prove their antiquity. I was greeted by a combination of words of sympathy and stares of curiosity. I was the young widow on parade. One of Edward's more junior partners greeted me and brought me to his office, the view and the furnishings recognizable.

I see you have taken over Edward's office. He looked a bit chagrined, but I continued without allowing a response.

I suggest that you replace the carpet. It was here when he moved in; and if you look behind the bookcase, the threads have worn through.

I sat down.

In his dark blue suit and Windsor knotted tie, he looked like a leading man playing the role of the family's barrister. Although they bore no resemblance, he looked like Edward. Or how Edward dressed and stood. I realized all of Edward's partners looked like they went to the same tailor, spoke in the same tone of voice, used the same hand gestures. I had never really noticed before. My thoughts were interrupted when I heard my name.

It is good to see you, Nell. How are you? We miss Edward every day. Richard McDermott, the senior partner of the firm who was handling my affairs, joined us.

I am managing, Dick, thank you. I need your help on a family matter and handed him Helena's letter. *I believe that you have a copy of my father's will along with our legal papers.*

He nodded slowly.

You will see Helena's name there. She is my mother's sister and was provided a sum of money by Father at the time of his death. I have not seen nor heard from her since she learned of his bequest. I see no reason to alter the terms of my father's will. Please advise her that her claim to any additional monies is denied.

He responded in his best lawyer's voice, I could hear Edward saying the same thing in the same way. *That will be taken care of. I will also contact the lawyers who reviewed the terms of your late father's will and advise them of your aunt's unsubstantiated claims.*

Thank you, but she is not my aunt.

His eyebrows raised in question.

I chose not to respond. *I plan to be meeting with my banker later this week. If you could be so kind, please have a copy of Edward's will sent to the house tomorrow.*

I stood up to leave.

Nell, I will be happy to do all of this; but may I suggest that you may be moving too quickly and without proper guidance as to how best to handle your financial concerns.

I smiled as I got up from my chair. *Edward would understand. Thank you for seeing me on such short notice. I am sure we will continue to be in touch.* I left the office with a confident stride.

Over the next few weeks and in a world of unbridled optimism, I took another path and became a fiscal conservative. That was the polite label. Despite the head-shakers who told me I had nothing to worry about, I was safe in their hands and their projections, investing in the stock market. I stood my ground.

I had lost my safety net when Edward died. I needed to touch, to see, to feel what I owned. I began a series of meetings with our financial advisor, a short, self-contained man, clean-shaven, and dressed in a pristine gray suit. He spoke about 'gains' and 'interest.' I heard a voice whisper in my ear – *nothing but poppycock. Buy land, invest in gold and short-term bonds.*

And so I did.

CHAPTER 19

STAYING ALIVE

I should have known better. I knew the pain of losing a parent, even if it is not my death. Mama didn't die, but she left me. I understood loss, a loss so deep that you know it will never be completely healed. White linen handkerchiefs remind me of her. As does the sound of a rattling cough.

I tried to keep the memory of Edward alive for Teddy. Teddy's bedroom hadn't changed in the five years since Edward's death. The seafarer theme Edward and Henry had surprised me with the day I brought Teddy home was still there. The only things that had been added were additional pictures. There were pictures of our wedding, of Teddy's baptism, trips to the zoo, the three of us playing in the ocean. Even Edward's old baby album that had been rescued from the sale of Mother Walker's estate was on a table. All reminders that once upon a time there had been three of us.

I thought Teddy was doing fine. I had worked through my grief, I missed Edward but life had taken on a new orbit. The library, once reserved for cocktails and raised voices debating today's newspaper headlines, was now the designated homework area. Teddy would sit at his desk, the only new piece of furniture that had been purchased, and its light oak finish somehow blended in the world of polished wood and Tiffany lamps. I would sit in Edward's chair and feel, at least for the moment, the three of us were connected as one family. These were precious moments.

I was taking on a more active role in managing our finances, a role that I found rewarding in more ways than one. Though I was no longer writing for *The Sun*, Rachel raised my hand to take on the volunteer role as the newsletter editor for the National Women's Party, a growing advocate for the adoption of the Equal Rights Amendment. The Women's Trade Union League opposed the ERA on the grounds it would undo the protective legislation it had fought hard to obtain. There were strong feelings on both sides of the issue, and I liked being in the throes of the debate.

Vacations were spent with Henry at his home on Long Island.

We were there on a hot and salty day, I sat under the umbrella watching Henry show Teddy how to body surf. My heart ached. I wanted Edward to be here. Henry had prepared Teddy for the adventure. *You are going to taste your first wave today. It will be briny and cold, and you will be addicted.*

By the end of the day, they were like a pair of dolphins, communicating in a language only the other could understand. Pointing at the wave Henry thought they could conquer, Teddy would shout his acceptance of the challenge. They floated over the top of the curl just as the surf broke, scattered, and disappeared. I couldn't stop smiling, I knew how lucky I was that day. I was watching a memory being made.

When the sand was out of our toes, we walked into town for ice cream. Teddy looked at Henry, with a mixture of wonderment and excitement. *This was my best day ever.*

Mine, too. Henry smiled

The world felt right. It had been a long time coming but for that moment, the world felt right.

CHAPTER 20

MORE LOSS

The weather was fine, and I had decided to see for myself what the newest monument of steel and glass was all about. My curiosity was getting the best of me. I wanted to see firsthand what Walter Chrysler had dreamed up. I was not disappointed. I walked up Lexington Avenue until I could get a good view. I wished that O'Brien was with me, as I would have liked his photographer's eye to direct my vision.

The automobile magnate had assumed control of the building now bearing his name. It kept with the current art deco fad, coupled with the recognition of the industry that had made him a wealthy man, the design incorporated wheels and radiator caps. The top of the building took my breath away. Still under construction, its series of shining arches rose high into the sky, as if an altar to the new gods of progress. Everything was soaring – people's spirits, New York City's reputation as the new center of the universe, the expectation money was to be spent rather than earned.

Historians look to October 24th as the start of the great crash of 1929. For those of us who were present and accounted for, there was not one day to point to but an epidemic of days. Too much cash had been placed in the market in the preceding years.

Edward had predicted the house of cards would fall. He had remembered the crash of 1907: *It is bound to happen again*, he opined on more than one occasion. The farming and commodity markets were weak and not as alluring with promises of easy stock market money. Banks and investment houses grew beyond expectations and need. Prices rose, as did greed. Edward would have been aghast but not surprised. Everyone seemed to be in on the game. Everyone would soon lose. As with all gambling casinos, the odds favored the house.

Following the war, the world of speakeasies, bootleggers, movie star celebrities, and bobbed hair socialites had heralded a world where pleasure had been the norm and hard work the exception. Especially in New York. Especially with those who pulled the strings who made us all dance to the tune they played.

The market collapsed on a Monday, the Dow fell over twelve percent. The next day was worse. Over sixteen million shares changed hands. The ticker tape machines couldn't keep up. Brokers had never seen anything like it. Investors were panicking, big and small were being wiped out.

———

1 932 entered a world that was trying to absorb the chaos that surrounded it. Disbelief and panic had replaced the optimism of the preceding year.

Brushing the newly-fallen snow from his coat, Henry came to dinner and began to complain that the city was looking untidy. *There are building sites wherever you look. No wonder flocks of born-and-bred Manhattanites are flying out to Westchester to feather their nests.* He was particularly upset that Columbia University had leased its land in midtown to John D. Rockefeller, Jr. *Hogwash*, was Henry's take on the plans to have the designated area torn apart to make way for a new opera house no one could afford. *Rockefeller will have the entire area in chaos, creating a monument to his millions over the next ten years. Once he gets these plans approved, you won't be able to kneel at St. Patrick's to pray without the sound of hammers and chisels interrupting your pleas to the Almighty.*

I laughed, *When did you start to worry about the Lord hearing your prayers, my dearest Henry?*

He shrugged, *Lately, it seems as if it is the only thing I do.*

I looked up, a bit startled, and tried to ask the next question. *Why?*

But Henry pushed the conversation aside. *Ah, my dearest Nell, one needs to keep all the options open. And speaking of opening, let's find a bottle of Edward's finest brandy and pour ourselves a glass or two.*

He had more than two that night. I wanted him to stay over, he had had too much to drink. An occurrence, I realize now, was happening more and more often. He refused the offer saying he had one more thing to do that evening. He held me tight as we said our goodnights.

You are my family, Nell, part sister, part mother, part wife. I have no better friend. You will love me no matter what, I know.

Of course, I will always love you. Even when you are drunk and a bit maudlin. I responded as I helped him put on his coat.

Promise? He said.

Yes, I promise, I sighed with exasperation.

Good, I will hold you to it, he replied as he tipped his hat and walked out the door.

The letter arrived by messenger the first thing in the morning. I recognized immediately Henry's handwriting. I poured myself a cup of tea and casually broke the wax seal bearing his monogram. I remember chuckling, *Well, he clearly wanted to make this private.*

My Dearest Nell,

I can picture you reading this letter. You are dressed in your morning coat, wearing the glasses only a privileged few of us ever see on your face. It is one of your few vanities.

I write to tell you that after our lovely and final dinner together,

I took my own life. Yes, Nell, this is not a cruel joke. By the time this letter is in your hands, I will be dead. As strange as it is to write, it actually brings me a sense of comfort. I have made the decision to end my life. It is not something I have done without thought and with full recognition that those I love most will be hurt and angry by this decision. I know it is selfish of me. Yet I can think of no other option. I have never feared death, Nell. Yet I fear dying. I fear it beyond rational thought.

There are many strings tying this package up for me. I hope to be able to explain them to you. Not that you will forgive me for the cruel and unexpected decision I have made to leave you. I just want you to listen. Please do that for me, Nell. Do not throw away this letter until you have read it. It is my one last request.

My hand started to shake, I thought I might get sick.

You are a realist, my dear friend. I believe once you get over your shock and anger, you will understand.

When I look back on my life, I believe my greatest flaw is I had no ambition. I am not alone in lacking this trait. Many of the men I went to school with, from private boarding school to university, fell into the same trap. All except those Roosevelt boys, but I am not going to spend my last few hours on earth berating their politics, each in their turn.

At this point, even as I couldn't catch my breath reading this nightmare, I had to smile. Henry abhorred TR, citing him as the cause of the Republican party's demise these past twenty years; and he would turn red in the face when Franklin's name entered into even the politest of conversations. I took a sip of my tea and continued to read.

I believe I am an interesting person, good to be with, and, as far as I know, have never done anything intentionally to cause damage to another human being. I leave no legacy behind, no testimony to my good works will ring from the pulpit at my leaving. Dinner party conversations may be a bit less vibrant, the wine not as properly chilled, the theatre lights a bit dimmer, but that is about all.

I know you will attempt to disagree. Or at least I hope you will, my dearest Nell.

Men like me, and I do mean men like me, need to have a fortune. And like so many known and unknown to us, I no longer have one.

Since Edward died, I have felt rudderless. You and Teddy are family, but I missed being loved. Loved in so many ways.

The night was warm, spring was in the air, the calendar confirmed the date. My birthday. You were at one of Teddy's school functions, and I was feeling particularly lonely. It had been years since I visited the baths. I met Edward there. He probably never told you. It never mattered. Once I met him, and I believe once he met me, there was no reason to return. That day I returned, paid my dollar at the door, and entered the steam room. Very shortly thereafter, my physical needs having been met, I was putting on my clothes when I heard a sharp whistle and someone yelling to freeze where we were. We were rounded up by local cops, and the door was locked. It appears that eight or so among us were actually detectives on duty. The carnage began, I was kicked in the groin, others were beaten, we were defenseless. One of the younger men, a stalwart fellow who appeared to know his way around a boxing ring, lunged at one of the officers and was winning the battle when two other cops, their bully clubs raised, smashed his face. The crunch of his facial bones was like the sound of nuts being cracked during the Christmas holiday festivities. Within minutes, more police arrived; and we were shoved and about to be pushed into the paddy wagon to go to jail. I had never been more frightened in my life.

I know who I am, yet I believe my secret life was mine alone. Public humiliation was about to unravel it all.

Just as one of the cops was jostling me into the wagon, I heard a voice, quietly but with an authority that couldn't be mistaken, say, 'He is with me'. Both the cop and I turned at the same moment to come face-to-face with your friend O'Brien, camera in hand. 'And who should you be?' was the quick response of the brute of the man wearing blue who had my arms locked behind me.

'My name is O'Brien, I am with The Sun. Captain Murphy wanted me to document the work of New York's finest in cleansing the city of this riff-raff. This gentleman is one of my colleagues, he was assigned to do the undercover work in preparation for the raid.'

The cop seemed somewhat skeptical but loosened his grasp on my arms.

O'Brien continued without a breath, 'Same as your boys who were found inside, heh?'

The cop let me go, shrugged, and said, 'Don't care much if he is a deviant or your deviant. We rounded up enough to give the captain the headlines he is looking for. Most of this lot will be looking to save their arses rather than getting their jollies from having it poked.'

When we got outside, O'Brien and I now side-by-side, I finally got the courage to offer my thanks and ask why. Why had he saved me from the unthinkable?

He shook his head ever so slowly. 'Well, the last time I saw you, you were more finely attired. You were with Nell Walker at the gallery showing my photographs.' I interrupted him here, my voice rising in admiration touched with relief, you are the infamous O'Brien, I should have recognized the name immediately, but I was clearly preoccupied with saving my life. I follow your work constantly. You are gifted. Nell has never been able to stop talking about you.

How can I repay you?

'You already have,' he shrugged. 'Safe journey home and a word to the wise, I'd stay out of these public baths for a while. Since the pressure on Tammany to clean up their act has intensified, the boys in blue are on a mission to prove themselves the guardians of all that is good and righteous in this world'. He smiled briefly, 'This is New York City, for God's sake. Not even sure the Archangel Michael

could defend the lot of us if he descended with the blessing of the
Almighty from the heavens above.'

And with that, he was gone. I am not sure your friend saved my
life, but he did save my reputation. The whole evening made me
realize how protected I had been. I had been so careful to keep who I
am and who I love hidden until I found Edward and you. It would
never happen again. It had been a gift. And life going forward
would be hard, harder than I could endure.

I had to stop reading for the moment. *O'Brien*, I mumbled. *O'Brien once again to the rescue.* My hand was shaking and my heart was breaking, but the inevitable quickening of my pulse when I heard his name occurred. I slowly got up from my chair and went to open the window. I needed fresh air. I needed to see the sun. I tried to imagine what the terrors of that night had been for Henry. He lived in a society where those who meet their membership requirements are not confined by steel bars but by the norms dictated by the few. Their rules are clear and their prejudices taught. They are free to walk the streets but are prisoners just the same.

I don't know how long I stood there staring into a world that was at once familiar and foreign. I returned to Henry's letter, hearing his voice on every page.

I was never as rich as everyone else. Not even as rich as others
thought me to be. What I have always had was the mystique of 'old
money.' That doesn't mean I ever had any, but it is (best to keep it in
the present for the moment) the world I was brought up in. I went
to the best schools where I neither shone nor embarrassed the family.
I was invited to the best parties and was the occasional item on the
society page. Nothing scandalous, at best it involved a charity event.
My one talent, I believe, is that I made easy look easy: easy living,
easy conversation, easy relationships. Even my relationship with you

and Edward was easy. He was easy to love; and you, my dear, are hard to describe. Beauty and brains all wrapped in a package that combines the strength of character with an iron will that charms while it surprises the eye of the beholder. You were both my refuge and my North Star. I was never happier.

When Edward died, not only did a piece of my heart die with him, but I was at a loss of purpose. My puttering in the theatre had been great fun but had drained most of the trust fund that had been my sole source of support. I began to dabble in the stock market, large sums I had never earned, so the dollars never seemed too real. I believe if Edward was still with us, his steadfastness and sturdy hands on the wheel would have steered me away from this path. That is all speculation and, perhaps, a slight bit of wishful thinking.

I got caught up in the excitement of trading. I would go into the back rooms with my brokers, where cigars and whiskey were standard fare and ticker tapes with their exotic alphabets clattered from the opening bell to the closing. In the beginning, I thought I had outwitted them all, even the experienced Wall Street mavens. Buy low, sell high. Even the dullest in the lot knew the mantra. I was making money. At least I thought it was money. Then it all unraveled as my stocks dropped and dropped again. Panic ensued, followed by men howling in pain and then sobbing as they fell to their knees. I did my best to appear nonchalant, grace under pressure, and all of that. I didn't lose it all at once, the market was still on its roller-coaster ride.

You probably won't remember, but we spent the evening together that same night. I was a bit beaten down and forlorn, but you attributed it to mourning Edward. As the conversation rolled around to the market and its fluctuations, you were your pragmatic best. A lesson I should have paid more attention to. I think I can still quote you. 'I took most of our money out of the market after Edward died. Brokers have never seemed much better to me than the rollers of the dice at the Monte Carlo table. When it comes to my money, I want to be able to know where it is. My investments are in land. We can stand on it, we can see it, and, if it all goes bad, Teddy and I can pitch a tent and live there.'

I remember I laughed out loud. Of all the places where I could see you living, somewhere in a tent has never been one. Yet the advice was sound. I went out to Long Island that week and changed the deed to my house there.

A year later, I was done. And my family fortune, or whatever was left, was gone as well. There is a stark reality when the realization finally hits that life as you have known it is over. It also got me questioning the meaning of life or the meaning of my life, to be exact. I didn't take long to ponder, for my recent doctor's visit gave me the most terrifying of answers.

Over the past few months, my body wasn't my own. I stumbled on the walk outside my apartment, my speech was beginning to slur, I had trouble holding onto a glass or lifting a cup. I initially diagnosed the cause as stress or my increasing reliance on alcohol to get me through the day and night. Losing both your lover and your fortune can do that to the best of us, and let us not forget the trauma of my experience with the boys in blue.

Well, after more tests than I could count, it was not what was going on in my outside world that was causing these symptoms. My own body is now betraying me. I have Amyotrophic Lateral Sclerosis, a rather long title for a disease that is attacking my motor neurons. The short form is that ALS is killing me, piece by piece. In a very short period, I will lose all functioning of my limbs, my voice, everything but my brain. I will need a wheelchair to get around and a ventilator to breathe. And I will be fully aware of all that is happening to me

There is no cure.

I am not a courageous man. The thought of being paralyzed, unable to enjoy the simplest pleasures like a walk in the park, a glass of fine wine, or the clasp of your hand in mine is too hard for me to envision. I will take my chances on explaining my decision to take my own life when I meet the Lord before the date he ordained. If he *is truly the compassionate God that is touted, I believe he will understand.*

And so my dearest, loveliest Nell, this is why I must say goodbye. I apologize for adding to your sorrow. As a way of atonement, the Long Island house is in your name. There is no will, so my creditors will not be at your door seeking their blood money.

One of my few regrets is not seeing Teddy grow up to be the fine young man I know he will be. I would have loved to dance with you at his wedding. Yet, I think it best that he remembers me as I am.

I am going to sleep now, thanks to all the pills a number of doctors have willingly given to 'help' me with my condition. My one last thought, and it will be your decision alone, is that a party in my honor would be a lovely send-off. Champagne and good music would be splendid. I leave this world with my last thought of how beautiful you would look and how gay the mood would be. My favorite flower is the calla lily.

I am looking forward to being with Edward. Look up to the evening sky, and the third star to the right is where we will be looking down on you. We will be twinkling.

I love you.
Henry

I don't know how long I sat there. I was unaware I was even crying. Bridget entered the room and seeing me in such a state came immediately to my side. *Is it Master Teddy?* she asked, her voice trembling. *No*, I said quietly. *It is my dearest friend, Henry. He has gone to the Lord, and I expect those gates opened wide to receive him.*

I needed to tell Teddy but not at that moment. *I must go to his apartment and see what must be done.* My tears stopped.

I stood up with a newfound strength. Henry had made the decision that was best for him, not one I would have allowed him to make if I had been given a choice. Henry, dependent on others to feed him, clothe him, and help him breathe was not a life he would want to live. I would miss him every day. When I go to a play that opens my eyes to a new point of view or see a painting whose artist has captured a moment that makes me want to hold my breath or listen to a musician whose soulful melody moves my soul, I will think, *Henry would love this.*

In some ways, I miss him more than Edward. Edward was my rock, but Henry was my light. It is hard to replace those who bring you joy.

Protestants didn't seem to shun suicide as much as Catholics. Henry was buried in the family plot amid all the trappings of a grand farewell. The press reported his death as an accident. I laughed out loud when I saw the article. Henry had been and done many things, but his life as well as his death was anything but an accident.

Less than a week after the funeral, Teddy and I were in the library. Teddy was sitting in front of the fire reading *Treasure Island*, his favorite book, a tall tale of buccaneers and buried gold. He looked up at me, pointing to its cover. *Whoever drew this, Mama, did he know what Jim Hawkins actually looked like, or did he make him up in his head? I think Long John Silver looks like an evil person, yet sometimes he can be a good person. I think sometimes people are not who they seem to be. You think they are nice but then you see them do mean things.*

Teddy didn't wait for me to reply, his voice became more measured. *I think Jim Hawkins and I have a lot in common. His father is dead, too. Why do people die, Mama? I heard someone say that Uncle Henry is now in a better place. Would I be in a better place if I died? I don't think death is better than being with you. I think death is stupid.*

My eyes betrayed my shock. *What they meant, Teddy, is that Uncle Henry is now at rest. And we don't say stupid.*

Why couldn't he rest here? We have plenty of room. He could have stayed here.

I pressed my hand to my mouth to stifle the sob I could feel about to erupt. *I know, Teddy; and I am not sure I can explain. We don't get to keep everyone we love, but we get to remember them. Our faith tells us that they go to heaven, and it sounds like a wonderful place. I think that is what people mean that it is a better place. When someone we love dies, we lose a bit of our heart. We still go on living, but our life has changed. What we can keep alive is our memory of that person. You were very young when your Papa died; but I think because of the stories I have told you about him, I hope you know him.*

Teddy nodded, *Do you miss Papa?*

Absolutely, every day. I still talk to him. I often sit in his chair. When I sit in it, I think of him. It is one of the ways I keep his memory alive for me.

Teddy crawled up on my lap, something he hadn't done for years.

I am going to miss Uncle Henry.

Me, too. I think of him when I hear music. He was a great fan of jazz; Louis Armstrong was his favorite. When I hear Satchmo's – that's what folks call him – gravelly-voice singing or his trumpet playing on the radio, I think of Uncle Henry. Can you think of something of Uncle Henry's that would always remind you of him?

Teddy got quiet, looking into the flames of the fire as if the answer would rise from its now dying embers. *Do you think I could have his golf bag? It is pretty big for me now, but I think I can handle carrying it. Then every time I play, I will think of him.*

That would be lovely. We will look for it among his things when we go out to Long Island. I am pretty sure we can find it there. Do you think I should learn to play golf so that we can play together?

Teddy paused. *No, I think we should ride bikes. I can play golf with my friends.* He picked up *Treasure Island* and continued to read. The conversation was over, but Teddy stayed on my lap until sleep overtook him.

Two weeks later, the golf bag was retrieved and Teddy replaced Henry's clubs with his own. The bag was big and cumbersome when he lifted it onto his shoulders, dwarfing him in both size and weight. Teddy smiled, *This feels perfect.*

Three months later, the party I hosted in Henry's honor had

most of the Manhattan crowd abuzz. The assembled crowd drank French champagne from crystal flutes and cocktails from slim-stemmed glasses. No one gave a thought to Prohibition or the Depression. Women with dresses with no backs, dared men in bow ties and slicked-back hair to touch their bare flesh. Calla lilies were everywhere. Laughter and conversation rose above the sound of the jazz band. There was no grieving, just celebrating. The only thing missing was Henry.

Anne had mentioned that O'Brien was back in New York. I invited him to come to Henry's party, he had essentially saved Henry's life. He was due an invitation.

CHAPTER 21

1933

O'Brien walked me out of the party for Henry. He really didn't have much of a choice. I told him I needed a gentleman's escort to find me a cab, and he was the closest thing to a gentleman I could find. I reminded him he didn't need to bring either his camera or his gun.

I gave the cab driver my address and pulled O'Brien into the cab. O'Brien started to say something, but I put my finger to his lips and kissed him. It just seemed like the most natural thing to do. He kissed me back, stronger, more passionate. He tasted of whiskey. I was getting dizzy, and I knew I couldn't blame it on the wine.

He put his hands through my hair and began to kiss my neck. He whispered my name, which came out more like a moan. He pulled me in, I could feel his heart beating. Or it might have been mine, I was losing myself in the moment. His hands seemed to be everywhere, I began to tremble with desire and anticipation. I thought I might lose control.

Then the driver's voice broke through, *This is the address you gave me, Ma'am, or do you just want me to drive around a bit. I got all night and you two seem to be having a good time back there.*

I caught my breath, *No we will get out here.* O'Brien fumbled for his wallet and paid the driver who winked when he said, *I would offer you my best wishes for a good evening, but it looks like you're going to have a very good evening indeed.* O'Brien climbed out. We were standing in front of the park, the silhouette of two people enjoined as one illuminated by the soft glow of the gas-light street lamp. I took out my house key and took his hand. The invitation to come in was not needed.

O'Brien stopped and kissed me one more time. He whispered in my ear, *Are you sure?*

Yes, Teddy is sleeping over at a friend's house tonight. There is no one home. There is one thing you should know, and I am not sure how to tell you. We were in the house. I dropped my coat on the table. Those violet eyes now searching mine. I took a deep breath, *I am a virgin.* I blushed the color of fuchsia.

O'Brien stopped cold. *You are a what?*

A virgin, trying my best to smile. *I just don't want to disappoint you.*

You are a widow and you are a mother, correct? I nodded affirmatively as he continued. *I wasn't great in biology; but unless the power of the Holy Ghost has been summoned again, the odds of you having retained your virginity are pretty slim.*

I took his hands to my lips and kissed them, I wouldn't let them go. *It is probably time I tell you my story. This is going to take a bit of time, why don't you come into the library. I think we should open a bottle of wine.*

O'Brien looked at me and nodded, *I think we should opt for a cup of tea. I am going to need to be fully focused on this discussion.*

Dawn was breaking when I finished telling my tale. O'Brien had remained quiet for most of the time, only asking questions when I moved too quickly from one scene to the next.

So, if I can sum it up, he said in his seasoned reporter's voice, *you were married to a man who loved another man, whom you also loved. You were all best friends. Your son is Irish, his father deceased, his mother is living in Ireland. He does not know he was adopted, which was also true for you if I recall correctly.*

I nodded, feeling slightly tainted and now quite tired.

I believe I am correct in saying that you have been loved but have not been made love to?

Before I could respond, he stood up, took my hands, and pulled me to him. He gently kissed me.

I will pick you up tomorrow at 4:00 p.m. Pack a weekend bag, bring your hiking shoes. You should go to bed and get some sleep. Your party celebrating Henry's life was a great success. Sleep well and I will see you in less than 12 hours. And with a final kiss, he was gone.

I don't remember going to bed. I felt giddy with happiness and anticipation. When I woke up from a deep and restful slumber, the clock showed the time to be almost 1:00 p.m. I picked it up to further examine it, as I could not remember a time that I ever slept that late.

I could barely eat the tea and toast Bridget brought to my room. I told her I needed my small suitcase and would pack it myself. She gave me a curious look but left me to my own devices. I knew the one thing I would take with me. Once again wrapped in the finest tissues, I found my wedding night peignoir, the one Mama had sent me. I tried it on and the softness of the fabric and the clarity of the color did not disappoint. It was as lovely as the first time I saw it over twenty years ago.

I got Teddy to spend the weekend with Victoria, an arrangement that suited them both, and waited for the doorbell to ring. I was a racehorse in the starting block, my cheeks burning with anticipation. I took a deep breath to calm my nerves.

There was a knock at the door at precisely 4:00 p.m., O'Brien was there. *Ready, Walker?* was his only greeting.

You bet, was my reply. We both laughed out loud as I handed him my suitcase and got into the car. We drove for about four hours, sometimes talking about nothing in particular, sometimes just settling into a comfortable silence.

O'Brien had booked a room for us at the Red Lion Inn in Stockbridge, Massachusetts. Spring was making its way north;

and on this early day in May, the Berkshires smelled of new earth and new awakenings. A perfect choice.

We have much to explore, was O'Brien's only comment to the clerk who welcomed us. I believed I blushed.

O'Brien took me in his arms as soon as the door to our room closed behind us. He kissed me gently on the lips, *We have a dinner reservation at 9:00 p.m. Let's not be late for I am famished in more than one way.*

I changed for dinner, feeling my heart race. Our conversation over dinner was easy but highly charged. I found myself looking at him with different eyes. He was about to become my lover. I was about to take a lover. I giggled out loud.

O'Brien's eyebrows raised, *May I ask what you find so amusing about your fish?*

Oh, the fish is delicious. I was just thinking if I should start calling you by your first name. I don't think I've ever done that either. I winked.

My mother used to say you can call me anything as long as you don't call me late for dinner, he responded, his eyes twinkling. *Perhaps we should be on a first-name basis from now on. Though I was baptized Timothy Patrick, my family calls me Finn. As the youngest of our tribe, I looked to boss my cousins around and became quite the gang leader. My brothers started to call me Finn McCool, after the mythological warrior. The name was shortened to Finn and stuck.* He picked up his napkin and put it on the table. *Since we now are on a first-name basis, I believe it is time for us to return to our room.*

I stood up. *I agree and as much as I like the name Finn, I am more comfortable calling you O'Brien.*

Any name you want, my darling Nell; and he took my arm as we walked up the stairs to our room.

My nerves took over. I had a thousand thoughts going through my mind at once. What was I thinking? What if he found me unattractive? What was I expected to do? The fears and doubts from my wedding night all those many years ago came flooding back.

We got to the room, and O'Brien left to retrieve the bottle of wine he was having chilled. My hands were shaking as I slipped on the peignoir and said a prayer to Mama this would all go well. I had not finished the amen when O'Brien returned.

I stared at him, fear, excitement, trepidation – I couldn't differentiate my feelings. He put down the bottle and came over and put my face in his hands. *You are beautiful. More beautiful than I ever dreamed of, and I have had this dream and not just at night. You crowd my waking minutes. It is your face I see when I close my eyes at night. I have longed for this moment.* He kissed me gently. I became bold, unbuttoning his shirt, running my hands over his tightly-muscled torso.

He gently undressed me, removing the silks covering my body, laying them on the chair with a degree of reverence I found both amusing and heartwarming. He took my hand and moved me to the bed and started to kiss me in places that now demanded to be explored. Dozens of kisses on my neck, my breasts, then he started to kiss my thighs raising his tongue even higher inside me until I succumbed to a swirling mass of desire. I cried out with the sweetness, the tearing power of it. I shouted sounds exploding from depths I never knew existed in me. I clung to him, trembling with each stroke. He made sure I was ready. I called *O'Brien* as I opened up to him. At last, I could feel him inside me. There was a brief moment of pain followed by a trembling running through my every being. He brought his hands under me and brought me closer to him. We were one, joined together by passion and what felt like love.

When we were spent, we lay together, entwined, worn out, and dazed. He was stroking my hair as I started to cry. Those violet eyes locked into mine with concern and compassion, *Oh, my dearest Nell, I hope I didn't hurt you. I tried so hard but I just couldn't control...*

I put my fingers to his lips. *Shh...wonderful, this was wonderful, you are wonderful. These are tears of happiness and a bit of relief.* I gave a bit of a grin, *Could we do it again?*

Kissing me gently, he smiled, *You just need to give me a moment to recover.*

I'll do my best, but don't take too long. You know me well enough to know that I am a woman who doesn't like waiting around. I kissed his chest and lay my head upon it.

True to his word, it wasn't long before he reached for me again. This time, our rhythms were stronger, more in sync, and he instinctively knew where to touch, where to guide me. I had never felt so free and yet so entwined. We fell asleep in each other's arms. I woke up to see the sun glistening through the windows, a spring morning welcoming me to a new world in more ways than one.

The day was too beautiful to stay in bed, no matter how strong the pull.

O'Brien knew the area, the hiking trails were a short drive away from the Inn. He took his camera. I saw the world differently from that day on.

We were searching for signs of the spring awakening, like buds breaking open with new leaves emerging, spring ferns popping up and new birds arriving. I learned to see these things with the eye of a photographer. O'Brien saw the same things I did but explored them with an eye that saw light, details, shadows.

He stopped in front of a limb of a tree whose leaves were just beginning to bud. I could just see the trace of green against the brown, weathered limb. *Look at this*, he exclaimed, excitement in his voice. *Magnificent the way the sun is capturing the green. There are still morning dew drops on the new leaves, so many shades of green,* and he snapped his camera, lost in the moment.

We hiked until the sun was setting. Walking hand-in-hand, sometimes stumbling over the rocky terrain, O'Brien stopping to describe how this landscape would look as a photograph. *It is all about the art of seeing, Nell. I see things in a way others don't. The pictures tell their own story and can make a difference.*

He was one with his camera.

On the road finding our way back to The Red Lion, we found an Irish pub that looked like it would be the perfect ending of a perfect day. The owners were recent arrivals from the old sod, as they called it. They recognized O'Brien as one of their own and started to talk with him in the old language, Gaelic.

You are a man of many talents, I exclaimed, wondering what else I had to learn about this man.

My grandfather spoke the Irish his whole life and made sure his grands did the same. I am not as comfortable with the language as my older brothers, but I made sure I learned enough so they couldn't talk about me behind my back.

I envy you, your family, I added wistfully.

You should wait until you meet them before you make that statement, was his quick reply, his eyes merry as he took my hand. *I still live with my sister and her family in the house I was raised in. That address will always be home.*

The fire burned bright and filled the night with good cheer. We were a couple, in love and in like with each other.

We could barely make it up the stairs to our room with our clothes still on. It had been too long since we had made love, and there would be no stopping us that night or the next. We spent the weekend exploring the woods around us during the day and each other in the evening.

At breakfast on our last morning, we talked about Roosevelt and our hopes that he could pull the country out of the ravages the Depression was causing. I poured myself another cup of tea. O'Brien took my hand when I had finished.

I leave for Washington, DC tomorrow. My train leaves at 7:00 a.m.

When will you be back?

I have tried all weekend to tell you but just couldn't find the right time. It will be months, most likely a year, before I return to New York. I have a new assignment.

The words rang as clear as shots to my heart.

I am to travel throughout the United States and photograph what this depression has done to people. Roosevelt's administration believes my pictures can move the government to act. I am to document how people are trying to survive, trying to find work, trying to care for their children. I need to capture their hopelessness in a country that should promise them so much more.

I pulled my hand away. *You are leaving me? You are leaving me after this weekend?* the words shouting in my head. I was sure I was screaming, but no one in the dining room looked our way.

I care about you, Nell, care about you more than I have ever cared about another person. But I can't stay still. I have to be where the action is. I never stop seeing the picture that needs to be taken, the one that explains what is happening without needing words. I believe if you search your heart, you understand this. You understand me. His eyes met mine, he covered my hands with his.

My darling Nell, I don't mean to hurt you. I just can't be anything else but me. I need to be on the move. I can't turn that off and on. I will get back to New York. We can be with each other when I am here. And once I know where I will be, you can meet me for a weekend.

Tears began streaming down my cheeks. The world once so clear became blurry. I shook my head slowly. *That is not enough for me, O'Brien. I need to be more than just convenient for you. I want to be with you. You. Not the memory of you. Not the dream of you. I want the smell of your pipe to permeate the house. I want you to show me how color and light dance together. I want you to touch me in places that make me lose my breath. I want you to be the first thing I see in the morning. I want you to be the last thing I see at night. I want to introduce you to Teddy.* I got up from the table. *It's time we get back to New York and our lives.*

We packed in silence. There was nothing more to say. We got into the car and O'Brien started to speak. I put my fingers to his lips. *No more talk, O'Brien. Tell me stories of Irish heroes, sing me Irish ballads.*

He nodded.

He told me of Queen Maeve of Connaught, a decisive and forceful leader, who assembled a mighty army when her equal status with her husband was called into question. O'Brien briefly squeezed my hand as he told of her famous beauty and sexual prowess. Then came the tragic love story of Oisin and Niamh who traveled to Tir na Óg, an island of everlasting youth and beauty. It was Oisin's desire to leave this Eden and return to Ireland that caused his death. In between the tales, O'Brien's tenor filled the space. He sang. Songs of love – for sweethearts, for the land. Songs of hope, songs of struggle. Songs that made you want to laugh, songs that could make you weep.

We pulled up to the house. My hands clapped my approval. *That was lovely, O'Brien. I now know what it feels like to be Irish. Happiness and sorrow, all at once. Just as you predicted.*

O'Brien took me in his arms and kissed me. A kiss I returned. One last kiss, one last memory.

He started to get out of the car, but I put my hand on the door and stopped him. I picked up my bag and looked into those lovely violet eyes. *Please don't. I need to do this on my own. Should you ever decide you can stay in one place, please let me know. I would like to share that space with you.*

Stay safe.

He mumbled in reply: *At mé i ngrá leat.*

I walked up the stairs and unlocked the door. I didn't turn around to watch the car pull away.

I didn't think my heart could break again. I was wrong.

Days later I got a picture. I was alone on the path that had brought us to the river. I was gazing ahead into the distance, and the photo captured both a sense of peace and a simultaneous sense of movement. O'Brien was both an artist and a reporter. He captured my spirit in this one shot in a way that I could not describe yet could be read. Attached was a note with his sister's address and a brief message, *If you want to reach me, Mary Ellen will know how to find me.*

I tucked the picture and the address with my Mama Letters for safekeeping. I swallowed my disappointment and focused on the future, a future where love would not be mine to hold at night. I had done it before, but it didn't get easier though the path was well-trodden.

CHAPTER 22

1935

The years went by quickly. Teddy was growing up. He turned 15 and was in that stage where you could see glimpses of the man he would become and the child that he was outgrowing

It was Christmas recess and he was home from boarding school. I had enrolled him in Edward's alma mater, St. Mark's. It was hard not to have him at the house, but I knew he was to follow his father's path.

I was caught up with the preparations for the holidays. Teddy did all the things I asked, helped host our annual Children's Christmas Party, accompanied me to Midnight Mass at St. Patrick's Cathedral, feigned some degree of enthusiasm when he unwrapped his presents. We were at the Monroe's for Christmas lunch. Anne's boys had always looked upon Teddy as a younger brother, and Teddy appeared to relish every moment when he was in their company. Not this day. He sat in the corner of the room, quiet and withdrawn, either not listening or not interested in the raucous tales of college life Benjamin and Franklin were sharing with us.

When we came home that evening, Teddy went right to bed.

The next morning, the house was quiet, as if it needed a

moment to catch its breath. It was snowing. The park looked like it was in a snow globe. Large white flakes drifted slowly to the ground, hanging onto the bare limb of a tree for one last second until they slowly drifted to the ground. Teddy came downstairs later than even his normal teenage wake-up time. I noticed dark circles under his eyes.

He shook his head when I asked if he wanted anything to eat.

Please tell me what is bothering you. You are clearly distressed.

He kept his head down. *I don't want to go back there, Mama. Back to St. Mark's.*

I was shocked. St. Mark's had been Edward's alma mater, and Teddy had thrived there last year. *May I ask why?*

He slumped into a chair. *There is a boy in my class, Roberto. He is not like the other kids, keeps to himself, doesn't play sports, a bit of a loner. Some of the other boys started giving him a tough time, calling him names like Guido, saying that his father probably shines their fathers' shoes.*

He looked up at me, *I wasn't one of them, Mama. Roberto is really good at science, my least favorite subject, so I asked him if would be my lab partner. I got to know him pretty well. He is at the school on scholarship.*

One night, things got carried away. One of the guys hid all of Roberto's uniforms so he had to wear his own clothes to class. He told the headmaster that he had left them at home. He didn't snitch, and he's the one who got detention. Things got even worse after that. It was as if the kids on the floor couldn't stop. Roberto had become an obsession. They locked him in the janitor's closet overnight. Then one day, Roberto cut across the football field as practice ended. One of the players told him he had no business on their turf and punched him. Roberto fell to the ground, his nose bleeding. As he lay in the snow, others stomped on him. One even spit on him. Roberto came to our lab the next day and could barely walk. Some of the boys snickered as he walked in. After class, I got out of him what had happened, but he didn't give me names. I wanted him to go to the headmaster, to tell him that this had to stop. Roberto wouldn't let me, said he would lose his scholarship; he would embarrass his parents. They were too proud of his being at St. Mark's. He said he could take it. We would be going home soon.

Teddy's chin began to quiver. *I got really mad, Mama. This wasn't fair. I figured out who threw the first punch at Roberto. He lives in my hall, boasts about being a tough guy, bragging that he can do pretty much what he wants at school because his father is a trustee. When I confronted him, he just laughed, telling me that Roberto didn't belong here, that he was taking a spot that should be given to someone more like us. He emphasized the word 'us' as if I was an accomplice in what was happening.*

Teddy looked into the fire, his gaze troubled. *I went to the headmaster. I didn't tell Roberto. I told the story in the 'what ifs.' What if one of our students was being picked on? What if the situation was starting to escalate? The headmaster told me my imagination was running rampant. That such things as I was describing didn't happen at this school. People like 'us' didn't do such things unless provoked.*

Teddy looked up at me for the first time. *I don't want to be one of the 'us,' Mama. I just want to be me.*

My heart was breaking. *You don't have to go back, Teddy. But do you think that will help Roberto? Would it not be better for you to stand up for him? To take a stand about what is wrong and try to correct it?*

Teddy got up slowly. *I know, Mama. I've read your articles and Aunt Rachel has talked about things like this forever. I'll go back. Maybe I can make a difference.*

Teddy went back after the recess. Two days later, I got a phone call from the headmaster. Teddy had been beaten, he was in the hospital with broken ribs and a slight concussion.

I drove to the hospital, horrible things flashing through my mind. The winter wind was cold, my icy fingers held onto the steering wheel in a death grip. Three hours later, I parked the car in front of the hospital. It was small, a former country estate that had been bequeathed to the school and whose exterior retained the look of its former grandeur. Once inside the doors, the air was stuffy, smelling of bleach and peroxide. I ran down the hall looking for Teddy's room, the walls were gray and scraped in places where the trolleys and gurneys had left their mark.

I found the room and rushed in. He was awake, his eyes opened wide as he cried out, *Mama!* I kissed his forehead and did not feel the tears that dampened his hair.

It's alright, Mama. I'm going to be okay.

Oh, Teddy, my darling son. What happened? The headmaster called to tell me you were in the hospital but not much else. I got here as quickly as I could.

Teddy looked at his bandaged ribs. *I am pretty sure I know who did this but there is no proof.* Teddy closed his eyes. *I had a confrontation with the football player, remember I told you about him?*

I nodded, taking his hand in mine, my eyes never leaving his face.

I warned him to back off picking on Roberto or I would report him to the headmaster. Teddy looked down at his bandaged ribs, *I didn't see it coming. I was hit from behind. The next thing I remember, I was here and then you walked in.*

Teddy flinched in pain. *What makes me mad is that I wasn't able to help Roberto. That is all I wanted to do.*

I know, my dearest love. You are coming home. We are leaving here as soon so you are well enough.

I made the preparations to bring him back to New York City, but this was an injustice I couldn't tolerate. I spoke with the headmaster who expressed his profound apologies. He dismissed my claim of who the culprits might be. *All our boys come from the best of families, Mrs. Walker. I am sure this sad event was caused by outsiders. We called in the local authorities, but they were not able to discover who attacked your son.*

I shook with rage. *Attack is the right word, Headmaster; and my son is withdrawing from this school as of this day. Whatever moral code St. Mark's once adhered to has eroded. My husband valued the education he received here. Sadly, what my son has learned is that there is a set of rules for one segment of the population and another set of rules for the others. I am taking my son home, but I am not done.*

Teddy came home to a celebration honoring his bravery. Rachel called him valiant, Victoria smothered him with affection.

Dear Mama,

> *When do people learn to be cruel? Who is their teacher?*
> *Teddy was hurt because he stood up for someone else. He saw a boy in his class being bullied, and he wouldn't just sit back and let that happen. I encouraged him to speak up. He ended up in the hospital, he was beaten up. I cannot help but feel that this was as much my fault as it was the boy or boys who threw those punches.*
> *I have written to the headmaster, to the board of trustees challenging them to stop this kind of harassment. I was summarily dismissed. If Edward were alive and the author of the same missive, I am convinced stronger action would be taken. It appears that I am viewed as a hysterical, single mother whose son lacks the proper male guidance in his life. The last letter from the headmaster implied that Teddy might be the cause for this clash, that he might be hanging around with the wrong type of people. I am furious and have no place to direct my anger except at me.*
> *I remember Grace's story about how her father had been killed for trying to make a difference. Trying to do the right thing. I had led my son down that same path and he had suffered for it.*
> *I failed to watch over my son, Mama. I failed to protect him. I cannot let that happen again.*

> *I love you, Mama.*
> *Your Nell*

Teddy had started at his new school, a day school that Anne had recommended. I wanted him to be home at night, I wanted to know he would be safe. I became fretful. He couldn't leave the house without me wanting to know his every move, where he was going, who he was going with, and when he would be home. I no longer trusted that the world would keep him safe.

Spring had finally arrived in New York. The days were warmer, brighter, but I was still wrapped in the darkness of the fear that would not let me go. It was a Saturday morning, Teddy had come in from a morning run. He had grown taller, fuller in the last few months, the boy shredding, the man forming.

I started my inquisition, where had he been, what had he been doing. Teddy pulled himself up and I realized he was now looking down at me, beating me in height by at least four inches.

Stop it. Mama, you must stop it. I am almost sixteen years old. I know what I am doing. What happened at St. Mark's was not your fault.

I shook my head, *I should have never sent you back there. You should have stayed home after Christmas. You wouldn't have gotten hurt. It was my fault.*

As Papa would have said, Poppycock! I'm glad I went back. You and Aunt Rachel have taught me that I should stand up for what I believe is the right thing to do. I don't want to grow up to be one of those people who run away, who doesn't try to make a difference.

But you got hurt.

I sure did. He grinned, a smile that lit up his eyes. *Next time I take on a football team, I won't do it alone. Lesson learned.*

I kissed him on the cheek. My son was becoming a man before my very eyes. *I've learned one, too. So, fewer questions, I promise; but I will still worry. I believe that comes with the role of being your mother.*

He gave me the okay sign and ran up the stairs.

CHAPTER 23

THE NAZIS

Rachel came to the house in obvious distress. She had been crying, something I had never seen her do. Thanksgiving was over, and my thoughts were focused on preparing for the upcoming holiday season. Teddy would be coming home from his first year at Harvard, and I wanted the house to look perfect. However, the look on her face told me all I needed to know. We were going to have a conversation and one that mattered to her.

The parlor was being turned into a forest of evergreen wreaths and pine. I moved us into the library. Rachel took her place in Edward's chair that remained in the same spot all these many years. *Have you seen the headline in today's papers?* she asked, waving today's *New York Times* in her hands. *It is only three weeks since the Nazis terrorized their Jewish citizens. The papers are labeling it Kristallnacht, the night of broken glass. Over 7,500 Jewish businesses and 1,000 synagogues were destroyed. I think the world is going mad.* She shook her head in disbelief.

I said nothing but couldn't agree with her more.

My father just received a letter from his cousin in Berlin, a doctor who treats patients no matter their beliefs. Jewish or Christian, he administers to them all. Rachel's hands started to shake. *He wrote he was on his way to the hospital when he saw broken shop windows and shards of glass lying in the streets. The fruit market in his neighborhood was destroyed, someone had painted the word "Jewish Pig" on the door and smeared a Star of David with mud.* She fingered that same talisman on a chain around her neck.

Across the street were three Nazi Stormtroopers. They grabbed a man who was doing nothing but walking down the street. He had the Yellow Star on his coat. For no reason, for no reason, they beat this poor man until he was left helpless and bleeding on the sidewalk. Without a second thought, our cousin went to help. One of these brown uniformed thugs pushed him aside as he began to help, questioning why he should want to help a Jew. Our cousin responded that he was a doctor, and he had taken an oath to help those in pain.

The Nazi spit on the man lying on the ground and then glared at our cousin. "Perhaps you should think of ways to help your Fatherland rather than saving Jews."

I shuddered at the picture Rachel was creating.

We knew life was becoming increasingly difficult. Three years ago the Nuremberg laws expelled Jews from public office in all of Germany. The Nazis had begun their systematic process to determine who was Jewish. Our family thought that my cousin would be safe as his mother was not Jewish. Although she had converted, she had been designated 'Aryan.' My cousin believed his 'first degree-mixed race' designation and his standing in the medical community would shield him.

Tears fell softly from Rachel's eyes; she looked vulnerable and frightened. This was a different Rachel than the one who laughed when she had come here drenched from the hoses the firemen aimed at her. She had seen injustice and faced prejudices but never had I seen her look and sound fearful. Until that day.

The Times and religious leaders are speaking out, condemning the violence. They are calling for their readers and congregations to support Jews in both Germany and here at home, but they are getting little real support. Everyone agrees it is outrageous, but no one is doing anything about it. She stood up and began to pace around the room, shaking her head in disbelief. *The German newspapers reported that the violence was spontaneous – a public retaliation in response to the assassination of a minor German diplomat in Paris by a Jewish teenager. Who had ever heard of that man, someone named Ernst von Rath? Clearly, he is only one of Hitler's henchmen who provided the excuse needed to start the assault.*

Powerless, I feel powerless. I don't know what to do. She stopped in front of the fireplace, staring into the flames as if they could provide the answer.

I picked up the paper and scanned the headlines and the pictures. While the photos were condemning, I knew what I was looking for. It was what I did in opening the paper each morning. I searched for the photo credit. There it was, the name O'Brien. He was in the midst of all that was going wrong in the world.

I shook off my combined sense of gloom and relief, focusing on the conversation as Rachel's voice got stronger. *My father called this morning absolutely distraught. The Daily News blames the violence on the German economy. As if killing innocent people and destroying their property was justification for the reparations the Germans had been forced to pay for starting World War I.*

And with only the briefest of smiles she added, *Poppycock, as Edward would have said.*

She shook her head, the tears gone and now sounding like the Rachel I knew and loved. *And our President, Mr. FDR, the one we worked so hard to get elected and we had such high hopes for, does nothing. The plight of the Jews in Nazi-controlled lands is getting worse, and our country does nothing.*

I started to say something and she slowly shook her head. *Thank you for listening, as always, Nell. But I need to think about what I can do. For now, I am going to Brooklyn. I need to be with my family. My father is heartsick about all of this, and he is an old man. I don't want him to be one more of Hitler's casualties.*

And with that, she gave me a quick kiss on the cheek and was gone.

I stared long and hard at the photos in the paper. *Where are you, O'Brien?* In the five years since he had left with his camera, the occasional postcard would be sent always with the same message: *Thinking of you. O'Brien.*

The weeks passed, the holidays were over and nothing seemed to be happening. Rachel was beside herself. Now back in true fighting form, she took off to Washington to lobby for a change in the immigration policy. Once again, as in the early days of labor reform, she turned to Frances Perkins and Robert Wagner, supporters of the progressive movements throughout their careers, to be willing champions.

The news from Europe was as chilling as the February winds that swirled down Manhattan's avenues. Rachel came back to New York flush with excitement. *Perkins has gotten Roosevelt to allow Germans here on temporary visas to extend their stay and Wagner is the man of the hour,* she proclaimed, throwing her coat on an open chair and not bothering to take off her boots. When she saw me look down at her feet and before she could step on one of Edward's prized Oriental carpets, she gave me a look of chagrin and slipped off the boots, leaving her stockings with holes prominently displayed.

Sorry. And for the look of my stockings, as well. My mother would be mortified.

I couldn't help but smile. *Continue, how does Robert Wagner continue to be your knight in shining armor?*

Quite easily. He has just introduced legislation that will admit 20,000 German children under the age of 14 to come to the United States outside of the immigration quotas. The best news is Eleanor Roosevelt has lent her support to the bill. It is the very first time she has ever done this. We will surely get it to pass. We are going to save children. Maybe we can make a difference after all. She was almost dancing as she delivered the news.

Then the tide turned and the bill was never voted on. Opponents argued that the legislation would take resources and jobs away from American children. Rachel's frustration was all-consuming and her anger at our government and its callousness was challenging her soul.

Dear Mama,

I am not sure what is happening in the world. My dear friend Rachel is going through the most horrible time. She is Jewish. She has relatives in Europe who are living through times that are hard to describe in a civilized world.

Her cousin and his family were seeking asylum in this country – this country that had opened its arms to immigrants for so many years. Rachel's father was able to secure passage for them on the German transatlantic liner The St. Louis, leaving from Hamburg for Havana, Cuba, where they would stay until their turn came up on the waiting list for a U.S. visa.

Despite all the work and high hopes, her cousin and his family, along with hundreds of others, never made it to safety. Our own country refused to accept them. The newspapers started to cover their plight that read like a diary of the doomed. Roosevelt chose to do nothing.

Then less than a month after it started its course for freedom, The St. Louis was sent back to Europe. Cuba would not accept its passengers. Neither would our own country.

I don't understand, Mama. I think about O'Brien's grandfather who had sailed to this country with a dream and a desire. I think about my birth parents who lost so much while hoping for so much more. We are supposed to be the land that welcomes those who need refuge, those who want a better life. What has happened to the country whose statue in the New York Harbor welcomes the huddled masses yearning to breathe free?

I am heartsick for my friend, for her family, and for my country. What is to become of us all?

> *I love you, Mama.*
> *Your Nell*

The day after I wrote the Mama Letter, Rachel called and asked if we could have lunch. *Absolutely, but why such a formal request? Don't you usually just come by and then we find time for some lunch? Should I ask Victoria and Anne to join us?*

Not this time. And she hung up the phone.

She came the next day, looking grave and determined. Our conversation was stilted. There was something in the air, I could feel it. I couldn't describe it. We sat down for lunch, she chatted with Mrs. Campbell and asked Bridget how her family was faring. Yet there was a cloud hanging over our conversation. Given the advance notice, Mrs. Campbell prepared one of Rachel's favorite meals, tomato soup with grilled cheese sandwiches.

Rachel's eyes sought mine. *I leave tomorrow for the Netherlands, If I can't do anything to help here, I may be of use over there.*

I couldn't catch my breath. *What will you be doing?*

Rachel took a bit of her sandwich, the grilled cheese oozing out of the bread and leaving a small trail of cheddar down her chin. *I am not sure. The Dutch are helping Jews as well as Catholics who need to go into hiding. I have a contact in Amsterdam whom I am to meet. I can't share much more, but I will be helping people to stay safe. I can't sit on the sidelines hoping someone else will do what I know needs to be done.*

I was finally able to articulate my worst fear: *I am afraid for you.*

I know and I love you for it. I am afraid, too. I am an American, so I will have more protection than most. I must do something, Nell. You, of all people, know me well enough that I can't be an observer.

I nodded, my voice thin. *And I am still afraid.*

Rachel nodded, *I am afraid for the world. The world in which we live and whatever world will be left to Teddy. Hitler and the Nazis must be stopped or civilization as we know it will end.*

Lunch was over quickly. All that needed to be said, was said.

I walked her to the door. *Promise me you will write. Promise me you will stay safe.*

She nodded slowly. *Best if you stay in contact with my parents, I will try to get word to them. I will do my best to stay safe, promise.*

We embraced fiercely. She stepped back, *We have come a long way since those days following the Shirtwaist Triangle Factory Fire. You are a good friend, Nell. You have made a difference in my life. I am a better person for having known you.*

And I, you, I responded, tears streaming down my cheeks.

She walked down the stairs, turned to give a final wave, and walked away.

CHAPTER 24

1942

I t was early afternoon, but the sky was darkened by thick folds of gray clouds. It felt much later. I was in the dining room, drinking my third cup of tea to take away the chill of the day when I looked up to find him standing there. It was Teddy, and he was in uniform.

Teddy, I'm so surprised to see you. I got up and gave him a hug, one he didn't give back.

I stepped back. Before I could ask a question, he simply said, *I've enlisted. We need to talk, Mother.*

Of course, but I don't understand. You said you planned to finish law school and—

Teddy raised his hand, stopping me in midstream of my sentence. *My plan changed. Much has changed. Who am I, Mother, who am I really?* His eyes never left mine. I knew what he meant. This was the conversation I prayed would never happen.

What do you know?

I received a letter from a woman in Philadelphia. She says that she is my Aunt Helena. He pulled out a letter, and I recognized Helena's writing on the envelope, even after all these years.

She is my mother's sister. I haven't seen or talked to her in years.

She wrote to tell me I am not your son.

Helena is many things, but she is not a liar. What has she written you? The word '*Why?*' screaming in my head.

She wrote she had recently met a woman named Phyllis Morgan who volunteers in the New York chapter of the same charity as this Helena does in Philadelphia. As they were talking, somehow your name came up in the conversation. Helena asked if she knew of you. This Morgan woman said that, while you had never met, you had become friends with her dressmaker over 20 years ago. It seems Helena made a comment that it would be like you to befriend the help as you never had regard for your social standing in the community. This Morgan woman continued that the situation was all quite strange. One day this dressmaker, she couldn't remember her name, just up and disappeared.

Maude, I whispered, *the dressmaker she was talking about is named Maude.*

Teddy seemed not to hear. *So this Mrs. Morgan said she asked the other servants what happened. While no one knew for sure, there was downstairs gossip that this Maude had gotten herself, as Helena described, 'in the family way.' The servants believed she may have gone to Ireland, the only place she ever talked about.*

This Aunt Helena wrote that Mrs. Morgan found it odd that this dressmaker never came back to retrieve the back wages due to her. Since I was born in Ireland at the same time this story unfolds, Aunt Helena believes this dressmaker was my mother, though my paternity is still in question.

Who am I, Mother, who am I? I believe I have the right to know. Teddy's voice was like steel, cutting me with every word.

The words gripped my throat like barbed wire. *Come into the library. I will tell you all.*

We walked into the room silently and separately, each trying to find our way through this tangle of emotion. I needed Edward by my side. I needed Edward. I sat in Edward's chair, Teddy remained standing.

I had always intended to tell you the story of your birth and all the women who loved you, most of whom have always been part of your life.

I thought someday I would find the right moment. Then Papa died. It never seemed like the right time.

Teddy snarled, *You'd better today.*

I looked him in the eye, eyes so like mine. *Teddy, I simply forget that I didn't give birth to you. I held you for the first time when you were less than an hour old. But yes, you were born in my heart, not under it.*

I told him Maude's story, with precision and clarity.

So, my father never knew about me? Never knew Maude was pregnant?

That is correct. Maude only found out that Billy Conlon had been killed through the newspapers. No one except Mrs. Monroe, Tory, your father, and me knew she had gotten married. Those were different times, Teddy. Politics and religion tore families apart.

Where is she now?

I shook my head, *I don't know. The last time I saw her, we were in Dublin. She was going to stay in Ireland, but I don't know if she did or where she settled. She wanted what was best for you. You were the gift she gave me. I can't imagine what my life would have been like if you weren't part of it.*

He walked to the door. *This is too much for me to reconcile. I need to get away from this, from you, from all that I have known, and figure out who I am. I have been accepted into the Officers Candidate School, and my train leaves in an hour. I will write to you when I know more about where I will be going and when.*

I took his hand in mine, putting it to my lips as Edward used to do to me. *I love you, Teddy; and never once did I mean to hurt you, to cause you pain.*

He gave me a brief hug. *This is hard, Mother. I love you, I do, but this is hard.*

I stood at the door and watched him walk away. He didn't look back.

I went back into the library and returned to my spot in Edward's chair. I pulled my knees to my chest and folded my arms on top, resting my head in the crook of my elbow. I was alone with my thoughts, my feelings, myself. Everything looked familiar and yet strange. What if I lose Teddy to the war? What if I have already lost Teddy? I blamed myself for not letting him know the truth sooner. I, more than anyone, knew the pain such news brings. I blamed Edward for having died too soon. He would have known the right thing to say or do. I blamed Aunt Helena. If her objective was to make my life miserable, she had exceeded her goal.

My vision blurred, too many tears, too much heartache, and enough blame to go around. Teddy was going to war. I knew we had to stand up to Hitler; I knew even before Rachel left for Amsterdam. I have seen the newsreels with the faces of thousands of women waving goodbye to their soldier sons and husbands. I understood Teddy would not, or could not, sit by and let the fight happen without him in it. But why now? Why when there is a rift between us? I was scared that something might happen to him. How could I live if this was the last time I saw him?

I fell asleep in the chair. The moon was shining through the windows, pouring a silver light through its panes. I felt cold and stiff. I found my way to my bedroom and pulled the covers close to my face. A fitful sleep ensued. I dreamt of Edward. He was taking my hands to his lips, telling me he was with me. I woke up with a jolt. Closing my eyes once again, sleep sought its rightful due.

The next morning, I woke up to face whatever the day would bring. The phone rang, it was Rachel's father. He had just received a telegram from one of his relatives in London, Rachel was missing.

CHAPTER 25

1943

It was mid-March and the world showed no signs of spring. A storm had been brewing for days; a steel gray blanket of clouds covered the tops of the buildings. I was looking outside as the smattering of raindrops gave way to a healthy downpour when the doorbell rang. I remember thinking whoever was there would be drenched from the relentless cascade of water now soaking all living creatures.

I was still lost in thought when Bridget came into the room. In her hand was a telegram, the envelope damp but no mistaking its origin.

This came for you.

I began to shake all over. There was not a mother, wife, or sister of a soldier who did not know what the telegram meant. The telegram sent off a siren in my head.

Teddy had written that he was in England and was learning to fly. A couple of brief letters followed with no mention made of our last conversation. The piece of paper Bridget was holding in her hand would tell me whether he was dead or alive.

I just stared at it.

Bridget asked if she should open it and read it to me. I must have nodded yes. After she tore open the envelope, I whispered, *Is he?* my heart beating faster than I thought possible.

Bridget walked over to me. *He is missing, ma'am.*

She handed me the small piece of paper, the words of dread blazing from it.

The Secretary of War desires me to express his deep regrets that your son, Lieutenant Edward John William Walker, has been reported missing in action since February 6, 1943. If further details or other information are received, you will be promptly notified.

He is alive, Bridget, I said. *I would know if my son was dead. We are not to give up.*

I gasped for air. I felt like I was suffocating. This was limbo. I was caught between the emotions of hope and hopelessness. Then hopelessness took over. I was swallowed into a black hole. The pain was too much to bear. Everyone was gone: Edward, Henry, O'Brien, Rachel, and now Teddy. I was grieving for the lives I had lost and the life I had never known. First came the night sweats where rivers of salty panic soaked the whole bed, then heart palpitations, blinding headaches, "explosions" in my eyeballs leaving me limp, and finally, full-body spasms resembling epileptic fits. The pain was just too much to bear.

For the next three days, I just sat in Edward's chair in the library. Bridget would come into the room with a tray of food that she would return to the kitchen untouched a few hours later. I didn't turn on a light, darkness surrounded me on the outside and in my soul. The people I had loved on this earth were gone or were missing. Questions from the past, still unanswered, tortured my soul. I began to wonder who I was. I was born in Ireland. Where? Did I still have family there? Was Margaret still alive? Did she know about me? Miss me? Love me? Why wouldn't O'Brien stay with me? Does Maude mourn the child she never knew? Is Rachel alive? Is Teddy alive?

I retreated from the world. I would see no one, talk to no one.

I heard the clicking of her heels. Victoria walked into the

library still wearing her hat and coat. Bridget following close behind. The two of them opened the curtains, letting the afternoon light find its way inside.

Victoria turned towards me, she looked taller, more in charge. *Nell, we are worried about you. You are not eating, not sleeping, not bathing. I cannot imagine the pain you are in. You are living your worst nightmare. But you are living, and those of us who love you dearly want to be sure you continue to do so.*

I shook my head slowly. *I am tired. Edward died and then Henry. Now Teddy is lost. Rachel is missing. I feel like I am a puppet whose strings have been cut. I can't find the strength to do anything to make my life come together again.*

Victoria tossed her coat on the settee, its fur lining looking like a bear that had found its spot to hibernate. Her hat then followed. My tiny sanctuary was looking disorganized and cluttered. I felt a wave of panic.

Victoria turned to face me. *I have given Bridget the number of a doctor I have contacted. His patients are women dealing with issues such as you are. He has a lovely spot in Westchester County where he attends to both their physical and emotional needs. I want you to think about it. No, to be exact, I have done your thinking for you. We should just agree on when you should go.*

Victoria looked over at Bridget, who was taking in every word and whose eyes never left my face. *Could you please ask Mrs. Campbell to make some tea and toast for us? If she has any of her muffins to add to the tray, it would be lovely.*

I continued to sit still, feeling more like an extra rather than a key player in the plot unfolding.

Victoria came over and took my hand. *While Bridget is getting us a tray, I am going to draw you a warm bath.* She walked me to my room. The drapes were drawn, the bed coverings removed, but the sheets untouched. She went to prepare my bath while I took off the only clothes I had worn for the past three days. Somehow, seeing them on the floor was like shedding skin, a layer that was dried up and used. I found my way to the bathroom and slipped into the tub. As the warm water washed over me, time became suspended. Victoria shampooed my hair, warm, soapy suds dripped down my back. I began to feel clean, I allowed myself to feel. Victoria handed me a robe as she stepped away from the tub. The mirrors, steamed from the hot water and the cool air, streaked our forms beyond recognition.

I walked the few steps back to my bedroom. Bridget had laid out a clean dressing gown that smelled of lavender. I slipped it over my head, the cloth felt soft and familiar.

I looked at Victoria, *Why? Why did you come?*

She gave a smile. *Because you need me. I am your friend.*

I sat down at the dressing table, and Victoria brushed my hair. Smooth, even strokes that made my curls, now streaked with gray, fall softly into place.

Victoria put the brush down. *Lovely. Now let us go downstairs to see what lovely tray Mrs. Campbell has arranged for us. I will read to you from Pride & Prejudice. Let us start when Elizabeth goes to visit her friend Charlotte and the insufferable Mr. Collins. That begins my favorite part.*

We sat in the library where a fire had been started and the tea tray delivered. The warmth of the fire, the tea, and friendship comforted me. Victoria read to me for hours. She had a voice for characters; and for the afternoon I was caught up in life in the English countryside, rooting for Lizzy and the proud Mr. Darcy to find true love.

Victoria left as the sun was setting. *This is better. We will see what tomorrow brings.*

I went upstairs to my bed and slept for the first time.

I woke up when the sun was well up in the heavens. I went into the dining room to find a pot of tea and the sound of bacon popping in its own grease. The smell was intoxicating. Mrs. Campbell came in and laid before me a soft-boiled egg sitting up straight in its blue and yellow trimmed porcelain cup surrounded by red and yellow bacon, charred and crisp. My mouth watered. I took my first bite.

As I finished eating, leaving only a few scraps of the meal I had just devoured, I looked outside my window to see a cardinal perched on a tree staring back at me. For whatever reason, connecting with this small, brightly-colored bird made me feel better. Or perhaps the sun coming through the windows shook my gloom. I felt less terrified, more focused. I opened the front door. The air smelled fresh and clean. I took a deep breath, taking in the scent of the late winter air. We were between seasons, too cold to be called spring but too warm for the snow to fall and the water to ice. The drifting clouds held a promise of afternoon sun. I needed exercise.

I went upstairs, changed my clothes, and climbed onto my bicycle. My mind slipped into a familiar trance, my motions effortless. There were shallow puddles, remnants of last evening's rain, on the sidewalk. As I passed through them, my wheels left their mark on the path of my journey. Within seconds, the morning sun erased these blemishes as if I had never really been there.

My front wheel got stuck in the mud. As I stopped to pull it out, my mind wandered. I felt that I had been stuck, but instead of mud, I was in quicksand. The more I struggled to get out, the deeper I sank. Perhaps it was the war, with all its uncertainty and fear. Perhaps it was my need to be a part of something again. To feel a purpose, not to have my mark disappear in the morning light. Rachel would understand, but she was not here. Edward would encourage me, but he was not here. Henry would support me, but he was gone, as well. I couldn't think about Teddy. For the moment, life was simply too painful.

I came home to find Victoria walking up the steps to the house. *Well, you certainly look better even though you and your bicycle seem to be covered in a thick, brown paste.*

I feel better, much better despite the fact my stockings are so wet. I feel like I was caught in a rainstorm. Let me go change, and I will join you for another cup of tea. I have already had my breakfast and, breaking in a smile, *left nothing on my plate.*

Taking off her hat and coat and hanging them on the rack, she shrugged. *Well, that is both good news and bad news. It looks like a recuperative stay in Westchester is no longer needed, and I was hoping to taste one or two of Mrs. Campbell's wonderful scones.*

I am sure that our tea tray will be adorned with Mrs. Campbell's delights, and I am not going anywhere. At least not in the near future.

She shouted up to me as I ran up the stairs to change. *I have an idea.* Like a true friend, Victoria found me in a dark place and led me back to the light.

I came back downstairs. Victoria was in the library, and the crumbs on her napkin and the edges of her mouth bore the evidence I needed – she had not waited for me to indulge the still warm sugar cookies that lay on the tray. She smiled as she poured me my tea. *Heavenly.*

I added milk and took my first sip. *You said you had an idea.*

Yes. You still own Henry's house?

I replied in the affirmative but had not been there since the war had started.

What if you opened it up to others?

What others?

Victoria shook her head. *I am not sure this would work, but I feel so helpless just sitting here. So I was thinking about the stories you wrote after the Shirtwaist Factory Fire. Do you remember?*

I picked up my teacup. *Yes, Victoria. I may have been depressed, but I have not yet fallen into senility.*

Sorry. What I remember most about the women you wrote about was their lack of a better future. Even when all the laws were adopted giving them safer workplaces and shorter hours, their futures still seemed bleak. They were lacking skills that could make a difference in their lives. So what if?

I was intrigued. *What if what?* I took another sip of tea.

What if we had provided those women with different skills? Skills they could use to get a better job, to move away from the life that has tied them down in so many ways. Her voice became excited. *With the war going on, women are doing all kinds of work. Our new mascot is*

Rosie the Riveter. But it is not true for all women, particularly those without the education needed to survive in this new world. I went to graduate school at NYU with a colored woman named Dorothy Height. She is now directing the YWCA in Harlem, and I heard her speak last week. She was talking about the struggles young colored women are having right here, right now in our own city. This is particularly heart-breaking for those colored women whose husbands have been killed in the war. Most of these women need to support their families but are lacking the skills to get a good job.

I believe we can help these women, these war widows. We could use Henry's house as a place where a small group of them could live for three months and be taught a new set of skills. Maybe five women at a time. I could set up the classroom and teach them the business skills they need. I was trained to do exactly that. Dorothy could help us find the right group of colored women that would be the best first group for us to start with. Victoria took a deep breath, pausing long enough for me to be sure I understood where she was going.

And Henry's house? I asked.

That's where all of this will take place. Away from the city, clean air, ocean breezes, and a new opportunity. Victoria's vision was captivating.

I stood up. My mind raced so fast I couldn't sit still. *I love it. We are going to do it. We can even add to the experience. I have a potato farm about five miles from the house that has not been worked on since the war started. The farmer who had leased it was drafted. I haven't thought much about it, but we could start our own Victory Garden. It would help us feed everyone. If they don't know how we could have someone teach them how to can the fruits and vegetables we grow. They would have food for their families all winter.*

Victoria clapped her hands. *That would be wonderful, and my mother can help teach the canning part. She was a whiz at it years ago. It is the memory I have of her growing up. I know she would love to have something more to do, particularly since my father's death.*

So out of the darkness came a light I had never expected. When Victoria left that afternoon, we had a plan or at least the semblance of one. I was to see my lawyers as to how we could go about funding the operation, Victoria was to meet with Dorothy Height to see if what we were discussing was feasible. We were to meet in the next couple of days to see what we had learned and what we had to do. I left her with two words to remember: *War Widows*. Those were the women we were going to try to help.

Two days later Victoria was back at the house, more excited than the day she had left. Before she could take off her coat, she began, *Dorothy thinks it could work. She knows at least seven women who would be perfect for what we are talking about doing – war widows with young children. We can help them, I know we can. Dorothy said she would be willing to help us select who would come. She is so smart and she knows everyone, including Eleanor Roosevelt.*

Come into the library, my friend. I have met with my lawyers; and although the news is positive, it is not nearly as exciting as what you have just shared. I took out my notes from my meeting the previous day. *My lawyer advised me to set up a Foundation to fund this adventure. I have plenty of money, and there is only Teddy to provide for...* My lip began to quiver.

Have you heard any more? He is going to come home, I know it in my heart. Victoria reached for my hand.

I agree, wiping away the tear that had found its way down my cheek. *I am not sure there is much more I can do than pray. Pray for him, for me, for all the sons who are lost and all the mothers and wives who have received the same telegram. I do know that Teddy would not want me to sit around gazing out into nowhere. Nor would Edward. I think the Edward J. Walker Foundation is the right thing for me to do on so many levels. I will be the trustee. I will have a sense of purpose, a reason to get up in the morning.*

I paused and looked out the window. These were the moments I still longed for Edward to be at my side, advising, counseling, encouraging. I knew his one answer to any doubts that I may have would be one word, *Poppycock!* I took a deep breath, *I will bequeath Henry's house to the Foundation, so there is no question of ownership. Then there are the potato fields. I am to retain ownership of these properties and lease them to the Foundation.*

Victoria smiled, *Edward would be amazed and proud. Henry, too.*

I agree, my heart filling up with the thought of them.

Victoria was having a hard time keeping still as I went through the details. *So now that we have gotten the green light from some of the best legal minds in the city, we are good to proceed. There is still paperwork to be signed and executed; but Dick McDermott, one of the best lawyers at the firm, said all the paperwork regarding the Foundation should be drafted and ready for my signature by the beginning of next week. In the interim, we should plan what we are going to do and what our next steps are going to be.* I finally stopped, *And your thoughts, my dear friend?*

Victoria was almost jumping up and down. *Hooray! I hoped we could make this happen.*

Hope is what it is all about, I replied. *And our project needs a proper name that captures that spirit. I think Rachel's Hope is fitting. No one has heard from her all these months, so it would be our constant reminder of her.*

Victoria's eyes shone brightly, *Oh, yes, Nell, yes. It would be as if she were with us and how she would love the project. Though she might exhaust us with her suggestions that are really demands communicated in loftier terms.*

I smiled, that was the perfect description of Rachel if there ever was one.

We were off on a mission. The days became too busy to think about the 'what ifs' pounding in my head. At night, I was too exhausted to do anything but sleep.

I went to the lawyers' office to sign all the necessary papers. No matter what the legal documents would proclaim, this house would always be Henry's. Like its former owner, it was a mixture of style – utilitarian like a New England farm building, gracious like a Southern antebellum mansion, and welcoming like our thatched cottage in Ireland. The road leading up to the entrance twisted its way through fields painted in myriad shades of yellow and gold from spring until the coldest of winter days. The lawn was lined with trees lush and vibrant, the sun sparking them with light that caused their colors to glisten and change with the seasons. You could see the water through their limbs. It was perfect.

I believed that Henry would have liked that it would now be part of the Walker Foundation. He and Edward connected even in death.

I walked into the lawyers' office with a series of questions that I needed to understand. The receptionist took my coat and hat, directing me to the conference room where the meeting was being held. She went to fetch my lawyer, Richard McDermott, to let him know that I had arrived. Two of his associates, freshly scrubbed and newly polished from their law school days, were already seated when I walked in. On my entry, one of the two who was puffed up like a bird waved his hand in my direction. *You can sit anywhere.*

I was about to thank him when he continued, *Where is your pad? I assume you have the skill to take notes from this meeting. The last girl we had was simply awful, she...*

Before he could finish his sentence, McDermott came in and rushed to my side, taking my hand in his.

Nell, how lovely to see you. I am sorry to have kept you. Please forgive me.

Always, Dick. Your young man here, pointing in the direction of the lawyer who now was turning the color of a fully-ripened tomato, *was putting me in my place.* Not taking my eyes off him as he stared down at shoelaces, I smiled my sweetest smile. *Since my place is at the head of the table and not 'anywhere,' I think it best that we find someone else to assist me in establishing the Walker Foundation. I am sure you have others with the same set of skills.*

McDermott's look to the associate in question would have wilted the strongest of men. *You may leave, Medwick. I will speak to you later in my office.*

Moving the chair at the front of the table out, Mr. McDermott said, *Please, Nell, take your chair.*

Medwick left the room, his shirt no longer looking quite as stuffed.

Thank you, Dick. I have made a list of questions that I hope can be answered, along with concerns that need to be addressed. Three hours later, the papers were drawn up, signed, and the Edward J. Walker Foundation was a legal entity.

Victoria was put to the task of coordinating with Miss Height to find our first volunteers. We agreed that seven war widows would be our maximum number. Victoria would live in the house, along with her mother. The former maid's quarters were set aside for me to use when I came to visit.

Victoria developed the curriculum, bought typewriters, notebooks, pencils, and pens, and raided my library. She organized a work plan: the widows would help with the garden in the morning; classes would be held in the afternoons. Her mother, Agnes, would organize and prepare the meals. One of the women would be assigned each day to help her and complete the household chores. The weekend was open time, the widows could go back to the city to be with their families or stay at Rachel's Hope. It was up to them.

We had our framework. By the first of May, we were up and running. The bedrooms had been painted a palette of soft blues and greens, bringing the color of the outside into the rooms. The kitchen and classrooms were neutral greys and soft whites. The overall look was both comfortable and serene, a clear departure from the dark and somber city colors that reflected the mood of the nation. I loved the living room best. A large sofa dominated the space, the walls lined with framed memorabilia of Henry's shows. They were alive with color and imagination, like Henry.

It took me more than an hour to examine them all, memories of days gone by came flooding back. I took Victoria's hand. *Wherever did you ever find these? I remember so many, so many memories. It is almost as if I can hear Henry laughing.*

Victoria gave me her best Cheshire cat grin. *They were in an old trunk that I found in the attic. I thought the trunk would be just the right thing to store the workbooks. When I opened it up, I found these and more. The trunk fits in the classroom perfectly. I put the rest of the programs in this box for you. I thought you would like to keep them.*

I twirled her around, our skirts flying around us like kites caught in the winds that plummeted this seashore. *These programs and you are a treasure.* My heart was light. This was a sign. A sign that Henry approved of what we are doing. I knew in my heart that if Henry approved, so did Edward.

My assigned task was the Victory Garden. Like my need for legal advice, I needed someone to show us how to plant, seed, and harvest the crops. I advertised in the local paper for a manager, noting that labor would be provided.

Only one person applied, so she got the job. She had been raised on a nearby farm, so I hoped she knew what I would be asking her to do. We spoke on the phone and agreed on a salary, a work schedule, and a layout for the garden. All seemed fine until the first morning I arrived with the widows to start the cultivating and planting. It was June 1st.

She came over to me, red-faced, eyes narrowed, and finger pointed. *You didn't tell me they were colored.*

What does it matter? They are here to work, along with me.

I don't work with coloreds. You gotta find other workers. The women stayed back by the car, hearing every word, their eyes downcast.

I couldn't believe what I was hearing. *No, indeed, I do not. I need to find another manager. You can now get off my land.*

She crossed her arms, the corners of her mouth tightening. *You city folk think you are so high and mighty with your fancy clothes and shiny new cars. Well, you are not welcome here. And,* looking over at the women who refused to make eye contact, *they need to go back from where they came from.*

My voice grew louder as I pointed to the women. *These women are widows of war heroes. Men who gave their lives for this country. Their husbands' blood was spilled on the same battlefields as your family and neighbors. They deserve your thanks and your respect.*

Go preach somewhere else, lady. I said I don't work with coloreds. She stormed off.

I was lost as to what to do next. I went over to the women. *I am sorry you had to hear that.*

Nothing we haven't heard before, one of them said.

Well, I am not sure what happens next. I have the plans but have no idea how to begin, I shrugged, when I felt a tug on my shirt sleeve. I looked to find a 10-year-old girl, her tousled blonde hair standing up like feathers on a startled turkey, looking up at me. *My daddy can help ya, Ma'am*, were her first words. The rest came out in rapid succession: *My daddy knows these fields better than anybody around here. They just don't like to hire him cause he's only got one eye that works. Wears a patch that makes him look more like a pirate than a farmer. That's why he is not shooting Nazis, though he's probably too old to do that anyway.*

Where is your father?

Just down the road working at Smith's garage, a job he hates. Likes being on the outside, my daddy, me, too. I could help you, as well, I am little but know how to seed and pull weeds. I can help teach your lady friends.

Knowing I shouldn't leave the widows alone, I smiled. *Well, can you go get your daddy while I wait here? The ladies and I will find a spot under one of the trees to sit.*

Yes, ma'am, I will be back in two shakes of a lamb's tail. And she was off. Only then did I realize I had never asked her name.

Within a half-hour she returned, accompanied by a weathered-faced man whose eye patch made him look both mysterious and dashing. His flannel shirt was neatly tucked into a pair of denim jeans that hugged his tall, lean body. He came up to me, taking off his faded red cap as he approached. *I apologize, ma'am. My daughter can be a bit too bold, though I try my best to watch her manners.*

I gave him my hand, *I'm Nell Walker and I own these fields. Your* daughter, I am afraid I don't know her name, said you could help us plant and grow our Victory Garden.

Faith, my daughter's name is Faith. My wife thought she would be extra blessed if she carried that name, though I'm not sure it is working. He smiled as he tried to tame Faith's hair, still standing straight up.

My mama watches over me from heaven, the now-named Faith replied while touching her head, *I'm not very good with a hairbrush.*

It's a learned skill and if you can teach me to plant, I can teach you how to brush your hair. That is if your father approves. Mister...?

Martin, John Martin, though most folks call me Jack, now taking my hand that was still extended.

Your daughter tells me you can help us. My friends here are widows, two of their husbands were killed in Italy and one lost her husband in the Pacific. Three of their husbands lost their lives in France. There is one more back at the house where we are staying who lost her husband in a plane fire before he even left this country. Together, we are looking to turn this land into a Victory Garden, though we have absolutely no idea how to even begin. I looked over at the women, now relaxed, and put my hands up as if in supplication.

The seven of them smiled.

We call our project Rachel's Hope; and now it looks as if we could have Faith on our side, as well.

Well, a small smile relaxed the lines around Jack's one good eye, *guess you have already found out you won't find much charity around here, but two out of the three virtues are a good start. I believe I could help you, Mrs. Walker. The garage has been looking to cut back my hours, so I could spend the mornings with you and then afternoons and evenings there.*

He scanned the field with his one good eye. *Looks like you got strawberries already trying to poke the heads up, and something else is sprouting over there. Needs tilling and weeding but I think you have a better start than most in getting this garden blooming.*

Please call me Nell. We are all on a first-name basis. We have a deal. Perhaps we could meet after your shift at the garage ends today and confirm the particulars. Until then, could Faith help us get started? We have tools and lots of energy. It is the know-how we are lacking, and somehow I think Faith could fill that gap.

Jack extended his hand that I shook. *There is a diner in town that stays open until 8:00 p.m. I could meet you there at 6:00 if that works for you. Faith can stay with you this morning. The first thing you need to do is till the land. She can show you how to move the earth, and then we can take it from there.*

And so we did. Jack Martin was just what we needed. Rachel's Hope was off and running. Under Jack's skillful guidance, we learned how to sow, weed and cultivate. Faith worked with us in the mornings when school wasn't in session; and on those days when she was in class, she came as soon as the school bell rang at the end of the day. With the attention of more adult women than she had known in a lifetime, she learned to brush her hair.

We started to see the fruits of our labor: the strawberries were plump and juicy, the asparagus right green and tender when Sonia proposed a new venture. *We got ourselves some of the best cooks and bakers I have ever tasted,* she began, *and with the orchards and the gardens starting to produce so many good things, we could bake cakes and pies and sell them. Agnes could help with the jams and the pickling. I think we could make some good money if we tried.*

There was universal agreement among the women. I checked with my lawyers who confirmed that if the stand was on my land, selling my products, we should be on safe ground. By July, "Walker's Pies and Cakes" hit the market. By the end of the third day, we had sold out of everything that had been made and had orders for the following week. Work schedules were revised, allowing more time in the kitchen.

The second group of War Widows had been selected and would be joining us on Monday. It was our last Saturday evening with our original group, the women who had been with us since the start of this journey over three months ago. Victoria decided we needed to celebrate, celebrate all we had done, all we had learned. It was a perfect summer's day and we moved the party to the lawn. A warm breeze gently moved the leaves, providing a quiet lull of background music. The cloudless sky rejoiced in the sun's return to glory. There were flowers everywhere, making the tables look like scattered rainbows. After the champagne had been popped and the cake cut, Sonia stood up. She had the bearing of an African goddess, almost six feet tall, her long body had an unexpected gracefulness to it even when she was weeding in the field. Her face was shadowed by sadness, having lost her husband and two of her brothers to a war that she never quite understood. She raised her glass for a toast, the buzz of the celebrants quieted.

I was asked by the other women to say a few words of thanks to Victoria and Nell for giving us these months at Rachel's Hope. You all know me well enough that a few words are a lot for me. Sonia's smile lit her face. *I believe there are angels all around us. God sends them down to guard and protect us, to show us the way in our times of need. They are here to help us become the best versions of ourselves. Most times we don't see them. That is not true today. Our angels are called Victoria and Nell.* Sonia's eyes searched for and found Faith as she added, *and Faith.* Faith looked as if the buttons on her shirt would burst.

Thanks to you, we have learned so much. We are ready to start a new journey, with new skills and new hopes. Only the Lord above knows where this path will lead us. We pray He will watch over and guide our every step. We will miss you, we will miss this house.

All eyes turned to me for a response, I wasn't sure I could speak. My voice broke. *Sonia, your kind words fill my heart. I know I speak for Victoria when I tell you that saying goodbye to you is very difficult. We have had to say goodbye to so many, and you each know the pain of having said that final farewell.*

I took Victoria's hand in mine. *We live in a time when hatred and fear are engulfing our world. Our friend Rachel left the comfort and security of her home and friends to stand up to this terror. I think of her often and pray that the angels guard and protect her each and every day.*

Rachel showed me that humanity persists even in the darkest of times. She was optimistic that we could make the world a better place. That is why we call this Rachel's Hope. She would be so proud of each of you. She would see in you what we know to be true – you are courageous, you are kind. You are our hope for a better world. God bless you today and always.

Our final farewells were hugs mixed with tears. No further words needed to be spoken.

———

The weeks and months went by quickly. 1944 dawned with the headlines that the tide was turning, the Allies were winning. There had been no word about Teddy or Rachel. With the exception of a couple of bumps along the way that Victoria had to smooth out, Rachel's Hope was doing what we had planned. Our 'alumni widows' were going in many different directions. Most went back to the city with the skills to become stenographers or telephone operators; one was looking to get a scholarship to fulfill her dream of becoming a nurse; Sonia had started her own bakery in a welcoming community a few towns away.

It was an early July day, Rachel's Hope was over a year old. The sun had set but left her heat as a reminder that she would be returning in the morning light. I was at the farm stand by the house working with two of the women when Miss Beekman drove by. I heard she had left New York City for the country, citing the need for a quieter life. With it went the prestige of being the Benevolent Miss Beekman. I caught full sight of her as she slowed down her car, her eyes narrowed, her mouth twisted. She looked straight at me but gave no hint of acknowledgment. I thought nothing more of it.

The Walker Foundation was taking more and more of my time, making me feel that Edward was still a part of my life. That particular day, I was on a personal mission. I had driven in from the city, my first visit in over a week, carrying with me the telegram that I had received the day before. Teddy was alive but had been captured by the Germans. He was in a POW camp. I thanked God that he was alive while trying unsuccessfully to keep the nightmares about what his life must be like from clouding my every thought. I needed to share the news with Victoria.

I was lost in that train of thought when Faith spotted me coming up the walk. She was growing tall, the traces of the young woman she would be emerging.

Can I talk with you alone, Nell? I heard stuff around town you need to know about. Best if the others don't hear.

Sure, let's walk down to the beach. What's happening, Faith? You look like the crops are about to fail.

It's bad, Nell. Real bad, and a tear slowly fell down her cheek.

Oh, my dear Faith, tell me. We can make it better, whatever it is. I promise.

Kids around town know I spend my time with you and the widow ladies, and they call me names. That's been going on for a while, and Pop told me to just ignore them. If I get into a fight, it would just make matters worse.

Your father is a wise man, taking her hand in mine as we continued our walk. Memories of Teddy and his lying in a hospital standing up for what he believed in overpowered me. I held her hand tighter.

Faith looked around to be sure we were alone. *One of the older boys found me as I was coming over today, said the folks in town weren't going to stand for it any longer. You and the widows, though that's not what he called them, were going to be thrown out and the farm stands shut down. There is some kind of letter people are signing saying you and them have to get out.* Faith started to cry.

Oh, my dear child, taking her in my arms, *we are going to be alright, Faith, I promise you. I pay a lot of money for lawyers to protect us. So no matter what the townspeople want to do, no petition can stop us.*

Are you sure? her eyes reflecting both the depth of her fear and her wanting to believe.

Well, we may not be dressed as soldiers but we can put up as good a fight as anyone, and I softly kissed the top of her head. *My husband was a lawyer, and he taught me that it always pays to have the best lawyers in town on your side of the battle.*

Faith paused for a moment. *Maybe I'll be a lawyer when I grow up.*

I think you can grow up to be anything you want. And I can't wait to see what you decide.

After supper, I shared Faith's fears with Victoria.

Is that why you were so distracted over dinner?

Yes, that and this. I pulled the telegram from my pocket.

Victoria cried when she read the words. She looked up at me. *I don't know if I am happy or sad. I am going with scared. But he is alive and there is hope.*

I carefully refolded the telegram, now damp with Victoria's tears. *Hope seems to be the only thing we've got going for us these days.*

The next day we shared Faith's fears with the other women. We agreed to adopt a 'wait and see' strategy. We didn't have to wait long. Two days later, we received the signed petition. The townspeople were demanding Rachel's Hope be shut down. The first signature on the document was Miss Beekman's. I felt I was back thirty years ago, only then it was the factory owners who were looking to keep others down. I called my lawyers.

Mr. McDermott advised me the petition was not a legal document, the house belonged to the Foundation and could be used for any purpose the Foundation sought fit. The fields were my property, to do with as I pleased. That night at dinner, we agreed that we would continue what we were doing while recognizing that things could get difficult.

Not getting what they wanted by simply signing their names to a sheet of paper, some of the townspeople retaliated and the harassment began. We found the graffiti on the stands – awful, hateful words. Children threw eggs at the house as they drove by on their bicycles. My car was smeared with feces, the words 'nigger lover' painted on its hood. A noose was hung on the limb of the tree shading our front lawn.

It was the end of September, and there appeared to be no let-up. I feared for our safety. I decided to visit Miss Beekman, thinking that a direct conversation might ease the tension and stop the harassment.

There was no answer when I rang the bell, but I heard voices coming from the back of her house. I followed the line of rose bushes where traces of their earlier blood-red bloom lay withering on vines now brown and yellow, struggling for their one last moment in the sun. Miss Beekman was sitting next to a woman who shared the same sharp features but whose eyes were vacant. I immediately knew that something was wrong. She was dressed in a light pink dressing gown that no longer fit her thin frame. She had the look of an old crystal vase, one that was too fragile to hold anything other than a single stem.

Miss Beekman?

She looked up, startled as if I had caught her in an illicit act.

I rang the bell, but there was no answer. I heard voices so I found my way back here. I hope we can talk about what is happening.

Before I could finish my sentence, Miss Beekman interrupted, her voice colder than the glass of ice tea resting beside her wicker chair. *Indeed you are, Mrs. Walker. This is my mother's quiet time in her garden. We have nothing to say to each other. You have always been rude and impertinent, with your holier-than-thou manners and your self-righteous ways.*

The woman in pink suddenly looked up. *Bernadette, who is your friend who has come to call on this glorious day?*

Before Miss Beekman could answer I walked over to where the older woman was seated. She took my extended hand between hers, hands that were as gnarled as the limbs of the ancient oak that provided her shade.

Nell Walker, Mrs. Beekman.

The older woman shook her head slightly, *I know that name.*

You write articles for that paper we get delivered. My Walter reads those articles to me.

I saw this as my opening. *You are absolutely correct. It was The Sun, though many years ago.*

Her milky eyes were closing. *Yes, Walter loves to read those articles to me.* Her head fell backward, a drop of drool appeared at the corner of her mouth, and slowly began its journey downstream.

My mother isn't well, Mrs. Walker; and you barging into our private time is unforgivable. This is a woman who lost her husband and her son to other people's greed. My brother came home from the first war, having fought on the fields of France. Nothing we could do would calm the nightmares of what he had seen, what he had done. We found him here, in his room, three months after he returned with a bullet in his brain. It was the same gun my father used to shoot himself the day he lost most of our family's fortune.

Miss Beekman's mouth curled, *His only act of kindness was that he killed himself in his office so we didn't have to clean up the mess. His death didn't even make the papers. What loss have you had that shatters the only world that you have known, the only one you have ever wanted? This is the only place where my mother finds peace, where she doesn't scream through her nightmares shouting out the names of the two men she thought loved her.*

You arrive here with your crusader mentality to make the world better for others. We are desperately holding onto the world that we know. It is the world we can survive in. I have nothing to say to you, Mrs. Walker, other than to leave my property. You will be able to make your case at the town council meeting. I will do the same. You should receive the summons by the end of the week.

Please find your way out the same way you came in. Uninvited and unwelcome.

I walked out. I knew this was a war, a war that would be hard to win. This wasn't a fight with factory owners and their lust for profits, requiring legislation to right the wrong. This fight was against something more ingrained, a deep-seated intolerance to accept these women because of the color of their skin. This was not the world I knew, or perhaps it was and I had never seen it stripped of its veneer of civility. I couldn't reconcile this narrow-mindedness at a time when my son was in the hands of the enemy, when Rachel was risking her life to help others being persecuted, and when these women who had lost their husbands to the cruelty of war were being victimized.

———

J ack was increasingly worried about our safety. I told him it would be pretty cowardly to attack women but agreed to his recommendation that we should not go out alone but stay in pairs. He wasn't convinced that was enough. He started to spend evenings at the house.

He and I were sitting on the porch one evening watching the sunset when I started the conversation. *Are you okay, Jack? How are the townspeople treating you, knowing you are working with us?*

His body stiffened in his chair, his one good eye not looking in my direction. *Lost my job at the garage. According to my boss, local folks said they wouldn't use him any longer while I was working there.*

Why didn't you tell me?

Not much you could do about it. Faith and I will be okay. Your wages are good, and we can just tighten our belts a bit more.

I could smell freshly-brewed tea and strawberry pie. Their combined scents teased my nose. Victoria joined us, straining the tea, pouring each of us a cup, staring at the leaves as if she was willing them to tell us our future.

The first sip of tea was warm, comforting, and unleashed my senses. *I don't know why I haven't thought of this before. Why don't you and Faith move into the maid's quarters? I can stay with Victoria when I come to visit. It would give us a bit more security, and Faith is here more than anywhere else. It would keep her off the roads, so no harm would come.*

The fork that Jack was using to stab a juicy red strawberry paused in mid-air. *That would help, Nell. Faith would love it. Me, too.*

I looked over at Victoria, and I swear I saw her blush.

By the end of the week, Jack and Faith had moved in.

CHAPTER 26

1945

Our New Year's present was a court order that Rachel's Hope was to cease and desist operations. The town council had passed an ordinance that only a 'family' could live in a house within its incorporated village. The residents at Rachel's Hope clearly did not meet that definition.

I turned to my lawyers for guidance. McDermott was blunt, *This is small-town governance, Nell. We can try to throw up roadblocks; but in the end, I have found that local governments have their own set of rules, their own etiquette. They reflect the values of the people in their community, their neighbors. Our best strategy would be for you to appeal directly to the town council. Get them to understand the purpose, the mission for Rachel's Hope. See if you can persuade them to make an exception in this case. This is not my legal opinion. It is just my personal advice.*

He was right. I needed to stand up and defend Rachel's Hope. I was to present our case at a special town council meeting to be held on the first of March.

The town council met in a building that was as old as the town itself. Originally it had been erected as an academy for 'preparing young men for college' and where young women were 'schooled in spiritual reading and the finer points of being a lady.'

The building was square, brick, devoid of the large manicured lawns and wrap-around porches of the houses that surrounded it. The original iron posts where visitors could tie up their horses were still in place along the front sidewalk. Nothing about the place evoked a sense of wanting or accepting change.

Victoria and I were directed to the meeting room, with its high ceilings, crown molding, and one very long cherry wood table. Victoria whispered as we sat down, *there is something foreboding about this whole place. You can almost hear the walls tell us that we don't belong here.* She shuddered. I squeezed her hand, she was right – though the fireplace burned brightly in the entryway, this building felt cold and unwelcoming.

At the table sat three men, the members of the town council, all fit with summer tans still visible though the calendar read March 15th. In the middle sat its chairman, his slightly graying blonde hair framing a face that smiles too quickly and shows no warmth. He had the look of someone who traced his heritage to the arrival of the Mayflower. He opened the meeting in a voice clear and measured. *Mrs. Walker, thank you for meeting with us this evening. I am a great admirer of your late husband, a fine lawyer, and a mentor to his younger colleagues such as myself.*

Shall we begin? was a statement rather than a question. *Rachel's Hope is the only item on our agenda for this evening.*

I blinked. I was not prepared to hear Edward's name. It was unsettling and perhaps not well-intentioned. I said a brief prayer to Edward to give me strength, touching the gold cross hanging from my neck, as I stood up.

Thank you, gentlemen, for taking the time to hear our appeal. As you know from the brief we submitted, Rachel's Hope is part of the Foundation that was established in my late husband's name. Looking straight at the man in the middle, *I believe he would have supported this endeavor with all his heart and with all his skills.* The man nodded while keeping his eyes focused on the papers in front of him. I then summarized the key points in the document McDermott had prepared.

We had agreed that if we were to win this appeal, we would have to change people's hearts, as the law was clearly written. My last comments I hoped would do this. *Gentlemen, do we not stand together as a nation and as one people to battle a common enemy? Is that not why husbands and sons are shedding their blood in foreign lands? My son, my only son, has been captured by the Germans and is being held as a prisoner of war.*

The women staying with me are good women, women whose husbands served this country. Women whose husbands died for this country. They are widows, most with children. Many of their grandparents were slaves, men and women who had no rights until a war was fought to give them the freedoms we are now fighting to preserve. We established Rachel's Hope to try to make a difference in their lives, to give these women who have lost so much the chance to become all they are capable of becoming. I believe we owe them that. It is a debt that all of us should be proud to pay.

I sat down. It was my best, and I knew it wasn't good enough.

Thank you, Mrs. Walker. We will keep your son in our prayers. As is our custom, we ask if any other members of our village would like to speak.

I was not surprised when I heard a rustling behind me. I looked to see Miss Beekman rearranging her dress as she moved to the front of the room. Standing next to the next table, she never took her eyes off me as she began. My first thought was that I had never seen this woman blink; that evening would be no different.

Mrs. Walker echoes Mrs. Roosevelt in believing that our soldiers are fighting to change the world. I think that you and our neighbors will agree with me that these brave men are fighting to preserve the world we know and cherish. A world free of Hitlers and Japanese emperors. We have lived in this town for generations, we have supported its schools, its library, its merchants. We know and trust each other.

Mrs. Walker lives in a house bequeathed to her. She has no ties to our community, to our way of life, to what we know is important. It is a life our fathers and their fathers worked hard to give us. Mrs. Walker doesn't understand that. Until she opened her house as this Rachel's Hope, she seldom even visited.

She brings strangers into our village. Strangers who simply don't belong here. They are not her guests, they are outsiders who are going back to where they came from. It is not in our village's best interest or really in these women's self-interest to live here for even a short time. These colored women are not, and never will be, our neighbors. There are other towns, not far from here, where they might be welcomed. Where they would find more commonality with those who live there. I say again, that is not our village.

No matter what Mrs. Walker's motives are, whether we consider them to be noble or not, her stated objectives about this so-called Rachel's Hope are not in the sustained interest of our village and our residents. Your neighbors elected you. Our village ordinance does not allow for the likes of boarding houses to dot our roads. That is what Mrs. Walker is running. It matters not that she is not charging rent.

It is your role, no, it is your obligation to sustain those ordinances that our townspeople have voted for you to enforce. You must vote tonight to close the doors of Rachel's Hope.

Miss Beekman sat down. I looked once again at the three white men who were presiding at the table. They were not my friends. They were hers. I knew that we would lose. The meeting adjourned while the council made its decision.

Our fate was decided within the hour. The chairman looked at his watch as he started to speak.

While those of us on the council have read your brief describing Rachel's Hope and applaud your efforts to help these poor women have a better opportunity in life, our village ordinance clearly prohibits the occupancy of a house by others than its rightful owner and the owner's family.

We can come to no other conclusion that while you, personally, would be a welcome addition to our village, Rachel's Hope is not. Recognizing that your intent is one of a selfless heart, we are giving you 90 days to desist operation. Thank you for your time this evening. We will send you a written determination at your home address in Manhattan.

He emphasized the word 'home.' I was stunned but not surprised. It was a flashback to a time in the courtroom when Blanck and Issacs were set free. I thought back to that first speech, the one Rose Sneiderman gave following the Shirtwaist Triangle Factory Fire. She accused the owners of having the judges in their pockets. I now understood the frustration of fighting against a system that was stacked against you.

———

F aith was having a difficult time. She just kept saying it wasn't right that Rachel's Hope was to close. Jack and I agreed a weekend in the city might lift her spirits, as well as mine. It was early April, and I was driving her back home that Sunday afternoon.

The highway soon left the concrete of the city, giving way to fields and woodland. The meadows looked ready to start anew, the soil reflecting the brilliant yellow of the soon-to-be-setting sun. Then came the pine barrens, their trees scorched by the fires they need to flourish again. I was lost in thought, thinking that, like these trees, I gain strength when threatened, when I face the heat of battle. With Rachel's Hope closing its doors, the Foundation was looking at what to do next. At times, there were too many options to have to choose from; and I was having to decide what direction we would take. Faith's voice jarred me from my thoughts.

I need to talk with you, Nell.

Goodness, Faith, isn't that what we have done all weekend. There is still more you want to say?

Yes, and I am not sure how to begin, her face grimaced. *It's about my Pop and Victoria.*

And? My eyes stayed on the highway.

Well, I don't know much about love between a man and a woman, but I am pretty sure Pop loves Victoria and I think she loves him. They are good together, and I have never seen him so happy.

So, what is it you want to talk about?

We're not like you, Nell, not you and Victoria. We don't have nice cars, apartments in New York City, and fancy clothes. If I know my father, and I think I do, he probably doesn't think he is good enough for Victoria. So, he'll just stay quiet and do nothing. Faith turned her head to the window.

I smiled to myself. Faith was wise beyond her years. *My husband Edward was a sensible man, and he had a favorite expression he would use right now.* Faith's eyes widened while I screamed at the top of my lungs, *Poppycock!*

Faith started to laugh, a deep hearty sound, *I don't even know what that means.*

Me, neither. Never understood it then, don't understand it today. I took one hand off the wheel of the car and gave her hand a quick squeeze.

I agree with you. I think they are smitten with each other and are good together. I got quiet for a minute. *I think our plan should be 'Divide and Conquer,' not unlike what our troops are doing. Let me talk to Victoria and I think you should start giving your father hints about making Victoria feel special, to convince her of his love. You know, taking her for a walk on the beach, bringing her a bouquet of spring flowers. I will then talk some sense into Victoria, and we can bring them together. This may take some time, but I know we can make it happen. We are a powerful duo.*

Thanks, Nell. I'm glad we have a plan. I would love to have Victoria as my mother. Can you add that to the list of things you will talk to her about?

You can count on it, my fellow conspirator. And thanks for spending the weekend with me, I had a great time.

Me, too. I love you, Nell. The lull of the road made her close her eyes, and she fell into a light sleep.

Our plan worked, although not overnight.

May brought sunshine, longer days, and peace. The war in Europe ended. The world, once ravaged, was now filled with hope. We had beat Hitler, and our boys were coming home. I prayed Teddy would be with them.

The New York papers showed pictures of celebrations, sailors grabbing hold of nurses in New York's Times Square and kissing them. In marked contrast, O'Brien's published pictures were of destruction and ruin – European cities in near collapse, parents without homes, children without parents. Once again his message was clear. In war, there are no real victors.

In September, MacArthur accepted Japan's formal surrender and the headlines no longer heralded battles won. The Victory Garden was bountiful and Rachel Hope's was closing its doors to the war widows. Victoria decided we needed to mark both occasions with a party. Try as I might, my heart wasn't ready to make merry. I had heard nothing from or about Teddy.

Though Jack and Victoria were spending more time together, they seemed to be at a stalemate. With Rachel Hope's closing, there was every possibility that they would walk away from their love for each other.

Victoria and I were alone, putting the last finishes on the party. I was polishing the silver that hadn't been put out since before the war. I stopped what I was doing and blurted out: *Enough, my friend, just tell him you love him and get a move on. There is not much time left.*

Victoria dropped the cloth she was using to wipe off the good china. *What do you mean?*

You know perfectly well what I mean, Victoria Remy. You are clearly in love with Jack Martin and he with you. His pride won't let him ask you, you are too rich. You are going to have to be the one to start the ball rolling. You need to take the first step.

I dropped my buffing cloth and put her hands in mine. *My dear, dear friend, if we have learned nothing else from these years at war and our own battles with the Miss Beekman's of the world, it is to embrace any happiness that comes our way. Relish the moment and thank the dear Lord that he has given us the opportunity to do so.*

Victoria looked up at me. *What if he doesn't love me back?*

Poppycock, I whispered and we both broke out laughing.

So, do I just tell him? I don't even know how to begin. Victoria looked at me for answers.

You will know the right moment. Just be brave. Faith and I are in your corner.

Faith, Faith? Have you two been talking about us? What did she say?

In my best nonchalant manner, I shrugged my shoulders. *Faith is the one who brought up the topic months ago. She told me she would like you to be her mother.*

Victoria started to cry.

Oh, Faith also observed she had never seen her father so happy. So, my dear friend, if you want these wonderful human beings to be a part of your life forever, you are the one who has to step up to the plate. Got it? I said, my hand raised in a salute.

Got it! Victoria saluted back.

The party was a great success. A month later, Jack and Victoria announced they planned to get married. I was to be their matron of honor, Faith their bridesmaid. My thoughts ran to Edward, to Henry, to O'Brien. I had loved three men, all different, all differently. O'Brien's postcards over the years always ended with the same line, *Thinking of you.*

I had never stopped thinking of him.

CHAPTER 27

FORWARD

We were back in Manhattan, having lunch with Anne to toast Victoria's engagement. We hadn't seen Anne much during the war years once we became involved in Rachel's Hope. Benjamin and Franklin now ran the paper, as their father had died of a sudden heart attack the day Pearl Harbor was attacked. All three boys and Grace were married and producing grandchildren at a startling rate. Anne spent most of her days with them, and she seemed at peace with her life. She had done her duty, the family tree was thriving.

I looked at Victoria, now wearing sensible shoes and no longer complaining that her feet hurt, and asked, *What took you so long after our kitchen conversation for you and Jack to announce you were getting married?*

Jack and I agreed we needed to ask Faith to give us her blessing, and then we went to my mother. Faith was easy and asked if she could start to call me Mother. I said, 'Absolutely' and questioned whether she could try calling Agnes, 'Grandma.' Faith said that it might take a bit more work, but she would do it.

My mother reconciled years ago that I was never going to hobnob with the Vanderbilt's. She likes Jack; and when she heard that Faith would call her 'Grandma,' she was over the moon with excitement. Life is wonderful! Victoria's eyes shone with happiness.

I couldn't agree more, and I have had more good news today. Rachel's father called me this afternoon. Rachel is alive. She went to London once the Germans invaded the Netherlands. Given her work with the Dutch Resistance, she thought it safer to have everyone presume she was dead or missing. According to her father, she is well; and I have an address where I can write to her.

Wonderful! Rachel's Hope was what got us through the war, and now that hope has been rewarded ten-fold. Do you think she will be back in New York in time for my wedding? Victoria was practically clapping.

I don't think she will ever return. She is actively involved in the politics and policies to give the Jewish people their homeland back. Rachel will be one of the first to settle in Palestine. I thought of my firebrand friend making a new life for herself in a new country. I was torn – happy beyond belief that she was alive and sad beyond words that she has chosen to spend her life away from me.

I thought of what O'Brien had said, to be Irish is to feel joy and sadness at the same time.

I came back to the moment as Victoria continued. *We will toast her as if she were beside us. Jack and I have agreed upon a date. We thought June 1ˢᵗ would be appropriate, the anniversary of the day we first met. It will be small, just you, Anne and her family, my mother* and, she smiled, *the widows and their families.*

Sounds perfect, and I would like to have the reception here. Phillips, Mrs. Campbell, Bridget, and all the others would love to share in the celebration. After all, they have known you all these years, my heart breaking a bit as I didn't add Teddy's name. There was still no word as to when he would be returning home.

That would be wonderful, the perfect day. And it keeps my mother reined in. She was talking about having the wedding at the Plaza which is the last place I could see Jack and me reciting our vows. He is not much for wanting to be around the swells you rub elbows with.

Rubbing fewer and fewer of those elbows these days. My focus is to run the Walker Foundation. And run it I will continue to do! I smiled.

Victoria took a deep breath. *Speaking of the Walker Foundation, and now that Rachel's Hope is closing, Jack and I have an idea that might be of interest. You know I loved teaching the widows, and Jack liked working with them in the garden. So, we were thinking of establishing a school, a boarding school for the children whose fathers never came home from the war.*

She sounded as excited as when we were planning Rachel's Hope. *We would limit enrollment to a small number, both boys and girls, from everywhere and all on scholarships. They would live as well as learn there. I would be responsible for the classroom instruction and will hire other teachers. Jack will teach them how to farm, fix automobiles, work with their hands. We would be giving them the skills to both survive and thrive in this new world. I have enough money in my trust fund to get us started and if the Walker Foundation was to support...*

I raised my hand to stop her in mid-sentence. *Consider it done. Let's get the lawyers more involved before we take a step. I have them working on turning Henry's house into the official offices of the Walker Foundation, not sure if the Miss Beekmans of the world will like it any better; but we will get it all wrapped up before it goes public.*

I smiled, *I've learned that lesson the hard way.*

———

The next few months flew by in preparing for Victoria and Jack's wedding and their new school, now called Henry's House. Amid all the planning, I received a telegram that Teddy was in the hospital and was recovering from a leg wound. Days later, I finally heard from him. It was a short letter but was the proof I needed that he was indeed alive. He signed it '*Love, Teddy.*' It was the very best I could hope for.

It was Victoria's wedding day. The smell of fresh-cut flowers filled the air while a gentle breeze rustled through the house, cooling the guests. Jack and Victoria walked into the parlor, arms linked, with smiles on their faces that competed with the brightness of this June day. A local judge led them through their vows. When it came time for the exchange of rings, Victoria and Jack exchanged their rings and then turned to Faith. Jack slipped a ring on her finger as Victoria held her other hand. The judge then said the words, *'By the power vested unto me by the State of New York, I now proclaim you husband and wife.'*

I turned to Faith, we had practiced this moment. *Faith, is there anything you would like to say?*

In a voice loud and clear, so there would be no mistake, Faith smiled as she looked at her newlywed parents, and proclaimed, *Okay, Pop. You may kiss the bride!* Jack did as he was commanded and we all started clapping and cheering. Happiness filled the room. We were in the midst of what might have been the third toast when the front door opened unexpectedly, and he walked through the door. My lip trembled as I whispered his name. *Teddy.*

Victoria and Anne cried in unison, *Teddy is here!*

I stood up, stretching out my arms, unsure if he would come. *You didn't tell me.* He took me in his arms and held me tight. I closed my eyes, thanking God for this moment.

I didn't know until the last minute I was to be put on the transport out of Bristol; once on the ship, I couldn't get in touch. He looked tired, ravaged. The war had taken not only his strength but also a piece of his soul. He paused and looked around at the crowd assembled.

I took his arm and brought him over to Jack, Victoria quickly coming to his side. *Teddy, may I introduce you to John Martin, known as Jack, newly married to our beloved Victoria.*

Impossible! Teddy pulled himself up straight, the command in his voice quieted the crowd. Everyone, including me, gasped.

He kissed Victoria on her cheek, *You promised me when I was 10 years old that you would marry me. I am heartbroken.* He smiled as he shook Jack's hand. *My Tory is as special as they come, so if she chose you over me, you must be worthy of her love.*

Victoria beamed, she had been given the perfect wedding gift.

Minutes later, he went up to his room. I had seen a flash of the old Teddy, the charming young man who always seemed to know the right thing to say. I wasn't sure who had come home. I wasn't sure if he had forgiven me. I only knew that I had not forgiven myself.

In the days and months that followed, Teddy spent most of his time in his room or on lone walks. He was polite but distant. Though his leg was regaining strength, the doctor predicted he would always have a slight limp. It was his eyes that told the story. They had a vacant look, reliving memories of what he had seen and what he had done. His body was healing, but his spirit was still shattered. He never spoke of his time in the war. He was going through the motions of living but was not alive.

CHAPTER 28

THE STORM

I went to Mass alone that Christmas morning. Teddy had decided not to join me; his faith was one more casualty of the war. I prayed that 1947 would be the year that Teddy would find his way back to us.

On Boxing Day, a quiet descended upon the city, as if it needed a nap after eating too much of a holiday meal. The morning sun has just entered my bedroom windows. I sat up, staring out the window. I got up to see my known world swallowed up in a great white blanket. The wind was whipping tornadoes of snowflakes across the empty street. I had never seen anything like it before. I was mesmerized. *Where on earth*, I wondered, *could such a blizzard have come from? And so quickly.*

The radio confirmed that it had come from the west. A great snowstorm had found its way across the continent, linking the Pacific and Atlantic coastlines with an icy airstream. Then the South entered the fray with its warm, moist air. The two collided and Mother Nature took control over our lives. The temperature had fallen suddenly, and the rain that had dampened last evening's Christmas farewells had become a blizzard. It raged all through the night.

Most of the staff were still on their Christmas holiday, and the few expected would not be able to forge their way here. I made tea and sat in the kitchen, staring at a world I had never seen before. We might just as well be sitting in a cloud.

I was lost in thought when I heard the front door close. Startled, I looked out to see Teddy dressed in his warmest coat and boots forge his way into the arctic landscape of the neighborhood. The street was empty. My first thought was that I should follow him, but the howling winds were too strong. He had only just left, and already he was hidden by the swirling snow. I couldn't sit still. My head conjured up every conceivable horror imaginable. Teddy would be found frozen just steps away from our door. He would never be found, lost again; only this time the weather, rather than Hitler, was the enemy.

I went into the library, started a fire, sat in Edward's chair, and prayed.

The clock was striking noon when I heard the door open. Teddy stood in its frame. He removed his jacket and hat, so frozen they were stiff when he peeled them off. I ran to his room to get the warmest robe I could find and silently handed it to him. He nodded, wrapping it tightly around his chilled body, and followed me into the library, taking his place in Edward's chair.

Can I get you a cup of tea? Or something stronger? were my first words, trying hard not to sound either worried or inquisitive.

Brandy would be best.

I will join you.

I brought back two glasses and the bottle and poured us both a healthy snifter.

This day reminds me of when I was shot down, staring intently at the honey hue of the liquor in his glass.

I said nothing.

It was the beginning of February, and the weather became brutal. I was on the docket to fly my sixtieth mission, and then I would be eligible for a rotation home. I thought I would take the time and go to Ireland. That thought kept me going. My buddies from flying school hadn't fared as well. Paul, Doug, and Mervin had been killed or were missing in action. Other names I recognized were being added to those same lists every day.

All the macho talk that had permeated the airfields when we were in training was gone. We yearned to be home, away from causing death and destruction. Away from the fear. A fear that never left. We had arrived in England as young men, brave, and ready to take on the enemy. In the months we had been there, we had aged far beyond our years. We had seen so much. We had done too much.

He took a sip from his glass. I am not sure he even knew that he was telling his story to me. He was in his own world. A world where I was merely an on-looker.

We were scheduled to do an armed reconnaissance near Berlin. I was leading a squadron of four P-47 Thunderbolts. We were now stationed in Belgium, and the day was iffy for flying combat, the cloud cover so thick I couldn't see the ground once I was in the air. When there was finally a break in the overcast, I spotted a railroad yard. I radioed my bunch to follow me and drove down through the hole. I then spotted locomotives and knew we found what we were looking for, and I set out on the hunt.

Then it started to rain, sheets of rain. Pellets hitting my window sounded like bullets leaving a machine gun. I began to panic, I couldn't see where I was or where the other planes were. I released my two 500-pounders and broke away in a steep left-hand climbing turn. I squinted through the water-splattered window to see the havoc I had wrought.

I cursed out loud. I had missed my target, and my bombs had landed in a farmer's field blasting anything that the cruel winter and hunger hadn't already ravaged. I could see nothing else. I tried to climb out of the weather, making a 180-degree turn. It didn't work.

I heard a sound. I thought at first it might be thunder. Then I realized I had been hit. I was confused. I didn't even know I was being fired upon. There had been no indication of the enemy. I had thought I was the only plane in the skies. The engines were on fire, and the flames were beginning to spread.

I gasped as he continued. *Nothing had prepared me for this. I knew I didn't want to die, but there was not enough time to figure out what I was going to do.*

The temperature continued to drop, bringing with it a heavy snow-fall. I was forced to rely on my instruments to fly whatever was left of the plane. I couldn't take my eyes off the fire; the flames were mesmerizing, flickering up through the snowflakes. I shook myself out of my stupor. If I was to live, I was going to have to bail out.

I started to recite the bailout procedures out loud as if I was the class-room instructor talking to a bunch of newbies. The sound of my own voice began to calm me.

I could barely breathe as the story continued. Looking at him, I realized he was no longer in the room with me but some-place else. Teddy was living his own nightmare, his nightmare of survival. He took another sip of his brandy, tying the robe a bit tighter around him.

I ripped off my oxygen mask and rolled the plane upside down. I was doing it point-by-point, as the rulebook directed.

I had forgotten one thing. You just don't drop out of a plane going 150 miles an hour that is diving towards the ground. I was slammed inside the cockpit. I yelled for Papa, as crazy as that sounds. I can't remember what happened next because, all of sudden, there was a pow, like the sound of a champagne cork on New Year's Eve. I was loose and out of the plane. The slipstream, the air rotating around the plane, grabbed me. This was like a rush I had never felt before. I was being pulled upward as if ascending into heaven. I could see the snow falling to the earth, and for a split second, I believed I was dead.

Then the need to remain with the living took over.

Thank you, Edward, I mumbled, refilling our glasses.

I pulled the ripcord, yanked it is probably the better description. The chute opened with a soft whoomph, making the sweetest sound I had ever heard.

I calculated my plan as I surveyed the world below me. I felt like I was watching all of this as a spectator. It couldn't really be me, para-chuting into Nazi Germany.

I saw the plane crash into the ground. It erupted into flames. My first thought, and he looked up as if seeing me for the first time, *was of you. They are going to tell my mother I died or at least am missing. This will break her heart. Then I realized, I could be either one of those alter-natives depending upon what happened next.*

All went quiet, even serene. I was floating amid the snowflakes. The strong winds were whipping my parachute all over. I was on a carnival ride, being tossed and turned with no control. I gave myself up to the wind, an act of faith; and then the ground came up fast and everything was white. I landed in a heap on top of a large snowdrift. I was cold, bitterly cold, but I was alive. I checked to see if anything was broken and slowly stood up. I had no idea where I was.

I saw smoke rising in the distance and made my way in that direc-tion. I couldn't imagine what I was going to do next but knew staying still was not an option.

As I started to make my way, I stumbled. I must have shrieked out, as the next thing I knew, I was face-to-face with four German civilians, one of whom had a Luger pointing straight at me. My arms shot up in surrender. We stared at each other, wondering who was going to do what next. They seemed as frightened as I was.

It was as if I was listening to a story on the radio, spell-binding and frightening. I added more logs to the fire, a task I had mastered since Edward's death.

They motioned me to go in front of them. We started down a long hill, where despite the grueling weather, a crowd began to gather. I was leading the parade, the grand marshal with a gun in my back. Schoolboys began hooting and hollering at me. I had no idea what they were saying, but their tone and their gestures sent the message. I remember thinking that this must be what it would feel like to be seated on the opposing team's bench while wearing my home team's jersey.

I responded in my best military manner, stood taller, my eyes looking straight ahead. I was an officer in the U.S. Army Air Forces. I was a pilot, and I was a gentleman. I would hold myself as a man of honor.

I raised my glass in salute. This was the boy I raised.

They led me to a small factory near the edge of town and brought me into a basement room maybe eighteen by eighteen feet with solid concrete walls. Despite its grimness, I breathed a sigh of relief. I was finally out of the cold and the snow. My sense of warmth didn't last long, as the first thing they had me do was strip off every stitch of clothing. They must have thought I was hiding secret papers, an absurd idea if they had seen the plane burst into flames; but I did as I was told. I didn't have much choice. Though I had been in and out of team locker rooms while in school, this was the first and only time that I was stark naked in front of people with whom I had not been properly introduced.

I let out a chuckle. Here was the Teddy humor I remembered, quick and a bit self-deprecating. Teddy chuckled. I was mesmerized while reminding myself this was not some random author's tale, this was happening to my beloved son.

Finally, they let me dress. Putting on my wet, cold clothes would normally have been less than appealing; but anything was better than nothing. They led back to the icy road. The snow had stopped; and the town looked like a postcard from the Alps, picturesque and charming. I realized it could be my final resting place. We were heading over to what I soon learned was the local authority's office.

Two uniformed officials looking self-important and officious entered the room and began questioning me. At least I thought that was what they were doing as I could not understand a word. My sense was they had no idea what to do with me, so I kept repeating "Luftwaffe, Luftwaffe" and pointing to the stripes on my now-frozen jacket.

If captured, we had been told to get in the hands of the German air force, comrades-in-arms so to speak. We were to stay out of the hands of the Gestapo, the SS, and civilians, and in that order. I must have said the right thing, for the first officer picked up the telephone.

He greeted the person at the other end of the line with a 'Heil Hitler' and gave the Nazi salute. This was the first and what I hoped was the only time I would see such an action other than in movie newsreels. I had no idea what was being said, but the atmosphere in the room seemed to lighten. The officer finished the call, and he eyed me covetously, gazing at his cigarette. He gave me one from his pack and I said 'Danka.' He responded 'Welcome,' in a thick German accent.

It reminded me of the time during the First World War when the English soldiers and their German counterparts laid down their arms on Christmas Eve. Any thought I had to break into singing Silent Night, though, was quickly extinguished as a man screaming' Murderer' in German came storming into the room. He smashed the cigarette from my hand, his eyes never leaving mine.

'Warum? Warum?' He yelled.

I realized it might have been his fields I had bombed, perhaps killing his wife and children. And if they weren't my bombs, it didn't matter. His rage had to be directed somewhere and at someone and that someone was me.

I shrugged and came up with the only answer I could think of: It is war.

My response put him over the edge. He pulled out the rifle he had hidden under his coat and cocked it in my direction. The first bullet missed, the second found its way into my leg. Within seconds, the guards took control, grabbed the rifle, and shoved him out of the room.

One of the men must have been a medic of some kind. I was in pain and bleeding but conscious. A tourniquet was made and the bleeding subsided. I was given a clean pair of pants and a shirt, two sizes too big but dry and bloodless.

Teddy grimaced, his mind reliving the horror. *I am sure If I had been shot prior to that phone call being placed, I would have been left to die, the second time in one day that I barely escaped death. I prayed there would not be a third.*

In the next 15 or so minutes, I was unceremoniously dumped into a wagon driven by an old man in uniform. The sun was beginning to set as we found our way to an airfield where I was turned over to the Luftwaffe and, without ceremony, dumped into a cell. I stayed there for a couple of days, being fed but having no contact with another human being.

I was then sent to Staling Luft, the prison camp for air corps personnel. My wounded leg began to fester and swell, and I became feverish. The camp doctor was a British officer who immediately had me transferred to the POW hospital for treatment. I became unconscious.

When I finally revived, I didn't know where I was or how long I had been there. I remembered being shot in the leg, so the first thing I did was look down to see if I still had two legs. There they both were, thin, bony, and with yellowing, decaying nails, but intact. *I wasn't sure if I could walk. but at least I still had the equipment*

Teddy closed his eyes.

You are tired, I whispered, trying not to break the spell, *let me fix you something to eat, and then you should try to sleep.*

His eyes met mine, *I will take you up on that only in reverse order. Let me sleep for a bit, and then we can continue where I left off. You can fuss over supper.*

I got extra blankets and a pillow and let him sleep on the divan. The room was warm, the snow had stopped as I watched my boy, now a man with so many demons driving his soul, fall into a slumber.

Dear Mama,

War doesn't end when the peace treaty is signed. The war is still raging within Teddy; no names on a piece of paper can end his nightmares. He has seen his friends die, he has caused the death of others. Innocent people died because it was war, and his job was to kill others. Horror and fear constant companions then have been replaced by guilt and sadness.

Today Teddy told me about the day he got shot down. I am not sure he knew he was talking with me, he just needed to tell someone. I thank God that someone was me.

A major snowstorm has brought this city to a standstill. May this blizzard find a way to quiet the tempest brewing inside Teddy.

I love you, Mama.
Your Nell

CHAPTER 29

THE NEXT DAY

Teddy slept through the night. I was up at dawn and the city looked like a wonderland, the sun was bright, and the snow glistened.

I thought I could smell coffee, were his first words as he poured himself a cup.

I've gotten quite proficient in making scrambled eggs with toast, as well, I replied.

Sounds perfect, let me get out of these bedclothes and I will join you. Taking his cup to his room, I noticed a difference. His voice sounded stronger, and he was walking without his cane.

I was just finishing getting our meal together when he returned and sat down. He had taken a shower, and his hair was still damp. I restrained myself from kissing the top of his head like I did when he was a boy. His eyes were brighter, the circles that had darkened his face all these weeks were fading.

He poured himself another cup of coffee and I placed the breakfast plate in front of him.

He continued his story between bites. *I was released from the camp's hospital but was still on crutches. By early spring, the word was out that the Allies were winning. There was a state of euphoria around the camp. My mobility was still pretty limited. Though both legs were attached, I couldn't put any weight on my right foot. I didn't want others to know how much pain I was in for fear I would end up on the operating table and the leg would be removed.*

I grimaced but remained silent. Teddy had eaten every bite, and I took the plate from the table. He hadn't stopped talking.

Our German guards were visibly more nervous and a bit more friendly. The propaganda had stopped, Hitler had killed himself, and their world was collapsing. The camp commandant met with our senior officers and proposed we march, Germans and prisoners together, to the Allied lines. Our guys immediately turned down the request; it would be a suicide mission. Our forces were some 100 miles west, and a line of unidentified marching males coming down the road would be great target practice to our mates in roaming planes.

Like Lee at Appomattox, the commandant knew there was nothing left to do but to surrender with as much dignity as he could muster. He agreed that he and his soldiers would leave that night. The guards would unlock certain barracks, and we would be given keys to run the camp.

I was one of those selected to manage this transition. By 1:00 a.m. the Germans were gone. We met as planned, and I was assigned an office. I felt strange. For months we were prisoners, unable to make our own decisions, and now we were in charge. While the more senior officers quickly assumed the confidence and command of their roles, I was still inexperienced in leading others. I soon learned to cover any look of anxiety my face might betray by shrugging my shoulders and pointing to my leg. The constant pain might be a blessing in disguise.

The first thing I did was unlock the prisoners' cells. I had heard that one of my buddies from flight school, Ron Carman, had been locked up for months in solitary confinement for spearheading an attempted escape from the camp. I found him in the first cell and shook him awake. Ron was stunned to see me. He had no idea I was in camp and what the latest news coming from the front was. Once he seemed somewhat cognizant, I explained the Germans were gone and the Russians were coming. He yawned: 'Are they here yet?'

No, I replied, but any time now.

'Great, Walker, but this little spot has been my home for six months

now. Why don't you just leave the door unlocked, and I will see you later this morning.' He turned over and went back to sleep.

My first action as a leader in the new regime had not gone as well as I had thought. Ron found me later in the day, and I filled him in on all the headlines he had missed. He was alert and hungry. I saw him regularly after that; but to the amazement of all of us, he returned to his cell to sleep each night.

Supplies, particularly food, were getting scarce; and we had many mouths to feed. The decision was made to send out a patrol every night in an effort to link up with the Russian forces and make them aware there were 1,000 Allied POWs not far away. On the third night, our patrol encountered a Russian advance troop. After a tricky and somewhat harrowing exchange of recognizing each other as comrades rather than enemies, the two patrols started back to our camp together.

The next day the first of the Russian troops showed up, five soldiers on horseback armed to the teeth and looking no more than 16 years old. We saluted them as professional warriors and brought them to meet with our camp leaders. A picture of Hitler was still hanging on the wall in the room. When the Russians saw it, they went berserk. They took turns smashing it with their rifle butts, putting holes in the wall, making it look like it had been a woodpecker's feast.

Other Russians arrived, their revenge clearly visible. Horses and wagons overflowing with silver, linens, and the remains of the homes they had looted along the way were being driven by soldiers who looked identical to their five compatriots who had arrived the day before. They were young, and they were drunk.

I shook my head as I began to clean up the kitchen. *It sounded like you were going from the frying pan into the fire*

Yes, indeed, was Teddy's response, *and my job was to see we didn't get burned. One of the older Russian soldiers appeared to be senior to the group and spoke some French. I was the only one in the camp who had the language skill, so I found myself in the role of communicator between the two groups.*

We agreed that one of our colonels would accompany him to their headquarters about 80 miles from our camp to get the food and supplies we needed. Despite my bad leg, I was to make the trip, as well. The next day the colonel and I commandeered a battered Volkswagen and started the journey.

There was no sign of life anywhere on the road. All I could see were dead horses, burned-out fields, and abandoned farms. Teddy got quiet. *Have you ever wondered what hell would look like, Mother?*

In my head I responded, No thanks. Fire and brimstone and a thousand women looking like Aunt Helena.

My hell was that road. It was deserted; nothing was alive. It looked like the earth had been scorched, and I was the only one left to put it back right.

I broke in, *Did you finally find the Russian headquarters?*

Yes, an old farmhouse, surrounded by a sea of mud. My vision of Dante's Inferno was now complete. A Russian MP met us at the door and escorted us into a side room of the house. The room was fashionable with a beautiful round cherry table and chairs commanding its center. There was a matching sideboard. The table was set for lunch, with linens, candles, and flowers. I assumed this was meant to impress; but it reminded me of home, of this house and your dinner parties. I thought of the family that once called it home, and a sense of sadness overcame me. I was lost in thought when the colonel asked me to translate what our host was saying. The same French-speaking Russian and I resumed our roles as translators.

We presented our request for so many pounds of meat, potatoes, vegetables, and flour. The Russians approved, our mission was a success but was not over.

We were to stay for supper. There was some food accompanied by a number of bottles lined up at the table. The first toast needed little translating. Our new Russian friend stood up and raised his glass to Franklin Roosevelt, the American-Russian alliance, and our victory over the Nazis. I took a sip of whatever I was served and thought my throat was on fire. The Russians all drained their glasses and insisted I do the same. I was trepidatious. It had been a long time since I tasted alcohol, and I could immediately begin to feel its effect. The glasses got refilled, and I motioned to my colonel to stand and propose a toast to Joseph Stalin, the great Red Army, and particularly to the unit that liberated us. Again, we went through the same drinking drill. I was beginning to see shooting stars.

I knew I had to get some fresh air or else the potential existed that I would embarrass my country, my division, and me, in that order. My fellow French speaker raised his eyebrows as I was leaving, and as he translated my farewell. I am not sure what the Russian word for wimp is, but I am sure that term was used to describe me.

The next morning I was clear-eyed and ready to return to camp. That is more than I can say for the colonel. He had the look of someone who was trying to figure out who and where he was. I realized whatever details needed to be finalized would be up to me. My senior officer needed coffee, aspirin, and a cot.

I was seated back at the cherry wood table across from a small mountain of a man. He was about six foot five inches tall and weighing in at almost three hundred pounds. There was not an ounce of fat on him, his arms looked the size of tree trunks. He reminded me of Joe Stydahar, who played for the Chicago Bears. Teddy stopped and looked up at me, *Uncle Henry took me to see him play and used to refer to him as a 'Monster of the Midway.'*

I remember, longing for Henry and Edward to once again be at my side.

Teddy continued, *The other interpreter, looking no worse for wear, was at his side. The big guy told me they had meat ready to deliver, but he was in need of some manpower. I let him know we could do whatever he needed, thinking he just wanted some of the guys to load carcasses on a wagon. It took me a minute or two to understand that he needed cowboys. He had 80 head of cattle staked out throughout the countryside, and he needed six or seven men to help drive the herd into camp. All of a sudden, I needed ranchers, real cowboys who knew how to round up and take care of cattle.*

I was a pilot and a New Yorker, so I was in way over my head as to what to do. I remembered Carman was from Texas, and I was sure he could rustle up the needed manpower. I agreed we would have our men ready by the end of the next day.

When we got back to camp, I found Carman who couldn't stop laughing. 'I can get a posse together, and we will get those varmints corralled,' he touted in a drawl I swear I never heard before. I wasn't sure how or who got tapped; but by the end of the day, the cattle arrived and those boys drove them through the front gate. The men in the camp started whooping and hollering, you would have thought we were starting a rodeo. All I could think of is that we were going to be fed meat. Five or six butchers were found, vegetables and flour arrived the next day, and the cooking began. We had some real chefs in the crowd; and the smell of steak on a grill, no matter how roughly constructed, was the aroma that brought back memories of home.

I reached for his hand across the table. This may sound naïve. No, it is naïve, I continued, shaking my head, but I never thought there would be moments while you were captured that we could laugh about. I also never thought of how you were going to get fed except for the Red Cross packages we heard about.

Teddy squeezed my hand before letting it go. Remember, the Germans were gone by then and we were back in charge. You can find your lost sense of humor when you no longer are worried about whether you are going to live to see another day.

I simply nodded.

There was a local airport about six miles away. We sent a team of the best we had to clear the airfield. They needed to check for booby traps, demolitions, and the like. In the middle of the runway was a German bomber. One of our guys started tinkering with it and soon had the engine running. We took our newfound Russian friends to the site. When they saw the airplane, we asked if we could fly it. They responded with a quick and resounding 'Nyet' that needed no translation.

One of their more senior Russian officers showed up the next day with the stated purpose of inspecting the plane.

There was a group of about five of us, all pilots, who were assigned to take him around the airbase. The first thing he wanted to see was the plane. He climbed up on the port wing, settled into the cockpit, and asked if it had been cleared of booby traps. We assured him it had. He peered around the instrument panel and finally found a wire attached to the *landing gear lever and disconnected it. He then pulled out a box of nitro-glycerine all fused up and ready to explode if the gear was retracted. He detached the box, and we all looked at the ground, our faces shades whiter but embarrassed. He then disconnected the fuse and tossed it about 100 feet. He looked down at his watch. Nothing happened. We were beginning to feel that perhaps there was nothing to worry about after all and started to breathe easier. Then the fuse detonated. We hit the ground, it sounded like a bomb. The Russian just shrugged his shoulders and walked away.*

He pointed to bushes outlining the perimeter of the airfield. The Germans had strung 1,000-kilo bombs in threes, placing them across the runway to make a barrier to landing aircraft. Our guys had dragged the bombs over to the bushes and had defused them. The Russian insisted we all go look at them. He gestured for more tools while we fidgeted. Getting all the equipment he needed, he unscrewed a fuse for the first one and detonated it. This was repeated until he was on the last three. By this time, the group of us was getting bored with the operation. The Russian clearly knew what he was doing, and we were merely his audience.

We moved into the grassy area, just north of where the bombs were being defused. My leg gave out, and I tripped and fell. I was lying on the ground, face first, swearing at the world and my weak leg when I heard the Russian yell. His voice was lost by the sound of the landmine going off. Three of the guys were killed instantly, the other died on the plane they used to evacuate us to the military hospital. My leg was shattered; the same one that had been shot. I was unconscious, but I was alive.

Why did God let this happen? It isn't fair. Teddy started to cry, his body racking with sobs. *These guys were about to go home in one piece. And they died. They were my buddies. We were planning the evacuation of the camp and they died. Maybe if we had stayed watching the Russian defuse the rest of the bombs, they would still be alive. Maybe if we had been paying more attention, we would have noticed the landmine. There are a thousand maybes and no answers. They were supposed to go home. I am the only one who did. I don't know why I did and they didn't.*

I took him in my arms, holding him as tightly as I could, and just let him cry. I could find no words that might give him comfort. The pain in his heart was too great.

We stayed that way until he looked up and gently broke away. *I haven't been able to talk about that day. Even when I was in the hospital, the shrinks wanted me to describe what happened. I couldn't. I tried not to remember, but I cannot forget. I cannot forget them. I won't let that happen.*

Nor should you, my voice softening. *Have you thought of writing to their families? I know that if I had lost you that terrible day, it would have given me some comfort to hear from someone who was with you in the last hours.*

Teddy looked at me. *I can do that. I can do that.* He kissed me on the cheek and left the room.

I was unable to move. I looked out the kitchen window. Children across the street were building a snowman, couples were walking hand-in-hand under the snow-capped trees, brave taxis were making their way through the one-lane passage. By tomorrow, New York will be back to normal. *May that be true of my son,* was my fervent prayer.

The next morning, Teddy came down for breakfast looking more rested, the letters he had written to his comrades' families resting in his hands. There was more of a spring in his step and his eyes, though still having witnessed too much sorrow and hardship, were brighter.

You were right, Mother. I feel better, he said as he looked down at the still-unaddressed envelope. *Writing about each of them allowed me to say goodbye, something that I was never given the chance to do. I will get their addresses and mail these out today.*

I said nothing, my role was to listen.

Over the next few months, Teddy's body and spirit became stronger. In September he announced that he was returning to Harvard to continue his law school studies. He told me it was time to pick up the pieces of his life. When I started to protest that it was too soon, he shook his head. *I know what I am doing,*

Mother. This isn't going back to boarding school to prove a point, this is me taking my life back, one step at a time.

CHAPTER 30

1947

I t was the first of the year, and Teddy was home from law
school. We were talking about what he might do after his
graduation in May when he took a deep breath. *There is something
I must do before I begin. I want to meet Maude. It is a missing piece for
me. The war taught me how fragile life can be. When we arrived in
England, we were young and brave; but by the time the war ended, we
had aged beyond our years and had done things that weren't the least bit
courageous.*

He took my hand in his. *This is my home and you are my mother,
whom I love and cherish. I am not looking to find something or someone
to replace what I have known. I have questions that may never be
answered, but I would like the opportunity to ask.*

I tried to find my voice. *I understand, my wanting to know more
about Ireland and what it would have been like to have grown up Irish
is what led me to Maude. And then you,* I took his hand and pressed
it to my lips. *Maybe it is time we both get our questions answered. I
only know my parents came from Cork and my last name was Clancy. I
could have family still living there.*

May I come with you on this journey? I held my breath until he
answered.

I can think of no one else who should be with me.

We need to be prepared, Teddy. As much as we might want to meet them, they might not feel the same way about meeting us.

You are talking about Maude, aren't you?

I nodded. *Yes, I don't want you to be disappointed if she doesn't want to meet us. You need to remember that all this happened a long time ago, and Maude was looking to start a new life. It is why she chose to stay in Ireland. We have had no contact since the day you were born. If she had wanted to get in touch, she could have written me or Victoria. Our addresses are the same. She may not want to be reminded of the pain, of the sorrow of those days. Are you prepared for that?*

Teddy bit his lower lip. *If that is her decision, I will surely accept it. I have a 'however.' Even if Maude doesn't want to see me, I still want to visit Ireland. I would like to see Ireland.*

We agreed that I would try to find our missing pieces.

———

I was meeting with my lawyers regarding the Walker Foundation. We had finished the meeting when I asked for their advice on how to find my missing family in Ireland. There was general agreement that this was not something they could assist with until one of the more junior partners came forward, a bit sheepishly. *I know someone who may help. He is my mother's second cousin who runs a detective agency. He is a bit of a character but seems to be pretty successful at what he does. I can call him on your behalf and set up a time for you to meet.*

Thank you, I replied. *That should work.*

The next day, I received a call that Frank Webster would be pleased to meet with me. I met him in his office, a two-story walk-up just off 14th Street, a neighborhood that had declined throughout the years. I knocked on the door to find the owner, Mr. Webster, behind the desk. There was no receptionist, no introduction. I felt like I was in a movie and not a very good one.

Webster was almost entirely bald except for a fringe of brown hair circling his head, making him look more like a monk than the head of a private investigation firm. He motioned me to sit down and try as I might, I couldn't take my eyes off his vivid red plaid shirt and stained dark blue tie. Traces of his morning coffee and perhaps his last night's supper were still evident on both.

However sloppy the office and his attire, Webster's mind was sharp and piercing. Before I could even begin, he explained, in an accent that alerted you immediately he was from one of New York City's outer boroughs, that the confidentiality of his clients and their requests were of his utmost concern. I liked him immediately.

He was clear this would not be an easy task and would take time. Europe was still in turmoil after the war. I told of my family coming from Cork. He asked if I was Catholic. I said, *Yes but why was it important? Church records are usually a great starting point,* was his quick reply. I told him the last time I saw Maude was in Dublin. At that time, she was planning to open a dress shop. I remembered that her mother's family name was O'Shea and that she still had relatives in Ireland.

He took copious notes; but from the looks of the piles of paper surrounding him, his desk was the only filing system in his office.

After two hours, we were finished. We agreed I would pay a sum of money up front and then at the end of the assignment. If he was successful, the amount would be four times the initial payment; if he was not, there would be no further bill. *Ya see, Mrs. Walker, I intend to find out what you're lookin' for. That's how I make my livin.' And like the Pinkertons, this private eye don't sleep. I'll get you a report in six months.*

True to his word, six months later, Webster called. The report was finished, and he could mail it or I could retrieve it by coming to his office. I was not going to rely on the postal system to deliver its contents so we agreed to meet the following

Monday morning. Teddy came home from school to join me. I cautioned him not to be deceived by Webster's appearance.

I was pleased to see Webster had changed his shirt and tie from the one he wore at our previous meeting. I realized it was Monday, the start of a new week, so probably a new shirt. He moved a bundle of papers off the only other available chair so Teddy could sit down. Webster handed me an envelope.

The report is all in here, but let me give you the particulars. I was able to find another P.I. in Ireland who did the leg work, a guy by the name of McManus. There is a successful dress shop in Dublin named O'Shea's that caters to O'Connell Street's finest. It got started about a year after your Maude arrived. The young woman who runs it is named Cate. We did not pursue any further inquiries, as I wasn't sure what you would want to do next. The shop's address is listed in the report.

I didn't look at Teddy. *I believe that could be her shop. Her mother's family was named O'Shea.*

The Clancy piece has gotten us somewhere, he began. My heart almost jumped out of my skin.

McManus found a record left in a Catholic church in Cork. It took a bit of digging, but the best we could make out is that you had a brother James who lived in Dublin, and a sister Margaret. Seems like your brother visited the church and left their names along with yours in the church registry. A major flood about four years ago ruined most of the church's records. The paper your brother left survived but was badly water-stained, and the letters were blurred together. McManus wrote that if he didn't know we were looking for the word Clancy, he wouldn't have recognized the name.

I knew about my sister; but it is wonderful to hear that I have a brother, as well. *This is what I prayed for*, I almost shouted out.

Webster continued. *Not sure there is much we can do to follow up on your sister. The records are too vague. It looks as though your sister got married, as her last name didn't appear to be Clancy; but the name was blurred, so he couldn't make it out. As far as your brother, there was a*

James Clancy from Dublin, a respectable banker with a good reputation. He died before the war.

My lip started to quiver, I had lost my brother only minutes after learning I had one. *Is there family left?*

Webster shook his head, *His son died in an airplane crash, and then his wife, Annie.*

Tears filled my eyes. Teddy took my hand, *I am so sorry, Mother.*

Webster went on, uninterrupted by my display of emotion. *They are all buried in Dublin. All the particulars are in the report.*

Thank you, Mr. Webster. You have done all I have asked. I stood to leave. Teddy did the same.

My pleasure. My bill is attached to the report.

Teddy and I walked out of the building. The day was unusually warm even for July, the heat and humidity draining the city of its energy. Our fast-paced New York walk was replaced by a leisurely stroll. Teddy and I walked in silence, each of us lost in our own thoughts, and soon found ourselves near our neighborhood.

Teddy suggested we stop at an outdoor café for a cold drink and talk over what we had heard. We placed our order, and Teddy lit a cigarette. My eyes must have registered my surprise; he smiled. *I don't really smoke, Mother; but I find it gives me something to do when I don't know what to say. Comes in handy most times when I am out on a first date.*

I grinned. *Well, I am flattered that I am in the same category as the young and beautiful women who seek your attention.*

Teddy smiled and put out the cigarette. *I am sorry Webster couldn't find more information about your family.*

I nodded, *Well, it is more than what I knew. It is strange to think I had a brother as well as a sister. How different my life might have been had they been a part of it. I believe the shop will lead us to Maude. I think it best that I write to her.* Teddy nodded in agreement.

I shook my head slowly. *I am not sure what her response will be.*

Teddy was thoughtful, *I understand and will take the risk. I don't want to enter a life where I am not wanted.*

I will write to her this week and we shall see.

Dear Mama,

> *I mailed a letter to Teddy's birth mother this morning. A private investigator we hired believes that he has located Maude in Dublin. Teddy wants to meet her. I understand his wish. He needs to know her. She is his family. I do not doubt his love for me. There is room in his heart for both of us.*

> *I have a brother and sister who are lost to me. This same investigator sourced a church registry in Cork that listed three names: James, Margaret, and mine, though the paper itself was badly damaged in a flood about four years ago. My brother James and his family are dead. There is no information on Margaret that I can follow up on.*

> *I should have told Teddy about Maude from the very beginning. The truth is not always the easiest path to follow, but our secrets are bound to be exposed sooner or later. I believe in my heart that Teddy has forgiven me, as I forgave you and Papa for not telling me that I was adopted. It is only through forgiveness that wrongs can be put right.*

> *Whatever will come next, will come. I will be fine.*

> *I love you, Mama.*
> *Your Nell*

F all was on the horizon. Teddy was back at Harvard for his final year when the letter arrived postmarked Dublin, Ireland. I looked at it for a long time before I had the courage to open it. I knew that whatever the message, we had chosen the path we were going to take. I thought of O'Brien. Joy and sorrow, all at once. That is what I was feeling.

———

October 1947

Dear Nell,

Your note was not unexpected. I have always known our past never truly goes away. It is as much a part of us as we are part of it.

I believe it is time that Teddy and I meet. Yet, it is going to take me a bit of doing to get it sorted out. I am married for close to 20 years to a wonderful man named Padraig. He was a widower with three strapping sons, so I inherited a family to call my own, as well. He and I have a daughter, Cate, who helps run the shoppe in Dublin. She is 16 and brings us much joy, most days.

Padraig knows of my past, though we only once had the discussion. The boys and Cate only know that I was born and raised in New York. They do not know they have a brother. I have my mother's family still living in the countryside, and so it made sense for me to return home to Ireland.

Padraig and I will tell them. We have agreed it is best to do it when we are all gathered at one time. The boys see the world through their own unique lens and are often at odds with each other as to what picture they are viewing. We never quite know if a conversation with the three of them will merely spark one single match or produce a flame that could torch the entire village. The one thing all three of the lads universally agree upon is that their sister is to be worshipped and protected beyond all reason. I am grateful for the shield they provide, though I fear our Cate is chomping at the bit to have her own independence. We shall be together over the Christmas holidays and will share the news then.

Given that timing and the rough seas, I think it best if we wait until early summer for you to plan your visit, perhaps in June of next year. It would be best to meet in Dublin. The Shelburne Hotel would again be the best choice as a place to stay.

I grieve for the loss of your Edward. He was a good man, and you stood well together. It is a hard world to navigate alone.

Thank you, Nell, for reaching out to me. Teddy sounds like a fine young man. I am looking forward to meeting him.

With kindest regards,
Maude

CHAPTER 31

1948

Teddy and I began the voyage over in May. I sent Maude a note that we would meet at the Shelburne Hotel on the afternoon of June 8th. I would introduce her to Teddy and then leave them. She wrote a brief note back that she would meet us there.

The sail over went well. We were celebrating Teddy's graduation from law school and the opening of Victoria and Jack's new school, Henry's House. We were comfortable together, a mother and her son traveling together.

Our first stop was London; we were to see Rachel. London was battle-scarred and bruised, there was rubble everywhere. Rachel told us to meet at her flat, the British term for a small, three-room apartment that was cold even in June. Teddy and I had picked up a 'hamper' at Fortnum & Mason, as Rachel had written that it would be best if we brought lunch. She had no time for cooking, as she was leaving in early July for Israel. She would be one of the first to settle in Palestine.

It had been almost 10 years since we had said goodbye, but it was the same Rachel who answered our knock on the door. Her hair was grayer, her body thinner, her spirit not diminished. This was still the woman who knew her own mind and sought to make a difference in the world. She gave me a hearty embrace and then stepped back, *My word, Nell, have you taken a cue from Dorian Gray? You haven't changed a bit. Though I remember your hair being a bit brighter.*

I laughed. *It is the only way I can cover the gray or I would look more like Whistler's Mother than Teddy's.* Rachel took a long look at the handsome man standing next to me. *Not possible,* she cried, *I wanted you to be a boy. When did you grow tall?*

She did not wait for a response. *If only you had arrived two weeks earlier, such a celebration. During the war, I never thought I would smile or laugh again; but now we have our own country, our own land. It is going to be difficult, already there are wars, but we shall win. If we learned nothing else from these past years, we understand survival.* Her eyes caught Teddy's and he nodded.

Nell, can you open the hamper? And you, young man, pointing her finger directly at Teddy, *I want to hear all about why you have become a grown-up. What are your politics? What is your take on Truman and this doctrine of his? Is he merely a haberdasher from Missouri or a brilliant statesman who no one recognized?*

Over a lunch of biscuits, cheese, and chutney, I listened to the two of them debate the issues, agreeing, challenging, laughing, and sighing at the other's opposing view. I was thrown back to another time, a time when Rachel and Edward would do the same. My heart broke with joy and sadness. Teddy was now a man with ideas, opinions, and a life of his own. I knew Edward would be pleased with his son. I prayed that Maude would be the same.

Our time with Rachel was ending. It had been a lifetime since we sat next to each other that fateful day following the Triangle Shirtwaist Factory Fire. She had opened my eyes to the world around me. I tried to thank her, to say a last goodbye. She would have none of it.

Really, Nell, enough of the dramatics. It is not like you. As Edward would have said, and together the word *Poppycock* came out of both our mouths and we laughed. *We shall write. You are my dearest friend.*

Turning to Teddy, her voice grew serious. *I can only imagine the horrors you saw during the war. It is true for both of us. You cannot erase the sorrow. Hold on to it, recognize it, turn it into good. It is up to your generation to make a difference in the world. Your mother and I tried our very best, we expect no less from you.*

And with that, she gave each of us a quick kiss and a hug, opening the door, she gave a quick salute. Her final words were addressed to me. *As we told you at our Seder, Nell, next year in Jerusalem.* She closed the door, and we walked back down the stairs.

Teddy shook his head, *She is something. I had almost forgotten – her wit, her opinions. Her energy consumes you when you are in her company. She is like no one else.*

I took his arm as we headed back to the Savoy. *Always has been, always will be. I am not sure I would have had the energy for a lot of Rachels in my life, but I am sure glad I had this one.*

Two days later, Dublin welcomed us with a charm and a warmth that offset the 'soft rain' that had dampened the ferry ride across the Irish Sea. We checked into the Shelburne Hotel.

Teddy and I had an early supper at the hotel. We talked about the weather, the charm of the people we had met, the headlines in the local newspaper. We talked about everything but the reason we were in Dublin, his meeting with Maude. It would happen the following afternoon. I was to introduce them and leave.

I went to my room and poured a glass of wine. I vowed I would not think about tomorrow. How my life could change. It would be what it would be. Life is like a game, we draw from the deck we are dealt and decide whether to keep that card or discard it and take our chances on the next. It is the hand that we choose to play that shapes our lives.

The evening sun was casting its final light on the manicured lawns and leafy green trees in the park below my window. I was reminded of Rittenhouse Square and that day in May, so many years ago. I try to picture that young girl, alone, naïve, sitting on a bench deciding what to do. I laid down on the bed, closed my eyes, and wondered if I would have been happier had I decided to leave Edward. My heart heard only one word.

Poppycock.

The pale light of dawn was tumbling into the gaps of the curtains when I opened my eyes. I found the postcard of St. Stephen's Green that the Shelburne had provided. I wrote, *Thinking of you,* and addressed it to O'Brien at his sister's home. I got dressed, asked the hotel clerk to post the card, and left the hotel.

The morning was cool and crisp, with no dark clouds threatening to drench the roads with mud. Dublin was quiet, but you could feel its pent-up energy. In a few short hours, Teddy would meet Maude. There was no script as to how this day would unfold.

I walked past Trinity College, behind its gates housed the Book of Kells, across its quad was Oscar Wilde's dorm rooms where imagination and the unimaginable mingled into one. I walked slowly, taking it all in. I thought of O'Brien's admonishment, *You couldn't learn to be Irish, you had to feel it.* I could feel Ireland that morning, like a breath of fresh air it was calming my body, strengthening my soul.

I had the address and found the church where my brother had worshipped. I stopped and lit two candles, one for James, the other for Margaret, whom I now thought of as Maggie. I knelt and prayed to the brother and sister I never knew, the family I never had. I asked them to watch over and guide me through the day.

I decided to walk to the cemetery where James and his family were buried before returning to the hotel.

That is where I saw her. She was standing by James' gravestone, next to a newly dug plot of earth. I stood staring and then summoning my courage, approached. My first question was direct – why was she at the Clancy gravesite. She seemed a bit taken back, but in a decidedly American accent told me that James Clancy was her uncle, and she had come to honor him and to fulfill her mother's dream to return to Ireland. The newly-dug grave was where she was burying her mother's favorite teapot.

My vision blurred with tears. *Are you Maggie's daughter?* She nodded yes. I took her hands in mine and pressed them to my heart.

I'm your Aunt Nell.

AUTHOR'S NOTE

I find the first half of the 20th Century to be a fascinating period in our country's history, especially for women. Women in mink coats supporting worker's rights; women raising banners marching to gain the right to vote; women new to our shores leading their fellow workers to demand better working conditions. And then there were the less fortunate whose dream of a better life ended in such senseless tragedies as the Triangle Shirtwaist Factory fire. These were the women who started the journey that generations later we continue to travel.

In today's world, the internet enlightens and informs. It was my major source of research for the topics covered in this book. Cornell University has a special collection devoted to the Triangle Shirtwaist Factory fire. Books on the politics of that era read like works of fiction. Tammany Hall shenanigans were not for the faint of heart. Al Smith's humor and down-to-earth approach to life made him a man of the people. As the first Catholic to run for the presidency, it was said that the country was not ready for "a man who carries beads in his pockets" – Hoover trounced him. Frances Perkins was the first woman to hold a cabinet post when she became a member of FDR's cabinet. Twenty years would past until another woman took a chair at that table. Glass ceilings cracked but still not broken.

I am thankful for the many people in my life who encourage, advise and comment as the story begins to unfold. My publisher Stephanie Larkin at Red Penguin Books is a force to be reckoned with, and I am grateful to have her in my corner. A special word of thanks to my first-round readers: Candi, Carol, Colleen, Erin, Kathy, Louise, Mary Ellen, Rolaine, Sandra, and Sandy. This is neither the first nor the last time your wise counsel will be sought. You define the word friendship.

To my husband Russ, no matter where the journey takes us or how difficult the ride, it is only you I want by my side. And to all my family, I am blessed to have you in my life. You raise me up.

ABOUT THE AUTHOR

Following a career that led her from managing colleges to Fortune-500 companies, to major international law firms, award winning author Maureen Reid began writing the kind of novels she loves to read. Blending fiction with historical facts, Maureen is inspired to write about strong women who by sheer will and spirit become the best that they can be. A storyteller, Maureen's characters have been described as flawed but determined as they try to make a difference in their lives and in the lives of others. The issues they confront are as current as today's headlines.

When she is not somewhere else, Maureen lives in the metropolitan New York surrounded by family and friends. She is blest that four of the world's most beautiful, smartest and kindest girls call her "Grandma."

Visit Maureen's website maureenreidauthor.com to check out her latest *Musings* and the date for the release of her next book.

ALSO BY MAUREEN REID

Becoming Herself

Winner of the 2019 Best Indie Book "Notable Indie" from Shelf Unbound

Nautilus Book Award Silver Medal, 2019

www.ingramcontent.com/pod-product-compliance
Lightning Source LLC
Chambersburg PA
CBHW050617110726
47899CB00001B/143